The Captive

A Story of Franco's Spain

The Captive Summer

David Quarenden

LandAstrum Publishing

Published by
LandAstrum Publishing
PO Box 183
Gravesend
Kent DA13 0WJ

www.landastrumpublishing.co.uk

Natalis edition April 2004

A CIP record for this book is available from
the British Cataloguing in Publication Data Office

ISBN 0-9546447-0-0

Cover design and typesetting by Ant Graphics Design Services

Printed and bound in Great Britain by
Antony Rowe Limited
Eastbourne

*Like as the waves make toward the pebbled
shore,
So do our minutes hasten to their end*

Shakespeare

Acknowledgments

Any mistakes relating to historical events are mine alone. The RAF sent both Hurricanes and Spitfires to Gibraltar in the manner described, as part of the reinforcement effort for Malta. But by July 1942 the air defence of the island lay with the Spitfires, although a few Hurricanes remained and carried out bombing raids on Sicilian aerodromes.

I wish to thank the staff of the Royal Air Force Museum, Hendon, for their help in locating material relating to the training of RAF aircrew, and air operations in Gibraltar.

And many thanks to Susan Loudon and Joy Haigh for their encouraging and helpful comments on earlier drafts of the book.

Rafael's story of the blind men and the elephant is taken from *The Teaching Of Buddha*. I am happy to credit this source to Bukkyo Dendo Kyokai, Tokyo.

No pasaran!

The Captive Summer

The Fall

The wave struck him, salt stinging the cut above his left eye and his swelling lip. Confused, he was momentarily aware of a submerged rock crowned by fronds of sea weed and then the warmth of the sun on his neck, as his head broke above the waves. He dared another breath; with his left arm and leg he grasped at and kicked against the surging waters. The onshore wind was aiding his slow passage to the land now, as if in inadequate apology for denying him as the dying aeroplane had slipped from the sky.

The next wave rose up before him, a mass of churning foam thrown back from its assault on the beach, into which his body now fell. He tried to swing sideways, his right leg and arm trailing almost uselessly: a drowning ragdoll on a hot afternoon. Again he held his breath, and the chill water broke over him; through blurred eyes he saw a looming rock, like a sea monster, almost below his feet. As the water sluiced around it and the disturbed sand billowed, he was thrown down. In terror he stared as the rock, dark and jagged, rushed at him, then fell away, and he was carried clear. He was aware of the crushing weight of water on his back, he had become a powerless spectator to his own sucking death. But through the boiling sea he made out a change in the sea bed. The vaguely defined bottom of varying hues of blue-green had been replaced by rippling golden sand, its surface marked out as if small submarine ploughs pulled by teams of sea horses and marshalled by drunken crabs, had uncertainly slewed across its surface in preparation for a harvest of sea shells. He thought of what it meant to drown; his racing mind crazily reviewed stories read in childhood of shipwreck and storm, finally alighting, as if it had found the perfect passage for his predicament, on the dream of the Duke of Clarence from Richard III: *"O Lord! Methought what pain it was to drown, What dreadful noise of waters in my ears, What sights of ugly death within my eyes."* With an effort he shut the words out, and fought again for the hot air in the rippling world above his head.

The lack of buoyancy in the life-jacket, and his incapacity, meant that his body ascended only with reluctance. He struck at the water with his left hand in a strange action, as if waving in farewell to the field of ploughed sand beneath him. He held back the pain of lungs and facial muscles which strained to contain the breath that threatened to erupt from between his teeth; but just as he thought that he could no longer hold out, his head broke clear of the sea. As he spat the corrupted air from his lungs, he gained a glimpse of the country beyond the water. The beach was compact: from the air he had been aware of a series of small coves at a distance, with a larger bay lying to the east. He could not tell which of the coves he had reached. Beyond the sand, rocks like broken stone teeth gave onto a rising table, and beyond that a rockier incline. To his right he saw something out of place, a narrow band of blue and white amongst the sun bleached bands of grey and amber; then he was jolted by the next returning wave.

There was a slow rhythm to his struggle; as he drew nearer across the shelving beach the rhythm increased but at the same time the effort required at the peak of the cycle abated. He learned to judge the moment when he should draw in breath and stop up his mouth, grabbing and kicking against the waves to propel himself closer to salvation. One half of his body obeyed his will, while the other half tried to: his right leg rose and fell but had no conviction to its movements, his right arm was heavy and there was little movement in the fingers. The drenched cool of his submerged body contrasted with a head that was subjected to sharp bolts of pure light, heat, and the stinging water. He felt the currents as they flowed through his clothes and around his body, his trousers lazily slapping against his shins, his shirt billowing under the parachute harness straps like a sunken sail.

He was exhausted, but survival's imperative forced him to take another breath and kick and grasp and splutter through the pain. His foot touched the rippling sand beneath him, and for a moment, he stood up to his chest in water. He fell forward, as if the waves themselves had now formed an alliance with the wind to bring him to shore; coughing the sharp sea water from his lungs he resumed the struggle for his life.

He found himself on his knees in the wet sand, head bowed down, weak of limb, breathing heavily, unable to think, unable to speak, aware only of the sound of the waves and the heat that bore through the life-jacket, the straps of the parachute harness and his tunic, to confirm his deliverance from the sea. He slowly raised his head, was aware of bands of heat sweeping across the rocks and stones of this foreign shore, offered up a weak laugh in thanks for his life, and collapsed.

While in this unconscious state, he nevertheless at some point rolled over. Perhaps the clawing waves in a last gesture of goodwill to the young man they had so desperately tried to claim for the god Neptune, agreed that his chances of survival would be further enhanced if his mouth and airway were clear of their life denying effects. The wind, being more fitful, did not have the necessary strength that afternoon to turn his body. However it came to be, Neptune would not claim him that day, although at that point in human history there were many other candidates for the dream of the Duke of Clarence. The young man lay on the wet sand and the sun poured down on his face. He lay in a death like slumber, unaware of the raw symphony of waves and wind that crashed around him, on that afternoon in early June, on the coast of Andalucia.

Much later in the afternoon, once the intense heat was spent, and the shadows of the larger rocks began to fall across the land to mark the passage of the sun toward its home beneath the western sea, two figures made their way down through a rough and indistinct path between the rocks and onto the rocky table. They were fishermen and they were returning to their hidden boat, the blue and white band glimpsed earlier by the young man. The fishermen were brothers, Jesus and Antonio Gomez. They had been born and brought up in the neighbouring town, and had fished the local waters together for several years. That they were returning to the cove and not the harbour had nothing to do with the elusiveness of shoals of silver backed fish, and everything to do with a cargo of cigarettes, which both paid better and took less trouble to land. However, in comparing the two catches, the issue was not ease of attainment, but its consequence. Few people, even in Franco's Spain, were arrested merely for the act of catching and landing fish. This was not true in the case of a catch of contraband supplies.

The cigarettes had been landed during the night, packed in bags of oil cloth that were placed on boards laid in the boat to keep the cargo dry; the two fishermen had moved with practiced caution around the little craft as they rowed toward the shore at midnight. The cove was their favoured spot due to its sheltered topography and absence of any obvious path to the beach. There was a handicap to this however, which was that if they had to move their cargo by mule, the animals could not reach the shore. Therefore, with some sweating and silent cursing against rocks which grazed their shins, they carried the oil cloth bags on their backs up through the rocks to a point where an old path marked out the original highway. It was here that they met their accomplice and transferred the effort to the mules. They had done this on several occasions, and had become practised at moving in the dark, feeling their way over the rocks and through the gullies, recognising larger formations by distinctive marks they had chiselled: precise tactile maps which meant nothing to an untrained eye.

Antonio walked before his brother; as the elder of the two by some years it was his right to take up a position of leadership. Antonio was tall, with a thick mass of curly hair partially concealed under a woollen cap, but thin. He wore rope soled shoes, a pair of worn dark blue trousers heavily stained from gutting fish, a white shirt which had two buttons missing, under a jacket of coarse cloth. There was a tear in one leg of the trousers, through which his leg could be seen when the material flapped as he descended over the rocks. He had fought for the Republic in a militia company which had held a trench in the Sierra Nevada for over two years. At the end of the fighting he threw away his rifle and walked home. His brother Jesus was seventeen years old, and his youth had spared him from the trenches. But the gap in their ages measured by the passage of time, was nothing compared to the gap measured by the horror Antonio had witnessed in the mountains.

Jesus trusted his brother's judgement without question, whether it was where they should seek out shoals of sardine or what contraband to bring ashore. Similarly attired save for a patched jersey in place of a jacket, and carrying a sack in which were deposited the ropes and straps by which they had attached the oil cloth bags to their backs, he followed the well practised route to the beach and their waiting camouflaged open sailboat.

Without warning, Antonio halted. In an instant he threw himself down amid the rocks with a speed and precision learned during nights of glistening frost and spitting death. Jesus dropped and crawled beside him. Antonio watched the beach, Jesus followed his line of sight and his eyes fell on the body at the water's edge.

"Where did he come from?" asked Jesus. Antonio paid no heed and continued to watch, daring to raise his head a little as he looked around the beach from right to left, the muscles in his neck standing proud, ready to pull his head down at the first report of a shot.

"A ship has sunk, he must be one of the crew," he replied. Jesus made to speak again, but Antonio raised a finger to his lips. Antonio had always thought that their luck must run out, perhaps today it had. They lay for some time watching the body.

"Is he dead?" Jesus asked.

"Perhaps dead, perhaps wounded."

"Should we go to him?" and Jesus now studied his brother's face intently.

Antonio knew that the body could be a trap, perhaps the Civil Guard had placed it on the beach to draw them on, and while they examined it, shoot them. There was no sign of the presence of others, no footprints in the sand that were visible from their vantage point. A rock pool lay between them and the body; Antonio noticed the rippling of the water as a puff of wind passed across its surface, mimicking the action of the waves in the sea. The rocks on which they lay were oven hot and there was little shade. Neither had a watch: they told the time by the passage of the sun. They waited and sweated, and watched the cool waves slapping into the sand. The body lay without any sign of life save for the illusion caused by the shimmering air.

"Not even the Guard would wait this long," Antonio at last said in a sharp whisper. He stood and looked about him. Jesus followed his example; then they dropped down onto the sand and walked to the water's edge. Antonio's shadow fell across the body. The young man wore a khaki tunic and trousers with light suede boots, on his shoulders were the chevrons of a sergeant. His face was swollen and bruised, and blood oozed from a head wound. Antonio knelt down and raised a wrist; through his pressed thumb he detected a weak signal of life, a Morse code signal of one repeated character.

"But yet he lives." He looked at Jesus, then out to sea, in search of an explanation for the stranger. He began to unfasten the life-jacket and the other straps which bound his chest. The deflated yellow jacket fell away to reveal on the left breast of his tunic a wing and crown emblem, with the letters 'RAF'. Neither Antonio nor Jesus could speak any English beyond the labels on the packets of English cigarettes which they smuggled. The young man might have come from Gibraltar, but Gibraltar was over one hundred and fifty kilometres to the west.

"What shall we do?" Jesus enquired.

Antonio reflected on images of comrades left behind in shallow ditches of baked earth. He sat down in the sand beside the body and looked to the boat, the white hull almost invisible under a tarpaulin and branches of driftwood. Jesus crouched down opposite him.

"We cannot take him in the boat, but we cannot leave him here," said Antonio.

"Will he live?" asked Jesus, concern flashing in his eyes.

"Jesus, I am not a doctor, nor am I blessed with the gift of prophesy."

Antonio opened the breast pockets of the tunic, and removed and examined their contents. There was a silver cigarette case; a small lined book which contained entries in different hands, now obliterated by the sea water; a wallet with a few photographs and two folded pieces of paper, these being English bank notes. Antonio kept the cigarette case. Jesus looked up to the rocky incline and the screen of ilex trees that started beyond the old coastal highway and continued beyond the new road.

"We could take him to Dona Consuelo," he said, still watching the trees.

Antonio looked down at the body. The young Englishman was probably going to die in any event; if he had been on a ship that had been torpedoed, then he would most likely have taken fuel oil into his lungs, and his lungs would burn. But they could not leave him for the Civil Guard to find, because that would arouse interest in the cove, and result in more frequent patrols.

"Antonio, we cannot leave him to die, the Virgin would not protect us if we abandoned him." Jesus now looked intently at his brother, who at first would not meet his gaze. Jesus, perhaps because of his namesake, believed in the practice of the faith into which he had been baptized. He regarded the unconscious young man as a Spanish baby Moses, whom they had discovered if not among the rushes and in a basket, then at least sheltered in the cove and borne onto the shore in a life-jacket.

At length Antonio raised his face, and said, "Help me move him into the shade. Then go to Dona Consuelo, I will stay with him."

The Captive Summer

Life's Ebb

Jesus retraced his steps, and threw his light body from boulder to boulder as he ascended to where the old road cut into the rock. The road was disused, and so thickly sown with grass and scrub, that the route was only discernible by the way the heaped earth twisted and fell as it sought out a safer passage away from the devouring sea. The rocks he grasped as he hauled himself up were like rough loaves newly taken from a vast oven and spilled randomly over the steep ground. At the point where he gained the level ground he threw himself down and looked out from under the branches of a carob tree, peering to left and right through eyes that strained against their sockets, with urgency and a dry mouth. Satisfied that no one was in the vicinity, he stood wiping dust and dry leathery leaves from his clothes, and then ran at a trot along the old roadway until it joined the new metalled highway.

Here he repeated the cautious exercise, for although there was little motor traffic, apart from the bus to Granada, the Civil Guard maintained regular patrol by horse; and were sure to question a man travelling alone. On the far side of the road was a plantation of ilex, which reached up tier upon tier as the ground rose at their feet. Kicking up dust he sprinted across the road and into the trees, not stopping until he was deep inside the plantation. Panting, he hugged one of the trees, digging his fingers into the bark and pressing his face against the unyielding yet protective trunk. Closer to the road he made out a clump of broom through which he had run, the long stalked spikelets waving lazily in the clear air. He waited, but no shout or call came, and there was no muffled sound of approaching horses. He turned away and carried on with short quick strides across the rising ground, keeping a watch all around him, but less afraid than before in the screen of trees.

The Spanish were a people under surveillance, and when they believed that they might be watched, they modified their behaviour; but modified behaviour, and love and respect, were two entirely different and separate things. The Guard, unable to detect true loyalty and model behaviour from the counterfeit kind, maintained a sullen and intrusive presence; each and every man and woman was a potential candidate for a Labour Battalion, and the reborn Spain needed many enforced hands to repair the damage inflicted on it by the Reds.

The ilex thinned out as he climbed; he could see now the outline of the Sierra La Contraviesa, the last barrier between the Alpujarra and the sea. He reached a ridge, which gave him a better view of the country for several kilometres. To his left, over a long distance, the ilex was replaced by stony hillsides peppered with olive trees; to his right, the ilex thinned further into a piece of open land that was still communally farmed by people from the town. And immediately beyond the open land was the farmhouse of the owner of that land, Dona Consuelo Arranquez, hidden from the coast road by a screen of ilex and cypress trees. This was his destination; pausing only briefly for breath and to wipe perspiration from his face with his sleeve, he hurried on.

Jesus and Antonio were well known locally. As he ran, Jesus reasoned that there must be people working on the communal land, and he therefore had to make a decision. He could either emerge through the ilex trees, and calmly walk past them, dispensing greetings in a voice which did not betray his agitation. Or he could run and scramble down the slope through the ilex and scrub, traverse the open land out of sight, and climb back up to the house. With the sun flickering through the branches onto his back, Jesus dropped down the slope, and traversed the ground. Through the trees he heard voices, and instinctively dropped to his knees. The voices were those of women; he realized that some of them were singing folk songs, powerful laments of love and abandonment. But no figure appeared on the skyline, and he rose up once more and moved on.

Dona Consuelo was the owner of the land and farmhouse in absentio of her husband, Don Arturo Bonar. He was in exile in southern France, in an internment camp for Spanish Republicans. Although by their social position as landowners they should have been on the side of the Nationalists, Arturo possessed one serious flaw in his personality: he had been a lawyer before the civil war. This echelon of people had shown an irritating tendency, from the point of view of Francoists, of being liberals or socialists. They were derided as delinquents, Masons, non-Christians, democrats: they had betrayed the *Patria*. Spain had spurned them like errant children, and they had fled to France and Mexico and Russia. Although now separated and alone, Dona Consuelo held to her husband's ideals because she believed that by so doing she was keeping not only his memory but his body alive; and that one day, perhaps tomorrow or the day after that, he would appear on the twisting coast road that led to their home.

Jesus walked briskly to the main door, and tugged at the bell. It was only then that he realized that he did not know what to say. He had met Dona Consuelo briefly before, but his brother had spoken then. The heavy door opened to reveal an African Cuban of about fifty years of age, whose broad face was crowned by a wave of greying hair, and whose sharp eyes scrutinized the youth without betraying emotion.The man was Rafael

Sabio, one of two servants to Dona Consuelo.

"Good day," said Jesus, and he instinctively bowed his head slightly. Rafael said nothing. "May I ask if your mistress is present?" Rafael looked at the sweating boy with suspicion, like a father alarmed at his daughter's choice of dancing partner.

"She is. Do you have business here?"

"If by that do you mean am I expected, then I must say that I am not senor. However I would ask to speak to her on a most urgent matter."

Without answering Rafael closed the door on him, and Jesus was left standing with the sun on his back, not sure whether he should remain or return to his brother. Dappled sunlight fell on the ground at his feet, and turning round, he could make out the sea through the trees as the waves refracted and broke up the light falling upon them. A few minutes passed; he started and spun round as the bolts in the door were pulled back, and the portal reopened. Rafael escorted him into the courtyard, and then via a narrow passage out onto a terrace of large flagstones, which overlooked an ornate garden, both encompassed by a high wall. A woman in a yellow dress sat at a table under an awning, the yellowness of the garment complementing a group of sunflowers in the garden beyond. Her head was turned from him, and although her long dark hair was drawn up, one lock hung down unnoticed, and brushed against the side of her face. She turned to Jesus, her dark eyes betraying a combination of inquiry and consternation. She recognised him, but did not know his name.

"You asked to see me," and as she addressed him she placed her hands on the table in front of her, her head turned very slightly to one side.

"Dona Consuelo, you may know me. I am Jesus Gomez, my brother Antonio and I are fishermen, from San Cristobal."

In his nervousness Jesus halted, and Consuelo regarded him with a cool stare. She was nearly twice his age, composed, elegant, but thinner now than she had once been, and dark shadows beneath her eyes had been carefully disguised with a little make up. She had seen several boys like Jesus leave the little fishing town in the dark years, most had not returned. She knew his brother Antonio better; she had once given refuge to both Antonio and a consignment of contraband cloth when, exhausted from flight, he had almost been caught by a passing Civil Guard patrol. Her instinct was to listen, and so she waited, raising a hand to encourage Jesus to go on.

"We have found someone Dona Consuelo, at the cove," and he turned and pointed to the southern wall of the terrace and garden.

"Who is this someone at the cove?" she asked.

"We do not know, he is unconscious," at which Consuelo shuddered a little, "and he will not wake up."

"Why have you come to me?" she asked, leaning a little forward on her seat, her figure pressing further in the dress.

"Antonio says that you may help us, the man on the beach needs a doctor. Antonio says that he is a soldier, he has wings on his chest," he traced out the outline of the brevet on his own left breast, "and there are three letters R - A - F." He stood before her, looking between Consuelo and Rafael, who had remained throughout the audience, standing a pace or two away.

Consuelo realized that the man at the cove was a foreigner, probably English, a pilot. There had been many Englishmen who had come to help Spain during the war, men who had given up their livelihoods, or come away from the dole queues, because they believed in the struggle of the Republic. She had known some of them, men who had fought with Arturo, men who were now gone, like her own husband. She turned aside.

"Rafael, what should we do for this man?" she asked.

This was no trivial question. Rafael was silent for a time; his eyes surveyed Jesus, then he coughed and answered.

"Madam, to bring the man here places us all in jeopardy. Once, some would have dared more, did dare more. He may die, he may live, but if he is to die we can at least ensure that he does not die alone. I will go with Jesus. When it is dark, and only if it is safe, we should bring this man to sanctuary."

Consuelo paused before replying; they were safe now, not bothered by the Civil Guard unless they wanted water for their horses or a little information. This unexpected development in their secluded lives of self imposed emotional exile threatened that fragile safety. But the man on the beach might be dying, as thousands of others had died; and by their intervention they might yet save him. She wondered what sanctuary Arturo had enjoyed, what unknown people had perhaps helped him escape to France. She looked up, and in uttering a few words, changed the course of their lives.

"I agree Rafael. I will send word to Dr Hernandez, and ask him to visit this evening, but give him no reason."

This concluded the conference between them, and Consuelo went to find the other servant, Maria; Rafael and Jesus departed by the route which Jesus had taken to reach the house. They carried with them water, two blankets, some rope and a small axe.

At the beach Antonio continued his lonely watch over the young man whose life ebbed as the sun set. Once he stirred, and mumbled in a low voice; Antonio held his head down close, but could not understand what he said. He had rigged, from some oil cloth and branches, a rudimentary tent to keep the sun and wind from the man's face. He scanned the rocks and the sea, all the time wondering where Jesus was, and what Dona Consuelo's decision had been.

It was Rafael who came first onto the beach, which vexed Antonio as he had taken care to select the secret route through the rocks. Rafael examined the young man, as blood fitfully coursed through his veins; and with a light and sensitive hand, which belied his impassive countenance, brushed away his bloodied hair to look more closely at his bruised and cut scalp.

"I think that his head is broken," he said looking up at Antonio and Jesus, "it will be very dangerous to move him, he may die."

"But he *will* die, if he stays here," and Antonio looked now with some fierceness, for he resented being told what should and should not happen by a Cuban. Rafael met his gaze, and Antonio looked away.

Rafael stood up and looked back above the rocks to where tree line began. They needed a stretcher, and would have to improvise one from the oars in the fishing boat, the blankets and the rope. The making of the stretcher was the work of a few minutes, then they lifted the body onto it, having removed the life jacket and harness, and waited for night.

The journey back was slow and tiring; they stopped at every sound, every crack or whisper. Rafael and Antonio carried the stretcher, while Jesus scouted ahead. The night was unpleasantly warm, and they felt the heat in the rocks and burned earth at their feet. They perspired, and could not rid themselves of their body heat, trains of sweat running down Antonio's back underneath his shirt. At the point where the old road joined the new highway, they waited, crouching, the stretcher still between them, as Jesus walked along the new highway in the direction of the town, to warn of the approach of headlamps. They were fearful that their casualty would regain consciousness and cry out, as he was tied into the stretcher, but he remained silent, and to all appearances, lifeless. At a signal they crossed the road, and were engulfed by the low branches of the trees. They negotiated a passage, fighting to keep their footing in the darkness, Jesus now walking beside them and holding the side of the stretcher. Eventually, with a cooler wind washing their faces from the mountains, they sighted the farmhouse silhouetted against the sky.

They kept within the copse of ilexes which lay just before the main entrance, and again lowered the stretcher to the ground. Rafael looked once more at the young man for signs of life. To his relief there was still a pulse, and he appeared a little flush in the face, but his lips were thin and lined with a blue tint. They had used Antonio's jacket to make a pillow, and there was blood on the cloth. Rafael went forward to the house and pulled twice then once on the iron ring, which was the signal that all was well. The door was opened by Maria Ortiz, the maid, and standing close behind her in the darkened hall was Consuelo.

"Is he alive?" asked Consuelo in a hushed and anxious voice.

"Yes madam," he answered, "his grip on life is unbroken, but is weakening."

"The doctor has still not come Rafael, but hurry and bring him here."

Rafael signalled, and Jesus and Antonio rose and came forward, stepping through the threshold. A room had been prepared on the ground floor, in a deserted part of the house. The room was musty, square and high; it was sparsely furnished, with whitewash over walls of stone, and brick. The bed had been stripped of clothes save for an undersheet and pillow, and now combined the functions of examination table and couch. The room had no electrical supply, and was illuminated by two oil lamps. Under their warm and yellow light, the wound to the left temple took on a darker hue, the clots of blood appearing maroon, particularly where the blood had dried above the hairline and was mixed in with a quantity of dust. The body lay limp, a seemingly broken form without connection between the bones and muscles beneath the skin. Consuelo gently brushed away the hair as Rafael had done, while Maria stood across from her, and held a lamp close. Without warning, the body moved in a spasm that rippled from head to foot; and they started back with thumping hearts. Consuelo looked around at the others, and asked Maria to bring hot water and a bottle of iodine.

Maria had left a message at the house of Dr Hernandez earlier in the evening, but he was away assisting with a woman in labour, and it was not known when he would return. Consuelo leaned once more over the young man, and Rafael held the lamp, both conscious that their intervention might indeed only ensure that he would not die alone.

The Captive Summer

Into The Ring

The young man whose broken body lay within the walls of the farmhouse had started his life far away from Spain. His name was Tom Roberts. He was a native of London, and like Jesus, his youth had spared him the horrors of the Spanish civil war. But as his father had once reflected, wars were like buses: all that humanity had to do was simply wait for the next to come along. In peacetime he had been an apprentice electrical engineer, an obscure commuter grateful for a job with some prospects, who left his native Denmark Hill each morning to travel to the Southwark factory of his employer. Before the war he had spent little time on beaches, extensive leisure not being a way of life widely known in post-Depression Britain. He was lucky to have an employer with a philanthropic impulse that ensured that each July the company directors dug deep into their collective pockets, and rewarded their employees for two hundred and sixty days of untiring effort with one day of unstinting generosity at the Brighton races: by the standards of the times a fair rate of exchange.

In July 1937, while Spanish Nationalist and Italian forces prepared to attack Santander, Tom put his name down to go with his fellow apprentices to the racecourse. One of his closest chums was a sandy haired youth by the name of Charlie Morris. Charlie loved motor cars, and used to fool his friends that he was related to the car manufacturer William Morris, the apprenticeship being only a prelude to going into the 'family' business. The ploy wore off after a while, but it impressed the typists in the main office. He proposed that a group of the apprentices travel independently of the main party, which was due to go down to Brighton on three charabancs. When questioned as to whether that would mean a journey by train, he advised that: "I've got something cooking boys, I've got something cooking," but would be drawn no further as to his meaning.

Tom had inherited from his father an interest in horse flesh, at least as a form of taxation for the poor, and considered it prudent to find out as much as he could as to how it was levied. His father obliged him by providing an explanation of the types of bet, betting tactics, the conditions over which the horses would run, and what to look for in a winning horse. In spite of the accumulated equine wisdom of a lifetime, Mr Roberts was still only neck and neck with the bookmakers, and approaching the final furlong in the life stakes handicap.

The race meeting was to be held on a Friday, and as the factory would be closed on Saturday, this gave the employees the luxury of a long weekend. Morris had arranged for a subscription from the apprentices, to provide for extra crates of beer, but as Tom walked up the road to the factory gate that morning, there was no sign of Morris, his alternative transport, or the alcohol. A group of the other apprentices were huddled together on the pavement, excitedly talking about Morris and what they would do to him when they found him; Tom joined them. There were three of them: Samuel Burrage, Joe Watkins and Fred Hope. They were trying on the attitudes of manhood in their heated discussions like a new suit of clothes, and were all keen to get their hands on Charlie Morris and *their* beer. But just as they had agreed on a suitable form of torture, there was a blast from a car horn, and turning round they saw Morris drive up, at the wheel of a gleaming new Austin open tourer. Open mouthed they crowded round the car, ownership of which was so far outside their resources, that they immediately suspected that it had been obtained by deception at least.

"Well boys, didn't I say that I was cooking something!" and Morris leaned back, every inch the (suspiciously) wealthy young lad about town.

"You stole it!" accused Joe, running a finger over the front wing.

"No! No, no," and Morris now shook his head from side to side in quick little jerks, to emphasise his disdain for the idea.

The questioning continued, but to no avail. They exhausted every possible means by which Morris could have obtained the car, and repeated several; all he would say was that it was due to family connections.

The charabancs moved off, and they followed for a few kilometres, until Charlie decided that he had enough of following the typists, who crowded to the back of the last coach and blew kisses from the rear window to the boys in the tourer. Tom, Joe and Fred were in the back, enjoying the freedom, and the possibility of adventure on a warm day, particularly when exiting London. Samuel Burrage sat in the front with Charlie, who clearly revelled in his role as a South London Great Gatsby. Tom had read the book at school, and recalling a few lines, called out.

"Hey old sport! Where's Daisy?" but Charlie did not understand the reference.

Fred looked at Tom quizzically, and Tom explained the outline of *The Great Gatsby* to him, at which Fred exclaimed: "Yes, we are all beneficiaries of the generosity of the Great Charlie! Ha, ha, ha!"

When the tourer reached the South Downs, Charlie stopped at the first roadhouse they came to, and they got out to stretch, and open a few bottles of the beer. This day in their lives was exciting: it was not a day regulated by work, or study. They laughed at jokes and discussed the prospects for the racing; when the serious business was concluded, they turned the discussion to the state of the nation. They argued about Stanley Baldwin, whether King George would popularise the Monarchy, and how they would spend the single man's unemployment benefit of some fifteen shillings a week, if the need arose. Then Charlie shepherded them back to the tourer with a gracious wave of his hand, and Tom spent the rest of the journey to the race track wondering which Hollywood star he was impersonating.

The day passed all too quickly, a blur of horses' hooves, flashing bright silk, men parading in their best suits, women parading in their best dresses, bottled beer, a picnic, jokes shared in bright sunshine, lost betting slips, horses winning, horses losing. At the end of the day, thousands upon thousands filing out, stumbling onto charabancs, tripping over, regretting the amount of beer they had consumed, being sick. Tom had not been drunk before, but as he tried to focus on the sky and keep his footing he reflected that life could be good, and looked forward to the next time they would follow the road south from London. They sang songs as they drove home, the dying rays of sun flashing in the windows of the buildings they passed; and each imagined himself to be a Great Gatsby, and each was happy.

But the outside world forced itself more rudely upon them as the decade closed, as threatening as a housebreaker in a stocking mask. Tom's family could have changed the door locks, fitted bolts, screwed down the windows, taken coshes to their bedrooms at night, but it would have made no difference. Tom's father, Sidney, a veteran of the Great War, became more subdued, and the quiet gaiety of earlier years left him. The announcement that the Government had opened a factory to manufacture gas masks for every child and adult in the country, 'to be distributed should the need arise', compelled a fatalism in him, and he became more prone to sitting out in the garden, gazing skyward, as if waiting for the first mustard gas bombs to fall. The topics of domestic discussion revolved more now around political issues; German expansion, and the progress of the war in Spain were recurrent themes; as they talked Sidney Roberts could see in his two sons, the shapes and attitudes of his brothers lost in the trenches of France and Belgium. He was adamant about Spain, and although he appreciated the validity of the claims of the Spanish Republic, he would not sanction that either Tom or William, his younger brother, should volunteer to fight. There was only one occasion when he said anything about his own experiences of war, in an attempt to deflect them from fatal choices about their own lives.

"Can you imagine walking along a road that was a collection of pestilent slimy holes, carrying the remains of your best mate in two sacks on your back, and looking up through eyelashes so caked with mud that you could barely open your eyes, and seeing an artillery horse broken in two pieces by an exploding shell, and those two pieces trotting separate for a step or two until they realised they were dead?"

As Tom had grown older he had become aware of a schism between the world he saw around him, and the world that was reported to him. This was coupled with an awareness that others did not seem to notice or to be troubled by the deceit. It was as if they were all standing on a railway platform at a terminus in London, and an approaching steam train was speeding up not slowing down, yet no one cared or noticed. The desire amongst the parliamentarian class to avoid another war was unimpeachable, but Tom quaked with rage when he read the newspapers, in the expectation that there would be detailed reportage of the situation in Europe, to find so little, or what there was condescending in its tone. At least the popular Press had stopped praising Mosley, and the BUF was not treated with the indulgence in some circles which it had previously known. However, the general public did not know that Lord Halifax had an informal arrangement with the Press that arose out of concern in Berlin at reports of the German regime's policies.

As part of his eighteenth birthday celebrations, William invited Tom to accompany him and some of his friends to a boxing tournament which was to be held at Mile End. William had followed his father into a position in the City, into a stock broker's office, which sounded to Tom as particularly grand, although William vehemently denied this, observing: "Why do you think we need to go to boxing nights, it's the only way a man can get some excitement?" The hall was full when they arrived, and a stale tobacco and sweat atmosphere assaulted their senses as they entered and took their seats.

Hundreds of men shouted the odds, joked, and called for blood. Eager pinched faces shone underneath the shaded lamps, which threw pools of watery light over small clusters of men, those just outside each tight circle merging into the general gloom. Tobacco smoke wafted like great bands of sea mist, through which distant heads appeared as rocks breaking above waves. In the centre was the ring itself, bathed in a harsh light which flattened colour and form. William jostled his brother's elbow, and winked; Tom felt that he had been granted access to a special place of male ritual, and looked about him to take in everything that was happening. The harsh murmurs became a roar as officials in suits processed in, followed by two robed fighters. The whole group was almost lost to view as rows of men closest to the procession stood to applaud the boxers. The crowd settled, but the atmosphere changed, the innocent jocularity disappearing as if someone had clicked their fingers to signal that an hypnotic trance should be ended. Tom felt the breath from the men seated behind him, heavy with alcohol, tobacco and greasy food.

The first fight was a dreamer's dance, as the combatants, neither of whom looked to be older than William, circled each other swapping punches and trying to avoid running into the referee. The crowd watched with polite expectation, and shouted encouragement if they thought that the two youths offered up to them were not trying hard enough to kill each other. When it was over the referee held aloft the arm of the sweaty victor, who drew in great gasps of air, his ribcage riding up and down within his slight frame as he breathed.

The next match was as different from the first as day is from night. The fighters were older, and carried the scars of earlier conflict; their fight was also for a minor area title, which whipped up the crowd to a true blood fury. That night Billy Sampson, a red haired thug with a face over which someone had driven a truck, faced up to George 'The Tornado' Tucker, a wall of muscle topped by an oily mass of black hair, in an attempt at lawful murder. There was clear animosity between the two fighters, mirrored in sections of the crowd; Tom looked keenly from the crowd to the ring and back to see where the fighting would start. He would remember years later the muffled sound of the blows, and the rasp of air spewed out of a man's lungs. From the start the fighting was vicious and intense; after several rounds they simply clung to each other, dripping blood and saliva and trading punches into each other's head, as the referee struggled to separate them. But through the smoke and the bellowing crowd Tom realised that he was witness to more than the senseless struggle of two sentient beings reduced to an archaic savagery. It was as if through their blood hate that these two men played out the history of Europe before his eyes. He looked about him, to see if the others realised what was happening, but they didn't. Then he noticed one man, wearing a wide brimmed brown felt hat and blue suit, who was seated to his left. The man had a thin pencil moustache, and had a cigarette to his lips. He pulled a cigarette lighter from his pocket and cupped his hands before his face to light up; he hesitated and his eyes narrowed as punches fell on bone and flesh, then light radiated behind his fingers and died away. He wore a signet ring; in that moment light passed across his eyes, and the ring caught the watery light from the lamps. One moment, and the light died; whether it burned for one instant or one human lifespan, Tom understood that the light of consciousness would inevitably be extinguished.

The Captive Summer

Flying School

By September 1940, Tom was an apprentice engineer by day, and a firewatcher by night. His days as an engineer were however drawing to a close; he had visited an RAF recruiting office, and put his name forward for aircrew selection. As he had walked home that afternoon he wondered how he would explain his actions to his parents. He did not know whether he would be accepted; RAF pilots were drawn from an elite, and he could hardly have been said to come from an elite social background, no matter how favourable a picture he drew of Denmark Hill. But the officers who subsequently interviewed him had either only passed through that part of South London on a train, or had made a connection between electrical engineering and aviation that he had not: he was accepted.

He completed the ground element of his training, incongruously, in Brighton. He never even got close to an aerodrome, nor for that matter returned to the Brighton race track, but gained promotion to leading aircraftman in compensation. Then he, and scores of others, waited. Waiting was a common element of service life: waiting for the next available course at an Elementary Flying Training School, waiting for the next available course at a Service Flying Training School, waiting to be released to a squadron, waiting for their chance. Eventually they would either join a squadron or, as the joke went, be discharged on grounds of age and infirmity. They wanted to fly and they wanted to fly in anger; there would be opportunities enough, but for many those opportunities would be tragically brief.

But these thoughts were far away from the mind of L/AC 200443 Roberts T.H. when, on a freezing February morning in 1941, he and a detachment of other airmen crowded onto an express train at St Pancras station for the journey to their EFTS in Scotland. They had been reliably informed that if they considered London to be cold, they should wait until they got north of the border. The informant, a Liverpudlian with traces of blond hair still evident beneath his forage cap, sat opposite Tom and his close companions in the carriage; with exaggerated chattering teeth and rapid pounding of closed fists on his chest he provided a demonstration of the likely effect of the Scottish air on their bodies. "It's like breathing ice!" he reliably informed them, rattling for good measure.

"It can't be that bloody cold!" came the retort.

"It is! It's so cold the farmers have to light fires under the cows before they milk them!"

They were shepherded by one sergeant and one corporal, who had harried them from the aircrew reception centre at St Johns Wood, into and out of motor transport, and onto the railway platform. They had been drawn up two deep along the platform, each man with his kit bag, bathed in light filtered grey through the besmirched panes of glass high up in that utilitarian cathedral. The only heating on the platform was an occasional jet of steam from the locomotives drawn up on the tracks on either side. They waited for the order to board the train, as impatient now as they had been when they had first enlisted. Two young women passed them, both elegantly bound in fur as they made their deliberate way to a carriage close to the front of the train; many pairs of eyes followed them, not a few out of a sense of envy at their apparel.

"You there, Roberts, eyes front!" and the menacing form of the sergeant came into Tom's vision, a glaring red face beneath a fringe of cloth. "Did I give you permission to admire the scenery?" he shouted into Tom's face.

"No sergeant," and Tom looked directly ahead, with the well practised technique of looking at but yet not seeing his tormentor.

"This is the Royal Air Force, not a...," but at that moment the whistle of the locomotive behind them let out a peal which completely drowned out the stream of invective, leaving the NCO frustrated and the other airmen struggling to contain their gratitude at the intervention of their mechanical ally.

As they left the northern suburbs of London they could make out that although it was as monochrome as the rest of the city, the level of bomb damage it had sustained was lower, and Tom was relieved that his brother-in-law had persuaded his sister and his parents to move away. Then they were in open country, and being lulled into sleep by the incessant 'clickety-click' of the express, spoiled only by the corridor patrol maintained by their guardians, who perhaps feared that the airmen would escape at the first opportunity that arose.

The pantomime warnings of the Liverpudlian airman, now formally introduced as Leslie Nash, were borne out. They found themselves billeted in a village on what appeared to be the edge of an enormous snow field. The village was at the head of a long sea loch; lying beneath distant snow capped hills they saw a dark green mass of water troubled only by patrolling herring gulls. The aerodrome was situated a few kilometres away from the village, and comprised the farm buildings and house of a local laird, generously donated to the nation. A protective plantation of fir trees thrown around the estate went some way to break up the cutting gusts that whipped in from the North Channel; although the land had a blanket of snow, no new falls had been experienced for two weeks, and the skies were clear: they might freeze, but they would fly.

For all its hastily put together features, a lecture hall converted out of the laird's library or the maintenance hangar from a barn, the flying school was equipped with sixteen pieces of equipment beyond value: DeHavilland Tiger Moth trainers. Closer in spirit to the Great War, they were yet adequate to the task of testing the aptitude and temperament of the often scared young men who placed a booted foot onto the port wing and stepped up and into the bucket seat behind the instructor for the first time.

The next morning Tom found himself paired with a fellow Londoner, Patrick Lytten, who protested against the weather at every cutting gust. In spite of wearing extra underclothing beneath their Didcot flying suits, and looking the part in gloves and flying helmets, they longed for a little more warmth. Their instructor was Flying Officer Browne who, while sympathetic on the issue of pinched extremities, was quite clear that they would pay attention to the job in hand. They made their way out to inspect the Moth that they would share, a weak sun struggling to rise on the horizon. Browne stepped up on the lower wing, dropped the side flap of the rear cockpit, and motioned to Tom to climb into the seat. Tom's breath came hard and in short gulps, which rapidly condensed, as he pressed himself down and felt the airframe around him, his mind contemplating what it meant to command the machine.

"This," said Browne with a finger pointing into the rear cockpit at a point in front of Tom's chilled face, "will be the most important school room you ever have the privilege of sitting in. Listen to what I tell you, and observe what I show you, and you will learn what it means to be a pilot. There is no experience to compare to flying, none whatsoever; you will see the world in a way only known previously to God. Remember that." He looked from Tom to Lytten and back to make sure that the message was received and understood. "Good, let's go through the instrumentation."

That concluded the first day's instruction, and to Tom's disappointment he climbed out of the cockpit; they returned to the hangar to collect their parachutes and flying log books. The war, although a defeat for humanity, had still bestowed on some opportunities that would otherwise have never come their way. In peace time, flying lessons at three pounds per lesson were beyond the reach of either man; now they would be paid to fly, and to break with a world of social and physical limitation.

There are two moments in any flying career, no matter how distinguished or mundane, that live with the pilot: the first flight, and the first solo flight. The first flight came three days later. After breakfast, motor transport took them from the village's only public house and hotel through still darkened lanes to the aerodrome. As Tom and Lytten looked out over the tailgate of their transport the dimmed lights of the following truck cast a grey tint onto the compacted snow, which bore the ridge marks from the tyres of many vehicles. Through the trees they saw the first signs of activity; the trucks passed through the gates and pulled up abreast, their headlights now faintly illuminating the runway. They pushed aircraft from their hangar while the dawn was breaking through, and waited. Browne emerged from the main house, which served as the officers' mess, greeted them and offered them the spin of a coin to decide who would have the privilege to fly first. He took a florin from a pocket on his flying suit, and held it up between thumb and forefinger; Tom could see that it bore the face of George V.

"Well Roberts?" he asked.

"Heads sir," replied Tom confidently, and Browne looked to Lytten to confirm that he accepted Tom's choice. Then with a graceful short sweep of his arm the coin flashed into the air, spun and fell onto the ground. They crouched down to see in the early light: the dead king's face lay firmly pressed to the snow.

Tom watched as the Tiger Moth pulled away and taxied out, a light spray of snow thrown up in its wake. The Moth turned at the end of the snowfield, and the engine tone rose. The aircraft bounced and rolled, the tail lifted, then slowly the airframe rose and the wings cut into the frosted air. Tom reflected ruefully that his Royalist instinct had cost him the first flight on the first day of the course. For some reason this bore a significance, even though there would be a hundred more training flights to come before he would be able to take his place in an operational squadron. The Moth grew smaller, and banked away; he tried to imagine what it must be like to be in the air, but nothing in his experience came close.

The aircraft returned; he and Lytten exchanged places, the propeller slipstream washing over Tom's face and tugging at his flying suit, adding to the sense of urgency as he climbed up on the wing. He pulled and fastened the harness straps as tightly as he could and lowered his goggles over his eyes; Lytten said something to him with a smile that was lost in the engine noise, and stepped away. This is it, Tom thought, and he put his gloved hands out in front of him to check through the small panel of instruments: airspeed indicator, altimeter, compass, turn and bank indicator, pitch indicator. A voice came out of his earpieces, to compete with the sound of Tom's thumping heart.

"Are you ready Roberts?" Tom looked up, to see Browne's face reflected in the mirror ahead of the instructor's seat.

"Yes sir."

"Always volunteer information about your status, don't expect me to assume that you have control, or don't have it."

"Yes sir, understood sir," and Tom took pains to hold his head close to the Gosport tube mouthpiece.

With a short chopping gesture of the hand from Browne as a signal to the aircraftman beside the wing, the wheel blocks were again removed and the aeroplane rolled forward. Tom felt the pull on his chest from the harness, and his heart beat faster still. The aircraft stopped cross wind, and they made one final check, as several other aircraft were now in the sky around them. They turned into wind, and swept forward, the engine noise and vibration through the airframe rising rapidly as Browne applied full power. Tom looked from side to side as the ground rushed past, the cold air stinging his exposed face and rippling his flesh.

Then they were free, and rising up into the clear blue sky. As the earth fell away, creation expanded to fill the void. The world below them was white, with blotches of darker colouring to signify houses, and threads of dark where a field was divided, or a road cut the land. When Tom looked into the cockpit he saw the controls working without his intervention: the throttle moved forward, the engine responded, the control column fell to the left, and the aircraft banked. He sat laughing to himself, hardly able to believe the forces which kept them suspended above the ground. Outside, they had gained sufficient height to clearly see the loch. Browne's voice came through again.

"Roberts, it's time to go to work, the holiday's over. Can you see the head of the loch?"

Tom looked ahead between the mainplanes, and then ducked down to the Gosport tube.

"Yes sir, I see the head of the loch."

"Good, you are to make for that point. Now this is the drill, when I give you control, I advise that you've got the aircraft, and you confirm that you have the aircraft. Is that clear?"

Tom acknowledged, and they handed control from pilot to pupil.

The elementary mistake of any student is to over compensate movement on the control column: the light caressing touch of the experienced pilot or instructor, is replaced by the death-fear grip of the pupil. Where the aircraft glided before on seams of air, it now bucks and wallows as if in the face of a storm. This was Tom's first experience, but the aeroplane still returned to the ground in one piece, and Browne waved him away. He walked through the compacted snow back to the hanger, and stood with a group of the other student pilots observing the sky. Several of the Moths were in the air, dots comprised of fabric and wire that were suspended by a magic power. As he watched the aerial circus, Tom vowed that he would learn to fly, and to fly well.

The Captive Summer

Arrival

On a November evening of intermittent rain Sergeant Tom Roberts reported at the guard room of RAF Benington in Dorset. The aerodrome had been constructed in the late 1930s, part of the response from a reluctant Air Ministry to the annihilating potential of attacks by heavy bombers on major cities. At that time the aerodrome was the station for a Hurricane squadron, a Spitfire squadron and a Lysander flight. Situated close enough to make Dorchester a walking proposition, the utilitarian brick buildings and steel framed aircraft hangars struck forlorn and incongruous silhouettes in the empty countryside. He arrived after night fall, and gained little detail as he walked alongside the perimeter fence from the local railway station. Challenged at the main gate by a guard in steel helmet and greatcoat, brandishing a rifle with fixed bayonet, Tom was directed to the front office of the Guard Room. A corporal sat at a desk with a telephone and two trays; Tom presented his papers. He had expected his arrival to be the signal for some commotion; but none arose, and after checking through a list of names on a sheet in front of him the corporal looked up.

"We have no record of you sergeant, I'll have to call the Orderly Officer."

"There must have been a mistake, my papers are clear," replied Tom, disappointed that at this moment in his service career the expectation and experience had parted company so abruptly.

"As I say, I'll have to call the Orderly Officer," which he then duly did.

There was nothing for it but to wait. The room was heated by a wood stove set in a corner behind the desk and its occupant; placing his kit bag against the wall and removing his gas-mask case, Tom went across and stood by it, rubbing the feeble warmth it gave out into his hands. He was annoyed; what should have been a moment of triumph and pride, had become fouled by a clerical error which prevented him from taking his rightful place in the squadron. A clock on the far wall mocked him as its second hand swept round, and round again. The corporal worked through some papers, but in acknowledgement at the inclement weather put down his pen, briskly rubbed his hands together as if in an attempt to set them alight, picked up the pen and carried on with his work. The telephone rang; he put down his pen in a very deliberate way, as if he had read the procedure for putting down pens in an RAF manual, picked up the telephone receiver and spoke in a deferential tone for a moment or two. Then the corporal replaced the receiver with the same precise action, and turned around. It was done; and Tom was given directions to the accommodation block where the aircrew sergeants had their quarters.

As he walked across he saw that the doors of a hangar were open. Inside fitters were working on the airframe of a Hurricane, its fuselage little more than a wooden skeleton. At that distance Tom could still make out their condensing breath, as it spiralled into the night air, and with his free hand pulled the collar of his greatcoat closer. Once at the block he was given fresh directions to a room on an upper storey and climbed; he knocked at the door, to be answered by a man with a Welsh accent, bidding him enter. There were two beds, one on each side of the doorway. On one bed was deposited a tall man with jet black hair and piercing eyes, older by a year or two, intently reading an RAF manual on pilot etiquette.

"Another pilgrim!" he said looking up, then levered himself from the bed and seized Tom's outstretched hand and pumped it vigorously, adding, "Don't mind me, my parents were devout Methodists!"

"Tom Roberts," offered Tom in reply, slightly taken aback.

"I'm sure you are, never doubted it for a moment," came the lyrical response, "I'm Thomas, George Thomas, pilot in this crusade of the common people against the forces of Teutonic darkness."

Tom sensed that he and his new companion would become friends. He unpacked, and they exchanged the histories of their brief service careers. Thomas was from Cardiff; in two months with the squadron he had flown nine sorties across the Channel and into Northern France. Like Tom, he had attended his SFTS in Ontario, where the RAF had relocated part of Training Command when flying became too dangerous in the British Isles. He had been a mine engineer, an occupation which could have exempted him from war service; but he wanted to go because, as he put it, "I have a temperamental objection to that short arsed Austrian with a moustache that looks like a rat has crawled up his nose and died."

"What's the squadron commander like?" asked Tom hesitantly, but reasoning that it was better raised now than not.

"Squadron Leader Bruce is, in my humble opinion," and George paused to see the reaction from Tom, "a most noble gentlemen, for a Scotsman that is."

Seeing that this produced only a quizzical expression he relented, adding, "Oh! He's not so bad, you'll meet him tomorrow."

Tom's first introduction was to the other sergeant pilots in the mess the following morning. There were four of them: Kenneth Maguire and Bill Mitchell, both Australians; Neville Longhouse; and James Stanley. George waved introductions with his knife, while Tom shook hands with each man in turn. Both Maguire and Mitchell possessed trademark rugged

Antipodean masculinity; but in truth Mitchell had been a school teacher in Sydney before the war, while Maguire had sold typewriters. The occupations of the two Englishmen were as diverse: Longhouse had been a draughtsman, and Stanley had worked as the manager of a repertory theatre. Breakfast completed, Tom reported to the squadron commanding officer in his office overlooking one of the aerodrome's three grass runways.

"You've chosen a good time to join the squadron Roberts," Bruce said, a statement that struck Tom as not being strictly correct, as the timing of his release to the squadron was not under his control. Bruce was a peace time aviator, and had joined when closed canopy Gladiator bi-planes were the best that were available. He had a narrow face, with thinning sandy hair, and grey eyes. He appeared tired, and opened Tom's file and picked papers from it with the slow deliberation of a man fighting off sleep; Tom wondered when he had last taken any leave.

"I want to fight sir," offered Tom as his rationale for being in the room.

"That's good laddie, the Hun has provided us with plenty of opportunities," came the reply in a measured soft Edinburgh accent. Tom met his gaze, he wondered how many times Bruce had gone through a similar meeting with other fresh pilots, only to compose letters to their parents weeks later which began 'Dear Mr and Mrs X, Your son was a fine and brave airman, and I offer my condolences to you in your loss...' Perhaps some day a more senior officer would compose a letter which began 'Dear Mrs Bruce, Your husband was a fine and brave airman and I offer...'

"I want to have a go at the Hun sir," was Tom's next attempt to convince Bruce of his sincerity.

"That will come soon enough sergeant, but," waving in the direction of the window through which a low impenetrable cloud base could be observed scudding over the broad expanses of Dorset heath, "operations will be interrupted if the weather worsens, and in any event I'll want to know from Flight Lieutenant Breeve what his assessment of you is. He is your flight commander. That is all, dismissed."

As Bruce predicted, the weather worsened. Fog, heavy rain, and cloud over the targets resulted in the cancellation of many operations. Tom's elation at being with an operational squadron ebbed; that by this reprieve he might live a little longer, did not occur to him.

The pilots took whatever opportunities arose to entertain themselves. The nearest pub was *The Falcon*; when operations were cancelled it received a surge in patronage and it was understood that within its walls the distinctions of rank and length of service were largely forgotten, although squadron loyalty was not negotiable.

The Captive Summer

The railway line from London to Dorchester cut across the main road a short distance from the public bar. The railway level crossing barriers were unmanned, and impending trains were announced by a bell still audible within the seventeenth century stone walls. It was only a matter of time before the higher intelligence of the pilots devised a game which combined beer, alarm bell, crossing barrier and speeding train. This was 'Scramble', and it arose out of the rivalry between the Hurricane and Spitfire pilots. Each squadron nominated a team of five men; for most of the evening the rival contestants assiduously promoted the publican's efforts to retire wealthy. However, the first railway bell to be heard after ten o'clock was the signal for the game to start, as one or other team captain shouted "Squadron scramble!" across the din. On this command contestants and spectators ran, staggered or crawled outside to the near barrier. The objective was simple: to see which team could send the most men across the railway line and back before both barriers fell.

If attempted while sober, it presented clear dangers but a degree of exhilaration; if attempted while drunk it offered the possibility of one or more airmen becoming detached from his head or legs as the train cut through the crossing. Inclusion in the team was a rite of passage, of the kind beloved by those who understood the futility of caring whether they lived or died. Tom's initiation had been shortly after he joined, and his speed over the ground while mildly incapacitated had gained the Hurricane pilots an advantage over the Spitfire team that had proved decisive. His second participation was almost his last. The cold on that early December night was intense, and sheltering in the warmth of the public bar, the airmen were matching spirits, which Tom was not used to, with half pints of beer.

At some time after ten the electric bell tolled out in the frozen fog that cloaked Dorset to the sea at Portland Bill; the unlikely athletes, who were by then generally so drunk that they couldn't make out the time on their wrist watches, staggered outside. The cold air ambushed them, felling one Hurricane pilot and two of the Spitfire pilots as if they had been hit from behind with a sock filled with wet sand. The survivors formed into two swaying columns, with Breeve standing between them as umpire; his giddy gyrations around a spot on the road matching the slow deliberate rotations of the drunken competitors, who tried very hard to focus, control the motion of their eyes, and not pass out. The mist that had slowly fallen across Tom's eyes in the bar, momentarily fell away, and he found himself staring intently into the broad back of one or other of his comrades, the wall of blue cloth before him admitting no neck or other distinguishing feature. Alcohol had rendered him dry mouthed and sleepy; he was placed as the fourth man in the revised team order, with Neville Longhouse as fifth. The team was led by Pilot Officer James Hilliard, the resident squadron poet, whose own unfamiliarity with drink owed greatly to his own father's temperance pledge.

Breeve raised his arm, and then let it fall in a waving motion not unlike the action of patting the rear end of a nervous donkey. Screams and yells let out as Hilliard, and a young Canadian pilot from the Spitfire squadron, lurched forward; Hilliard looked around him as he ran, clearly not certain where he was or what he was doing. His left foot connected miraculously with the road without the leg attached to it crumpling, then his right, then his left again. Behind him cheering and ragged roaring rose steadily, shouts of "Hilliard! Run man, run!" and "For God's sake look where you're going!" were hurled at him for comfort and inspiration. The Canadian, perhaps more used to the cold air, made determined if erratic progress across the road, reached the far side and turned about, while Hilliard lagged several feet behind. The next runner for the Hurricane squadron was Pilot Officer Boyd, who teetered forward with his right arm outstretched waiting to take up an imaginary baton from Hilliard. As the two men shook hands, they collided, which winded Boyd and put him on his back. The desperate situation called for a superhuman effort, so to make up ground he effected a curious long stride, as if crossing the deck of a ferry caught in a storm in the English Channel.

The bell rang out again through the fog to insist that the train had almost arrived, and a faint light pulsed along the curving rails. The barrier on the far side of the road came down just after Boyd had turned, and he was faced by a barrage of shouts and urgent gesticulations from both his team mates and concerned onlookers. He leapt forward, but instead of placing his foot on the wooden decking either side of the near rail of the Dorchester bound track, placed it squarely on top. His foot slipped as he transferred his weight forward and he fell face down, rendering himself unconscious but perfectly arranged for the removal of both feet under the locomotive's front wheels.

The juxtaposition of unconscious airman and locomotive electrified his comrades; rivalry forgotten they ran forward, some to hold up the near barrier, others to pull Boyd clear from the train. As they carried him off, they were illuminated by the lights from the express, providing the startled driver with a scene from an infernal funeral procession, as six figures bore away a limp body that they held at shoulder height. But Tom's attempt to take part in the rescue were thwarted by a powerful force that held him to the spot. Looking round, his dim eyes made out the face of the publican, who held him fast by one hand, while with his other he held Neville

Longhouse.

"You're too drunk! You're not going anywhere tonight," he said in a Dorset burr. He shook each of them in turn and escorted them back to the warmth and safety of the public bar, muttering as he went.

The publican was as good as his word; when Tom awoke in the early hours of the morning he was not in his bed in the familiar room with lime green walls, but lying on a bench in the darkened lounge bar, his nostrils assaulted by the stale odour of tobacco, and the rapidly cooling vapour of human revelry. He sat up slowly and swung his legs off the bench; the room was illuminated only by the faint embers in the open fireplace. He shuddered as he looked about, momentarily transported to other places. There were at least two other prostrate occupants, but he could not make out who they were; one breathed heavily on a bench across from his, while the other sat at a table, snoring gently, his head cradled in his arms. Tom sat at the edge of the bench, moodily looking from left to right, trying to decide whether to stay or go, and uncertain what effect the drink was having on his digestive system. He thrust himself upward and stood quietly surveying the room with a blank mind; but slowly the remembrance of the evening came back, and he smiled to himself. He adjusted his tunic, and using the bar for support, he made his way toward the door which let out onto the road. He turned the handle and stepped out into a night of bright stars and scurrying clouds. The fog had lifted; the Earth was empty, from somewhere beyond the trees he heard a fox call. Beneath his feet the frosted ground reflected the light from the sky, as if the Milky Way were laid out before him, and he a voyager contemplating its vastness. Hugging himself, as his greatcoat was lost within the building at his back, he looked to find a bearing home, and advanced.

The Captive Summer

Departure

The first reports of the entry of the United States into the war reached Europe late in the evening of the first Sunday in December. Tom and George Thomas were playing chess in the sergeants' mess, while Neville Longhouse sat across from them, thoughtfully sucking at a pipe and composing a letter to his wife. Occasionally Longhouse looked up, and offered suggestions to one or other of them, depending on the balance of play. He regarded chess as a game of beautiful and intricate variation, and saw in the flow of the pieces across the chequerboard an analogy with the detailed technical drawings by which he used to make a living. To his mind chess was a game of structured movement, leading to a 'resolution' in terms of an 'inevitable form' of the pieces. A technical diagram, say of pistons and crank shaft in an aero engine, depicted a system for structured movement, which would be 'resolved' when the 'inevitable form' was transferred from two dimensional representation to three, from paper to aluminium or light steel. He attempted to explain his scientific philosophical beliefs to his friends at the low baize table, but to little avail. George nodded and raised an eyebrow at one interjection, and it was with an effort that Tom stopped himself from openly laughing at the comedic exchange.

Tom scoured both the chequerboard and his mind for a means to save his queen from capture. George leaned back, tapping one foot on the floor, and sipped a glass of beer, apparently heedless of his opponent's discomfiture. Tom looked up at him, and down at the pieces, then repeated the exercise. There was a commotion outside, and Alan Stanley hurried in, dragging the cold with him like a blanket. The mess radio would normally have been switched on and tuned to band music from London, but that night the NCOs preferred only the accompaniment of their own voices.

"Have you heard, have you heard?" he said. He had a habit of repeating short statements, which perhaps arose from spending too much time memorising the verses of popular songs, or calling out "Five minutes please, five minutes!" at dressing room doors in theatres in provincial English cities.

"Heard what?" asked George. Stanley ignored him, and told the steward to put the radio on and tune it to the BBC Home Service.

"The Japanese have attacked the Americans at Pearl Harbor!" he announced as he threw off his greatcoat.

"What?!"

A few minutes later the disembodied voice of the BBC announcer spoke to a silent and attentive room. "Reports have been received," and no one in the mess breathed, "that Japanese Air and Naval forces have attacked the American Naval base at Pearl Harbor in the Hawaiian Islands."

They listened in stunned silence. As news spread throughout the aerodrome, ground and air personnel gathered in the messes to listen, the brief pronouncements now giving rise to longer periods of speculation among the servicemen. But the only tangible immediate impact of the events on the other side of the world was that the station commander increased the number of sentries on duty.

As Tom, George Thomas and Kenneth Maguire made their way to the mess the next morning for breakfast, the talk was only of Pearl Harbor. To their surprise they found an armed sentry posted outside, a polished Lee-Enfield rifle with glistening bayonet held a little way from his face. They passed him, but just as they were about to enter the building, Maguire turned back to question the sentry about his orders.

"And if," he asked, "a Japanese saboteur were to approach the mess hut, what would you do?"

"I'd challenge him sergeant," came the not too certain reply.

"And what if he didn't speak any English?"

"I'd challenge him in a louder voice."

At which Maguire turned away. Shaking his head, he was heard to mutter, "It's just as well that the Japs don't have any aircraft that can fly as far as Dorset."

But the pilots were also expected to fight in the propaganda war. A journalist arrived one day from a Canadian newspaper and, escorted by one of the station intelligence officers, met the Canadian pilots of both squadrons. No sooner had the journalist departed, than the station commander gave notice that the aerodrome had been selected for a visit from a documentary film crew from the Ministry of Information.

The Ministry had identified a gap in the RAF's propaganda war effort, and believed that issues of public morale demanded a short film portraying life at an RAF fighter station. All that was needed was a suitable title, and agreement with the Air Ministry. For the film makers, an aerodrome in the heart of the Dorset countryside had a desirable aesthetic quality. It was also close to the homes of T.E. Lawrence and Thomas Hardy, Dorset being the mythical Wessex of *Tess of the D'Urbervilles*.

The project gained a working title, *The Winged Sentinels*, inspired by a Jagger statue of a Great War soldier wrapped in a rain cape that enveloped his body like furled bronze wings.

"And just what type of damned war do they think we are fighting here?"

The station commander threw down the note from Group HQ, picked up his cap, strode to his office door, stopped and turned about, then called for his clerk to come in. Perched on one corner of his desk he tapped out on his fingers, as if practising Morse code, his thoughts on the unsuitability of the aerodrome for filming; his concerns were noted, but ignored. The film crew and their equipment arrived in two light vans one morning in March. The Hurricane pilots had been briefed by Bruce as to what to expect. As the only person in the squadron with experience of the arts, albeit theatrical not cinematic, Alan Stanley was pressed as to how the budding Hurricane stars should deport themselves, and which profile they should present to the camera. On the first morning they waited at a dispersal hut, as they joked, to be screen tested and called to have their makeup applied by the station's WAAFs.

"Who knows," offered Cameron, a Canadian veteran from Ontario, "when the war is over and the RAF no longer needs the aerodrome, this place could become the Hollywood of England!"

"Have you, my friend from the beyond the Rockies, never heard of Pinewood?" enquired Hilliard.

"Heh, that's last year's story!" and in jest Cameron took a swing at Hilliard with the back of his hand.

"Perhaps they want a record of the place for when we're all gone...," interjected Purseglove, a new and untested pilot officer, not realising the impact his words might have. Those who were seated shifted uneasily, those who stood looked away to the hangars. Then Hilliard leaned across to Stanley, and said, "Alan, as we must defer to your wealth of wisdom in issues artistic, do you think there might be, just might be, a chance that my next role could be opposite Ingrid Bergman?"

"I think that you've seen *For Whom The Bell Tolls* one time too many."

"That might be so, but I *do* think that Gary Cooper has the screen presence of a five day old corpse."

Laughter exploded and radiated outward, bouncing off the blades of new grass, rippling and dispersing with the mist. In truth they were as anxious about their impending appearance in front of the cameras as they were about the next operation over France.

The station commander still smarted at the imposition, and a memorandum from Group HQ that instructed him to provide 'every assistance and facility' to the film makers. He had defined those places within the perimeter fence where the film crew were not to be allowed; this included the bomb dump, his own office, and the officers' mess. He gave orders that the film crew were to be chaperoned at all times by one of the intelligence officers, to make certain that they did not come to any harm, and were kept away from the defined 'sensitive locations'. He had another reason to suspect the civilians in their midst, as he had been advised that the director, Ernest Houseman, had once gone by the name of Ernst Hausmann, a transformation that did not sit well with his sense of just who the enemy was supposed to be.

He had a staunch, if unknown ally, in the senior ground crew NCO of the Hurricane squadron. Flight Sergeant Murray was a long service veteran, and traced his career to the days of the Royal Flying Corps in France. He took issue with those of a 'Bohemian disposition', and consequently warned his ground crews.

"If you observe anything, mark you anything, which appears untoward, you are to report it immediately," he said, his burning resentment of the unknown flashing in his eyes. This left the nonplussed ground crews expecting that the sound technicians and camera operators were enemy agents, who perhaps had been dropped by parachute in the night; an impression enforced when the director appeared wearing a dark blue beret, dishevelled corduroy trousers and a sleeveless sweater, making notes at a furious pace into a little black notebook.

To his surprise, Tom was selected for a scene which was to be shot in one of the hangars. The premise was that one of the 'gallant pilots', in Ernest Houseman's own words, was to brief ground crew on battle damage sustained to one of the aircraft. The first problem was that none of the Hurricanes had battle damage of a kind suitable for the storyline; however, one of the Spitfires did. The second problem was that Tom had never flown on that aircraft type, and the ground crew selected as being most photogenic to receive the intelligence from him had only limited experience on Spitfires, which required much more intricate work to repair. These considerations were not regarded as serious enough to prevent the filming going ahead, Houseman being keen to capture the 'spirit' of the drama. There was to be no sound recording for this scene, as a commentary was to be provided at a later date, so Tom and the attendant ground crew enjoyed a certain freedom as to the dialogue they provided to match their actions.

"Well corporal, what do you think this is?" asked Tom as he pointed to a series of bullet holes in the tail of the Spitfire which was the principal property.

"I can't rightly say sergeant, I have seen one before, but never at this distance."

"Looks to be in working order, and appears to be a type of flying machine," Tom said to the jubilation of the Hurricane pilots gathered behind the camera, and fury of the Spitfire pilots, "but I wonder who in their right mind would fly in it? He would have to be mad, quite, quite mad."

When the scene was completed, Tom walked over and stood next to Murray while the camera and lights were taken down and moved.

"Tommy, there'll be hell to pay when the Spitfire C.O. hears about this," whispered Murray out of the corner of his mouth. Tom turned his head, and winked. Needless to say, there were protests from the commanding officer of the Spitfire squadron, which Bruce politely refuted.

The film crew were billeted at the aerodrome, and had the use of the sergeants' mess; apart from being challenged by nervous sentries on two occasions, there were no incidents. On the last night, Houseman hosted an all ranks party in *The Falcon*. The station commander made a brief speech, punctuated with references to his own service in the Royal Flying Corps and the need to know where the enemy was at all times; then they all drank to the publican's health. The Ministry technicians packed the cameras and lighting gear into the vans in the morning, and drove away, leaving the RAF personnel to ponder how much screen time they would have. For Alan Stanley screen time was all that he would have, as he was lost over the Channel returning from a raid later that week.

Quite suddenly, their tenure at Benington was brought to an end. Bruce called the pilots and ground crew officers and senior NCOs to a briefing, they convened in the operations hut. Squadrons were regularly posted to alternative aerodromes, or sent for specialist training or re-equipment with new aircraft types, or even disbanded. In truth the squadrons were almost as expendable as the pilots who flew with them. From his seat Tom could see the wind sock lazily flapping against its mast; a truck passed, changing gear with an awkward grinding noise; and a couple of WAAFs strode purposefully past a hangar. George Thomas sat down next to him, a little self conscious as he had recently become the victim of a stunning haircut, that had given him an unfortunate profile resembling that of a carrot. Bruce stood up and addressed them, advising them that operations were suspended. This set off a rapid murmuring, which he silenced, before continuing.

"All that I am able to advise you, is that the squadron is being posted overseas," which brought forth some cheering, "but, for reasons of security I cannot advise you to which theatre of operations. However I can advise you that you are all to receive embarkation leave."

The leave was welcome. Bruce again quietened them, holding his hand up as he surveyed the ranks of young faces before him.

"I am allowed to pass on one other piece of information, which is not to be discussed outside this room," and he looked with stern displeasure to his left and right before continuing, "all pilots will attend a short training course prior to embarkation in take-off and landing procedure from the deck of an aircraft carrier."

Silence. Tom and George exchanged glances, George with a slightly furrowed brow, Tom with the muscles around his mouth pulling tight over his jaw. They were dismissed, filed out of the room and along the corridor to the door onto the apron. The wave that had borne them up to this place, now carried them further on.

The Captive Summer

Gibraltar

That Gibraltar remained physically attached to Spain was due in no small measure to the failure of the plans of Oliver Cromwell. In 1656 it had been the intention of the Lord Protector of England to dig up the land bridge, and cast Gibraltar adrift in the Mediterranean. The plan failed, due to the capture of the ship carrying the wheel barrows and spades to be used to remove the thousands of tonnes of earth, sand and rock tethering Gibraltar to the Iberian peninsular. But the failure of the seventeenth century expedition had much to recommend it from the perspective of the aerial defence of the Western Mediterranean and the Straits in the twentieth century: the flat strip of land separating Gibraltar from La Linea was the only suitable place where a runway could be constructed.

The Fleet Air Arm emergency landing strip set in the middle of the racecourse was replaced by a new runway capable of handling four engined heavy bombers. Hewn from rock blasted out of the Rock itself, it jutted like an accusatory stone finger across Algeciras Bay. For much of 1941 the engineers blasted and tunnelled, and the laden trucks threw splinters and pieces of rock into the sea; the German spies in La Linea got little sleep. Protest by the Gibraltar Jockey Club was futile: the race track had gone forever. As the RAF built up its strength, aircraft had to be parked wing tip to wing tip around the perimeter; air and ground crews tired of cramped troopships found accommodation in Nissen huts, aircraft crates, or those hotels or apartments not already claimed by the Army or Navy.

By 1942, Gibraltar and Malta represented the only British presence in the Mediterranean beyond the shores of Africa. Their fates were linked but separate. Gibraltar was immediately surrounded by 'neutral' or non-combatant countries, but perhaps the aircrews shot at by Spanish or Vichy French gunners would take some convincing of that. Malta was the floating fortress of the Mediterranean; the island that could not be allowed to fall, but set less than one hundred kilometres from the Axis aerodromes of Sicily. Gibraltar was the staging post for Malta relief convoys; its Sunderland and Catalina flying boats provided anti-submarine patrols as the convoys ran the gauntlet of Axis air and naval forces. But few merchant ships reached Malta, and for a time, the convoys were suspended. Without reinforcement, the defenders of Malta had little option but surrender. Spitfires and a few Hurricanes were sent to Gibraltar in crates, to be assembled, and then ferried on an aircraft carrier until they reached a flying off point still several hundred kilometres to the west of the besieged island. And in that consignment were the Hurricanes of Tom's squadron.

The pilots arrived on the merchantman *Adelaide Ranger* from Liverpool in early May. The vessel had not been designed as a troopship, and the sergeants in the RAF detachment found themselves sleeping in a mess deck close to the water line, the officers in cabins some decks above them. At one end a companion way led to the upper decks, and in the event of an emergency would be their only escape route. At night they slept in hammocks, or for those unable to master the technique, on the mess benches or even the cold and not infrequently wet deck itself. The fear of U-boat attack was ever present; as they played cards, or read or lay in the hammocks rocking back and forth, many minds considered the prospect of a torpedo passing through the dark waters beyond the steel plate, and erupting among them. The Bay of Biscay honoured its reputation; the contortions of the ship in the heavy seas, together with the cramped conditions, and food of uncertain origin, brought forth a stream of complaints from Maguire and Mitchell.

"And just what," enquired Maguire at dinner one day, sniffing at a plate on which mashed potato was complemented by a meat dish of uncertain origin, "are we to make of this?"

"I think it's a new way of preparing pork," offered Neville Longhouse, looking up from a letter he was reading from his wife.

"But it tastes like a new way of preserving explosive," commented Mitchell as he purposefully chewed on a piece cut with some effort from the main portion on his plate.

"And just how do the senior officers and politicians who are running this war expect Britain to win if this is the best they can do for the serving men?" retorted Maguire, pulling in his chin and pushing out his chest as he spoke, to emphasise his distaste both for the food and British military leadership.

"I'm sorry lads," said Tom as he looked up from his own plate, "the catering would have been better, but the Queen Mary was needed to carry an urgent consignment of champagne to the Australian Prime Minister." This retort produced the expected uproar and protest from the Australian contingent; the argument raged for a few minutes, allowing all the men the chance to take their minds away from the churning sea, and the grey spectres following them beneath the waves.

But no attack came, and in early misty light one morning the ship and the others in its small convoy sighted Europa Point. There were plenty of opportunities for them all to complain once they were ashore and taken by truck to the new runway, which had become RAF North Front. While accommodation had been found for the officers in huts, the sergeants had to make do with camp beds thrown down in aircraft crates, which were arranged side by side like chalets at a military holiday camp. The base area was a raw open piece of land, with no shade, few facilities, and the incessant din from the construction of the runway. They would have climbed into their aircraft then and there and flown away, but for the fact that the Hurricanes were in bits. They passed one of the squads of ground crew on their way into the base, and witnessed a dozen or so under the command of a corporal, straining to insert the port wing into the wing root of a Spitfire.

"I hope they remember which way round the wing goes, or we'll never get off the bloody ground!" commented Maguire, the incident instilling further misgivings in his mind.

Gibraltar was unique because of its proximity to a neutral country, and its dependency on labour from Spain for the docks. It provided employment for several thousand Spaniards, desperate for work, and the chance to buy luxuries like English cigarettes and bread. But German agents in La Linea and Algeciras did what they could via Spanish informers and agents to find out what was going on in Gibraltar, and sometimes to sabotage the Naval and Air facilities. On their arrival, the first priority for the pilots was a briefing from an intelligence officer attached to Air HQ. No sooner had they dropped from the lorry, but they were all shepherded into a Nissen hut overlooking the bay.

"I must impress upon you," he began, "that the enemy is quite literally not only at the gate, but walks amongst us."

They were addressed by a flight lieutenant, apparently humourless, with dark hair close cropped and plastered down on his head with too much oil. He had a twitch in one eye, and gave the impression of being a novice priest offering up a sermon on moral delinquency. However, the danger was tangible, and the message was clear and simple: "Keep your mouths shut!" No aircrew would be granted permission to go across the border into Spain on any grounds; no information gained about the nature or details of operations was to be discussed; and no questions were to be asked about other operations centred on Gibraltar. The civil police and intelligence forces, he assured them, were vigilant in monitoring those they suspected, their efforts given greater urgency by the activities of agents just across the perimeter fence. Suitably chastised, the pilots were then briefed by Bruce about their role in preparing and testing the aircraft prior to embarkation on the aircraft carrier. Until that moment, their destination had been classified information, but they had not expected to be sent to North Africa; Gibraltar was the ante room for only one other theatre of operations.

Most of the civilian population had been evacuated, so the day time population comprised the British garrison and the hungry Spaniards. Gibraltar could not decide whether it was an armed camp or a town under siege. The airmen could still buy a pint of beer, a packet of twenty Players cigarettes and go to the cinema; but they slept within a few hundred metres of a constantly patrolled fence, and had been warned that high powered telescopes incorporating the finest German optical technology were trained on them from villas alongside the road to Algeciras.

Each Hurricane or Spitfire under assembly was allocated its own ground crew, augmented in some cases with Army personnel. The limited amount of space meant that construction and testing had to be conceived as a type of Chinese puzzle: one aircraft at a time could be moved, and the objective was to move each one so that full power engine tests could take place without threatening to blow ground crew, loitering air crew, spare parts or other aircraft clean off the runway and into the sea. A second problem was that surrounding dispersal and working areas were made up of compressed dirt, resulting in choking sand and dust storms as the engine of each aircraft was run up and held at full power. Tom, George Thomas, and Bill Mitchell worked as a group to test the Hurricanes they would eventually fly to Malta. The aircraft were pushed across to the verge at the side of the runway on a cloudy morning, turned to present their tails to the sea, and lined up a few metres apart. With brakes on full, and the weight of two aircraftmen holding down the tail of each, the pilots climbed into the cockpits unburdened by parachutes and life-jackets, and started the engines. As mechanical life flooded back into the airframe, Tom felt the vibration rise up through his legs, and into his hands as he held the controls. He pushed back the cockpit hood, pulled down his flying goggles to protect against the dust, and communicated with the leading aircraftman who stood by the aircraft at the edge of the wing, by hand signals.

His aircraft was the middle of the section of three. As they went through the test sequence of idling, running up and holding at full power, he looked between George and Bill Mitchell, laughing at the absurdity of the three of them in perfect formation, and at full power, but going absolutely nowhere fast. In the deafening roar Bill gestured back to him, holding one hand to his throat, then raising his hand to his mouth to indicate that it was time they had a drink. George had leaned forward in his cockpit, and when Tom turned to him gave the thumbs up sign to announce his agreement. The first test sequence completed, the engines were silenced, and they climbed down for warm sweet tea.

One of the two aircraftmen who had struggled to hold the tail down passed round mugs of tea, and the little group gratefully washed the dust and sand out of their mouths. The leading aircraftman who had stood beside the Hurricane was Indian, and his black hair and dark skin were now peppered with dust, apart from two rings around his eyes, which had been protected by his goggles. His job was to check the engines for signs of leaks of oil or coolant, the propellers for signs of wear, and the blades for excessive movement as the pitch was varied. He was L/AC Kubai, as young as Tom, with keen bright eyes, made all the more intense by the contrast in skin tone on his now dusty face.

"Sergeant, how does the engine respond?" he asked Tom.

"Straight through with no loss of power, I can't wait to get into the air again," he answered, washing his mouth with the tea.

"At one moment I thought we were," commented the tea dispensing aircraftman, as he rubbed a sore stomach with one hand while offering a tea mug with his other to the sky.

"You will just have to try harder, or I'll nail your boots to the runway," offered Kubai, not prepared to accept any slacking.

"Do I look like Johnny Weismuller?" he replied, and in truth he didn't.

"Then you should eat more and do extra PT."

The aircraftman winced and turned his back on the others to drink the contents of the mug he held in peace.

Kubai wanted to fly. He had applied for aircrew selection, and waited for news. The object of some joking, he had exiled himself from the ground crew huts, and taken to sleeping in, on, or in close proximity to the aircraft at their dispersal points. One night he had improvised a hammock and slung it between the undercarriage of a Spitfire, sleeping like a baby in a crib until rudely awakened with a prod from a bayonet wielded by a member of a passing patrol.

The name of the underweight aircraftman was Matthews, and he had become the camp's unofficial bookmaker. The passage of thousands of Spaniards each morning and night along the Spanish Road into and out of Gibraltar, was regularly halted due to air operations. If this occurred in the morning, the assorted dock workers, shop assistants and household staff, would accumulate, impatiently waiting for the police to raise the barrier. The ground crew soon appreciated that if they then became late for work, the raising of the barrier acted as a starting pistol for a short sprint race across the runway and along the road. Matthews kept a form book, scrupulously noting the details of each entrant. The betting became sophisticated, and the event was divided into separate races: 'Dockers under the influence of alcohol' and 'Assorted shop staff subject to medical supervision' being two quotable examples. The pilots were sometimes allowed to wager a shilling; George succeeded in winning ten shillings one morning, but Tom, Bill Mitchell and Ken Maguire parted company with part of their pay. By the time his tour of duty was completed, Matthews had become a successful businessman.

The ground and air tests were completed over a period of two weeks. They provided Tom and the others brief opportunities to fly along the burnished coast of Spain and into the Straits, but extensive patrols were not encouraged. Testing completed, the aircraft were moved across the runway to dispersal areas awaiting the arrival of the carrier. Too soon the day arrived; the Spitfires and Hurricanes were taken to the docks, and the pilots were briefed about the sea journey, take-off procedure and what to expect when they arrived in Malta. That evening they were taken to the docks for embarkation. They walked up the gangway to be drawn within the towering bulk of the ship, and made their way through dimly lit companionways.

Assisted by three tugs, the carrier pulled away from No.1 Dock, passed through the boom, and joined the escort group of a cruiser and four destroyers. Standing in the stern with Cameron, Hilliard and some of the others, Tom strained to make out the blackness of the Rock against the blue-black of the summer night sky. A few minutes passed until, as if by common consent, as no words passed between them, they gave up their vigil and stepped back into the shadows of the vibrating ship.

The Captive Summer

Confinement

Toward midnight on the day that Tom was discovered on the beach, the inhabitants of the house heard a car approaching along the drive. Consuelo had stayed with the young man in the room of warm wavering light; although in need of sleep, she continued to watch over him, sitting at a chair drawn up beside the bed. She had cleaned the wounds to his head and face, and watched as the bandage she applied slowly changed colour from white to pink. With slow care they had removed the khaki tunic and his boots; Maria had found an identity disc attached to a chain around his neck, and from this they had learned the name of their invalid, his military number, and blood type. Consuelo spoke English, but it was useless to her now. No communication was possible, but she waited patiently in the hope that he might regain consciousness.

They had learned nothing of how he had come to be in the cove; the salt water had obliterated just about every scrap of writing in his possession, and the only connection to the outside world was a photograph of a man and woman with two small children. They assumed that this must be a family portrait, until careful inspection showed that the man in the photograph and the young man on the bed were not the same. Consuelo sent Maria to prepare some food for Rafael, Antonio and Jesus, and so she was left alone.

She was roused from near penitential silence by the sound of the main door being opened, the drawing of the bolts resonating through the ground floor, and hoped that this heralded the arrival of the doctor. Doctor Don Federico Hernandez was one of only two physicians who served the people of that area, and more importantly, he was an old and close friend. Like Consuelo and her husband, he was sympathetic to the Republican cause, and for now escaped censure or arrest because there were few doctors in that part of the country. Maria had tempered urgency with a need not to arose suspicion as she walked into town to find him, as Consuelo possessed no motor car. When she arrived at the doctor's house she was cautious yet insistent as she rang the bell, paying attention to who might see her. The door was opened by Dr Hernandez's housekeeper, Senora Lopez, who correctly interpreted the anxious expression on Maria's face and ushered her within. Maria had no choice but to leave a message for him, and returned to the house.

Consuelo heard heavy steps along the corridor; the door opened and Dr Hernandez entered, closely followed by Maria, who was still explaining that it was not Consuelo who was ill. The doctor was a tall man, of late middle age, but still robust, with greying hair receding around the temples.

Deep channels cut underneath his eyes, which bore the signs of too little sleep, too much work, and the effects of bearing witness to much suffering. His cheeks were hollowed, and there was stubble on his face. In profile he had an aquiline nose, and although a proud Spaniard, there was an air about him of ancient Imperial Rome. His hands were powerful and broad, with strong fingers. He wore a grey suit with a double breasted waistcoat, but carried the jacket over one arm. His shirt cuffs hung loose, and the collar of his shirt was partially detached and unbuttoned. Overall he gave the appearance of a man who had dressed hurriedly, whereas in truth he had been working all through the day, as spots of blood on his sleeve bore witness. In one stride he took in both Consuelo, now standing pensively by the bed, and its occupant.

"My dear Consuelo," and he advanced to her, and kissed her lightly on each cheek, "I thought that something had happened to you."

"No Federico, not I, and I am sorry to have called for you so late, but he," now pointing, "is very sick."

Dr Hernandez put his jacket and bag down on the chair, as he did so Consuelo noticed the blood on his sleeve. He knelt down beside the young man, and looked up to ask Consuelo something, but seeing that her eyes were drawn to his shirt his own eyes strayed there.

"Forgive me, it was a difficult delivery, and I did not have time to change my shirt when I returned to the house."

Consuelo called for Maria to get a clean shirt for him, and a basin, hot water, soap, and towels.

"How did he come here?"

"We do not know, two fishermen found him in the cove and one of them came here to seek our help. All that we know is that he is English, from his uniform, and we know his name, Roberts, but that is all."

"Were there other bodies?"

Consuelo did not know, so she called for Antonio, who confirmed that his was the only body they had seen. As he washed and changed into the fresh shirt, which had belonged to Consuelo's husband, Dr Hernandez questioned Antonio about the young man; whether he had regained consciousness; whether he had struck his head while on the beach, and any signs of life or movement. They had almost forgotten the sudden spasm which had gripped his body as he lay on the bed, but when they related that to Dr Hernandez he straightened up from drying his face, and asked them to confirm precisely what had happened. Then he examined the young man as Consuelo and Maria both held lamps, and Rafael went to bring other lamps to the room. As Consuelo watched she noticed that a dark wisp of smoke arose from the lamp on the dressing table across from the bed; she shuddered a little, hoping that in its ascent to the ceiling it was not an omen for the ascent of the young man's soul.

Dr Hernandez probed the skull with great care, using his fingertips to feel for bone protruding near to the skin. He found none, but his sensitive fingers found a very slight depression in the bone, which ran close to where the skull had suffered a long cut. He shone a small light into the young man's eyes, and seemed satisfied with the response. He asked for a shaving kit, and shaved the scalp, leaving an area of bare stubble like a field after harvest. He cleaned the wound, and applied a dressing. Then he cleaned the cut and swollen upper lip, and stitched that. Finally he sat down; clearly exhausted he held the young man's limp hand and felt the pulse, checking against his pocket watch. Relieved that he had at least survived the initial examination, Consuelo withdrew to the kitchen and Maria went in search of linen. The night was still warm, and the only ventilation in the room was provided by two small rectangular windows set high, which were filled by wooden lattices; as a consequence the air in the room had become oppressive.

Maria returned to put a counterpane over the bed, and found the doctor just on the point of sleep. She placed a hand on his shoulder and shook him twice in quick succession, and he revived. At her suggestion he rose and went out, walking along the windowless corridor to the courtyard, drawn by the clean night air. The house was familiar to him, as he had been a frequent guest here with his wife in happier times. As he emerged into the courtyard and looked through the rectangle of roofs to the stars, he was assaulted by the ghosts of the house; they chattered and laughed and drank and danced, swirling unseen around him, as in a phantom carousel. One of the ghosts was his wife, Constanza, who had died several years before. He crossed to the far side, and passed into the main reception room. Throwing himself down into a chair, he stretched out, craving sleep but mindful that he had a journey yet to travel back to the town. Consuelo came into the room bearing a tray containing dishes for a cold supper, which she set down beside him.

"He may not live through the night, you know that," he commented through closed eyelids.

"I know. If he dies we will bury him," and she looked away through the windows onto the silent garden beyond, the upper branches of the fruit trees seemingly brushing against the stone balustrade of the terrace.

"Consuelo," and now he opened his eyes and looked at her, "it may be better if he does die. Have you considered the consequences of looking after him, for you all?"

She turned toward him now, her face impassive, but with set feature __.
Hernandez remembered a younger woman, in love, and loved; a woman
who shone and laughed, and talked quickly, and lovingly chided her
husband. There was little of that woman now, just set features, and a care
numbed expression.

"I have thought of that. To harbour an enemy of Spain is an act of
treason. We could all be shot, or sent to a Labour Battalion."

"Is it worth the danger Consuelo?"

"Federico, when we lost news of Arturo, I prayed and prayed every night
for him. I prayed that if he should be found half dead in a field somewhere,
that whoever found him would take care of him. Perhaps, this young
Englishman has someone who also prays for him. You may think this a
token of madness on my part, but I hope that by showing mercy to this
young man, that by some way, mercy will be shown to Arturo."

The doctor reached across and took Consuelo's hand. "I understand; I
only wanted to be sure you appreciated the consequences."

"Will he live Federico?"

The doctor's countenance became grave, and he released Consuelo's
hand and sat back. "Yes he may live. He was strong enough to survive the
journey from the beach. He has a fracture to his skull on the left frontal
bone. However in striking his head, he may have suffered an injury to his
brain. I cannot tell yet. I am concerned about the seizure, I would like you
and Maria to stay with him, and let me know in the morning whether he has
regained consciousness. But do not move him, he must not be moved."

"I understand, I will send Rafael with word tomorrow," and she
contemplated the enormity of the deception they would carry out, over
weeks, perhaps over months, to hide this man; a man about whom they
knew nothing bar the briefest details, in the hope that by this act of
compassion she could win an unseen bargain for the life of her husband.

They ate together, then he collected his case and jacket and went out to
his car. He drove a fine, almost antique, sleek black Mercedes; when he
opened the door the smell of the leather upholstery slipped into the air like
jasmine. Consuelo watched as the car pulled away, until its lights were lost
within the trees screening the house.

Antonio and Jesus had not yet departed; Consuelo made her way to the
kitchen, where they were eating with Rafael. A couple of glasses of coarse
wine had made them both drowsy, when Consuelo entered the room she
found that Jesus lay with his head on his folded arms, while Antonio was
endeavouring to engage Rafael in a discussion about Spain's neutrality in
the war raging across the Mediterranean. Antonio possessed the true

Spanish temperament, he also disliked those who were not of Spanish blood; these, taken with his tiredness in the late evening, were a dangerous combination. Rafael knew that Antonio would have wished to raise the fire in his Cuban blood, but would not be provoked; Maria maintained an uncharacteristic silence, but watched both men closely.

"You must understand, Moro," and Antonio used his finger like a dagger and pointed it in Rafael's face, "when Imperial Spain in her glory conquered half the world, and gold spilled from the pockets of the conquistadors, we had no need for tribes of goatherds from the Atlas mountains, we...," at which point Consuelo intervened.

"Antonio, thank you for your help in bringing the Englishman; may I speak to you privately?"

They stepped out into the corridor, and Consuelo addressed him. If the circumstances of life had been different for Antonio he could have become a successful man, and worn a suit of good dark blue cloth; but his face was worn and pinched and his eyes untrusting. There were however still traces of a greater humanity, and the sharp remembrance of the sound of bullets from Civil Guard rifles passing close to his head. He sobered quickly.

"Antonio, if the young man lives, he will have to remain here, perhaps for weeks. If any word should leave these walls, then we are doomed," she said.

"Neither I nor my brother are informers Dona Consuelo, and had it not been for your intervention we would have been sent to a Labour Battalion a year ago. No word of this shall come from us. You have my word as a Spaniard."

That night they watched, and into the next day, and the next night. And so for several days.

Tom opened his eyes. The room was darkened; across from him he could make out a bar of intense light on the floor where a shuttered window admitted the sun. The ceiling was high and he could see the rough hewn rafters. As his eyes adjusted he could make out that the walls were whitewashed, roughly rendered, ancient. There was a smell of wax and flowers. His lips were dry, and in an effort to wet them he ran his tongue across them, but no saliva came; his tongue felt alien to him, as if a small scaly creature had climbed into his mouth. He turned his head to see if there was water nearby and regretted it immediately, as a pulsing of blood like the beating of hammers returned in his left temple. He felt sick. Scared, he felt himself slipping down into a cold pit. He gripped the side of the bed with his left hand under the sheets. Then the sweat came, and for the first time he could smell himself: he stank. Nausea rose as he felt himself continuing to fall, as if in a tail spin in that dying Hurricane. Was he now dead? But he felt pain, he could not have died.

Footsteps in the corridor without. Then a loud crack as the door handle turned, and light reflected from the opposite wall of the corridor diffused throughout the room. A figure of a man was briefly silhouetted, the door closed. He was unable to make out anything further; soft footfalls approached the bed, and he was aware of a dark face looking intently down at him. The figure reached for something out of Tom's sight, while at the same time a hand slipped under his head and raised it very slowly and by a small degree only from the pillow. A glass was held to his lips, and Tom drank, the little river of fluid washing his tongue like the first snow melt over a dry stream in a high valley. Then the man departed as he had come, to be replaced after an interval of time by the figures of two women. A voice spoke to him from the darkness, in English, but not an English voice.

"Good morning Mr Roberts, we're so glad to have you with us."

The Captive Summer

Remembrance of Things Past

Remembrance of Arturo was never far from Consuelo's consciousness; and many waking hours were punctuated by thoughts of him or his situation. She had made a bargain, possibly in vain, in the hope that the salvation of one life could be traded for another. Following Dr Hernandez's departure on that first evening, she had visited the room where Tom lay, to see that Maria had all that she required for the first period of vigil, which would run through the remaining night. Maria was seated just inside the door; a single lamp illuminated the room now, and the faintly undulating shadows thrown up by its light gave to the room the atmosphere of a cave set in a sheltering mountain. Maria was sowing, repairing a shirt which belonged to one of her children, and the tiredness in her face was softened by the gentle yellowish light. In reply to the concerned entreaty of Consuelo's eyes she shook her head in a constrained way, in case even this action should disturb the unconscious figure.

Consuelo approached the bed; the wounds appeared worse now after treatment than they had before, which owed much to the bare strip of skull where the hair had been shaved away to expose the cut being adorned with a ribbon of congealed blood. Saddened, she left and retired to her own room, the room which had been the marital bedroom of herself and Arturo. She kept many photographs of him on the dressing table: some in his lawyer's robes; in others dressed casually or in suits; at a cafe table in Madrid; leaning easily against the garden wall with the sun bathing his face, a pair of sunglasses in one hand and a cigarette in the other; photographs of them together, photographs of them apart. If she had not these remembrances of him, his image would still have been illuminated in her consciousness, and it was the presence of his image which gave her hope that he was still alive, and would one day return.

She did not know how the years of separation had changed him; she knew that he could not look precisely as he had done more than four years before, and she attempted to imagine him even thinner in the face, perhaps tired, haggard even; but she dreaded to imagine him wounded, disfigured, scarred, with sunken lifeless eyes staring out to her from a face that was a pallid mask drawn tight over spectral bone.

When the Spanish Republican army had been finally beaten in the spring of 1939, its remnants joined several hundred thousand refugees who moved across the border into France to escape the advancing Nationalist forces. The French authorities were initially reluctant to allow Republican soldiers entry; but as the tide of desperate men built up, it became clear that the only alternative would be deploy the French army to fight them, which the French government recognised it could not do. However, these men were segregated from the civilians, disarmed and forced into internment camps, where they remained, even into the period of the Vichy government. The most encouraging statement that could be made about their condition was that they were alive, although this could not be attributed to the generosity of spirit of the *gardes mobiles*, who were eager to demonstrate their contempt for the internees. And this, it was understood from the fragments of news which reached them, was the fate of Arturo and the men in his company.

The most recent photograph had been taken in 1938 when Arturo, then a *comrade capitan*, had enjoyed a brief period of leave. He was already notably thinner than he had been before, and his eyes were two deep pits of colour which concealed horrors he would not relate, but which no soul could bear alone. His tunic was a little ill fitting, and his collar rode up, in spite of Consuelo's efforts. Whereas at any other time Arturo deliciously anticipated his wife and lover smoothing the cloth lying across his breast or combing his hair, as Consuelo would softly say, "My darling, you're too good for Hollywood!" as she did this, he now regarded these loving acts as pointless distractions, although he tried to conceal this from her.

When she came to look at this photograph in the months and years which separated them, she was struck by the melancholy in his face, almost a reluctance to face the camera, as if the camera lens were the muzzle of a machine gun, and he a condemned man running breathless and sweating up a slope seeking, yet shying away from, oblivion.

They had married in 1931, another year of turmoil in Spain that saw the abdication of King Alfonso XIII and his replacement by the Second Republic; and they believed that in their life together they would see Spain transformed. This at least came to pass, but not as they had hoped. Arturo was older by four years, and came from a family of lawyers and judges; Consuelo's family were merchants, apart from one uncle who also was a judge, and it was the law which was responsible for them meeting. When they had first met, Arturo pretended to ignore her, holding a book up to his face and slyly observing her from around its edges. What he did not realise was that in his agitated state he was holding the book upside down, which Consuelo noted and coolly played up to.

This meeting took place in the drawing room of her uncle's house in Seville, where Consuelo and her family joined her uncle Eduardo's family and close friends to celebrate his appointment as a criminal judge. Spain's legal tradition did not include trial by jury; during the dictatorship of Primo de Rivera the system had again been suspended, so that major trials were conducted by a panel of three judges only: Eduardo Arranquez would now take his place as one of the three judges on the local panel.

Whether it had been her uncle's intention to act as matchmaker she never discovered, but he took pains to introduce the haughty law student who was the son of his closest friend. He regarded his niece, still only nineteen, and a pure statement of expectant innocence, as a jewel without equal, made more precious in that he and his wife had only succeeded in extending the male line of succession. Arturo had displayed the warmth which one would have expected of a stranger with whom one shares a large room for a short period of time. And Consuelo was not impressed by his attitude, with an excess of hair oil and deficit of good manners. While they waited for lunch, there being a number of guests who were yet to arrive, polite conversation and fino sherry passed round the room in the way that fuel impregnated gases pass round an engine until they combust and the pistons shiver into life.

As most of the guests were lawyers, the topic of conversation was the law, which presented Consuelo with a deficit of knowledge and anecdotes. She sat close to her mother, and looking around tried to take an interest in the details of the proceedings; she noted that the haughty young man was seated at a couch next to an alcove in which were a collection of books, one of which he was purporting to read. She did not know anything about the law, which may or may not have been a handicap in the conduct of a happy life, but she was intelligent and had sharp eyes. It was clear to her that the book he held was either written in a language like Castilian but with characters suspended from each imaginary line, or that he held the book upside down and was not aware of the fact. She turned her attention elsewhere; however, curiosity drew her eyes back to that part of the room, although she took pains to give the impression that she was merely sweeping her gaze over the chattering, boisterous, prosperous and congratulatory gathering of humanity. It was with an effort that she stopped herself nervously laughing and drawing attention to herself, pressing her fingernails into the palm of one hand, and straining earnestly to listen to her mother's conversation.

What Consuelo observed was a routine taken from the *commedia dell'arte*, a pantomime, a naked man holding his hands over his eyes to shield his nakedness from himself. First Arturo's right ear, then the tip of the eyebrow and the corner of the eye came into view; for a moment he hesitated, then slowly the pale green iris and the dark pupil reached beyond the cloth bound edge of the book. Consuelo found herself blushing as she realised that she was the object of his attention; she lowered her gaze, then in a series of quick glances she took in the tortoise like movements as the eye appeared and then retracted, to re-emerge after a minute or so. The book played its role faithfully as the instrument of the prospective lover, although the lover remained oblivious to the absurdity of the device. They were summoned to lunch; and as they entered the dining room she took the opportunity to question him as to his reading habits.

"I see you lose no opportunity to widen your knowledge," she said without looking directly at Arturo. He, affecting an air of scholarly virtue, replied, "I hope to follow my father's occupation," to which she countered "As public prosecutor or spy?"

Thereafter she would say to him, "But it isn't fair that you treat me so: do you think that I cannot read?!" whenever he did or said anything which implied that he was toying with her. She remembered the lightness of his touch when he placed a hand on her shoulder to gain her attention; he had a particular way, not as a father or brother or less still another woman would have. He would first place his palm, then pivot his hand forward on her collar bone and finally gently squeeze with his fingertips. It denoted more than a desire or need to communicate, his touch was the simplest and most innocent statement of his love. There had been many days following his departure when, in a quiet reverie, she would sit with her legs drawn up under her on a garden seat at the edge of the terrace, with her arms embracing her own body, and the warm wind sliding and murmuring through the almond trees beyond, and remember his touch.

She imagined him walking amongst the fruit trees; she remembered Arturo and Rafael digging and planting, Rafael trying to gain leverage under the root of an old dead olive tree while Arturo pulled against the bridle of a mule they had harnessed to tear the root out of the ground, and cursing the animal. She was happy with her memories, but she gave little outward sign; to show recaptured joy through the avenue of memory could as easily grant access to uncorroborated grief. Arturo had loved the house, had indeed been born there; it had been purchased by his grandfather, as a sanctuary from the Carlist Wars and military coups which punctuated Spanish political life in the nineteenth century. It had gained the name by which it had come to be known in the locality, El Faro, the Light, because the ancient tower had once held a burning brazier to warn of the treacherous sea.

When Tom was recovered sufficiently to be allowed to sit on the terrace under the awning, he would sometimes observe her as she sat a little way from him; knowing so little about her he could only wonder who rather than what encouraged these periods of reflection. He remembered the words of Brabantio in Othello, "*But he bears both the sentence and the sorrow, that to pay grief must of poor patience borrow*", his elementary Spanish preventing him from communicating these sentiments to anyone else in the household. As his Spanish improved he risked asking Rafael in formal Castilian, "The lady is sad, indeed?" To which the reticent Cuban would only answer, "My mistress has many memories."

In the early morning Consuelo rose from her bed and relieved Maria; as she crossed the courtyard a faint crimson light stole through the air, lightening the dark spaces and giving form to shapeless matter. She remembered what she had been told as a child, that each day is a resurrection, that each day in some way we approach the world for the first time, and that each morning an angel walks beside us until we are sure of our way. The effect of the acoustic of her footsteps on the floor gave her the impression that someone else was walking with her; although she knew that it could not be yet she turned before leaving the courtyard and looked behind her; but the masses of cool air hung undisturbed in her wake. Maria, stiff from hours seated on the hard chair, whose unrelenting spindles allowed no comfort, rose gratefully as Consuelo entered the room. Together they came close to the bed; only a shallow rising and falling of the counterpane across the young man's chest assured them that he was still alive.

"Go now Maria, sleep until the late morning, Rafael will prepare food for us when he rises."

Maria departed and Consuelo took her place, composed, attentive, yet aware of the morning which was gaining outside the room. When she judged that there was sufficient external light she turned down the lamp and opened the two small shutters set high up on the wall, stretching a little to reach them. The room radiated the massive strength of the outer wall into a still space which contained a frail and broken human form; whether that strength could be applied to heal and repair the young man she did not know, although she was conscious of the cruel disparity between the room and its sleeping occupant.

There were wild flowers on the dresser, collected by Maria and her children, and Consuelo quickly recognised the yellow flowers of Spanish broom mixed with blue cornflowers. She wondered whether she should leave them or take them out, and decided for the moment to let them abide. One day when she and Arturo were walking out together, and had reached a degree of intimacy in their early courtship such that she accepted when he took her hand rather than instinctively pull away, they passed flowers at the roadside still heavy with rain; the heads were bowed to the earth as if in prayer, and the earth around them now steamed as the sun resumed its assault. Arturo had taken some broom and shaken out the droplets of rain from the flowers, making this action as an anointment across Consuelo's brow. She stood with the pearls of water in her hair, and felt them warm on her cheek, then he leaned forward and kissed her.

The morning wore on, but there was no change in the sleeping man; when Rafael woke he prepared breakfast for them all; once this simple affair was concluded he went into town with the oblique message for Dr Hernandez that there had been no change in the situation. In a very narrow interpretation this was correct, but considered more broadly, all their lives had changed.

The Captive Summer

Dr Hernandez

Dr Hernandez woke early, in spite of receiving little sleep. His habit was to wash, dress and retire to the garden of his house with a cigar and a book before his housekeeper was about and preparing breakfast. Senora Carmela Lopez had worked for him for in excess of twenty years, and for the last five of those she had lived at his house, following the death of the doctor's wife. Dr Hernandez entered the garden from his study, his habitual route, as it gave him the opportunity to select a book from his library and a cigar from the cigar box on the desk. The flagstones of the terrace were littered with dry and brittle palm leaves, that made a curiously reassuring cracking sound as his feet pressed down breaking their spines. He kicked a few leaves away in a half hearted attempt to clear a space; with the cigar clamped between his teeth and the book in one hand, he pulled his garden chair across so that its back was against the palm tree and it faced the still hidden sun. He surveyed the arrangements briefly, and content with his work, sat down and deeply exhaled. This action was not to be confused with a sigh, as the doctor was not a man given to such gestures; the expulsion of air from his lungs was a statement, his only explicit acknowledgement that he had regained some fleeting contentment with the world. Before lighting the cigar he sat with his eyes closed and his head resting against the high backed chair, and listened to creation, keen to detect any indication of imperfection or sickness.

Above him the palm leaves made a rustling like the whispering of conspirators, and the water droplets in the air hung heavy before the scything rays of the morning. He felt the hairs on the back of his fingers caught by a teasing breeze, and he relaxed. His house was situated in a narrow street that was a tributary of a wider road leading into the main square. It was a square Spanish Victorian villa with a small garden hidden behind a stone wall. The wall had one opening, and in that was set an iron gate. He positioned the chair so that he faced away from the gate, and although not entirely hidden from view by passersby, he had a reasonable expectation of seclusion. He tried hard to detach himself from his body, in the sense that he attempted to become only conscious of how his senses, with the exception of his vision, described the world to him. He inclined his head the better to hear a cicada. Thus immersed, the world around him became once more without limit or fault, and he could not fix a position in it for himself. It was, and he was, and above him he could hear the palm leaves conspiring.

Yet he knew that his position within the world would soon become a fixed point; he knew that the sick would obtain that reckoning and turn toward it. He opened his eyes, and for a moment half lay and half sat in contemplation of his next action. He bit the end from the cigar and spat it away, then searched in a pocket of his waistcoat for matches. His cigar now alight, he took up his book; this morning his choice was poetry, a selection of the work of Antonio Machado. His position fixed, he endeavoured to ignore it, drawing on the cigar and letting the poetry, like the smoke, wash through his consciousness. He read for a quarter of an hour; the printed words before his eyes occasionally obscured by slowly wafting smoke, as he allowed the warm and acrid vapours to roll across the yellowing paper. His nose and mouth were so suffused with tobacco that his awareness of the warm mustiness of the garden and the sweet odour of the flowers in baskets on the far wall was quite deadened. Then, at the extreme periphery of his vision, he saw movement. Closing the book with one finger caught between the pages to mark his place, he turned and cleared away a small cloud of smoke with two brisk strokes of his hand. Close to the wall of the house, where a low stone trough held water for the plants, there was a cluster of palm leaves. The palm leaves shuddered; Dr Hernandez watched, a faint smile rising on his lips. The leaves moved again; he rose and stepped over to the pile of yellow-brown vegetation, but halted as the thought occurred to him that the leaves might provide cover for a snake. As he was considering how best to proceed, and looking around for a stick, a small olive green blob erupted from under one of the fronds and landed halfway between it and the water trough. Man and frog faced each other; the frog's air sac filling and emptying, the jet eyes fixed and absorbing every detail of its new adversary, and judging its next move. For reasons which the doctor was never able to fully explain to himself, but may have had something to do with his awareness of his own lack of close companionship, he engaged the animal in conversation.

"Good morning Capitan Mendoza, I am pleased to see that your vigilance to protect the Patria is undiminished! Do you now suspect the flowers?"

The frog made no reply, but continued to observe the doctor with a cool police like disdain. Dr Hernandez turned his head, the better to enable him to look about for other intruders, while keeping one eye on the amphibian; the amphibian considered it prudent to keep both its eyes fixed on the doctor. He remembered when he was a young medical student at the University of Madrid, and carried out experiments on innate animal reflexes using stripeless tree frogs such as this specimen; casting around in his memory for the Latin name, it came to him attached to the image of the twitching hind leg of a decapitated frog on a laboratory bench.

"*Hyla meridionalis*, of course," and he straightened up, but then leaned forward again to add, "but to me you are El Capitan."

He reflected that this little animal, which he could have placed comfortably in the palm of his hand, had yet a cardio-vascular system in miniature, a system of perfect operation and function. He wished that he could have shared his joke at the expense of the local Civil Guard commander with his wife; the smile on his lips faded, as he remembered that he could not. He wondered how it had gained access to the garden; he reasoned that it had used its acrobatic prowess to progress from a neighbouring place, perhaps drawn by the smell of the water trough. Further, albeit one sided, communication was ended by the arrival of Senora Lopez, who showed her surprise at the conference in the garden by arching her eyebrows, her habitual public display of emotion.

"Dr Hernandez, is something wrong?" she asked.

As the doctor faced her, the frog, sensing both heightened danger and faint opportunity, jumped and reached the water trough, landing in it with a faint splash. It lay with only its head above the surface, bulbous black eyes regarding them both.

"Good morning Senora Lopez. No, nothing is wrong, but we have a visitor, perhaps even a police spy," but seeing her momentary alarm he pointed to the frog and continued, "please do not worry, even if he made a full report against us he could not be understood."

Her face softened, but she was concerned at the tiredness evident in his face, which was matched by the slow deliberation with which he drew himself up to full height. On his instruction she had retired for the night before he returned from El Faro, although she was aware of his arrival from the shuffling slow footsteps as he ascended the stairs to his bedroom. But his weariness was not borne out of one night, but many days and nights; of seeing women die in childbirth because they were too weakened by their pregnancy, of repairing the smashed and gaping bodies of young men on bloodied stretchers, of children with cholera dying in pools of their own bodily fluids. For all of his mantle of exhaustion and hastening old age, he still retained a quality about him, a small boy's capacity for delight in a specific moment, and it was through this that he clung to his humanity. His pleasure in the mysterious arrival of the tree frog was a manifestation of this, and it transported him to a realm where the bitter sorrows of this world had no place. In short, for a moment, he had remembered what it was to be happy.

As they entered the house he drew out his little joke at the expense of the local police chief, although Senora Lopez cautioned him against such dangerous depredations, with unflattering allusions to the frog's sexual technique during the mating season. Humour, even dangerous humour, was his principal relief for the sense of frustration and rage at the continuing barbarities, and daily wastage of life. The Nationalists had not only taken the country, they saw it as their mission to cleanse and purify it; the police wielded the force to accomplish that aim.

Senora Lopez was a small spare woman, of some sixty years of age, silver-white hair pulled tightly back from her forehead into a comb of coiled silk. Permanently in mourning for her own husband, she habitually wore either black or deepest grey, and prayed every day for her husband's soul. Her room at the top of the house was sparely furnished, and enlightened only by a vase of dried flowers and photographs of her three children, all now moved away to more remote parts of Spain. A locket kept at her breast held a faded photograph of her husband, Alfonso, then a young man with a waxed moustache, high collar and look of captured surprise, taken in a photographer's studio in Seville many years before.

This morning breakfast was to be a special feast, as Senora Lopez had obtained a small packet of real coffee, and some eggs. The doctor did not ask how she had come by the contraband, for precious little was available legally, but had come to appreciate that beneath her wrinkled features this woman possessed great powers of resourcefulness and determination. While waiting at the dining table, he busied himself in reviewing some of the mail from the day before, which he opened with an ornate silver letter opener. When Senora Lopez had placed the coffee before him he lightly tapped the side of the cup with the tip of the blade, and lifted grey eyes still marked by a want of sleep, to meet hers. Although they had an agreement that he did not need to know where various items or goods may have originated from or who provided them, he still had a legitimate interest in the cost of procuring them, if only to demonstrate his notional control over household expenses.

"Was this expensive?" he asked, as the aroma of the coffee began to rise before him, enticing and invigorating him at the same time.

"The bag of coffee and the eggs were in settlement of a small debt," she cautiously replied.

"And was this debt being settled directly?" he asked.

"No doctor, it was not settled directly," and thus ending the discrete exchange and turning her back, Senora Lopez returned to the kitchen.

The intelligence yielded indicated that the provider of the feast was probably Enrique Morales, the most active local *contrabandista*, an occupation still with attendant dangers even if most of the local police could be bought off with a percentage of the goods in transit. However, he did not owe any money to the doctor directly, but had evidently taken over a debt for medical expenses from one of the poorer citizens, for whom he acted as an unofficial banker of last resort. There was no universal State provision of health care in Spain, and access to treatment and medicines was controlled by access to money, although payment in kind was not unknown. Physicians such as Dr Hernandez treated the poorest on the simple grounds that they were suffering. Some charitable sources of finance were available, but were often under the control or influence of Falangists if not the Church, who extracted an ideological price for compassion. As a physician he was aware that the medicine which was most difficult to obtain was food; an agricultural labourer's wages of ten or twelve pesetas a day would provide a family with nothing more substantial than a few vegetables, bread and olive oil. He had protested to the regional authorities about the consequences of widespread malnutrition, and the number of children in the town whose pallor and listlessness were only general symptoms to be placed next to bleeding, mouth lesions, diarrhoea, dementia and cardiac malfunction. Such protestations were unwelcome in the new Spain, where the shining promise was as tangible as the deed.

There were only two doctors in San Cristobal, to tend to a population of over eight thousand, although the poverty of most put them outside the boundary of adequate medical care. The town had no hospital, and the only medical facility was the clinic run by nuns of the Order of the Sacred Heart, which both Dr Hernandez and the second physician, Dr Marin, attended. Today Dr Hernandez was to attend; completing breakfast with a second cup of the good coffee, which he drank off with extreme reluctance, as he wished to savour the bitter taste for as long as possible, he prepared. Conscious that Consuelo may try to get word to him about the young Englishman, he spoke to Senora Lopez. He knew that he could trust her, but yet decided that it would not be wise to be too precise as to the reason for his return along the coast road. There was an understanding between them, and so he had only to approach the subject obliquely.

"It is possible that Dona Consuelo may need to speak to me about some matter. Should that arise, call me at the clinic, but only ask for me to return the call if I am not immediately available."

"Yes doctor. And if Don Octavio should call?"

At this, Dr Hernandez admitted to something closer to a sigh. Don Octavio Montero was his oldest friend, but also a man of an extreme nervous disposition, subject to fearful and dark imaginings.

"That will not be necessary. I will attend to it upon my return."

And with that he took up his case and hat, entered the street, and strode briskly away.

The Captive Summer

San Cristobal

The sun that had risen on Consuelo, and now poured down on Dr Hernandez as he made his way through the streets to the clinic, ran swiftly across fading terracotta roofs of the crowded and insensible houses. The crumpled buildings jostled each other for a view of the small breakwater and the sea beyond, as if they had once been living creatures petrified in the act of rushing down the sloping ground and out to the deep waters of the Mediterranean. A similar petrifaction had overcome the people living in the houses, but one that was not immediately apparent from the dilapidated condition of the buildings, or contour of the land, or change of season. Eddies of dusty wind still tugged at the corners of sun faded posters hastily splattered across the walls and windows of abandoned houses; but now instead of revolutionary slogans, they bore the visage of the *Caudillo*, the saviour of the Spanish people, the man who would not be distracted from his purifying mission even if he bled Spain white in the process: General Franciso Franco y Bahamonde.

Spain was a police state; and San Cristobal was an amphitheatre in which local tragedies were played out, the encircling mountains indifferent onlookers. The stage was represented by the harbour and main square, while the houses set in the avenues, streets and lanes which radiated out and upward, had become the rising terraces of stone seats. The town was divided into three *barrios*; those toward the west and north were moderately prosperous, that in the east was the slum district, and home to a few shanty brothels. Most streets were narrow, some so narrow that only humans and donkeys could traverse their tortuous and treacherous worn stones. This was entirely practical, as the jostling houses threw shade onto each other, as playful children might throw splashes of water on a burnished shore.

The petrifaction of the inhabitants was evident in the caution, in the deference, shown by people in the street; in the want of food; in the apprehension late at night in shuttered houses at the sound of a vehicle or approaching footsteps. The town possessed two lives, and one patron saint. The patron saint had been claimed for the Nationalists; one of the lives was the public life of a small provincial Spanish town, carried out under the gaze of the Civil Guard. In this life officials bustled and organised; output increased in a fashion which would do credit to Joseph Stalin's tractor factories and collectivised agriculture; the forces of law and order watched benignly over the people, who then reciprocated by adorning the smiling policemen with garlands of flowers at street corners. This perfect Spain, a land of brazen sun, of sweet oranges, of newspapers with little crime or discord to report, of the Church, was the land that Franco wanted to believe was a tangible realm. Perhaps, given Franco's interest in the cinema and the power of the image, he came to believe that he had only to imagine such a place and it would be so. Certainly his representatives in San Cristobal worked hard to place before their eyes the vision Franco himself would have wanted to see.

The town was home to four of Franco's apostles: Eduardo Castellon, the local Falangist party boss; Jose Oleanza, the Mayor; Capitan Franciso Mendoza, the Civil Guard commander; and Father Ramon Abarca, the local senior priest. Franco's belief in his destiny as the ruler of all Spain was in part influenced by his experiences as a young army officer fighting Moroccan tribesmen. On one occasion it was claimed that a cup was shot from between his fingers, and many bullets left him unharmed in their search for a resting place in his tissues. The Moroccan tribesmen believed that he was blessed by *baraka*, that is divine protection. How the course of human history in the Iberian peninsula might have been changed had that good fortune deserted him just once, can only be pondered by historians.

The other life, the hidden life, of the town was not represented within the publications or statistics of the Ministry of Labour. This was the life of the black market, of the smugglers, of the prostitutes and the racketeers, of malnourished children, of agricultural workers too weak from hunger to work a full day in the fields. This also was the life of summary arrest and imprisonment, of whispered denunciation, of the Labour Battalion. This was the life of the defeated. Subsequently the Spanish would have to contend with rapid price inflation, drought and famine: but for now they just had to contend with the intensely personal consequences of losing the civil war. Spain was a country under occupation, but the occupying force was Spanish. It is against this background that the pattern and quality of daily life was judged.

The lack of food was a daily consideration of human survival, in spite of Franco's pronouncement that: '[W]e have the Patria, which is something that is worth much more than anything else, and a Patria in which our children will have bread and justice, and power, and pride in its strength and in its glory.' There were two elements to the problem of the lack of bread. The first was that agricultural production had fallen in the aftermath of the civil war; the second, was that the corrupt State system to control prices encouraged the withdrawal of wheat into the black market. And so people were hungry.

The main sources of employment were agriculture and fishing, closely followed by whatever other means people found to procure food. This final category embraced the prostitute, and the teacher barred from teaching for his political beliefs who repaired shoes, the tradesman, the bar tender, the domestic servant, and those who hunted for and hawked whatever trinkets they could. There was one class of person who could look to a more assured future than these, if a precarious one from the perspective of police activity: the black marketeer. If a writer has a job for life, although no certainty of income, then a black marketeer in a hungry land has some surety of income, but the prospect of interruptions to his business on a regular basis.

As Dr Hernandez walked through the streets from his home to the clinic, all these facets of life pressed upon him. He reached the habourside, a place where the unemployed congregated. Most of the men he saw were unemployed, and they lounged against the walls of the small fish market or loitered outside the cafe, each man possessing a vacant spectral quality. He noticed a young woman with an infant and a baby, who had crouched down by the harbour wall; the baby sucked at one tired breast, while the infant chewed a piece of orange peel at her side. The young woman looked at the fishermen who were unloading sardines from their boat, not quite believing the reality of the silver parcels of food they poured out. Dr Hernandez knew one of the fishermen, and walking up and exchanging social pleasantries with him, asked him to spare some of his catch for the woman and her children. Then he turned away to enter the labyrinth of streets at the heart of the town.

In all the years that he had lived in San Cristobal, he had never lost his amusement at the anomalous, and absurd, name of the main square. In Spanish, *plaza de toros*, is the expression for the bullring. However, for reasons lost in medieval history, the town's main square had come to be known as the *Plaza de Toros*. Whether it marked the site of an ancient bullring, or a place where cattle were once corralled, he did not know; but it was the spiritual home of the Falangists, and that made some kind of sense to him. In one of the tributary streets lived Dr Hernandez's oldest but most troubled friend, Don Octavio. The doctor's reticence to accept a call from him did not denote that Montero was a difficult or unpleasant man, or that he wilfully wasted the doctor's time. He simply suffered from what Dr Hernandez believed was a nervous condition brought on by the strain and impoverishment of Spain's recent past: he was subject to hallucinations.

This was not assisted by his fondness for brandy and vermouth, although he maintained that he needed these medicines to keep the hallucinations at bay, not invoke them. He was a retired municipal official, and survived on his pension and the little income which his bonds provided. As he lived alone, and did not have the services of a domestic servant, he maintained a state of tarnished respectability, most evident in the laundry and repair of his clothes.

While Dr Hernandez passed unknown in the streets outside, Don Octavio prepared to leave his apartment, to stroll to the square to take a seat at one of the two cafes, where he would drink coffee and read a newspaper. He ate little, so that he had money to spend on brandy, which he then drank through the early afternoon, in spite of the summer heat, until he either judged it desirable to step out of the sun, or ran out of money. Sometimes his judgement, impaired by the quantity of alcohol he had consumed, his age and general health, or the strength of the sun, failed him; then he would slump forward at the table, requiring the intervention of the cafe owner or the waiters, who had often placed him in the storeroom to take his siesta among sacks of onions. He favoured one cafe, *La Alverjilla*, as the whimsy of the name, suggested to him a better time, a time when he was a boy, a time so long ago that Spain's earlier dictator, Miguel Primo de Rivera, was a lowly army officer chasing bandits through the jungles of the Philippines. He was mildly surprised that Gabriel Soto, who owned the cafe, had not been obliged to change the name to something more in keeping with the times, something more redolent of victory and annihilation. But he was pleased that it had not changed, and considered that by choosing to drink there he was in a small way still defying the prevailing orthodoxy.

He did not care for the local newspaper, *Ascenso*, so would make the best of either *Marca* or one of the more 'informed' national daily newspapers. *Marca* was the daily national sports newspaper, with a Fascist perspective; that meant, for example, that it did not report incidents of foul play in soccer matches. The substitutability of one article for another, that is to say the phenomenon that sporting achievements existed in a loop of consciousness that could be endlessly repeated without losing their emotional impact, meant that it did not particularly matter whether one was reading the current edition, or one which bore a date from some months earlier. The triumph or failure of sporting heroes existed as an emotional catalyst complete in itself, not an historical pageant, and the Government used this to divert attention from more pressing issues. He therefore selected a copy of *Marca* from the previous April, an edition that carried the stories of Spain's soccer matches against Germany and Italy.

He would always pause before leaving his apartment, as if holding a vigil for a missing friend, but in truth to make certain that no taunting visions would rise up before him. Tucking the newspaper under his arm he locked the street door behind him, and carefully turned round to face the world. He had a theory, which Dr Hernandez was sceptical about on the grounds of the prevailing medical understanding of brain chemistry, that sudden physical movement could provoke an hallucination, as if the blood and chemicals flowing through the cranium would collide with unpredictable consequences. He turned round with his eyes firmly shut, as if he could not bear to observe the street or the people in it. His first communication with the outer world was by way of smell and sound, and the sensation of touch. The air brought to him the complex aroma of laundry, drains and cooking that sought escape from the street by scaling the walls of the houses, thereby to be carried away by the fresher air tumbling over the rooftops. To his left there were children playing in a desultory way, their voices meek and prematurely aged. He opened his eyes; the children, two boys and a little girl with grey pleading eyes, looked up at him; he smiled, and nervously moved away.

He was served by Andres, one of the two waiters, a tall gaunt Galician whose thick crown of black hair seemed incongruous on his spare body. They made an interesting comparison, for Don Octavio was short and portly, sweated profusely and struggled to keep his own pate respectably covered with grey remnant strands of hair. At another table, one of Gabriel Soto's children, Elena, was helping her father to spread the cloth, and set the glasses and cutlery.

"Don Octavio, it is going to be very hot today, do you think that you should sit outside?" Andres asked.

Don Octavio, the newspaper spread before him on the table, considered for a moment, reviewing the advantages of shelter from the fierce sun, against the opportunity which shadow gave for the generation of dancing images, in a mind which could be upset by the sudden transition from light to shade.

"No Andres, I thank you for your concern; however it is such a fine day I would not wish to hide from it," and he relaxed in his seat and waited for the hot brown sludge which masqueraded as coffee to be served.

When Andres returned with the coffee, a patrol of two Civil Guards happened to be making a circuit of the square and were passing in front of the cafe; with his eyes averted from them he placed the glass down before Don Octavio. The two Guards, solid squat individuals whose fleshy necks rubbed up against the collar of their tunics, and who were prone to spitting to clear their mouths, sauntered past, coldly arrogant in their unassailability. Andres only raised his gaze once the imminent danger was past, and then looked down again at Don Octavio, the tension evident from a pulsing muscle in his hand.

"Spain is truly a great nation," offered Don Octavio, sipping the hot liquid in front of him, "we grind donkey shit for coffee beans, and employ psychopaths to guard the cribs of babes."

He winked, and Andres, not in the least affronted by his pronouncement on the origins of the dubious brew, withdrew to serve a recently arrived customer. The old man was well known, and from his vantage point, which placed him across from the Town Hall, spent his time either reading, or talking to other customers or to people passing by. He felt secure there, and any agitation of mind that he had experienced when he made his preparations to go out deserted him. The sun rose higher, and heat rippled through the square like a phantom, distorting space and reducing human effort to the drowsy minimum necessary for life.

The Captive Summer

An Unexpected Visitor

During the days and nights that Tom lay unconscious in the darkened room, and through the hours of silent vigil, Consuelo had not lost hope that he might live. They had learned little of his life from his possessions; as Jesus had said, it was as if Moses had been delivered up to them. They therefore had no idea of his character, or of the memories that urged him to hold onto life even as the waters had closed over his head. They could not tell what chaotic dark nightmares raced through his mind, what monsters pursued him across beaches of powdered black onyx under a sun of blood red embers, or how he silently screamed until his lungs could tolerate the pain no longer. His wounded brain, and its child of electrical impulses and fantastic chemistry, the mind, were as inaccessible and yet as tantalizing to them as a casket of jewels thrown from the stern of a sailing ship into deep and unknowable waters. They waited, and they watched over him, each one by a simple ritual taking their turn as sentry.

The night before he regained consciousness, when the world slept uneasily in the far houses around the harbour, Consuelo sat with him, fighting sleep. She imagined the fishing boats moored up in the harbour, bobbing in the blackness, as lights from the shore skittered over the surface of the waters. In that dead hour of the night a vision imprinted itself of a solitary boat moving across the sea without assistance from oar or sail, a figure in a grey shroud lying between the cross boards. She awoke suddenly, realising with horror that she had been lost in a dream, and pressed a hand hard to her mouth. She looked about the room, expecting to see that her vigil was shared by the Angel of Death. Satisfied that she was alone, she composed herself. She was determined that if Death appeared she would be awake; and by whatever means, with whatever weapon she could find, she would drive it away, to seek a companion on the journey into eternal blackness amongst the dying in the jumbled houses in the town.

As dawn arose Rafael came to the door, which was never fully closed, and stole into the room. He had prepared coffee and washed pomegranates for her breakfast; he bowed to her with his habitual slow reverence, and took up his position. As Consuelo sat in the cavernous kitchen with its stone floor and scrubbed and scored table, the thought came to her that she had not spoken English in years. Why at that hour she should have troubled herself with this matter, she could make no sense. She reasoned that it could only be explained by fatigue; however she remembered that somewhere in the library were an English dictionary and grammar primer. She resolved to find them, and while she chewed the flesh of the pomegranate, rehearsed such standard English phrases as 'How pleased I am to meet you,' and 'Could you show me the way to the railway station?' Therefore, later that morning when Rafael had knocked urgently on her bedroom door to advise that the young man was awake, she desperately tried to compose a little message of greeting as they returned to the room with Maria, who repeated excitedly, "Thank God, thank God, he's awake, he's awake, he is awake!"

Had Consuelo read *Pygmalion*, she would have been aware of the absurd parallel drama that she now played out as a Spanish Eliza Dolittle. The croaking voice that replied was not that of a cultured English gentleman however, and although Tom had read far more widely than many others of his age and background, he had not yet turned his attention to the major works of George Bernard Shaw. In spite of the water he had drunk his mouth was still barely moistened; he tried to speak, and a dry rasping emerged, to his own ears like the sound a file made when dragged over a piece of tin. Consuelo correctly guessed that he wanted to know where he was; she stepped beside the bed, and looked into his watery desperate eyes.

"You're safe now. My name is Consuelo Arranquez; this is my home, we have cared for you since you were brought here by the fishermen who found you." His first instinct was to try to rise from the bed, but Consuelo called out, and strong arms pinned him down.

"Senor Roberts, please do not move, the doctor says you must lie still," and for the first time Tom was aware of her breath and the warmth which exuded from her body as she helped to restrain him. He did not require much convincing of the efficacy of doing as he was told, as the hammers started up immediately in quick sequence beating out on his skull, not like the tamping hammers he had used on metal as an apprentice, but heavy claw hammers driving long nails through the very bone. He lay still, again aware that the dark face had returned to the room, and that this man had ensured his compliance with the doctor's instructions.

Consuelo did not wish to pass messages to Dr Hernandez via the telephone, because she knew that at the Telephone Exchange all conversations were listened to by those who only revealed themselves by clumsy and accidental coughs, or by faint clicks in the wire. So Rafael made the journey, on the pretext of buying some nails and rope. Later that day the sound of the doctor's car was heard approaching. Night had changed for day, and the young man whom he feared was about to die had opened his eyes, but in other regards the visit followed the pattern set earlier. Dr Hernandez re-examined Tom, looking for bruising, tenderness in the bone, evidence of bleeding. He cleaned the wound area and dressed the wound; the skin was melding, but there would be a scar through the hairline once the stubble grew back. The cut lip was puffy, and he was concerned that bacteria in the mouth could cause an infection; he advised that the mouth had to be kept clean, and that they make up a saline mouth wash. Dr Hernandez spoke no English, so Consuelo translated for him as he explained to Tom the extent of his known injuries, and the need for immobility while the bone healed. Dr Hernandez sat beside the bed, leaning forward in the half light, intense, using his hands to make a structure like a skull, and then flexing his fingers slightly to illustrate the impact forces and their effect. Tom watched the doctor, and nodded at Consuelo to show that he understood.

Satisfied that the young man was past the initial crisis, the doctor then lightened his tone, and with almost a smile on his face spoke to Consuelo.

"Dr Hernandez says that we know nothing about you apart from your family name Senor Roberts. What is your Christian name?" she asked.

"Tom," he replied, with a faint lisp owing to his bruised lip.

"Yes in Spanish we have the same name, *Tomas*," and for the first time Consuelo also admitted to something like a smile.

"Do you remember what happened to you Tomas?" she asked.

For a moment his mind was blank, and he stared at the ceiling, trying to find an explanation out of the timbers and whitewash. Then a hazy recollection asserted itself, and he remembered being flung about in the cockpit of the Hurricane, and the engine missing, and the aeroplane falling through the sky as he coaxed and fought to cross the limitless sunlit sea.

"I was trying to get back to Gibraltar, but the engine failed," and now tears came, tears of relief at being alive, tears of shame that he had not gone on with his comrades to Malta. Dr Hernandez reached out and squeezed his shoulder.

They sat together on the terrace under the great flapping awning, drinking pale sherry from delicate crystal supported on bluish twists of glass as if it were an ordinary summer day, and the civil war and the European war had never happened. Far beyond the garden walls the mountains hung in the air, the developing haze rendering them less palpable. Dr Hernandez spoke first.

"I asked you before whether you were prepared to take this risk Consuelo; it will not be safe to consider moving him for some weeks. Do you know what will happen if he is found here?"

"What will happen to him?" she countered.

"As a British serviceman he will be arrested, interned. You will be arrested and shot."

"I made a bargain Federico, I made a bargain for Arturo."

"Do you have any idea how we will get him out of Spain?" he asked turning toward her.

She shrugged her shoulders; they were surrounded on all sides, apart from the sea, by enemies, and there were only a few people she could now truly trust.

"We will find a way," he said, "we may even be able to get word back to his friends."

In the weeks that followed, Dr Hernandez made as many visits as he could to El Faro, without drawing attention to himself or the occupants of the house. As he had been a long term friend of both Consuelo and Arturo, it was easier for him to pass these off as the renewal of social contact on a regular basis, particularly as people had long wondered whether the widower doctor and the lonely and isolated woman in the great house, as Consuelo was referred to in the town, would deepen their friendship. However, the doctor was aware that he had to be discrete, and was privately pleased that people had considered and given the interpretation to his actions of those of the suitor. He even encouraged Senora Lopez in this belief, as he knew that she discussed his situation with her circle of friends, and that if this idea subsequently radiated outward in society to the ears of the informers, it may then assist them in deflecting police enquiries.

While the virtual relationship developed their patient did as he was told. Tom's world was limited now by the walls and ceiling of his sanctuary; where before he could look to the sky, he now picked out only the aberrations and curves of the open timbers above his head, which twisted like petrified snakes. Boredom was relieved by brief periods of exercise, supervised by Rafael. He wanted to ask questions, but Consuelo parried them, promising to talk at length when Dr Hernandez said that Tom was strong enough.

But they all now shared a desperate secret. In times of suffering, such secrets proliferate; identities, locations, deeds, thoughts or aspirations: all have the power to extinguish lives or cast them down into misery. Spain had proven a fertile realm, and millions now carried secrets within them like fire spitting demons, what the Moors referred to as *jinn*. Consuelo had taken upon herself such a secret. The issue now was how to keep that demon closed up within the walls of El Faro, at the same time as relying on those walls to protect the wounded airman from what lay beyond. She trusted Rafael and Maria implicitly: they were her co-conspirators in an act of resistance; they would ensure that domestic life continued as it had before, albeit now making allowance for a convalescing foreigner whose discovery could send them all to a firing squad, or condemn them to years of imprisonment. Spain espoused moral belligerency against Britain: they were all now enemies of the Patria. But who else could they trust in a land of hungry informers? During the war San Cristobal held out for the Republic; the Republic had perished, and with it the more certain loyalties forged from blood and political conviction.

For a farm labourer to change the route home that he took on his way back from the fields at the end of the day, could raise suspicion of him being a black marketeer; for Consuelo, who had taken an active interest in the affairs of the town, to now withdraw within the walls of El Faro without explanation would be calamitous. She laughed at herself when she considered instructing Rafael to put up a sign outside the house with words daubed in red paint: 'Silence please! Sick English airman in residence', but then reproached herself immediately. The first days were the most trying, a time when they were alert for any sign that people suspected or were intrigued by any change in behaviour or routine. None came.

The house was large enough, there were rooms on the upper storey that were hardly used, and that no visitor would ever have reason to enter. If they were vigilant, and yet did not show the strain, they could continue as they had done before. In the daytime Consuelo read or wrote letters for those possessing neither skill who had made the pilgrimage to the house from the town; in the evening she walked down with a jug of lemonade or leather bottle of wine to talk to the people tending their crops on the communal terraces, while their children played in the dust. The device worked, until one day in early July.

Andrea Perez was a prostitute. Her mind was not fully formed, and that, coupled with a lack of any living close family, made her vulnerable in a ruthless society. As a consequence of her occupation she had given birth to two children, both of whom had died before reaching the age of six years. The effects of irrecoverable years held captive by an abusive occupation, and the loss of her children, had deepened the wounds to her mind. Although still young, charm and beauty, which had never been present in abundance, had perished like withered fruit. She recalled in her childhood a solitary act of kindness from a nun, who told her that God loved and took to His personal care all children called to heaven. In the long darkness that was her life after her children died, she clung to this gift of thought as a drowning sailor will cling to a spar.

One day she received a letter, an unusual event, and one that caused her pain, as she had never mastered literacy beyond being able to write and recognise her own name. She turned the envelope over in her hands; it was made of coarse light brown paper, and on one side contained, apart from her own name, other words and symbols which she did not understand. She sat on the step outside the house where she lived with another prostitute, and her sole friend. The letter spun in her hands, the symbols on its surface flashing before her eyes; and as they flashed, her distress at not being able to understand them increased. Her friend was at work, and Andrea trusted no one else at the brothel; frustration, despair and fear took hold in her mind, and soon bitter tears flowed. She looked into the street, that curled like a crooked serpent in the sun, but she knew that no one would help her. Across the street a solitary pot of geraniums decorated a window ledge; as Andrea looked, the flowers seemed to vibrate in their terracotta prison. There was one other place where she had seen such flowers: the house of Consuelo Arranquez, some kilometres outside the town. Gripping the letter tightly she rose, and walked slowly down to the harbour and the road that ran beside the sea.

The Captive Summer

An Innocent Discovery

The heat reflected upward from the ground, was almost as intense as that pouring down from the sun as Andrea joined the coast road. She wore a dress of blue cotton, picked out with flowers in orange and peach, but dirty and faded, with a torn hem. Her hair was oily and unkempt, and she wore no scarf. As she walked she swung her arms, the envelope brushing against her dress as her arms swung in a determined arc. Few took notice of her; some men watched her with urgency in their loins, some women with contempt. She walked on oblivious to them, pleased to be leaving the town and dismal narrow streets, to enter into the open country.

When Andrea reached the house, she crumpled against the wall next to the doorway, and drawing her forearm across her perspiring face, panted as a dog would. The switches in her mind flicked between light and shade, hope and despair; she became convulsed by a fit of trembling, and looked down at the now crumpled and damp envelope with fear. She was on the point of running back to the safety of the step outside her lodging house, when she heard the bolts of the heavy door behind her being drawn, then a loud crack as the key was turned in the lock. A dark figure emerged, looked around, saw her, and hurriedly withdrew. More startled now she shrieked and ran from the house, to gain the path down through the trees to the road, until a woman's urgent voice called out.

"Andrea don't run!" Consuelo emerged into the heat, and walked in quick strides over to Andrea, who started to shake visibly. Taking her arm, Consuelo turned her about and guided her to the doorway and into the dark recess of the entrance hall. Andrea's arrival had caused momentary panic in the house, questioning their faith in the rippling heat of the afternoon as a deterrent against encounters with spies or informers. Rafael and Maria exchanged glances as Rafael emerged into the courtyard, then he followed Consuelo and Andrea across and into the reception room.

Consuelo had first met Andrea at the time of the death of her eldest child, when drunken and raging, she had been found outside Dr Hernandez's house.

"We didn't expect to see you," began Consuelo with a thumping heart after she had guided Andrea to a chair by one of the large square windows, and sat down opposite her, "Rafael only drew back to call to me to announce you." This was true, perhaps in the action but not objective.

"I have a letter Dona Consuelo," and she offered the envelope to her, "would you read it to me?" Her eyes darted from Consuelo to Rafael, expecting their punishment because she could not read the symbols.

Consuelo took the envelope.

"Of course, Andrea, and then perhaps," taking hold of her hands, "I could help you to read it."

Andrea twisted her mouth into a short uncertain smile; in some dark recess of her consciousness she recoiled from their imagined blows, as she physically recoiled from the men who beat her when she did not please them. Consuelo noticed the perspiration on Andrea's brow, and her spectral pallor.

"Rafael, I think that Maria is still attending to the laundry, please go into the kitchen and prepare a glass of lemonade for Andrea." Rafael left the two women alone. The expression 'still attending to the laundry' was in fact part of a code they had devised, and referred to Tom. They had agreed that to minimise any suspicion in the presence of guests, all references to their invalid would be coded in terms of the daily household routine. Therefore, 'still attending to the laundry' meant that Consuelo believed that Maria was still sitting with and watching over Tom, as he slept in the bedroom upstairs. Rafael knew but did not say that this was not the case.

Through the open door of the reception room, came the sound of the telephone. The telephone sat on a table across the courtyard in the entrance hall, and allowing for the fact that the door from the entrance hall into the courtyard was partly closed, the sound of the telephone was muffled, but still audible where the women sat. The telephone rang unanswered, filling the air with an insistent wailing. Consuelo began to open the envelope, but noted Andrea's rising agitation at the sharp discord filling the courtyard, which to Andrea's mind now seemed to grow louder. Consuelo rose and put the envelope down.

"Perhaps they haven't heard, please excuse me Andrea," and smoothing the folds from her dress she left the room. The wailing demon fell silent; Andrea waited, but Consuelo did not immediately return. Consuelo assumed that Rafael would bring the lemonade for Andrea, or that Maria would come down from the bedroom at the sound of the telephone. But neither of these things happened. Sitting alone, Andrea looked about her at the furniture and curtains, the room's gloomy aspect suggesting a place where the dead lay for inspection.

She did not want to be alone, she had not wanted to receive the letter. Since childhood she had come to believe that when she was left alone in a room, a demon might enter to torment her. She listened for the sound of its breathing, and heard it call softly to her. She spun around, terrified. The demon called again, more insistent now, and told Andrea that he had come to claim her and carry her to purgatory for her sins. She jumped up and ran, knocking over a table. The empty courtyard wavered in the heat, and other demons waited for her in the pillars of vibrating air. It had been a trap, she thought, the Devil had sent the letter, and he was now walking through the house looking for her. To her right was the staircase that led to the upper gallery. She spoke to herself, repeating: "The higher I climb, the closer I am to God," and harder yet for the Devil to find.

When she reached the gallery she stopped again. She heard another sound, like someone shifting or moving in a chair and calling out. Although she was afraid, she followed the sound along the gallery to a bedroom. The door was ajar; she pushed it open, but did not find any of the people she knew, only a man asleep in a chair.

Andrea approached the sleeping man. He sat in an armchair of broken wicker, that was placed near to the window, but at such a position that the chair and its slumbering occupant could not be seen from the courtyard below. A sly breeze funnelling through the shutter of the bedroom window now caught the hanging cord of the robe he was wearing over old striped pyjamas: it swayed like a pendulum, but twisted at the same time in the airstream, fighting to regain its point of origin. As she drew up beside him she lent a little over to study his profile.

His head was supported by a cushion, and lay to one side. She could see the vivid scar that ran from above his left eye and disappeared through the hairline. She could make out that part of his scalp had been shaved, the stubble hair growing back being a little darker than the rest. He was young, and beautiful, and not a Spaniard. She put out a hand to touch his hair, which had been lightly bleached in the sun, but drew back when he shifted a little. Although his face and throat were pinky bronze, she could see that the skin on his chest was whiter where the folds of the pyjamas shirt fell a little away. His lips were slightly parted, and his upper lip showed signs of bruising and clotted blood. Under his eyelids his eyes moved rapidly, and although he slept, she could sense a restlessness, as if in his dream he were trying to escape from a great danger. For some minutes she watched him, transfixed. She started swaying a little from side to side, holding an imaginary child in her arms; she could sense that he was not well, and her natural instinct was to cradle him, as she had cradled her own dying children.

Andrea was aroused from her reverie not by a voice but by a sharp intake of breath. She looked around to see Consuelo standing in the doorway, terror clearly lighting up her eyes.

"He is sleeping," said Andrea softly, her fear slipping away.

"Yes," answered Consuelo barely containing her panic, "he needs to rest, he has not been well."

"He is not Spanish."

"That is right Andrea, he is English."

Summoning composure she did not feel in her being, Consuelo walked over to Andrea and the sleeping figure, and placing her hand on an elbow, led her away; the latter still cradling the imaginary child. This was the first crisis they had faced hiding Tom, and had come so soon, and from such an unexpected quarter that Consuelo's mind went blank. That of all women in the town they might be betrayed by the simple prostitute, who lay with the police and prominent Falangists, now terrified Consuelo.

However, Consuelo knew that Andrea bore no ill will toward herself. They came down the stairs, and emerged into the courtyard once more. Maria and Rafael came up to them, and Consuelo indicated by motioning with her head toward the window of the room where Tom lay, that they had been found out. Anxious, Maria and Rafael stepped aside and Consuelo and Andrea continued across the courtyard and back into the reception room. She sat Andrea down, drew a chair beside her and sat also, gently taking the hands of the young woman in her own.

"Andrea," she began haltingly, "I have known you for many years."

"Oh yes Dona Consuelo," replied Andrea, "I remember when you and your husband first came here."

"I remember as well Andrea," Consuelo interrupted, but not harshly, and she pressed her hands. "In all that time we have trusted each other."

"Trusted, yes we have trusted each other," repeated Andrea.

Consuelo looked intently at her. Deep lines radiated out under Andrea's eyes, and her cheeks were prematurely sunken. She looked at Consuelo, but could not hold her gaze and turned away, troubled by a memory or the pain of close proximity. Consuelo was concerned in case she pulled away, but their hands continued in an embrace; Andrea looked at a point in space in front of her where the dust particles spun like stars.

"You saw the young man," whispered Consuelo, not sure what effect her words would have and illogically fearful that even in the privacy of the room they would be overheard, "he is sick and needs to rest."

Andrea looked back at her sharply, fear now returning and distorting her mouth, which twitched at the corners.

"But he is beautiful! Is he going to die? Surely God will spare him!" she pleaded, now strongly agitated. She was stung by the memory of the loss of her own children, in spite of her pleading to God to spare them.

"Andrea, Andrea! He will live, but he is sick, and we must help him get better. Will you help us?" and Consuelo indicated Rafael and Maria, who still stood a little back in the room, their fate bound together.

Andrea, afraid to speak, assented by vigorous nodding, the energy of which rippled through her body to her hands, and was transferred to Consuelo's body. Both women laughed and cried together.

"Then," and Consuelo squeezed her hands, "you must not mention to anyone, not anyone, that you saw him here today."

Andrea reflected on this for a moment before answering.

"Can I tell God?"

Consuelo was momentarily at a loss at what to say, so Andrea continued. "When I pray, can I tell God that I saw him?" The more reasonable reply would have been that God would have known that Andrea had seen the young man, but Consuelo ventured, "In silent prayers you may tell God." This satisfied Andrea, who became calmer, but tears still pricked her eyes. Consuelo released her hands and caressed her face. The first crisis had passed.

That evening Andrea knelt down at the side of her bed in the brothel. The room was small, dingy and badly lit. Beneath her arms the blanket had the texture of sacking, the pillow was soiled. There was a chair, on which her clients deposited their clothes, and a table with a pitcher and basin of water.

Andrea clasped her hands and lowered her head. In spite of the difficulties of her life, which mirrored the life of the poor elsewhere in Spain, she had retained her faith. Although she was regarded as half mad by others, deeply affected by the loss of her children, she had defined a rational universe for herself, one in which there was an explanation as to why prayers were not always answered.

Andrea believed that God lived in a fine house, as one would expect, and that the house had attached to it a garden in which the spirits of children played all through the celestial day. There were three kinds of spirit children: the spirits of those who had died in their mother's womb, the spirits of those who died at birth, and the spirits of those who had died as children on Earth. She took care not to share her beliefs, particularly as the Church was not known for its generosity of feeling or compassion for the bereaved poor; that is to say it was her own secret. Andrea believed that God sat at a window on an upper storey of the house, and that it pleased Him to watch the children play. His vantage point enabled Him to hear prayers as they rose up to heaven, even over the sound of the laughter of the children in the garden. If an offered prayer was not answered, this was explained because sometimes God, on official business, was called away from the window and withdrew into the recesses of the house. Andrea tried to imagine what games her own children played, and pictured them with the other children running round the olive trees (for there must be olive trees in heaven) and jumping to pluck oranges in the orange grove.

Silently, she composed a prayer for Consuelo, Maria, Maria's children, Rafael, and the young man. She asked God to send down His angels to watch over them, particularly the young man, who had troubled sleep and a wounded head. She would keep the secret that had been entrusted to her, and only talk to God about what she knew.

Then a knock came at the door; Andrea completed her prayer, got up and sat on the edge of the bed. She called out, and waited for the business of the night to resume.

The Captive Summer

Municipal Business

The town's Mayor, Jose Oleanza, was an appointed political representative of Madrid, like thousands of other officials throughout Spain. In spite of this, he still held to the delusion that his elevation to so important a position was a reflection of his skill and abilities as a civic administrator. His office was situated on the second floor of the Town Hall, a building the colour of weak tea from which the Spanish flag fluttered in crackling spasms, and which overlooked the dirty bleached stone facade of the *Plaza de Toros*. On days of quiet listlessness, when the air trapped in the building shied way from the heat and loitered in fluid masses around the stairwells, it was his habit to sit languidly at his desk looking out on the world, his waistcoat unbuttoned, perspiration slowly dripping in the musky space between his fleshy back and shirt, occasionally licking away the beads of sweat which formed on his upper lip. From his window he could spy on almost every other building: the cafes and the bank, the tailor, the offices of the notary, the haberdashery store. If the passage of humanity at these establishments provided no amusement, he either contemplated the cooling effects of the liquid diamond cascading from the fountain's mouth, or guessed at what the statue of Philip V might think, as another seagull used the crown of his stone head as a suitable place to defecate.

Today was a day of quiet listlessness. Before him on his desk were deposited the damp and finger marked pages of the official records of the new Spain; but secreted in his head were the truer records of corrupt contracts and furtive conversations. He had read a memorandum on the progress of the new orphanage for the town, a document whose dry tone contrasted with the patchy dampness of the paper, due to repeated mauling from his moist hands and the occasional drop of perspiration from his brow. He was the orphanage's principal benefactor and beneficiary, a novel and unexpected circumstance, which arose not because he had been an orphan, but because he had set himself up in the construction business; and construction required access to supplies of the grey dust worth more than gold: cement.

Cement was rationed in Spain, as was petrol, food, cloth and human compassion. It was in the interests of all that supplies should be used sparingly, and where possible, used more lucratively. Oleanza wanted to attract the new class of successful Spaniard, drawing them away from Granada, and other coastal towns. Successful people needed homes, and he just happened to own a piece of land suitable for an apartment building. He also owned a warehouse, where supplies of building materials for the

78

orphanage were held until required; all that remained was to ensure that of every ten bags of cement that the trucks delivered and the perspiring workmen carried into the store, seven subsequently found their way into the foundations of the orphanage, while three did not.

He turned his attention back to the memorandum. Oleanza was stocky, and he liked to give the impression by his lumbering and ponderous movements, and sly hints in unfinished sentences, that he had enjoyed an earlier career as a prize fighter. This was not true, but he was aware of the power of the suggestion of physical force. Whenever he encountered opposition either in his civic capacity or in his relations with humanity on any level, he would not hesitate to twist his mouth and bare his nicotine stained teeth, like a beast of prey. He possessed a square head, and wore a mantle of black hair swept back; his lips were thick, and protruded on his face like a blister. When he laughed, his narrow eyes all but disappeared in the folds of flesh. His threatening physical air was complemented by an attitude of contempt for all but his closest friends and political associates. Although he was Mayor, he was not an educated man; and yet it irked him that he had not been accorded the title of *Don*, to denote his elevated status in Spanish society.

The meaning of the memorandum eluded him. He looked out into the square, peering over the balustrade as a young woman navigated her way in the shade: the swaying of her body aroused him but he could not see her face, and he desisted with his lustful enquiry. He decided to summon the Town Clerk, Ferdinand Aguado, who occupied an outer office. He gave vent to a bellow which conveyed force, spittle and whatever he had consumed for breakfast but yet lingered around his teeth. Aguado hurried into his presence, stopped two paces short of Oleanza's desk, and adopted a stance of dutiful supplication. During the years it had been his misfortune to work for Oleanza, he had learned that praise was the absence of criticism: whenever he ventured into the Mayor's presence, like Daniel entering the den of lions, he hoped only for an abatement of the stream of snide comments to which Oleanza was prone at times of personal crisis or political misfortune. His hopes were rarely fulfilled. These ferocious preliminaries concluded, Oleanza's face softened, for although ignorant, he was mindful of his dependency on Aguado, who had the benefit of an education.

"So you can still hear," he commented, feigning a laugh through a slit like mouth, "*muy bien*, I need subordinates with good ears."

Between thumb and forefinger he held aloft a page taken from his desk; it was a report from an engineer on the load bearing characteristics of the new building. The reduction in the quantity of cement being applied in the work had been remedied by mixing additional sand, and bags of brick dust, into the concrete. Although this produced the same volume, the compound lacked the mechanical strength required to support a building with two floors above ground level. Cracks had appeared in one corner of the structure, but the work continued. Oleanza would have ignored this, but the local Falangist boss, Eduardo Castellon, had been informed by one of his spies that the workmen were nervous working in the higher storeys, and keen to embarrass Oleanza, had made reference to the rumours that the orphanage was unsafe. An engineer employed by the Ministry of Labour had visited the site from Granada to make an inspection.

"What does this mean," and he fluttered the sheet of paper like a dead and emaciated bird, "am I expected to take on the responsibilities of government and yet speak the language of sorcerers and Masons?!"

Aguado peered forward in an attempt to determine what was written on the poor quality grainy paper flapping in front of his superior's contemptuous face.

"I think that is the engineer's report Your Honour," he offered in an attempt to placate him.

"I know what it is *supposed* to be, but what does it mean?" and he threw the paper forward. It danced in the air briefly before slipping down in graceful arcs just out of reach of Aguado, who lunged forward to prevent it reaching the floor.

"Read it! Read the paragraph that begins 'from an engineering perspective', and explain it to me," and Oleanza sat upright in his chair, studying the blades of the ceiling fan as they made their desultory assaults on the warm masses of air close to the ceiling, another mystery of creation. By the simple device of hurling the report across his desk, responsibility for his incapacity of acuity was transferred onto Aguado, and by inference the engineer.

Aguado coughed, and held the sheet of paper before his face so as to provide a defensive barrier.

"From an engineering perspective," he began, trying to read ahead and comprehend at the same time, "the function of the foundation is to distribute the weight of a building's superstructure onto an area of supporting rock or soil not to exceed the loading capacity of the substructure. The soil bearing capacity is assumed to be uniform throughout the substrate..."

"You see, you see! What does that mean? This man is a Mason, he does not speak in terms which a Spaniard, a man of noble sentiments, a man charged with the responsibilities of high office can comprehend in the frenetic flow of official business!"

In apology for this error, Aguado bowed his head and folded the sheet of paper up.

"I will study the report Your Honour and prepare a summary of the important issues and findings."

Oleanza calmed down, the colour passing from his face, secretly pleased that he had concealed his own ignorance.

"While you are here Aguado," and he leaned forward now, adopting the serious air of a man thus burdened with the affairs of state, knitting his plump fingers in front of him, "have you heard anything further from Lozano?"

Alfredo Lozano had the distinction of being a veteran of the Army of Africa, and the town barber. He also was the Mayor's spy, a role for which he was well placed because of the number of the most important local men who submitted themselves to his razor. It was believed that the years of survival in the arid and heat blasted deserts and wastes of Spanish Morocco had affected his brain, and it was rumoured that he slept with an open razor under his pillow and his cash box in the mattress. There were many unsuspecting men who gossiped dangerously in his chair while he danced around them, scything soapy bristles at their throat or whispering in mock conspiratorial tones at their ears. A small man, he was intense, always in expectation, as if awaiting an infantry assault or artillery bombardment. He remained shaven headed as he had been in the Army, and blue veins stood clear at his temples. At night, images rose up before him of screaming tribesmen and comrades falling around him with a knife in their guts; he controlled these images with alcohol, which the Mayor ensured he never ran short of. On nights of pulsating heat when alcohol oozed through his pores, he was convulsed by nightmares of the African desert, yet in the mornings he could remember nothing.

Oleanza had a particular job for him, and that was to pass back any information that came to light about the new local delegate of the SNT, Carlos Lupion. The SNT controlled not only the supply and distribution of wheat, but other basic agricultural produce. Lupion had arrived a few weeks before, the model of a provincial civil servant adorned with hornshell glasses with circular frames, slicked unwashed hair and fractured teeth; but he possessed the miraculous power in a controlled market economy to set official prices for basic foodstuffs.

It was this power that set him apart from Oleanza or the other powerful men in the town like Castellon, or the journalist Bucaro, or the chief of police. Lupion at once became a threat to each man's position, and a potential ally to tip the scales decisively in favour of any one of them. He had to be courted, and that meant that it was politic to invite him to dinner, but he also had to be watched, so it was therefore politic to recommend a good barber. Running a finger around the collar of his shirt, as intelligence was passed back at the barber's chair while Lozano shaved him, Aguado cleared his throat.

"Lozano advises that he visited twice in the month of May, once to be shaved only, the second occasion to be both shaved and the have his hair cut."

"Is that all? What did he do, what did he say?!" and Oleanza brought his hands down emphatically on the desk and pushed back in his chair to show his frustration at the triviality of the intelligence activity.

"Lozano told me that he did not say very much, but believed that he was a good Francoist," seeing that he was not to be immediately curtailed he continued, "Lupion is short sighted, and so without his spectacles was unable to clearly see the framed photographs of Franco and Dona Carmen that were on the wall. Lozano passed comment during Lupion's first visit to the shortage of bread, and jerked his thumb in the direction of the photographs, which as I said Lupion could not see. Lupion replied that he felt that he was as safe in the barber's hands, as Spain was in the hands of the Caudillo."

Aguado again ran a finger around his shirt collar to ease the nicked and reddened skin away from the material; Oleanza regarded him coldly, as if he had been presented with an inmate from an asylum.

"And that was all?"

"Yes Your Honour."

Oleanza waved him from his presence with a flick of his hand, and sank back. He scowled at the papers on his desk, and checked his watch; he decided that he had exerted himself sufficiently for the morning, it was time for something to eat and then siesta, Spain would not fall during lunch.

As he walked down the stairs he scowled as he remembered the affronts and slights he had suffered at the hands of those he derided as cockroaches and leeches, but who still wielded power; and who, if they worked together against his interests could bring his career to an abrupt halt. In truth, each one of them was motivated by a distrust of the others, a hatred of Republicans, a desire to be looked upon favourably by their superiors, and money: the new Spain.

The Captive Summer

A Policeman's Lot

That Oleanza could cram his mouth with food in safety, was due to the efforts of Capitan Mendoza. Mendoza did not share the physiognomy of a frog, in spite of Dr Hernandez's beliefs, nor the ability to transform into one. But his posture was permanently hunched, which gave the impression that he was slightly shorter than he actually was. His enemies said of him that he affected this stance so as not to embarrass the Caudillo should he ever meet him, Franco possessing the physique of a short barrel. He was also an anxious man; and had reason for his anxiety, as he was a fugitive from the law he upheld.

By birth he was a Catalan, from Barcelona; as a youth he had taken part in the events of the *Semana Tragica*, the bloody uprising of 1909. Then he was a gut empty radical with a different identity, a textile worker giddy on the promise of Engels and Marx, desperate for Spain to be the country in the vanguard of worldwide revolution. In a cellar bar, he and his revolutionary brothers had plotted through clouds of tobacco smoke an attack on a mill owner; the man's fateful crime being that he had paid two thousand pesetas for his daughter's wedding dress, and boasted of it as he toured the factory. Huddled together, they became drunk on scorching tobacco and watered brandy, and the excitable talk of death, vengeance and blood. Their faces thrown into relief by the light of oil lamps, the fire in their eyes convinced them that the barricades of Paris had come to Barcelona, and that the workers would now be free.

The execution of the so called workers' decree was to take place as the mill owner returned home from the theatre in his gleaming new Packard; a symbol to the starving mill workers not only of wealth but the humiliation of Spain's defeat in Cuba by America. They expected him to be alone. Three men, including Mendoza, were 'democratically' selected by the drawing of lots to carry out the attack, but he would never know that the draw was manipulated to ensure that their leader and the political steward of the cell were both exempted. The plan was elementary: one of the men would lie down in the darkened road as if dead, just before car arrived. As the vehicle decreased its speed, Mendoza and his accomplice were to jump out and gain the running boards, then enter the cabin and stab their victim. It was not their intention to kill him, just to wound, to demonstrate the determination of the working classes in their political struggle; and to provide a warning

The plan unravelled as assuredly as a ball of string will unwind as it rolls down a slope. The man detailed as the road blocker never broke from his cover, and there was only a slight change of speed as the car approached the bend in the road. Almost unable to comprehend what was happening, and with his throat closing in fear, Mendoza and the third man ran for the vehicle from opposite sides of the road and clawed for a hold, the car rolling on and the road surface slipping past like a river in flood beneath their feet. They launched themselves into the cabin, Mendoza bizarrely clasping his knife between his teeth. He remembered screams in the darkened space, the smell of leather and perfume, and the presence of a second body in a dress of rustling silk: they had not expected the mill owner's daughter to accompany her father to the theatre. Then Mendoza forced open the door and leaped into an abyss. In the dark confusion it was the daughter who had been stabbed, although she lived, but her father was unharmed.

Terrified, shaken and alone, he made his way back to his lodgings through the city streets, avoiding the looks of the curious night people who staggered along in amorous pairs or clung to walls vomiting outside the bars; the exultation of revolutionary purity replaced by elementary emotion and the specific fear of being apprehended. He had fractured his left wrist jumping from the Packard, and the painful joint now swelled as if he had been bitten by a powerful snake. As he turned into the street where he lived he could see the Civil Guard already at the boarding house beating at the door; so he turned and ran away. He had been running ever since. He changed his name, came to the South, and in the sole moment of true intelligent insight in his life realized that the only place he would not be looked for was within the Civil Guard, so he enlisted. The revolutionary became a policeman, the youth who had chanted slogans now recited the law that he enforced. His old identity was subsumed, and no one suspected that he had any connections with Barcelona. He became an enthusiastic Civil Guard, proud of the traditions of the service and the uniform, yet still in nightmares detesting it; and although he saw the advantages in advancement to a position of authority, declined transfers to any of the northern provinces, citing his love of Andalucia. His wounded wrist developed arthritis when he became older; he liked to think of it as his 'conscience' although it was nothing of the kind, it was just that it became painful during the winter months, and was a reminder to him of his past; a past left behind in the blood soaked cabin of the cream coloured automobile.

In spite of the great gulf of years, his fear of discovery never departed. He lived in a villa close to *Avenida Isabella*, and had acquired a wife and four daughters. Away from the barracks, when he was surrounded by his family, he presented a different face. He could never be truly open with them, and gave the impression of a man who would have liked to join the dance, but was afraid to be laughed at. His attainment of the villa was the outward sign that police work had its rewards, but those rewards were not derived from his salary. The dusty rivulets of money that flowed through San Cristobal provided a comfortable additional income from the recycling of confiscated *estraperlo* goods, some of which found their way directly from the barracks to the villa; it was as if Mendoza was practising for Christmas, with gifts generously donated by the men and women who travelled over the country by day and night with food, cigarettes, brandy or whatever else they could carry concealed about them.

As a revolutionary he did not accept the possibility of the existence of God, but as a policeman it was necessary to adopt the norms of the society in which he moved and the class that he defended. He attended Mass, and drank sherry with wealthy landowners. He convinced himself of the virtuous nature of the struggle in which he and his men were engaged against starving farm labourers, and he likened the Guards in their olive green uniforms to wingless angels of justice. By whatever distortion of mental process this transformation of belief was achieved, he did not fully understand. Perhaps he did not perceive that there was a process, yet it was accomplished; he accepted the teaching on religious relics while remembering line for line the pamphlets of Engels, hunted down Reds while he could retrace his movements almost by the step as he made his way across Barcelona that night, soiled and sweating. But perhaps his experience only proved that political or religious beliefs, no matter how tenaciously held, are merely whims that can be reshaped, exchanged or transmuted at will.

His Nationalist superiors regarded him as reliable, an issue of life or death after the Army revolted in July 1936, and rewarded him after the war with command of the strip of coast that encompassed San Cristobal. He ensured that whoever threatened the legitimate authority of Franco in this part of Spain would understand the consequences of their action; he slept with a pistol beside his bed, but had not had cause to use it.

His satisfaction at the state of affairs was interrupted however when he received notification in June that he was to be assigned a new subordinate officer, an event as unexpected as it was unwelcome. Although he would normally have had a *teniente* as his deputy, he had for almost a year sufficed with the services of Sargento Pedro Pelean, an obdurate man of few words, who yet had an understanding with his superior officer as to how the law was to be enforced, and how confiscated goods were to be divided. There was little need for another officer, and as he read the note advising him of the change in personnel, he shook his head resignedly. He dropped the note from police headquarters onto his desk, turned to the slender service file which accompanied it, opened the file and studied its contents.

"Name," he read aloud, "Carlos de Rozario," he shrugged, "born Seville, age twenty three years. Graduated from the Civil Guard academy nineteen forty one, position in class fourth out of twenty three."

He shrugged his shoulders again, determined not to be impressed by the young man's achievements. He read through the comments from his tutors: they were clearly impressed by his enthusiasm and commitment.

He turned the page, looking for details of the young officer's active service. There was only one sheet of paper relating to this, and it was turned the wrong way in the file. Mendoza lifted the page up and regarded it without paying too great attention. Then he stopped; from the rows of black type one word came into focus: Barcelona. Dropping the file, he took the page in both hands and read it with great care. There was no mistake, Teniente Carlos de Rozario had completed his first year of service at the Civil Guard headquarters in Barcelona.

Although the old injury gave him no discomfort, Mendoza instinctively grasped the wrist, pushed back his chair, stood up, and walked back and forth across his office, in an effort to regain his composure. The wide gulf of years separating him from his deed of blind anger could not prepare him for this information. It was as if he had been presented with the confessions of the other men involved in the attack on the mill owner, and saw his own former name recorded on the page. He started to sweat heavily, and his eyes painfully pressed against their sockets. Then he steadied himself, reasoning that there could be no way that this new officer, this bright new coin stamped with Franco's fervour, could know anything about him. He stopped pacing, and stood in the middle of his office, gripping his wrist. Could it be a trap? What if his superiors suspected, or had been given information that one of the gang had fled Barcelona and taken a train to the South? But he had obliterated his past; and unlike Jean Valjean in *Les Miserables* he had hidden in the one place where not even Inspector Javert would seek him. But as Valjean retained the number branded into his flesh, so Mendoza retained his guilt branded into his soul. But guilt was neither confession nor evidence, and above all guilt was not the accusing face of either of the men with whom he had carried out the attack. Mendoza knew the value of caution, and decided that de Rozario would have to be another name on the list of those who were watched, until he could be certain that he had nothing to fear from him. He realised that his hand was throbbing, so tight was the grip he maintained; he released his wrist, and smoothed the sleeve of his tunic. He gathered up the papers, opened the door of the office, and called for Pelean. He could not question de Rozario's transfer, and had little time to prepare.

De Rozario arrived a week later, a mannequin in a new uniform, the stock collar buttoned so tightly that Mendoza afterwards wondered how he moved his head without cutting off the supply of blood to his brain. He waited pensively at his desk. There was a low knock at the door. Mendoza called out; as the door swung inward he maintained the appearance of indifferent authority, but heard the blood rushing through his ears. Should he feign pleasure at de Rozario's arrival, or maintain stoical indifference? Question him about his experiences in Barcelona, or his reasons for requesting a transfer to Andalucia?

The young man who entered the room and stood to attention before him, had the bearing of a prince; erect in stature, naturally elegant, yet slightly hesitant as to the correct protocol to be followed. He had a small thin face, his hair lay across his head as a neatly folded series of oiled waves, and his moustache was a perfect pencil line broken at the filtrum. He looked like a matinee idol from the days of silent cinema, or a young *torero*, hardly bloodied in the bullring. Mendoza rose and returned his salute; he could scarcely believe that this youth was twenty three years old. He instructed him to sit down, then came around the desk and offered him a cigarette from his own case, which he removed from a tunic pocket. He noticed that as he lit the cigarette for him, de Rozario's hand shook slightly; he was nervous and that was a good sign.

"I must say teniente," he began as he replaced the cigarette case, "I was surprised that you should request a transfer to Andalucia. The large cities or Madrid would provide more opportunities for you."

"Thank you capitan, but I was born in Seville, and I always intended to return here as a policeman."

Mendoza leaned against the desk, arms folded across his chest, head cocked slightly to one side to listen to the young man's testimony.

"May I ask why you chose the Civil Guard over the Army as your career?"

De Rozario looked up at him through dark eyes of youthful intensity and conviction.

"I think this is where I can serve Spain best. I regard the work of the Guard as of the utmost importance to the defence of the Patria."

Mendoza allowed himself a brief smile; he stood up and walked away, turning his back to de Rozario. He could detect nothing in the young man that suggested that he was anything other than an eager but inexperienced boy. He relaxed, feeling the tension dissipate in his face. He turned and faced him once more. He questioned him further about his opinions and motivation, but skirted around the issue of Barcelona. Satisfied with the responses, he concluded.

"I will arrange for you to meet the Mayor, and Eduardo Castellon, who is the head of the Falange here. Both men are exemplary, and we enjoy good relations with both the civil and political authorities. I think that is enough for today, Sargento Pelean will show you to your quarters."

When de Rozario had departed, Mendoza went to the window and watched as he emerged from the building and walked across the yard. Pelean displayed his trademark diffidence; at his side de Rozario was correct in bearing at every step. Not a spy perhaps, Mendoza thought, but that was never a good reason not to keep watch on anybody.

The Captive Summer

The Garden

The gallery bedroom in which Andrea had discovered Tom, bore clear but incomplete testimony to the Moorish occupiers who had yet vanished like phantoms centuries before. But only fragments of the Arabic motifs and inscriptions enveloping the chamber had survived the swords of the conquering Christians. Although Tom could no more speak Arabic than Spanish, at least as he cast his eyes upward he now had a mysterious but interrupted sequence of symbols and notations to occupy his mind; and he spent fruitless hours attempting to unravel their mystery. Where the stars had once filled his field of vision by night, the inscriptions now filled it by day. As he grew stronger he was allowed out of bed to exercise, and he practised walking unaided across the room, but always under Rafael's supervision. Consuelo talked to him each afternoon, sometimes reading stories from the newspapers, making many angry interjections to contradict the cult that had grown up around Franco, sometimes relating what had been broadcast by Radio Seville the previous night. When the opportunity arose Tom asked questions about the house.

"Oh! Yes Tomas, it is very old. Some claim that the Romans were here. From time to time a plough will bring a Roman coin to the surface on the terraces. It is because of the headland, it was a good place to set a fire to alert sailors of the entrance to the bay."

"Have the people here always been wealthy?" he asked.

"No! Spain is a faded dowager. When my husband's grandfather bought the house, it was little more than a hen coop."

Tom laughed.

"Why do you laugh? It is true, Arturo's grandfather chased the hens around the gallery. When Arturo was born there was no electricity, and the water was drawn from the well in the courtyard."

"And Arturo believed in modernity?" he asked.

Her face darkened. "Arturo believes in many things," she said, but then paused. "He believes that the house was built to an ancient pattern, a code. He spoke to me about Pythagoras, he had read the works of Alberti."

Tom look quizzical.

"Alberti saw a pattern, a cosmic harmony. Arturo believes in that harmony."

But she would answer no more of his questions.

That evening Dr Hernandez visited. Tom noted the physician's exhaustion, and wondered whether he should offer to exchange places with him. Afterward, leaning against the gallery balustrade, the doctor raised his own eyes to the stars that skimmed the rooftops, and then lowered them down into the courtyard, which was illuminated by a few oil lamps and long narrow beams of electric light escaping at the edges of the curtains in the rooms below. He felt the cooler air of evening sinking around him, its energy withdrawing to the Earth's core, and it drew him down. He reflected that this was now the time of silent healing for his secret patient, when the body became the physician, and the physician became its assistant. Dr Hernandez pushed himself away from the balustrade and walked to the stairs.

Details of Tom's condition were discussed over dinner, along with the issue of his fate; Consuelo was concerned that it would be unwise to prevent Maria's children visiting the house.

"Yes, I see that this could arouse suspicion, but," and Dr Hernandez raised a finger to emphasise his point, "children should know little of the bestiality of this world. For the sake of all of us and that young man," and he now looked intently at Consuelo, "it is safest that we alone know of such things."

"But what if the children stayed here with Maria?" she answered.

"Then they will become like Tomas, a captive of the house, for now at least. And once they returned to their home, they would talk to their friends about their adventure at El Faro, and their friends would talk to their parents, and if the mother or father of one of those children was in the pay of Mendoza..." At this he closed his eyes, to emphasise the vision of hell that he had invoked. Consuelo understood.

"Federico," she paused, "Tomas has been confined with little exercise for weeks now, couldn't he be taken out to the garden, or just say, to the terrace? He is not our prisoner."

Dr Hernandez reflected on Tom's progress; he had betrayed no immediate sign of a brain injury, and the proposed medicines of exercise and sunlight were readily available and easily administered.

"I agree, but not for long, not in the summer heat. Wait until he is stronger."

As if a furnace door was slowly opening, the July sun broke over the eastern horizon the next morning and climbed in solitary majesty into the sky. A few cirrus clouds marred the otherwise empty canopy, but they neither brought relief to man nor water for the parched earth below. The intensity of the heat, that punished movement, made the world drowsy; a fit person would not venture out, and a sick person only did so if motivated by a desire to unburden themselves and their family of the responsibility of life. As a consequence, Tom's introduction to the world that lay beyond the courtyard was restricted to the period before noon.

Rafael assisted him out of bed, into his gown, and onto the gallery; Consuelo waited for them in the courtyard, her face illuminated, her body in shade. It was as they stood together at the foot of the staircase that Tom became aware of the strength of the sun as it poured in torrents of pure light, as the furnace door opened ever wider. The exposed pale skin of his hands and neck burned under the solar torch, and barely able to open his eyes, he averted his head. Seeing his discomfort, Consuelo instructed Rafael to move him into the shade quickly, while she went in search of a pair of dark glasses.

Rafael turned and offered his arm; Tom accepted it, and like two ships lashed together on a calm sea, they made a slow passage to the mouth of the corridor connecting the courtyard to the terrace. As Tom looked ahead the far doorway appeared like an eclipsed sun, as a faint corona of light escaped around the frame. The door of eclipsed light drew them on; the corridor was cool, and the stones and rendering exuded a dry and crumbling dustiness. Rafael stopped, released his arm and drew back the door. Tom looked over Rafael's shoulder and out into the pulsating light that filled the terrace. His eyes were assaulted by a piercing white and ochre iridescence, and he was unable to clearly make out the shapes and forms beyond. He closed his eyes tight shut, and was aware that they were stinging from drops of perspiration that had run down his face. Rafael led the now blind man across the flagstones, toward the shelter of the awning, and the blistered wooden bench and chairs that lay beneath it. Tom's head spun as he leaned back in the bench; Rafael, his eyes fixed on Tom's face, waited for him to open his eyes. He spoke in Spanish, making a gesture of a drinking action. Tom nodded, and Rafael trotted back across the terrace and disappeared into the passageway.

He looked around him slowly and breathed in shallow gulps, afraid that the unseen waves of dry heat would prove too much, and that he would lose consciousness. But as his eyes grew accustomed to the light, and he focused on the world that had exploded before him like a grenade of colour, his consciousness turned outward and away from his own discomfort. In front of him was a stone balustrade overlooking a wide garden that fell away in steps to a far wall of terracotta tiles and sand coloured stone. Within that garden were rows of fruit trees, a central avenue of cypresses, large rectangles of turned ground pierced with sticks, that were evidently harbouring vegetables. To his left, and set against the south wall, there was a shaded flower garden with a small area of lawn, and bright clusters of flowering plants. There was precious little wind that day, but what there was plucked at the tips of the cypresses, which were so tall that they rose above the sheltering walls. Although his eyes were open now as far as he dared against the glare, his first delirious impression was in fact the sound the garden made; the slow rustling as if the trees and plants were alerted to the presence of the unknown energy that he represented, and had turned to scrutinize it. The tips of the cypresses rocked back and forth as if in greeting, and the sunflowers nodded their heads in agreement. As he raised his eyes beyond the far wall he could make out the outline of the mountains, which shimmered before him. He wondered whether Eden had been like this before the expulsion of Adam and Eve.

Rafael returned, bearing a glass tumbler and jug on a tray. He placed the tray down and offered up a glass of opaque liquid. Tom drank, and the cool lemonade cascaded over his tongue and down his throat. For an instant he was so happy that he wanted to cry. Rafael stood beside him, and although not able to communicate in a common language, started to explain the garden to him in Spanish, pointing and giving the names of the plants and trees. Consuelo entered the terrace through the french doors of the main reception room, bearing in her outstretched hand a pair of glasses with lenses of dark brown smoked glass.

"I'm sorry I was absent so long Tomas, but these were in my husband's study."

Tom set down the tumbler of lemonade and put on the glasses, an experience not altogether alien but still a little novel. He was immediately reminded of the day at the Brighton races; Charlie Morris had sported a pair, that he kept pushed up on his forehead as he swaggered about the paddock. He felt the warmth and open expanse before him seep into him, to become his new reality.

The old reality was quite different. The gardens he had known as a child were set in small Victorian suburban gardens and allotments. He had an early memory of venturing into the family garden with a teapot, to feed the plants with a cold dark slurry of wet tea leaves, and slipping an infant hand into the pot to draw out the last vestige of nutrient that his clumsy swishing action had failed to dislodge. As he grew older his father would take him and his brother to the allotment that he kept with Tom's grandfather. In autumn months the boys helped the old man keep his little brazier stocked up with newspapers, and dead leaves and twigs cleared from beneath the trees that overhung the site. Tom and William listened while their grandfather told them stories and passed cups of sweet tea from his vacuum flask, stopping occasionally to prod the smouldering pyre.

With a jolt, he realised that Consuelo was speaking to him.

"It's beautiful, isn't it Tomas?" she inquired.

"I have never been seated in a garden like this in England," he replied, and as he looked up at her his face conveyed his astonishment.

"Surely in England there are gardens?" she asked with some surprise.

"Yes, there are gardens, country estates, parks. But the colours here are more intense," and he held one hand out from under the shade of the awning, "so is the heat. And the air is rippling through it all."

He could only associate one type of fruit, the orange, with Spain, and he knew it was a cargo for which British merchant seamen now risked their lives.

"Are they orange trees?"

"No Tomas. They are lemon trees, and behind them are pear and plum trees. We grow as much of our food as we can."

"Do you tend to the garden yourself Consuelo?" he asked.

"A little, but mainly it is the work of Rafael. He understands the ground, and coaxes and pleads with the trees to bear fruit for us each year."
Rafael understood that they were talking about his work, and although they conversed in English, still maintained a keen interest in their conversation. Consuelo continued.

"In Spain, largely due to the Moors, there are many fine gardens. In Granada there is the Generalife, the name is derived from Arabic, and means the noblest of all gardens. But I think that this is also a noble garden. Do you not agree?"

"Yes, it's beautiful," he answered.

"When you are stronger Tomas you can walk among the cypresses," and now half turning to Rafael she added, "and Rafael can show you how to grow watermelons."

"I can't speak Spanish," Tom said.

"Then I will teach you."

The Captive Summer

A Time To Heal

Tom's command of the Spanish language incremented by degrees. But in the first days of patient tuition, he and Rafael were often reduced to the universal and timeless language of signs and grimaces to convey their meaning to each other. To facilitate their communication, Consuelo also taught Rafael a little English, in the hope that whether by broken English or broken Spanish, the pantomime of facial expressions and hand gestures could be brought to a conclusion. The first expressions imparted to Rafael were the utilitarian imperatives of daily life, that he practised with conviction in front of the mirror in his room, curious to see how his mouth coped with the curious sounds. Once mastered, he approached Tom's bedroom door with confidence.

"Good morning Senor Roberts. Are you ready?" he said, and waited for the reply.

"Yes Rafael, you may come in."

Rafael could no more have understood anything else Tom had said even if he had sung to him, but he knew that the reply was in the affirmative. He insisted on taking Tom's arm before they navigated the staircase, taking some of his weight onto himself, and guiding him step by step to the courtyard below. A small flame of humour, along with a larger flame of humanity, still burned within Rafael, but he guarded them well. The daily ritual of Tom's passage to the terrace provided an opportunity for this smaller flame to flare up, although still obscured by the language barrier between them; and so he passed comment on his young dependent.

"Oh Jesus but you're heavy. It's no wonder, you are eating more than the three of us put together, and Spain is a hungry country. Perhaps we should tell people in the town that we are fattening a pig!"

Rafael smiled as he said this, as the observations were made in jest. Tom, assuming that he was offering a commentary on life, in much the same way that a London taxi driver would on a wet afternoon, nodded in reply when he thought it appropriate to do so.

"If God had intended for me to be a beast of burden he would have given me the hoofs, tail and ears of a donkey. But then, if I had been a donkey I would have been added to the pot to fatten you up. Be grateful, for there is not much meat on me."

It was later, when Tom had learned the Spanish for donkey, *el burro*, that he began to wonder what had been the true meaning of the rasping lyrical bursts of sound emanating from the Cuban.

The iron framed terrace awning was covered in a withered cloth, the fibres bleached to a streaked salmon pink. From beneath it Tom observed the sun as a disc of pinpricks of light that slowly traversed across a pink heaven, while around him the narrow curtain of shade shifted across the ground.

There was little for him to do but sit, and watch, or sleep. His inactivity and needle sharp remembrance of the squadron's destination across the Mediterranean sea shamed him; but this was tempered by the knowledge that in his condition he would not be certified as fit for flying, perhaps for many months. The hammers beating in his head had slowly abated; he could walk unaided but did not trust himself to run; he could not face strong sunlight; he was still weak and tired easily. But when he sat looking out at the garden, pulverized and sterilized by the heat of a burning sun that made stone so hot that it forced the small lizards to seek shelter under the rail of the balustrade, their scaly sides moving with a deliberate slow rhythm, his mind still raced to debate what fate had befallen his friends.

The compassion of those who now sheltered him he could not repay. He could not offer to help Rafael as he worked in the kitchen garden, nor sit and talk with him under the shade of the fruit trees when he rested. His incapacity lessened his shame, but simultaneously broadened it to encompass his new situation. Inactivity forced him to re-examine himself. He was playing an unchosen role, living a scene from a motion picture, but he did not know when the reel would end, or what would be the final scene. He gave the false appearance of having become a languid English traveller, a poor man's Leslie Howard. But he wanted to fly again.

He was also conscious that he had taken another man's place, and now wore another man's clothes. His uniform had been the subject of a heated, and incomprehensible, argument between Consuelo and Maria; the former keen to retain it, while Maria cautioned that it should be burned in case the house was searched. Dr Hernandez settled the dispute by pointing out that if Tom was arrested wearing civilian clothes he could be shot as a spy. Without another angry word Maria repaired, washed and pressed the tunic, and hung it in Tom's bedroom in full view, as if it had become a talisman of cloth that would protect the house and all who lived there. For Tom it was his only connection with his earlier life, and a reminder to him that he was only a passing traveller in the new one.

One morning Consuelo worked at her desk in the study, composing a letter for the widow of an Army veteran, enquiring about the woman's pension. But the right phrase of patient supplication would not come to her, and frustrated, she put down her pen, and went out into the sun. As she advanced to the awning she saw the figure lying beneath it wearing Arturo's robe and pyjamas; she was distracted by the letter, but was unaware that she was distracted; she called out in Spanish.

"Arturo, will you help me? I cannot finish the letter."

The figure in the deckchair turned to her, surprise and incomprehension marked in equal measure, and removed the dark glasses he wore. She stopped; instead of Arturo's green eyes, Tom's blue eyes emerged, regarding her intently.

"Oh! I'm sorry Tomas. For a moment I thought....that you were someone else."

"Can I help you Consuelo?" he asked.

She came closer, and sat down in a chair beside him. She looked out at the garden, hiding her disappointment that this man was not the man she loved.

"No thank you, unless you are familiar with Spanish law."

"Not my area of expertise, I'm afraid," he said, folding his hands across his stomach and wiggling his naked toes.

"But I thought you knew everything," she offered in an attempt to introduce a lighter tone.

"There's a great deal I don't know. For example, the names of most of the plants out there, whether it ever rains here, why Rafael scoops up a handful of earth before he starts work, and lets it drop through his fingers very slowly, as if he is watching each grain."

The questions were trivial, yet searching, and they dispelled thoughts of the widow's pension and Arturo from her mind.

"Let me see," she replied, marking out on three outstretched fingers the queries he had put to her. "Does it ever rain here? In the summer, hardly ever; most of the rain falls in the winter, and in the spring the rivers swell with the melted snow from the mountains. What are the names of the plants? You know that we have several varieties of fruit trees," at which Tom nodded, "in addition to which we have jasmine, sunflowers, sweet violets, gum cistus and jacaranda. Can you see the date palms?" she asked.

"At the back, near the wall. What about the vegetables?"

"Oh! Tomas, more questions!" in a note of mock alarm.

"I'm curious," he said, affecting the air of the languid Englishman once more, as it suited him at that moment to do so.

"I will have to accelerate your language classes," she shot back, "then you can discuss horticulture with Rafael! Now, what was the other question? Why does Rafael pick up a handful of earth?"

"Yes."

"It is a ritual. Life is brought forth from the earth..."

"And to the earth we shall return."

"No. And from the earth we harvest life. He is acknowledging that."

"It must be hard to obtain enough water for the plants."

"We are fortunate. The Moors sunk a deep well here, the water is clean and cold, even in summer."

Tom wanted to ask further questions, but she stopped him, having decided that he should move out of the sun. He retired to the library, while she, still not able to find the words she needed for the widow's letter, went upstairs.

The library had bookcases on two opposing walls, and the air in the room was suffused with sulphuric mustiness. It reminded him of the converted lecture hall at the flying school in Scotland, although that was always cold, and there was no time to read the leather bound volumes by Sir Walter Scott. The library looked out onto the courtyard, which was paved in worn terracotta bricks. There was a colonnade which extended around all four sides of the ruined space, and the elegant round arches were supported on slender columns of rippled stone. Beyond the columns were pools of deep shade, which hid the full intricacy of the geometric patterns of tiles which made up ruptured mosaics on the walls. The courtyard pump and fountain had been spared destruction when the Moors were driven out, although the fountain had long since dried up.

He moved along the rows of books, all of which were in Spanish, trying to find something which would interest him. There was an atlas of the world, and an ancient guide to flora and fauna of the Iberian peninsula, which at least had illustrations to distract him. He picked out one volume, believing that he had come upon a copy of Don Quijote; but even though he could not read it, still determined that *Vida de Don Quijote y Sancho*, was not what he expected. Most of the shelves were given over to legal texts; he took one down and, casually skimming through it, found on several pages pencilled notes in a neat hand, that he assumed had been made by Arturo. He looked down, conscious that he was wearing the clothes of the man who had purchased the book he now held, and who had written on its pages the notes he could not read. He had become an impostor; he returned the book to its place on the shelf and turned away.

The appropriate phrase still eluded Consuelo. Before returning to the study, and with Arturo's image still with her, she decided to complete a task for which Tom's arrival had acted as catalyst: the division of his clothes. She was no more or less superstitious than others of her age and upbringing, but her motive was to separate those garments which could be given away, from those invested with memories, which could not. The latter included his wedding suit, a leather jacket and his courtroom gown. As she held the gown to her she recalled Arturo leaving her one morning to enter the court building in Seville, the gown billowing like the toga of a young Roman Senator entering the Forum. As he had reached the top of the steps he had turned around and waved to her, the garment caressing his body, then he disappeared from sight.

She set the gown aside, and reached for the last two suits that hung in the dark recess of the wardrobe. But one slipped from her grasp, and fell at her feet. She froze to the spot. In a sudden and cruel trick of her mind, the crumpled folds of cloth suggested a headless corpse lying on the ground, arms flung crazily. She stared in horror, momentarily transfixed, then backed slowly away, as if facing a snake. Desperate to dispel the portent of the haphazard arrangement of fibres, she bent down and scooped them into her arms and threw them onto the bed. The spell was broken; the suit once again became an arrangement of coloured fibre and thread. She composed herself, and quit the room; she returned to the study and the letter for the widow, her hand shaking a little as she took up her pen.

The Captive Summer

Where The Blue Of The Night

Tom dreamed each night while his brain struggled to renew the synaptic connections and repair the bruised tissue immediately beneath the healing fracture. It was as if he were compelled to attend a surreal cinema, condemned to sit alone in a darkened auditorium while flickering panoramas played before his eyes without any discernible order. He watched them all, an appalled, awed, confused, terrified or perplexed spectator. Most of the dreams were forgotten at the moment of waking, some lingered like friends he would have liked to get to know better but which still had to take their leave of him. A few so bizarrely straddled sleeping and wakefulness that he was left utterly confused as the first light probed the closed shutters, mimicking the electric spectacle.

One night he dreamed that he was walking in the English countryside; it was early in summer, the long grasses and dew heavy field flowers stroked his shins as he strode through them. He came to a style set in a wire fence, beyond which was a large field of blood red poppies. He crossed over, feeling the rough grain of the wood beneath his hand as he climbed up. There was no foot path, just the slowly undulating mass of flowers that radiated before him in bands of colour. He had crossed a third of the field when he saw a man emerge from the row of trees that marked out the far boundary. The distance was still too great to allow Tom to identify him, but they walked toward each other rapidly closing the distance. He discerned from his gestures and open mouth that the other man was singing, although the words did not carry to his ears. But with a jolt as if he had been slapped on the back, Tom suddenly realised that the man approaching him was Bing Crosby. The first words of the song reached him, and the familiar lines of *Where The Blue Of The Night* filled the morning air.

He walked eagerly on, and Crosby waved to him, singing still. But in an instant the field, poppies, sun, breeze, all disappeared. Tom was back in the darkened bedroom, but he was not alone. Crosby was now suspended in the air above him, arms outstretched, a microphone on a stand set in front of him. Tom struggled to break free from the vision and roll onto his side, yet he could not move. But as quickly as it arose, the apparition departed, like a bubble bursting in front of his face.

Tom lay in the familiar warmth of the bed, breathing easily and allowing his eyes adjust to the pink dawn light that was even then bursting around the shutters. He swallowed, and turned his head to look more closely at the light around the windows. The music returned, he shut his eyes tight, although why that should affect his hearing he couldn't quite explain.

Another verse came to his ears.

He opened his eyes, looking now directly at the ceiling, expecting Crosby to re-materialise before him suspended in the glowing air. But no figure appeared; he slowly rolled over onto one shoulder and shut his eyes once more. He reasoned that he must be awake, although he could think of no clear test that would prove the case one way or another. He felt his heart beating, mildly convulsing his body, the blood pumping in his ears. He thrust his face into the pillow in a vain attempt at escape, inhaling the dry warm musk of the duck feathers. He resolved to break the hallucination even if that meant propelling himself from the bed and risking further injury. He sat upright, alert for the sudden appearance of phantoms, regardless of whether they came dragging microphone stands, ball and chain or parachute silk.

The music played on, he waited for it to stop. The sound was no phantom emanation however but a tangible one, and he knew now that it came from beyond the walls of the room. He climbed out of bed, stepped unsteadily to the wicker chair, picked up his robe and drew it around his body, then moved toward the door. He paused to listen for signs that anyone was outside; satisfied, he opened the door and stepped onto the gallery. The roof and upper storey of the house was suffused with a gentle pink light; below him the courtyard was a well of shadows. As he looked across to the loggia both the source of the music and its sponsor were revealed to him in an instant. A gramophone had been placed on a small table; on the gramophone a whirling disc of black vinyl held the voice of the singer. Next to the gramophone was a wicker chair, whose occupant sat wrapped in a shawl and faced the terrace and garden. Tom walked noiselessly toward the steps leading to the loggia, his bare feet moulding to the worn stone. As he drew nearer he made out that the first rays of the sun were brushing the tips of the cypress trees, and morning was hurrying on. He climbed the steps but hesitated before entering the loggia, conscious that he was entering a private space, and considered turning back. Before he could do so a voice called out in Spanish.

"Rafael, is that you?"

"No Consuelo, it's me," he said and stepped forward. Consuelo turned her face to him; the silk shawl which she had draped around her shoulders caressed her neck as she moved her head. Even from this distance he could tell that she had been crying.

"I'm sorry Consuelo, I heard the music, and wondered where it was coming from."

She wiped her cheeks with the back of her hand to hide the emotion she had given vent to, and swallowed hard.

"It is I who should apologise Tomas, I should not have played the gramophone at this time of the day," then with a sweep of her hand to a pile of other records which lay at her feet she added, "as you see I have been reliving my life, such as it is. These discs are all that is left as a record that once I was happy here."

In the rapidly growing light Tom could make out some of the labels and covers: Spanish popular singers were mixed with American jazz and tunes made famous in Radio City in New York.

"The American records are some years old now, nothing after 1937, so I have to take care with them. Once they are broken they are lost forever." The final bars of *Where The Blue of The Night* died away, and after a few moments of scratchy silence *Buddy, Can You Spare a Dime?* replaced them. Consuelo turned away to look again over the terrace, one hand now to her forehead.

"It is four years since I last saw him. He had been able to obtain some leave in June, just before the festival, and came to see me here. He was so changed, so sad. When he left for the North we knew that the Republic would be defeated, but he still went. Soon after, San Cristobal fell to the Nationalists, and I knew that I would not see him again." She dug underneath the shawl and handed Tom a bundle of letters, held together by lilac ribbon.

He stood beside her with the crumpled and worn sheets of paper in his hands, but he did not want to look at them; he felt that he was eavesdropping on their love making, and more practically, he could do no more than read the dates and the places where they had been written. The earlier letters were set down in a neat hand, precise and ordered, with square blocks of words on each page. He turned the pages through hurriedly, ashamed at himself while she sat so close to him. The more recent letters were disordered, and the handwriting started to stray, with occasional blotches of black or blue ink. He noted that the date on the most recent was October 1941. He thrust the letters back awkwardly, as if he were giving flowers to a new lover.

"I don't think that I should see these, they should be between yourself and your husband," then searching for something more gentle to say added, "please tell me about him." These words aroused her from her thoughts; relieved at having someone to talk to who did not already know her story, she recounted their courtship, marriage and early life together.

"After the battle of the Ebro," she concluded, "we received no news, but then a letter arrived from France, not from Arturo but from a comrade who said that he had been wounded, but had escaped and had eventually made his way to the border, then into France."

"So he's safe in France."

"You may say safe, but in reality the Vichy hate the Spanish Republicans. He is in an internment camp at Bram. I have received three letters since he was interred. He is alive."

She looked at him; and for a moment Tom thought there was accusation in her eyes, as if she resented that her husband was far away behind barbed wire, while this sick Englishman was hiding in her home and wearing his clothes. In a moment the look passed, her face softened again, the lines of care that had started to form at the sides of her mouth becoming less severe.

"Tomas, because of me you have been roused from your sleep, and brought here to talk, when Dr Hernandez was quite clear that you should rest and not be disturbed. I am a bad nurse."

"I don't agree. I think that you are a very good nurse and what is more you and Maria and Rafael are risking your lives to protect me. I think that you are a good woman and a very brave one."

Consuelo raised her hand to silence him, as she did so the sun's golden rim broke above the rooftop.

"You see, the sun rises in tribute to you Tomas. We can do nothing more, Spain is lost, but the Fascists can still be stopped. Stop them Tomas! You and all your friends; where we failed struggle until you succeed! If you will do this it will be as if my husband were restored to me!"

He was taken aback at the strength of her feelings; uncertain what to say in reply, he nodded and turned away, conscious of the futility of his own situation. His father had ensured that neither Tom nor his brother had volunteered for the Republican cause during the civil war. This was not from indifference to the plight of the Spanish people, but a deep love of his sons, and scepticism as to how highly their lives would be valued by Russian commissars. As stories of ineptitude and manipulation started to spread with the return of veterans from the International Brigades, he regarded himself as vindicated. From the then safe distance of London they looked at the photographs taken by Robert Capa that appeared in *Picture Post*; stark photographs of laden carts harnessed to bullet riddled mules, that had died pulling the belongings of now equally dead Spaniards. Franco had taken his first small steps into the world arena and declared that the crusade had won out against the international forces of Bolshevism and Masonry.

The focus and direction of the lens changed, the agony of Spain faded from consciousness. It was strange now to be in that land and among those people and yet to be utterly incapable of rendering any assistance, in fact to be dependent on those defeated people, who were each day gaining a deeper understanding of what it meant to be cast into the pit against a devouring foe. Tom could not replace Arturo and he could not liberate him; he might in time become a constant reminder to Consuelo that he was not Arturo; he again became aware that he was wearing his clothes, perhaps even the clothes of a dead man. He shuddered even though the morning was warm and full of the promise of life. As he reached his bedroom door Rafael ascended to the top of the stairs, and let out a little gasp of surprise at Tom's presence. Tom nodded to him in acknowledgement, and stepped back into the shadows.

With the arrival of the sun, Consuelo concluded her gramophone recital, carefully placing the thin vinyl discs into their covers, securing the arm of the gramophone and closing the lid so that Rafael could carry it back to the house. She reasoned with herself that her situation was better than many in the town, at least she had reason to believe that her husband was alive. She looked out across the open expanse that rose kilometre upon kilometre to the horizon; her memory told her that these things had happened, but her eyes saw another reality. She wished that her mind had tricked her, that she had only to turn and look down and see Arturo, with a saw balanced on his shoulder, walking to the lower plot to cut down one of the old trees. But no matter how many times she looked, his form did not appear. She gathered up the gramophone records, and like Tom, returned to the shadows within the house.

Relapse

Rafael did not live in shadows; he faced the full abrasive power of life, and yet outwardly remained untouched by it. He quietly ministered to the needs of those he served, while remaining conscious of the misfortune and adversity that had marred their lives. Each morning he brought up a pitcher of hot water to Tom's bedroom, set out the razor and shaving brush on the dresser in front of the mirror that hung on the wall, its fading and blotched silver obscuring the world it presented to him; then he lay out the clothes that had been prepared on the bed, and with a short bow, departed. But one morning that routine was varied, as Dr Hernadez judged that Tom was well enough to have lunch with Consuelo on the terrace. Rafael was more animated, anticipating this event as something like a return to the old days when Arturo was resident and the house was a sanctuary for laughter and happiness.

"How are you feeling today Senor Tomas?" he asked.

"Much better Rafael."

"Good."

"Rafael," Tom began, "why do you refer to me as Senor Tomas?"

"Are not all Englishmen knights senor?"

"No, not all."

"But you are a pilot."

"I'm not an officer, I'm a *sargento*."

Rafael regarded this as an inconvenient fact.

"Clearly a mistake on the part of the High Command," he replied.

"I think that I would accept the judgement of the High Command for now."

"But are you not a leader senor?"

"I follow others."

"And one day they will follow you," he said, bowed low and took his leave.

As Tom held the shaving brush to his face he peered intently into the mirror. The face he encountered was not the boyish oval that had appeared over rising mists of steam in the mirror of the aerodrome wash-house. It was now thinner; there was a scar in his lower lip where the deep cut had been sutured, its companion scar rose at his forehead and disappeared into the now ripening gold of his hair. But it was his eyes that struck him most forcefully, for they had become the eyes of a man who had witnessed hell, and could not close his mind to what he had seen. His war had not been bloody; he had felt the death of Alan Stanley the most keenly, but when he was lost over the Channel, there had been no communal outpouring of grief, no haunting tale of a stricken aircraft plunging down in flames into the cold dark waters. They simply did not know what had happened to him; he didn't come back from the patrol and next morning someone cleared personal effects from his locker.

He had been changed not by Stanley's fate, but by his own; by his frantic struggle to separate from the Hurricane when he rolled the aeroplane over to fall clear away in his parachute. His rising feeling of panic, as the aircraft throbbed across the empty glittering sea, alone in the immense hostile sky, abated when he at last saw the coast of Spain emerge in the distance. He nursed the crippled engine, which was stopping with a cough like that of a dying horse, and fought to keep the aeroplane from dropping straight into the sea. When he judged that he could not hold above a safe altitude to jump, he turned the machine parallel to the coast, pushed back the cockpit hood and forced the stick across. But something held him fast to this flying coffin, he thought with cruel irony afterward that it must have been the dinghy strap; his desperate kicking against the seat had only succeeded in throwing him head first onto the port wing root.

In an instant he became a living puppet, the side of his face dragging against the wing as the aeroplane spiralled and twisted around him. He felt blood trickle down underneath the smashed lens of his goggles; he screamed silently, clawing his way from the cockpit as sky and water alternated at the periphery of his vision and the propeller wash tore at his harness. Then the partially deployed parachute tore him from the wing. He was caught between it and the dying Hurricane; now almost blind he could only hear the wind rush past him as he was dragged down. Without warning he broke free, spinning at the end of the parachute silk like a pendulum. Through one eye he saw the Hurricane tumble lazily through the air and hit the water; it slipped from view beneath the waves, one wingtip pointing directly skyward. His right side felt heavy; as he counted off the distance into the spinning sea beneath his feet, he discovered that the fingers in his right hand were without their usual strength; he later remembered looking down at his gloved hand as his body struck the waves.

He worked the meagre bar of shaving soap to produce a lather, and plastered his jaw. Rafael had sharpened the razor in his honour, and with quick short strokes he cut the bristles away. Then he stripped to his waist, and poured more of the hot water into the enamel basin set on the dresser; he luxuriated once more in the simple ritual of washing himself, but took care not to catch the eye of the face in the mirror. Once dressed, he allowed himself one more brief look at his altered self, but stood back a pace or two into the room, where the faded silver was less able to taunt him.

Satisfied with his appearance he went down onto the terrace. He walked over to the balustrade; Rafael was working in the garden now, and looked up as Tom appeared. The two men exchanged waves, Rafael returned to the precise working of a hoe along a shallow trench of earth; Tom returned to the awning. He settled himself in a worn deck chair, and took a book from the small table set alongside, an antique of equally historic lacquer over cane, that rocked from side to side due to a slight difference in the length of opposing legs. From the house came the sound of guitars, and a dark voice filled with pain and regret. He reasoned that Consuelo had decided to trouble the walls and air with one of the gramophone records in her mercifully small collection of flamenco songs, a style that she said was called *cante hondo*.

Consuelo had set the boundaries of her world outside the house, in opposition to the Francoist ethic of woman as the provider of the home. The official presumption against paid employment for married women did not prevent her from helping those, like Andrea, who brought letters to her to be read and replied to. Illiteracy was widespread, and the stream of those seeking assistance with letters, court orders, applications for State charity or identity papers, unceasing. He knew that she spent her mornings preparing responses to the letters and documents left in her possession, for which work she used Arturo's study; and referred to the law books he had left behind. As the Franco regime had declared the illegitimacy of many of the Republic's laws, the old statutes were of less use as a guide to procedure, but she believed that he had left his spirit impressed in the fading pages, and this gave her strength. As she worked, she often liked to listen to music, and pressed the gramophone into regular service. He could only imagine that she was working on a very difficult letter, for her to resort to flamenco at that time of the day.

By some miracle there had been no repetition of the incident with Andrea in spite of the stream of petitioners, the 'escape procedure' being now well rehearsed. Tom's resurgent strength meant that he could quickly get to his bedroom without assistance, while the others took care that they had not betrayed any sign of his occupancy. Those who came to see Consuelo were discreetly ushered in, and discreetly guided out again once the meeting was concluded. Consuelo herself had little need to visit anyone in the town, apart from occasional forays to the bank, or to visit some of those who had sought her help.

He should have been calm, but he could not resist a rising tide of agitation. He looked out to Rafael, looked beyond him to the mountains, lay back in the chair and listened to the music: he did not belong here. He could not avoid his military obligations, and resolved to raise with Consuelo during the meal the question of how he was to return to Gibraltar. She came onto the terrace and sat down beside him with a sigh, to demonstrate both her satisfaction at her labours and her awareness of the importance of the work she undertook. She wore a dress of dark green, gathered at the waist, with a small string of pearls at her throat. Her hair was gathered up and her face, although betraying signs of fatigue, still shone when she was happy, and she was happy that day. Maria brought out lunch, then retreated to the kitchen where she shared the same meal with Rafael. The bread had been freshly baked, and was still warm from the oven.

"Consuelo," Tom began. He chose his words with care, "I am much stronger now, and my wounds have just about healed. You know that I have to return to Gibraltar, if I can get there, or to North Africa. You have been very kind to me, and I would have probably died if the fishermen had not found me."

"No Tomas," she countered, but not maliciously, "Dr Hernandez believes that you would most definitely have died. I understand that you must leave Spain Tomas, and Dr Hernandez and I have already discussed how this could be done. While you were ill we couldn't tell you."

Tom reflected for a moment on the precariousness of his mortality, then took another piece of bread and drank a little more of the soup. His shirt stuck to his back in two damp patches, and the garden shimmered in the heat as the sun approached its zenith. Soon they would have to retire to the relative comfort within the walls of the house, chasing the afternoon breeze through the rooms, and blessing the shadows that made life tolerable in the furnace heat.

"I had thought that I could leave in a fishing boat, perhaps to North Africa."

"How would you pay Tomas?" and Consuelo looked at him keenly. Tom had no money, apart from the crumpled and salt stained pound notes in his wallet.

"I don't know, perhaps one of the fishermen would be prepared to help."

"Or betray you to the Civil Guard! No Tomas, that is too dangerous, for us all, but particularly for you. God must love you, because the men who brought you here can be persuaded to take you away across the sea when the time is right."

With this exchange they finished the meal, filling out the quiet spaces with casual talk, even with news about the progress of the war taken from the broadcasts of Radio Seville. Consuelo rose and left Tom to find Maria.

It was when he was quite alone that it happened. He stood up and walked over to the balustrade, having decided to eat an orange while looking out over the garden. He attacked the peel with vigour, eager to expose the soft sweet fruit that lay beneath. As he lounged against the stone, chewing and basking in the sun, wiping the juice from his chin with the back of his hand, he noticed that his spoon had dropped to the floor, and lay under the deck chair. He casually stepped across and bent down to retrieve it. As he straightened up he became aware of a tightening in his right hand, as if his fist were about to clench. The sensation started to spread along his arm, and simultaneously in his lower right leg. He had experienced cramp before, but instinctively knew that this was different; his mouth was still full of the flesh of the orange, and he immediately spun round and spat it out over the garden.

The pain in his hand and leg intensified; and his right hand closed up in a violent muscular contraction. He struggled to stop the fingers twisting but the fist closed tight, as if it had become a vice of bone. He felt his leg give way underneath him and his heartbeat raced. In a frenzied action he tried to reach the deck chair, but only succeeded in pushing it and the lacquer table over, the dishes and cutlery crashing and splintering to the floor. He fell; and lay in agony as one side of his body twisted and contracted against him. His breath came in short very rapid bursts; with his left hand he flailed and tried to pull the deckchair upright but gave up, and lay in blind terror while the spasm twisted him.

He became aware of the sound of a woman's shoes clipping hurriedly toward him. As he looked upward Consuelo's face was thrown into shadow by the sun; as if from a great distance he heard her calling, screaming for Rafael and Maria. He lay, the pain searing through his right arm and leg, and he thought that he could no longer breathe. Rafael came, knelt beside him; spoke in a Spanish that was too hurried, too urgent, to understand.

It ended; the violent convulsion abated, his hand opened once more. But he was now very weak and washed in sweat. He was taken to his room, Rafael and Consuelo sat with him; Maria was sent into San Cristobal to find Dr Hernandez. The atmosphere in the house became at once funereal; what joyfulness they had allowed themselves was replaced by a hushed and fearful silence.

The Captive Summer

Two Steps Back

Senora Lopez was reconciled to the arrival of supplicants at any hour of the day and night to seek the doctor's help; not every home had electricity, let alone a telephone. However, when she opened the door to Maria, she understood that there must be another reason for her making the journey from El Faro. She quickly ushered her into the hall, a large plain room, set with black and white tiles on the floor, and a solitary plant exploding from an earthenware tub on an iron filigree table. The silent space maintained the reverential air of a private chapel. There the two women took up a low conspiratorial dialogue.

"Is Dr Hernandez here Senora Lopez?" Maria asked, narrowing her eyes to speed their adjustment to the Spanish Victorian gloom of the hall.

"No Senora Ortiz, today he is again at the clinic, Dr Marin is away."

"Can you please get a message to him, say that Senora Arranquez needs to see him."

Senora Lopez, although formally untrained in medicine, had developed over her years of service a keen sense of the urgency and importance of the pleadings that she received on behalf of the doctor. In some sense she carried out the medical procedure of *triarge*, the dispassionate sorting of those who were going to die in any event, from those who might live if medical intervention was swift enough, from those who could wait. She instinctively knew that Senora Arranquez would not have sent Maria without good reason. Maria declined the offer of something to drink, and stepped back into the street, waved briefly and hurried away, her only concession to the day being to seek the slim perimeter of shade.

Before he could hear Dr Hernandez's car, Rafael saw its enveloping dust plume from the tower as it made its way along the road and through the trees. The black cabin melted under the heat, and adopted a rounder and more fluid line, as if a piece of jet were set upon four wheels and by some mesmeric power were being drawn toward the house. He relinquished his sentry post and hurried down, his hands held out against the stone walls, his feet balancing on each narrow step. Consuelo explained as she walked with the doctor how she had found Tom convulsed on the floor; Dr Hernandez nodded in reply but said nothing. Tom lay propped up in bed; his face had regained the haggard countenance of his first days in the house, although he made a pretence of hiding his fear. There had always been a danger of infection; given the lack of even elementary diagnostic tools, and the suicidal impossibility of transporting Tom undetected to a hospital with an X-ray machine, Dr Hernandez had resorted to blind skill and judgement in his diagnosis. That Tom had appeared to recover without neurological complications satisfied the doctor that he had sustained a simple fracture of the skull, any irritation to the brain tissue or haemorrhaging being localised and minor.

The doctor carried out a thorough examination, Consuelo acting as translator where Tom's Spanish failed to furnish the expressions he needed. The most stark symptoms were that he now experienced tingling in his right arm from the elbow to his finger tips, and that he had no feeling around his mouth or the toes in his right foot. Dr Hernandez asked Tom via Consuelo to grip his own hand, and to push against him, first with his left, then with his right hand. Although he did not say anything to either, it was clear that there was a weakness along Tom's right side; the motor nerve impairment being unmistakable. Dr Hernandez asked for a precise account of what had happened earlier in the day; he wanted to know whether Tom had lost consciousness at any time, which he had not, and for any unusual incidents.The only thing that Tom could think of was that he had started to eat the orange prior to the seizure coming on; and although it was unlikely as a contributor, Rafael was sent to find the remains of the fruit on the terrace, so that it could be examined for signs of disease. Although Tom had been put back to bed, Dr Hernandez wanted to assess his walking capability. When Rafael returned, they assisted Tom out of the bed and stood him up, Rafael at his side and Dr Hernandez a couple of paces in front of him. For Tom it was as if an electric current had been applied along his right side, from his finger tips to his toes, and this current had caused the switches and relays which controlled his movement to burn out. He instinctively knew that he would not be able to walk, but he did what had been asked of him. For a moment he gave the impression to his observers of standing without assistance, but actually he held his weight on his left leg. Dr Hernandez beckoned to him, and he swung his right leg, placed his foot and transferred the weight of his body.

Rafael caught him, swinging his weight up again in an arc as if he were tossing a baby. Consuelo stifled a cry, so changed had the young man become in so short a time. They helped him to the bed, and Dr Hernandez now took Tom's right foot in both hands and instructed him to push against him: the leg crumpled under the effort. Dr Hernandez lowered the leg and took his left foot, repeating the instruction; the left leg more clearly resisted the effort applied, the doctor's face reddening a little as he pushed. Dr Hernandez rapidly explained to Consuelo that he wanted Tom to rest, and that he was not to exert himself, he would arrange for the pharmacist to prepare a sleeping draught.

When they had departed, Tom lay in the profoundly silent room nursing his right hand in his left, running his finger tips across the insensible skin. His mouth felt heavy and alien, as if it had gone to sleep under a dentist's needle, and his tongue probed soft, warm but foreign flesh. He knew again the panic of the desperate struggle on the wing of the Hurricane, but this time he was not falling into a literal abyss. He had complimented himself on his progress and his returning strength, measured out in courtyard lengths; he believed that he had cheated death, and might start to give thought to how he could leave Spain and escape to Gibraltar. Then for the first time, because the topic had never arisen in conversation with Consuelo, he realised that it didn't matter. Whether he died now, or had been dragged under the waves, he would already be classified as 'Missing', and the appropriate telegram sent to his family. He was, in one sense, already a dead man awaiting burial.

"Consuelo, has he recently vomited or shown signs of nausea?"

"No Federico, he is still weak, but he walks," then correcting herself, "walked without assistance. I watched him as he crossed the courtyard each morning. His appetite was good, the headaches had stopped, he did not complain of any distress, and as you instructed we took his temperature daily. There was nothing, no warning." As she spoke she surveyed the wreckage of the lunch through the windows of the reception room, as Maria cleared away the debris.

"Why now Federico?"

Dr Hernandez, seated in one of the deep armchairs beside her, looked up through eyes burdened with the demands of another sick man on the cusp between this world and perhaps another.

"In neurology, with injuries to the brain, we refer to the lucid interval, to denote the period after apparent complete recovery and before the onset of traumatic stupor. This," he chose his words carefully, "denotes cerebral compression, caused by a haemorrhage." For Consuelo however, these words were not careful enough. In the early stage of the war Republican causalities from the front were placed in a field hospital close to the town, before being taken to Cartagena or Valencia. She volunteered as a nurse, and saw a number of young boys on bloody stretchers, for whom haemorrhage did not convey the spluttering, gushing, slopping, warm horror of bodies drowning within, of life ebbing without seemingly leaving the body. But she could not reproach him; they found themselves working in the same tent, and he had to see things, to perform butchery which she knew she would have fled from.

"Will he die?"

"You asked me that before."

"I ask you again because I still need to know."

"Consuelo, is this because of your bargain for Arturo?"

"No, it is because I have seen Tomas returned to life."

"The diagnosis is difficult, some of the other symptoms associated with haemorrhage are missing. His pulse, temperature and blood pressure are normal, had they been," and again he struggled for an appropriate word, "disordered, it would have been an indicator from early on. And also with his eyes, the reflexes have always been normal, and there have been no retinal haemorrhages. If there are any retinal haemorrhages present it is reasonable to suppose that there are haemorrhages elsewhere in the brain."

"What else Federico?"

"A blow to the head can lead to epilepsy, but this seizure did not result in loss of consciousness. We must also consider the possibility of cerebral abscess," but as he said this the unbidden memory returned of a war operation he had assisted on, where an incision to the scalp revealed a skull oozing pus, and he pushed the image away, "or perhaps even a mild stroke." He had intended to reassure, but he could see that he was only creating more alarm. Although outwardly calm, she quaked at this information. The darkest darkness had passed Spain, and the killing had abated. Terrible things were reported from other places, although Radio Seville took pains to emphasise the triumph of Spain's Axis allies. It was as if they had all passed into another dimension, with which it had become difficult to communicate; but Tom's arrival had opened a portal to their former selves.

"What can be done for him?"

"Consuelo, he has to remain here. I have considered how we could secretly extradite him to the main hospital in Granada or Malaga for an X-ray to be taken, but it is impossible. We might as well invite Mendoza here and ask him for his opinion. I could carry out a lumbar puncture, it would help with the diagnosis of the haemorrhage."

"Then do it, please do it!"

"I will."

"Federico, but what if he needs an operation?"

"I am not a surgeon Consuelo, I do not have a surgeon's skill or hands."

"But to save him?"

"I could kill him."

They parted, the doctor giving further instructions for the monitoring of Tom's condition. Consuelo went up to his room and looked in. He was sleeping now, and she closed the door with infinite care in case the slightest noise disturbed him.

The Captive Summer

A week passed. There was no recurrence of the seizure, and the numbness slowly departed, leaving a tingling sensation in limb and face, but a continuing lack of strength in his right leg. He did not like to stand, for fear that his leg would not bear the weight, and it was noticeable that when he did walk his foot dragged a little, although he tried to hide this. His courtyard exercises were now a memory, and the new confinement produced a more profound change in his outlook. Although not sullen, he was clearly quieter, and withdrew into himself. His mind was clear and unimpeded, but for the first time he had to seriously consider the possibility of being permanently disabled, if indeed he should live. Dr Hernandez permitted him to leave his room and go out to the terrace, and Tom took this opportunity for contact with the light and the mountains that still appeared to hang in the sky. He did not like the enforced inactivity, but like military discipline, had to accept it.

The one element in his daily regime which did not change was that Consuelo continued his instruction in Spanish. She was a patient teacher, and although frustrated that she could do little directly to speed his recovery, she believed that by this act she could at least prove to him that they had not abandoned him. He tested his pronunciation of the Spanish phrases he learned on Rafael, who went about his daily chores while the language school was in progress.

"*Yo no soy japones*," he intoned clearly, as Rafael was about to walk down the steps from the terrace to the garden. Rafael's response was to turn his feet outwards and tug at the corner of his eyes, and thus transformed, skip down to the lemon and fig trees in mockery, although strictly as a native of China, not Japan. He disappeared from sight before them, like an Oriental boatman going down the steps of a quay to the dark and oil stained waters of a distant harbour.

"You see, he understood you perfectly Tomas."

"I am sure he heard you tell me first."

"No, Rafael has very selective hearing, he hears only that which he thinks he ought to. The rest he ignores."

Then Tom decided, as a child will from a process of synaptic development imperfectly understood, to compose a short statement to demonstrate that his mind yet functioned, even if he had reason to doubt the brain and body which supported it.

"*Rafael esta en su huerta.*"

By this time Rafael was far enough away in the pulsating light, a hoe thrown over one shoulder, fitful puffs of dust at his heels, not to be able to hear them.

"Yes Tomas, and in spite of my pleadings he will stay there until the sun is so far in the sky, that the ground quakes and splits under the heat, until all colour is washed away, until the beetles and lizards crawl away into the shadow under a fragment of roof tile. Then he will rest, then he will take a siesta."

"How is it that he became your servant?"

Consuelo sat back, and folding her hands on her lap, replied, "I will tell you when you are well again, for now the class is over, and it is time to return to your room."

He deferred to her ministering power, closed the exercise book in which he had set out in a neat hand the verbs, nouns, adjectives and expressions of his new tongue, and prepared to return to the quiet sanctuary.

Will You Dance With Me?

Each day Tom emerged from his sanctuary to draw in the power of the shimmering Andalucian light; and each day started in hope. But hope was not enough: he suffered two further seizures. There was no pattern to the attacks; the first occurred while he lay in bed early one morning and the second a few days later while walking in the garden with Rafael. Dr Hernandez could do no more than prescribe rest; the curious nature of the incidents defying what he had been taught in medical school. For his part Tom was forced, at the age of twenty two, to confront the possibility of his own death.

Where he had previously readily entered into conversation with Consuelo, he now drifted away in mid sentence, or seemed to have difficulty in finding fresh topics to explore. His mind turned back to the black thoughts it had presented him with as he fought to gain the surface of the waves. The unknown territory lay before him, and he could only recall those passages or sonnets of Shakespeare relating to it. One sonnet, the sixtieth, seemed to him to describe his situation perfectly: "*Like as the waves make toward the pebbled shore, So do our minutes hasten to their end.*" Consuelo now deliberately kept discussion of the war in Europe to a minimum. She was concerned that Tom had resigned himself to his fate; and she looked for a way to introduce other diversions for him, but she would not admit to herself, that this also reflected her own emotional need to push away thoughts of Arturo's unknown parallel fate in a hostile land. The language school continued as before.

"Tomas, how would you say in Spanish," and Consuelo looked now full into his face one morning, her preferred technique for preventing his gaze from straying, "and let us assume that you are travelling with your wife, how would you say 'I would like two single tickets for the train to Madrid, senor'?"

Tom rubbed the right side of his face enthusiastically, in an effort to dispel the tingling sensation which ran from his nose to his chin, then he responded.

"But I have no wife."

"I know, but pretend for now that you have. If you cannot pretend, then think of your sweetheart."

He looked away, and for a moment Consuelo thought that he resented the request or the intrusion into his personal life.

"Very well," and Tom conjured up the image of June Ryedale, a WAAF corporal he had known in England. But she had never been particularly keen on him: they had shared a few dances and kisses at all ranks parties, ventured in Dorchester to go to the cinema, and spent one Sunday cycling through the Dorset countryside. Before answering he also considered the women he had known in civilian life; and then the thought came into his head: What's the point? He looked up, but realised with the first renewal of contact with Consuelo's calm but pensive face that his attitude toward a woman who had risked imprisonment to save him was ungracious.

He accordingly placed himself and his girlfriend in the ticket hall of a provincial railway station, where they were waiting to board a train for the capital. She was wearing a dress in lemon with a matching jacket, and a wisp of a hat in light grey felt secured with a pin. For himself he selected a linen suit, with a light blue shirt turned out at the collar, which he considered to be a fair compromise between English elegance and Hollywood chic. A smile came to his lips when he remembered something that Maguire had said about her. He recalled that she habitually strode around the aerodrome with a precise swinging action of her arms, and Maguire with typical Antipodean reserve had quipped: "If she does that a little faster she'll take off and clear the bloody perimeter fence."

"What is it that has made you smile?" Consuelo asked.

"Something about my fictitious wife."

"Is she beautiful?"

"No it isn't that, she has a way of amusing people that she is not aware of."

"What is this skill that she is not aware of?"

"She invented a new dance step," he replied, trying now to conceal his amusement.

Consuelo looked quizzical, unconvinced of the truthfulness of Tom's reply. She saw an opportunity to get the better of him, and formulated her next question.

"Tomas, will you dance with me?"

This was unexpected, and struck at his sense of his own incapacity.

"I don't think that I am ready for the dance floor Consuelo."

"But you do dance, don't you?"

"Of course, or did. But I'm not Fred Astaire."

She had to agree that he was not Fred Astaire. Now it was her turn to conjure an image, for her it was from *Top Hat*; Tom was in white tie and tails and a silk top hat, but with one leg inexplicably encased in plaster. He was making brave but ludicrous attempts to tap dance, and succeeded only in falling on his back, one leg kicking out at the air as he lay on the ground. She returned Tom's earlier ambiguous smile.

"I think that it is time that someone led you back to the dance floor, with or without the plaster cast," she said coyly.

"What plaster cast?"

"It is only a figure of speech we use in Spain."

"But you are already teaching me to speak Spanish, there won't be enough time in the day," he protested.

"By day you will learn to speak Spanish, by night you will dance. It would be good for you, it will assist your recovery. I am sure that Dr Hernandez will approve."

She had no knowledge whether this was true or not, but to her ears it had a ring of plausibility.

"Where will we dance?" he asked.

She looked at him, then surveyed the terrace around them; to her his question was as fanciful as enquiring where on an open mountainside he could find blocks of stone.

"Here. It would be perfect, don't you think?"

She was teasing him, and they both knew it, but she acted without malicious intent. Tom considered how he might escape this strange fate. He was an invalid, and an invalid that did not want to dance. She regarded him intently with a sly look of mild amusement, even mischievousness; the corners of her mouth turned upward.

"If I fall," he hesitated, "will you laugh at me?"

"No, I won't laugh at you Tomas, and I don't believe that you will fall."

"I might; I could topple over. Look, Consuelo," and he was more emphatic now, "I don't think that it is a sensible idea for me to start dancing classes at this time."

She considered this for a moment, then raised her gaze to the garden. Still looking away she said, "Then we will have to see that you don't."

"How?"

"Rafael. He's going to dance with us."

The precise details of how the dance academy would operate were left as a sublime mystery. Tom spent a listless afternoon in his room; through the window onto the courtyard he watched the slow transit of the sun across the sky by the slanting line of shadow which swept around the walls and the blistered shutters. He sat in the wicker chair, tapping his feet together as he practised steps he had learned in the local dance halls. Sometimes he practised with his eyes closed, sometimes with his eyes open as he stared at the ceiling. But always with the same question on his lips: "How is Rafael going to dance with us? I just don't see how three people can dance together."

The Captive Summer

Perhaps Consuelo had meant that she and Rafael would demonstrate the dance steps first, then he would replace Rafael as Consuelo's dancing partner. This did not seem likely: he doubted whether Rafael would agree to this violation of the proper relationship with his employer. He had once seen a dance band in London called the *Havana Rhythm Boys*, but had been told that it was made up of musicians who had formerly worked on transatlantic liners, and that the name of the band was suggested by a visit to a brothel undertaken by one musician when his ship was in port in Cuba. The recollection was passing, and of no use to him, as he tried to find a logical solution to the imminent physical dilemma he now faced.

Dancing had entered his life when he became an apprentice, where one of the rites of passage to manhood was attending the occasional social functions provided by the company's omnipotent guardians of social welfare on the board of directors. He went to these parties, and also attended South London dance halls with his workmates. One of the big British singing stars at that time, and a firm favourite, was Al Bowlly; the languid romanticism of his songs, such as *Time On My Hands* or *By My Side*, conveyed the aspiration and hopes of a frustrated generation caught by the Depression, but spared the trenches. Tom embarked on a new two year apprenticeship, one that required he shuffle under subdued lighting to such melodies, clasping the waists of shop-girls and secretaries, making polite conversation, but not truly enjoying himself. He knew that he was supposed to, and everybody else appeared to, but he didn't think that he was born to spend his life in a dance hall.

His early morning encounter with Consuelo, while she listened to Bing Crosby, had warned him that she might have a considerable collection of dance music records, and so it proved. After supper, as the sun slipped away and the sting of the day's heat abated, he made his way to the terrace; a space that had by now in his own mind folded down into an oppressive cell. He found Consuelo and Rafael in close and earnest discussion, rapidly disputing something in Spanish, which Tom had already noted on a number of occasions was a good language to dispute in. He watched them, as Rafael, shoulders hunched, made short sweeping actions with his hands, while Consuelo cajoled and pleaded. Her plan was simple: while she and Tom danced on the terrace to music from the gramophone, Rafael would perform a kind of shadow dance a few paces behind, ready to step forward and intervene if Tom needed help. But Rafael had doubts.

The request was outside his understanding of the proper relationship between himself, a servant, and Consuelo, his employer. Tom appreciated that Rafael was more than a domestic servant, he was also Consuelo's guardian, and only with great reluctance was he prepared to accept her request.

"Rafael! I am not asking that you dance with me, only that you help Tomas to dance with me," she exclaimed with vexation, "why are you both so afraid to do this thing with me? Am I an ogre?! Do you fear me?!"

Consuelo demonstrated to Rafael what part he would take in the evening's entertainment by gesticulating where she and Tom would stand, then stepping back to Rafael's desired position on the terrace and moving, slowly, a step to the left, then another to the right. She spoke quickly, her own hands flying to indicate the flowing movements of the dancing partners, and Rafael's expected response. It was a dance sequence in its own right. Using his imperfect knowledge of Spanish, and Consuelo's expressions, Tom quickly understood what was going to happen; the comical nature of the episode taking his mind away from any concern about his own ability. Tom decided to speak.

"Rafael, I should be grateful if you would help me. I am nervous about falling," and then he added, "Consuelo might be hurt if I fell."
These few words dispelled the affront to Rafael's dignity and sense of position within the household; as the request was made on the basis of protecting Consuelo, he consented.

"Now Tomas," and she went over to take a record from its paper sleeve and place it on the gramophone, lowered the arm and turned back to him, "you know I haven't danced since Arturo was here."

Then she held out her arms to him. Drawing her toward him was the sweetest and yet most anxious action of his life, and it was an experience quite different from what he had known before.

Rafael took up his position; as the music broke out from the horn of the gramophone the three of them began their slow shuffling under the stars. As she melted toward him, and Tom tried to keep his weak leg from robbing him of the moment, Rafael circled the dancers at a discreet distance, like a nervous bodyguard.

The Captive Summer

A Holy War

Spain was a Catholic country, and Spain was Fascist. Unlike Germany, the Church held a central position within the political ideology and machinery of the State. The Church fulfilled Franco's emotional need to believe that his actions were sanctified by God; it also provided a network of informers and propagandists. But Franco saw no need to disband the Army: he was loath to give up uniforms and ceremony; and although the bishops had learned to salute, they were not all proficient in handling bolt action rifles.

The defeat and expulsion of the Moors centuries before had deprived the Francoist crusaders of the new Spain of an object for their hatred differentiated by religious creed; the next best alternative was an object of hatred based on class and political affinity, the Republicans therefore became the new Moors. Those on the losing side were harangued in the chapels, pursued in their homes and places of entertainment by the zealots of *Action Catolica*, and indoctrinated in the classroom. Church officials also had influence in the distribution of rationed goods; they ensured that political loyalty, not hunger, determined the allocation of the loaves and fishes by which the modern Spain fed itself.

The senior cleric in San Cristobal was Father Ramon Abarca, who officiated at the town's main church, the *Iglesia de Santa Maria Magdalena*. He had been the parish priest for fifteen years; he knew the people and had known the town in times of peace and war. He had remained during the conflict, at some risk: many priests were executed by Republican militia as anti-clerical fury had swept the country. People said of him that both his eyes and his soul were hooded. No one who talked with him could ever say clearly what fundamental truths he did and did not ascribe to. He was both a clerical politician and a political cleric; he took as keen an interest in the appointment of the Bishop of Granada, as he did in the appointment of a minister in Franco's government.

He was grey and lined, with an untypically pallid complexion; but a frail body, tired of this world's temptations, contained a zealot's determination. He believed that Franco had saved Spain from darkness, and even went so far as to doubt whether Republicans had souls, so great was their crime and damnation in the eyes of God. And he considered it his duty to pass on to the Civil Guard any information he thought of use to them, no matter where or how it was obtained.

In the civil war, Abarca had kept a fully loaded pistol on a wooden shelf below the altar during Mass. He carried the gun with him secreted under his vestments; as he reached the altar he withdrew the weapon with a slow graceful sweep of his arm and placed it just beyond his fingertips, taking a few moments to survey the congregation. They beheld the messenger of the word of God, but in truth his dignified ascension owed as much to a desire to prevent the accidental discharge of the gun, as a need to convey the gravitas of the holy ritual that was about to unfold. When Franco came to power the altar became an observation post, from which Abarca surveyed a now sullen and hostile populace, and from which he delivered a liturgy that was a curious hybrid of dogma and political invective; he sometimes mentioned Jesus.

But the ritual that was most suited to intelligence gathering and surveillance was confession. Abarca conveniently forgot the teachings of his Lord when he heard the sins of his parishioners; he noted their failings and passed to Mendoza every piece of gossip or revealed indiscretion in which the Civil Guard would be interested. He also, as a good propagandist, took pains to extol the virtues of Franco and the rapid improvement in the quality of life he had brought about, as a manifestation of God's plan.

One Sunday he heard the confession of a young man who had admitted to lusting after a plump ham, and two loaves of bread, that he had seen in the kitchen of a neighbour. The neighbour had food to spare while the young man, who was a tailor, struggled to support and feed his family. By his careful questioning Abarca satisfied himself that no offence under the penal code had been committed, just an infringement of one of the commandments. He decided that the man would benefit from a short lesson in political education, and so prepared to provide it. He had only just composed his mind and decided what proud metaphors he should employ, when a low rumbling emanated from the other side of the partition.

"What was that?" he inquired with some annoyance.

"Father forgive me, for I am hungry, and my stomach has spoken without consent," came the reply through the wooden grill.

"A weak stomach is the product of a weak mind, a weak mind the product of a weak will, a weak will the product of a weak spirit," which seemed to Abarca such a splendid statement of cause and effect, that he duly noted it down in a little book which he kept beside him.

"May God forgive me for my sin Father."

"Indeed," and the priest cleared his throat. "The true spirit," and Abarca now shifted a little on his seat, "of the Spanish soul, the spirit of the explorer, the soldier-priest, the colonial administrator, is the spirit of the soul in turmoil which seeks salvation through suffering. Do you understand that?"

"Yes Father."

"And do you accept that you must suffer if you are to achieve salvation?"

"Yes Father," but the man's stomach let out another audible complaint.

Abarca, now rapidly tiring of the rebellious stomach and its owner, decided to curtail the audience; he admonished and dismissed the young tailor with some irritation, then spent a few moments recording the name and address of the neighbour who, he reasoned, must be in possession of contraband goods. As he sat back in the musty creaking confessional box he consoled himself that the tailor's sin had been minor compared to that of Don Octavio Montero, a drunk who was given to visions, and who had plagued him through the years with requests for help. Don Octavio no longer came to Mass, being either too drunk or too deranged; he was a man who was utterly beyond any help the Church could offer. Father Abarca coughed, the habitual sign of readiness, set the notebook at his side and inclined his head.

Don Octavio preferred to stay away from his apartment and amongst other people for as much of the day as he could. He was gregarious by nature, and age had not changed his outlook on life. He had never married, and could only offer vague explanations as to why he had remained a bachelor, the most specious being that the demands of provincial government precluded satisfactory family life. In truth he had never developed the necessary skills to woo and win a partner; added to this was his shortness of height, which was a practical handicap of an embarrassing nature. It was a common custom in Spanish society for the initial meetings between *novio* and *novia* to be conducted at the window of the house where the girl lived. This gave an advantage, as indeed in life in general, to those young men who were tall. Don Octavio quite literally came up short; in spite of his assiduous study of the arts of romance and his unrelenting early efforts, he could never rid himself of the comical nature of his lovemaking. An early rebuff when, half obscured by flowers adorning the window box, he had resorted to standing on tip toe, the better to observe the object of his infatuation, only then to fall backward, dented his esteem to such an extent that he rapidly lost interest in the pursuit of women. He became committed to his work, there being no other likely partner in life for him, and watched as his friends married, raised families of their own, and then one by one, died.

However, Don Octavio guarded a secret in its own way as terrible as that which his friend Dr Hernandez was party to. And it related to the departure from this world of his friends and acquaintances. He first became aware of it when, one morning, he passed a former and now retired colleague in the street. He raised his hat to him and called out from habitual politeness; but the man kept walking, making no attempt to acknowledge the greeting. Momentarily annoyed at the snub, he went on his way. Three weeks later he happened to meet the man's wife, but she was now dressed in the cloth of widowhood. His initial thought was, "Good, how dare he snub me and expect to enjoy a long life!" but being a civil man, he followed the appropriate etiquette and went over to her and expressed his condolences at her loss.

"I was not aware, please forgive me."

"There is nothing to forgive Don Octavio."

"May I ask from what cause he was taken?"

"He suffered a heart attack, a month ago. Yes, I have been a widow exactly one month!"

He did not dispute the length of time, and held back from making an obscure reference to seeing her husband at a somewhat later date. He let the matter pass, until something like it happened again. By now he was becoming troubled, and initially sought solace by going to visit Father Abarca. He decided not go into the confessional box, as he was not aware that he had committed a sin, but sought out his views in a private meeting.

This proved to be unwise, as Abarca, angered at his impudence, warned him repeatedly and volubly that to consort with Satan would ensure damnation; refusing to listen to any further instances of spectral sightings, Abarca threatened him with excommunication; and throwing open the door, ordered him out of his chambers. Don Octavio next consulted Dr Hernandez, who although more sympathetic, was inclined to believe that the hallucinations were induced by subconscious sexual stresses, having himself only recently finished reading a volume of the work of Freud. Don Octavio resigned himself to the visitations; but he took what comfort he could from alcohol, on the view that the hallucinations brought on by *delirium tremens* would prove indistinguishable from those that were not, and in some way they would work to nullify each other.

In an attempt at physical escape, he began walking expeditions in the mountains, leaving home early each Saturday morning, his pockets stuffed with fruit, his sagging body supported by a strong stick. But this failed, the apparitions simply visited him in his apartment when he returned. The war had commenced, and the hallucinations were accordingly ascribed by Dr Hernandez to a 'war psychosis', occasioned by the terrible facts of the conflict. But Don Octavio knew differently, because on every occasion that the form of a local young man, known to be away at the war, came to him, confirmation was shortly received that be had been killed. One morning he awoke to find a young soldier sitting at the foot of his bed, hand on chin, calmly observing him. He pleaded with the figure to leave, asking: "What is it, what can I do for you?" The soldier rose from the bed, and without saying a word, pointed to the bedroom window. Don Octavio looked from the young man to the window and back, trying to understand his meaning.

"Well yes, I know that they are dirty, but you see I am old and it is not easy to clean them. No? That is not you're meaning? Do you want me to leave the house? Is that it?" This produced a nod from the young man, and emboldened, Don Octavio climbed out of bed, to see what lay beyond the window pane. The young man pointed again, quite unambiguously, toward a house just along the street. "Do you want me to go to that house?" he asked. Again the young man nodded. Don Octavio looked at the house, and when he turned back found that he was quite alone again. He reasoned that he could not go and announce himself, so he made some discreet enquiries as to who lived there. He quickly discovered that it was the family of a baker, whose eldest son was fighting with the Republican militia. He regarded it as outrageous and quite unknown for anyone to go door to door telling strangers that their son or brother, husband, father or nephew had perished. And in any event he had no proof; the visitation could have been the effect of eating too late, or the last glass of brandy, on the chemical and electrical impulses which his friend Dr Hernandez told him poured through his brain.

Discretion and the desire to avoid offending innocent strangers prevented him from doing as he had been bidden. Then a week or so later he saw the baker and his wife in the street; she was screaming, and her husband was trying to restrain her, but out of love, and a shared grief for the son they would not see again. Don Octavio felt ashamed, he could not have prevented the death, perhaps he could try to take away its sting. However, the clear warning from Abarca, local superstition, and his own understandable desire to avoid ridicule held him in check. Twice more he saw figures, both of young soldiers. He decided to act, to communicate with the living. He still could not bring himself to visit their homes; and so he decided to write anonymously to the families, explaining that he only wanted to convey to them some hope that their loved ones lived yet, but in a place and in a form not readily amenable to communication.

He resorted to walking through the streets late at night, in the hope that a spirit would appear to him outside the house or apartment where the family lived. As San Cristobal was still within Republican territory, the immediate danger was of being considered a Nationalist spy. No one took too much notice of an old man who would occasionally stop suddenly in his night time wandering, and note down a house number and street name in a little note book. He placed two anonymous notes late at night under the doors of local houses, walking away briskly on each occasion to avoid discovery. In time word spread through the town, but as no one knew who was doing this, and gypsies were already feared and hated in the district, rumour spread that a gypsy fortuneteller was responsible. Then one day a gypsy was arrested for spreading despondency about the war, and later beaten up in the street. Don Octavio passed the man as he lay rolling like a drunk; ashamed that this man had suffered for his own actions, he resolved to stop. But the figures still appeared to him; in an effort to shut them out he drank more heavily; in response people started to shun him, citing his perpetual drunken state, filthy clothes, and incoherent rambling. As darkness fell across Spain, a dark shadow passed over his mind: the torment of many became reflected in the tormented mind of one old man.

The Captive Summer

Suffer The Children

Dr Hernandez had practised medicine in the age before antibiotics, or the widespread availability of blood transfusions; and he witnessed each day the fragile hold of sentient life in the universe. He had learned that no death existed in isolation from any other; whether the demise of two men who had drunk from the same contaminated well or a mother's heartbroken yielding of the will to live as she buried her child. For him the miracle was that so many did not die. His religious faith had declined as age advanced, although if questioned closely he might admit to a residual sense of the divine in a freshly opened flower. But his faith was checked when presented with the death of children; and he did not understand why the light of cosmic consciousness had to be extinguished so often in those who had barely begun to understand it.

He had lobbied to the extent of what was advisable for his own safety against an authority which could twist demands for improved sanitation as proof of political dissent. His heroes were Pasteur and Lister, and in their names he attempted to educate and cajole the municipal authorities to provide clean water and adequate sanitation throughout the town. That the slum district had neither, was to his conscience as sure a means of reducing the population, as harnessing the Spanish love of lotteries to the need to provide firing practice for the Civil Guard. But a pit and a bucket of quick lime were considered adequate; that the sloping ground to the east of the town was avoided by all except those who were ignorant of its use as a tip for the sewage carts did nothing to assuage his anger at its existence. At the clinic he treated those from that quarter whose ailments could easily be traced back to the bacteria laden ordure which festered in the sun. He believed that it was only a matter of time before cholera came; in this he was proved correct.

But he was still surprised when he was woken late at night by urgent banging at his door; clattering downstairs bare footed he found the cafe owner, Gabriel Soto, in a state of parental agitation.

"Dr Hernandez, please forgive me, I know that it is late doctor, very late, but Elena, my daughter, is sick, she has been vomiting and passing water. Doctor, she has a fever."

He was ushered inside, where Senora Lopez, grey hair coiled at the sides of her head, had joined the doctor. It was not until some days later that Dr Hernandez realised that the irregular tapping he had heard that night was due to Soto wearing one only boot, the other foot being bare to the ground. As he dressed he questioned him about the onset of the little girl's condition; he had eaten regularly at the cafe; the symptoms suggested to him some severe food poisoning, perhaps from bad meat. But when Soto explained how the bed sheets were stained with a watery diarrhoea, he started to change his opinion. He had seen the child only a few days before, walking between the pavement tables, taking cutlery and glasses for her father.

"For how long has she been like this?"

"Since this morning; my wife says that she would not leave the toilet, and she became weaker, but still she passed water, even when we lay her on the bed," and he lowered his head at having to discuss such a matter with the doctor, "and so we changed the sheets for they were very stained."

"What have you done with those sheets?" Dr Hernandez asked with a note of urgency.

"My wife will wash them."

"Burn them!"

"Burn them doctor?" enquired Soto, not quite understanding the significance of their soiling.

"Yes, burn them Gabriel! We'll take my car, we may have to travel on to the clinic."

And with that they left the house, Soto making a clip-clop noise in the doctor's wake as they strode in the darkened street.

The little girl's pallor and condition confirmed Dr Hernandez's worst fear. She lay on her bed half naked, cold to the touch, her skin translucent, the smell of her own bodily fluids strong in the little bedroom above the cafe. Her mother Julia held her hand, willing her to open her eyes, but crying silently. Julia's sister had arrived, and was looking after the other children, who wanted to know what was wrong with Elena, and howled when they were forcibly put to bed. When Julia looked up at Dr Hernandez she had the same imploring look of helplessness and faith that Dr Hernandez had seen in innumerable eyes. It was the look which encapsulated human incomprehension, fear and hope that a miracle would be performed and the dying restored to life. Dr Hernandez made no claim to divine skill, he did what he could, he appeared calm, but inwardly he was as traumatised as they.

"We must move her to the clinic," he said.

"Save her! In the name of our Lord, please save my child!" and Julia released her grip on the child's hand to claw at the doctor's chest; Gabriel pulled her away.

"Forgive her doctor," he said, restraining and comforting his wife at the same time.

"There is nothing to forgive, I will do what I can," Dr Hernandez replied, sitting down beside the sick child.

The child was weakening, and she had been afflicted from a position of weakness, the condition of most. She was wrapped up in fresh sheets, and carried to the car by her father. There was a small ward at the clinic; two nuns cared for any patients who were detained there. Dr Hernandez made arrangements by telephone and they drove to the outskirts of the town, where the clinic, one of the few modern buildings, enjoyed views across the sea. All through the night the child lingered, with her father and Dr Hernandez at her bedside. When day came, Dr Hernandez telephoned Dr Marin to advise him that the town had a case of cholera, and then left a message for the Mayor. Exhausted, he drove Soto home, collected his wife, and took her back to the clinic to maintain the vigil. On that afternoon Elena opened her eyes to her mother, smiled at her, sighed and relinquished her life.

Dr Hernandez was discussing with Dr Marin in their shared office his fears for the outbreak of the disease, and his anger that the Mayor had still not returned his call, when one of the nuns knocked urgently and asked him to attend. Julia Soto was cradling the child, shaking her almost, and it was with difficulty that the three of them were able to separate the woman from her dead infant. When Dr Hernandez brought Julia home later that day, she and Gabriel wept openly in the street and clung to each other in an anguished slow dance that attracted the attention of passersby. Dr Hernandez and Andres guided them inside; Julia was sedated, and put to bed by her sister, who had now taken over the running of the household.

Friends and neighbours gathered at the cafe, aroused by the open weeping and the presence of the doctor. Andres went out to speak to them, while Dr Hernandez spent time with Julia and examined the other children. He gave instructions to her sister about what had to be done to clean and disinfect the building. He needed to speak to Gabriel; but like the god Janus, Gabriel now maintained one face turned to the world and one turned to the blackness which was enveloping his mind. He relentlessly paced the bar, clenching and unclenching his fists; he was unable to accept or comprehend that his child was gone, that he would never see her again, and recited over and over the truth which he did not want to accept.

As he paced he looked out of the window, but saw nothing or no one, although from time to time people passed by and stopped to speak to Andres. The crashing of the door against the frame alerted those upstairs that his pacing was at an end, for Gabriel had at last recognised one of the faces in the square, and it was the face of Father Abarca.

"She is dead! My little child is dead!" he shouted into the priest's face. "Why was she taken from us?!" and then he spat, the veins on his temples standing proud from the skull. Abarca regarded Soto as if the matter was of little concern to him.

"It is not for us to question the will of God Senor Soto, only to submit to it."

"Submit, submit, to the will of a God that hides His face, that turns His back on the suffering in this world?!"

"Mankind is wicked senor, and is rightly punished."

"Wicked you say!" and Soto moved his face closer and clenched his fists in readiness to strike the priest.

"Was my child wicked? Was she in sin? What sin had she committed you lying bastard?!"

Dr Hernandez and Andres hurried across the square to restrain Soto, whose voice, like the steam from a boiling kettle, had reached a high pitched squeal. There was no pity in Abarca's tone, only a note of irritation, as if he were being questioned about a detail in a lease by a pedantic notary: it fuelled the desperate man's rage.

"We are all in sin, Senor Soto. As our Lord Jesus died for our sin, it is possible that this child died for the sins of another."

This was the breaking point.The grief and toil exhausted simple cafe owner, who had watched helpless beside his wife as the joy in their life was snatched away from them, leaving them bereft, lamed in heart and soul, rebelled against a tyranny of faith which he could contemplate no longer. As his right fist swung upward to strike, Andres launched himself forward, and succeeded in enveloping the clenched fingers in his own, but not in taking away all of the momentum of the blow. Whether Father Abarca was actually struck was a matter of conjecture, but he toppled backward, and would have fallen over into the square had not Dr Hernandez caught him and pushed him to his feet.

"Did you see that?! He struck me! He struck a priest!" cried Abarca, whining like a self righteous martyr, and already looking for witnesses.

"Father, he was not aware of his actions! His child has died; have pity on him, in the name of God have pity on him!" and Dr Hernandez looked closely into the priest's face to try to draw his attention away from Soto and Andres, who were now struggling violently together. Andres had succeeded in pinning Soto's arms at his side, while Soto spat curses at the priest and threw punches ineffectually into the air.

As misfortune would have it, Sargento Pelean chose that moment to enter the square, drawn by the sound of the altercation. He found Dr

Hernandez remonstrating with the priest, while Andres, who had been joined by the second waiter, Cano, was trying to drag Soto back across the square. Although his arms were secured, Soto was using his voice to continue the assault on the cleric.

"Who is this God, that allows the innocent to be cut down while the wicked walk the Earth exultant and unmolested!? Damn Him, damn Him for taking my child! Let me go, fuck you Andres let me go!" he yelled, expelling every molecule of air from his lungs.

"He is a heretic, do you hear he is a heretic!" Abarca called to the policeman. "Sargento Pelean! Arrest him, I order his arrest!"

Sargento Pelean had a number of failings, but blind obedience to religious authority was not one of them. He placated the priest, and pushed Soto, who was still grappling with Andres and Cano, into the cafe. Assuring Father Abarca that he would investigate the assault, he ushered him on his way, then went to speak to Dr Hernandez; the doctor explained what had happened.

"Will you arrest him Sargento Pelean?" he asked.

The policeman drew himself up, and saluted the doctor.

"No doctor, I also have children. Good day to you Dr Hernandez."

The policeman's compassion may have saved Soto from humiliation that day, but his mind could not contain the images of the child holding out her arms to him; and his mind slowly unwound like the mainspring of a clock. A week later he sat by himself in the darkened cafe while the town slept around him. He sat there for some time, a rope held loosely between his fingers, an insensible thing, as insensible as the body of his child, but not as cold. The electric lamp in the square threw a warped grid of light and dark shapes onto the cafe floor, which mirrored the warping of reason in his mind. The clock behind the bar struck two in the morning, stirring him, bringing him temporarily back to himself. His hands gripped the rope and he looked up to the row of hooks in the ceiling. He reasoned that there would have been room on the bar for half a dozen men, but he could not be sure that the beam would hold. He pulled himself up, breathing the rich mixture of tobacco, stale air, coffee, and grease. He stood unsteadily upright, feeling for support in the half light. He fashioned a loop in one end of the rope, and a larger noose at the other. It took several attempts to catch one of the hooks, as he had to stop himself toppling from the bar when he cast the rope out. He pulled on the rope to close the loop tight, then placed the noose around his neck. For a moment he stood quite still, listening to the room, and the sleeping town beyond. In his mind's eye Elena stood before him smiling, and holding her hands out to him once more. He opened his own arms to his child and stepped forward.

Andres found the body, when the day was still full of sleep, and unblemished. He had come to the cafe early, strangely conscious as he walked through the town in the early light that there was once a morning when all the Earth was clean and silent, before the first bird had risen into the sky, before the first child had cried with hunger. A sheet of newspaper blew along before him, as if announcing him to the sleeping town; it twisted round, lost form and lay dead at his feet. When he opened the door, his eyes were drawn upward, and in the aromatic gloom he saw the body, frozen in space. He walked across and stood beside the figure, shuddering as his glance revealed the opened blank eyes of Gabriel looking down on him. He turned, and leaning against the bar, aware of the shadow which fell across the polished wood at his side, a phantom companion, decided what to do.

Gabriel had not been missed in the grief, and clamour, of the other children and the need to care for them. Andres brought the step ladder from the storeroom, found a knife and cut the body down, clasping him under the arms as he took the weight, and removed the rope from his neck. For a moment he sat watching him, not wanting to believe that he would simply lie on the floor and not get up and prepare the cafe for another day. Eventually he succumbed to the truth, and rose to carry that mortal truth to the still sleeping and unblemished world beyond.

The Captive Summer

Enter The White Rabbit

Dr Hernandez arrived at *La Alverjilla* shortly before Felipe Escolar, the undertaker. He stood beside Soto's body, which now lay on a bench; once he had pronounced that the cafe owner's life was extinguished, he stood aside and allowed Escolar to take his place. He walked across to a table set close to the window looking onto the street, where Andres sat with Julia Soto's sister, Ana, and lowered himself onto a chair. A copy of *Ascenso* lay on the table, its headline proclaiming the success of a local tennis tournament, the doctor pushed it aside.

"This is a bad day senor," offered Andres, as Ana looked away in desolation.

"Yes Andres." Dr Hernandez turned to the silently weeping woman, but realising that she could not answer him, motioned to Andres; the two men rose and stepped to the far side of the room.

"Does his wife know?" Dr Hernandez asked.

"No doctor, she is still sleeping."

"And the children?"

"A friend took them to school."

"Good," and the doctor looked to the ceiling, to Andres, and then out onto the square, deciding which had prior claim on his time and compassion. "I have to go to the clinic Andres, let Senora Soto sleep, I'll come back later."

He stood outside the cafe and looked across to the desultory fountain that threw a meagre jet of water into the morning air. A flapping poster promoting a bull fight in Malaga caught his attention; the intense blue, scarlet and brown tones of the torero's jacket, his cloak, and the charging bull, standing in relief against the paler dirty sand colouring of the wall it was imperfectly pasted to. He walked away; as he did so he attempted to explain to himself the significance of the tennis tournament.

Dr Hernandez found time now for only brief visits to El Faro, but he needed these opportunities to talk with Consuelo, and to draw strength from the mountains. Cholera soon claimed seven children, most from the slum district, and one of the nuns working at the clinic was not expected to live. It was the needless death of the children that drew this anger, as Oleanza was not inclined to take action unless he considered it politically expedient.The Mayor had relented and allowed Bucaro to refer to an outbreak of illness on an inside page of *Ascenso*, but forbidden either the identification of the disease or publication of the names of the casualties. As they sat together one evening drinking coffee on the terrace, Dr Hernandez raged against his tormentors.

"Do you know what they are calling Bucaro now?" he asked Consuelo.

"No, Federico, but it must be a term of abuse," she replied, putting down her cup.

"They call him *el ascensorista*, the lift attendant, because he rises with the powerful, but descends again while they move forward! He is a prisoner of the machinery! Poor Bucaro!"

"Aren't any of them concerned about what's happening?"

"Concerned? No! Why should they be concerned when the dead are likely to be Republicans?! Damn them!" and he stood up and strode to the balustrade.

Consuelo looked to Tom, still struggling to keep up with the rapid stream of invective, and he looked at Consuelo. She shook her head, to counsel him not to take personally anything that Dr Hernandez said. The doctor turned to face them and continued his verbal assault.

"So I decided to go to Oleanza, to see what was the problem which was so insurmountable, which prevented the provision of adequate medical supplies."

He was animated, but appeared fevered, and was clearly exhausted from hopeless vigils in airless chambers. Consuelo, anxious at the exhaustion that was etched in his face, would have had Dr Hernandez stop, but he went on.

"He was in his office with Castellon, discussing that damned parade! The children are dying, and he discusses how he can best celebrate the capture of the town by the Fascists!"

"Federico, they cannot see what harm they do. They are proud men, they believe that they enjoy legitimacy. The death of the children is not your fault."

He looked at her, but with eyes which blamed himself; he quietened, stepped beside her, drew her hand to his lips and kissed it.

"We should have stopped them Consuelo, it is too late now, we should have stopped them," he said almost inaudibly.

Consuelo withdrew her hand, ashamed at her own complicity in the failed struggle. The Republic and its supporters had done all that could be expected of them, while the Great Powers stood by. Those who had died were spared the ordeal of life under Franco, those who yet lived hoped for the strength to outlive the nightmare.

"What did he say Federico?"

"He told me to leave his office. Castellon watched me with a look of contempt, as if it were I who had brought disease into the town. I asked him where were the nurses and the supplies I had been promised from Granada? He told me that I should concern myself with treating the sick; economic planning and production was best left to those who had the requisite skills! Then Castellon spoke, accusing me of spreading alarm, and all the while he had that look about him, as if I were filth."

He made a despairing gesture, offering his hands to the sky, as if asking a question he had no belief would be answered by any mortal or supernatural power.

"Will they do nothing?"

"The Civil Guard will ensure that no one leaves the slums without a permit. They do not understand that cholera is carried in the water, it needs no permit to move from house to house. It isn't enough to drink only bottled beer, we must find the source of the disease."

He was weary, and she would not question him further. But despite his exhaustion, he now turned and spoke to Tom, aware that he had sat throughout the political tirade without any opportunity to comment.

"And you Tomas, how have you been?" he asked, exhaling deeply.

"I think I am better doctor. I still have the tingling sensation in my hand and my leg, but I am getting stronger."

"When did you last have a muscular spasm?'

"That was three weeks ago."

"And are you taking the quinine?"

"Yes Dr Hernandez."

The quinine had been recommended by Dr Hernandez as a muscle relaxant, and Tom believed that it was helping to suppress muscular twitches which were the latest manifestation of his injury.

"Good. I cannot say when we can begin to plan to repatriate you. There is to be a parade at the end of August, there will be many soldiers in the town, it is better that we wait until they have departed."

"Why are they coming?"

"To help us celebrate our liberation," and he laughed cynically, "then they will return to the sierras to chase the Red guerillas. If they had any intelligence they would know that all they have to do is leave a few sacks of grain in a clearing and those starving men would come to them!"

"Do they suspect anything?"

"No, no Tomas, no one suspects, you are still safe here."

The doctor departed; as he took his leave of Consuelo she kissed his cheek, and laid a hand on his chest in a consoling gesture she had once reserved for Arturo.

"You need to rest Federico," she said.

"I will rest when no one needs me," he replied, and turned away.

Although he accepted the assurances offered by Dr Hernandez, Tom was still acutely aware of the vulnerability of his own position. He had now sheltered in El Faro for two months, during which time he had seen his own cause advance, only to be thrown violently back. His memories of his earlier life, although sharp, were now supplanted by his experiences within the sheltering walls of the house. He was conscious of the people who lived beyond the cypress trees, outside the warp in the universe in which the house was situated. With each day he felt greater guilt, afraid that not only would he be discovered, but that those who had sheltered him would suffer punishment for their compassion.

It was indeed a strange world, as it had struck him, a black *Alice in Wonderland* world. But he still doubted whether the White Rabbit would emerge from the lemon trees, skip up the steps to the terrace, and pronounce on how late he was in rejoining his squadron. He looked for explanations, and found none. He lay in the deck chair the next afternoon, with eyes half closed, so that the Rabbit could not arrive without him knowing, and considered the events of the recent weeks. The garden wavered before him, the pulsating air and rippling trees withholding their secret purpose. A thought jolted him like an exploding shell. Could he be already dead? He sat up, perhaps he had been in the sun for too long. He looked around. The house shimmered in the heat behind him, its stone face impenetrable. But if he were dead, then Consuelo, Rafael, Maria and Dr Hernandez must be dead also. He had been a pilot - they must, he thought, be the pilots for his soul; but it was nonsense. Stories had circulated for months in the RAF about Dowding's interest in spiritualism; some claimed that was the truth behind his replacement as C-in-C Fighter Command in 1940, that the notion of so senior an officer espousing those ideas was deemed unsuitable; others thought that he had succumbed to the strain of the loss of so many young men in the skies over England, and needed rest.

He laughed at his own ludicrous logic, but stopped again as other thoughts demanded to be heard. Why would the afterlife imitate Spain? He reasoned that the Spanish coast was the last land he had seen as the Hurricane fell out of the sky. He might have been dragged under the water by the fouled dinghy strap...

He pinched himself; he felt the pain in his hand and took that as conclusive proof of life. But the doubts made one last attempt to claim his attention. What did he know of the neighbouring town? Was it was made of plaster and plywood, like the cities of Babylon constructed by Cecil B DeMille in the foothills of California, but inhabited by spirits? No. He cursed himself to think more coherently. He couldn't know what the town was like because as a British serviceman he would be arrested if he walked through its streets. Spain was a police state. Franco was a dictator.

Something caught his eye, like a leaf which twitched momentarily on the ground. His reasoning would have been perfect had he been back in England on a wet and dismal November day; but he was in a burned land, sheltering from a near cloudless sky in a crucible of heat. The leaf twitched again; he spoke aloud: "It's the White Rabbit!"

The leaf spread an imperfect pair of wings, then flipped from full sun to the slim shade afforded by one of the cypresses in an effort to escape the furnace door. Rafael was nowhere to be seen, and Consuelo and Maria were in the house. He realised that this was no leaf, nor was it the anxious burrowing Rabbit of Alice's dream, but a bird, and a wounded or diseased one. There was nobody in view, but the doubts about his own mortality now raised a suspicion that he was being watched, as if an unseen spirit had set a test for him. He levered himself off the deck chair; his bare feet were stung by the hot stones; he made his way on the balls of his feet across the terrace to the steps, holding out one hand for balance. He had walked down to the garden before, but never unaccompanied. He halted on the threshold, unsure whether he should go on or turn back and resume his seat. The wings fluttered again beside the tree; he resolved to go on. In a rush took the steps two at a time, too late appreciating that if his legs failed to take his weight he would not stop until he reached the gravel path. He reached the bottom step, turned and looked upward, aware that Consuelo would not be pleased if she found out what he had done. He cautiously thrust his toes into the gravel; the small stones seemed cooler than the large flagstones of the terrace, and the sensation reminded him of a childhood visit one summer to a shingle beach.

The small bird was motionless, paralysed either by fear of the large predator bearing down on it, or by death. He walked over and crouched down, ran one finger tip along its outspread wing. It came to life, and dragging one wing attempted to scramble further away. Tom reached out with both hands and gathered up the weakly protesting bundle of feather and bone; it lay with its black bead eyes blinking at him. Olive green, with a white underside, and a yellow stripe along its crown, it had been well camouflaged, but did not belong on the dry and hard earth.

Rafael appeared at the far end of the garden, and surprised at Tom's presence, trotted up to him, emerging through the heat haze. Tom rose and held out the bird, but Rafael made a rapid clean action with his hands to signify that he would break the animal's neck. Stirred to anger, Tom turned his back.

"No Rafael, it would be wrong to kill it! Let us see if it lives, we can do that much!" he exclaimed.

"But, it is only a little bird."

"But it is a living little bird."

"It would taste good senor."

"Rafael!" Tom cried, and walked away. He called out over his shoulder as he made his way up the steps to the terrace.

"Do you know what it is called?"

"It is called a firecrest Senor Tomas, the bird is a firecrest."

"I'm going to find Maria, she said that there is an old birdcage in the basement, and I'll get this creature out of the sun."

"It might die in any event."

"It deserves a chance to live," he said as he reached the top.

It occurred to him, as he went on tiptoe back across the burning coal hot stones into the house in search of Maria, that he did not require the presence of Alice's Rabbit or any mythical creature to influence his mind. The weak pulse of life that he cradled in his hands convinced him that he remained firmly in this world; caring for the wounded bird might prove to be a futile gesture, but he would do what he could, nonetheless.

The Captive Summer

The Elephant's Tail

Tom attempted, and failed, to explain to Rafael the story of *Alice's Adventures in Wonderland*. Rafael could see no reason why the young man might have mistaken the wounded bird for a rabbit; and laughed at the notion of a rabbit in a waistcoat with a pocket watch. As Tom became more exasperated, Rafael only scratched his head and said, "A rabbit senor? Have you never seen a Spanish rabbit?" He did succeed however in drawing a murderous parallel between the Red Duchess and Franco, in spite of the problem of gender.

But intrigued by the story, he invited Tom to spend time with him the next day after he had completed his morning's work, and before he took his siesta. He wanted to hear more of these stories, which were so much more vivid and fantastical than the romantic novels he sometimes read in the library. Consuelo had said nothing more about his past life, and had not explained how he had come to be in the service of Arturo and herself. Tom's curiosity was tempered by his belief that he had no right to pry into the Cuban's history, but he remained curious nonetheless.

Rafael had created a little camp for himself in a far corner of the garden, close to the wall. Here he had secured one end of a hammock, which was so old it must have accommodated Christopher Columbus, to the wall, the other to a date palm. From this distance the house shrank a little in proportion; Tom sat down on the ground and observed it through the branches of the fruit trees. With a lock knife which he habitually kept thrust in his belt, Rafael cut two slices from a red watermelon, and passed one across; he tore into the flesh of the piece which he held almost before Tom had taken his slice of moist fruit in both hands. Rafael spat the seeds into the baked earth, and wiped his mouth with the back of his hand as the sweet juice ran down his face.

"Why did you want to save that bird senor?" he asked, closing the knife and replacing it.

"It did not deserve to die Rafael. It was afraid, and it did not deserve to die." Now Tom bit into the fruit, chewed and swallowed, avoiding Rafael's eyes.

"Did you imagine yourself to be that little bird?"

"Perhaps, yes perhaps I did."

"It is nothing to be ashamed of, a man who sees the suffering of others, even that of a little bird."

"Why then did you want to kill it?"

"I was in jest senor. In death that bird will fly away to a better place."

The wounded bird had not expired; and now showed signs of reviving in its new temporary home, the salvaged birdcage, which Maria kept in the kitchen.

"How can you know that?"

"Senor Tomas, do you think that I am just an ignorant Cuban, the son to an African slave taken by the Spaniards to grow tobacco in a plantation near Havana?"

"No, I have never thought that, but how can you know Rafael?"

Rafael, his piece of melon now devoured, produced a small cloth bag secured at the neck by a drawstring. He pulled out the neck, slipped two fingers inside, and retrieved a scrap of tobacco and some tobacco papers.

"You are afraid that you will die here," he said. "Perhaps you are afraid that you will die one day, and you don't know when, or how, or why."

"I didn't used to think about it," replied Tom, wiping his hands, "but I do now."

"Do you believe in God?"

"I used to."

"Then why did you stop?"

Tom could not find a suitable answer at first, and sat for a brief interval considering his response.

"I started to think that I would die, and I could no longer make myself believe that anything lay beyond this life."

Rafael rolled two cigarettes and proffered one to Tom. He reached out and accepted it, rolling the rough paper between his fingers. Rafael struck a match and both men drew heavily, Tom coughing on the unfamiliar and raw Spanish tobacco.

"Dr Hernandez would be very angry if he knew I was smoking again," Tom said.

"Why? Is he worried that it will kill you?"

They both laughed, and the tension between them evaporated as the tobacco smoke rose in grey plumes around them.

"Rafael," Tom hesitated, "do you believe?"

"Yes, but not in the way that you once did."

"Why?"

Rafael sat back and ran the hand which held the cigarette along one thigh; then he spat a scrap of tobacco from his mouth.

"Jesus came into this world to heal; the Church became corrupted when it forgot His healing mission, and turned to support the rich and powerful, twisting His words to suit that purpose. The Spanish bishops venerate Franco, they honour him as a man ordained by God to rule Spain."

Tom nodded, and turned his face upward to feel the heat of the sun.

"I don't know what I should believe in. In the Great War the Germans believed that God was on their side every bit as much as the British and French did."

Rafael sat back, his spine pressing against the date palm. He drew his legs up to his chin, and wrapped his arms about them.

"When I was a boy in Havana, that was the first time I became aware. It was a little before the war between the Americans and the Spanish for ownership of Cuba. I ran errands for the women in a brothel, brought them food and drink, anything they needed. There was one woman who," and he pointed with the tip of a forefinger to his forehead, "could see that which others could not. But you understand senor, she was still one of the prostitutes. One night a sailor from a big Spanish cruiser anchored in the outer harbour came to the house. She told him that he was going to die, to drown, that she could see the metal plates of the ship buckle and the water pour through. He wouldn't have her, or any of the other women. The next night more sailors came, and again she told them that they would die."

He leaned forward to share the joke, tapping the side of his nose. "Now this was bad for business, and the owner beat her."

"What happened?" asked Tom, intrigued.

"She was correct, they died as she had seen it, at Santiago."

This was a reference to the naval battle at Santiago, where the American Navy attacked and sank a Spanish battle squadron, effectively ending Spanish control over Cuba in the process.

"Did she see your future?"

"She told me that I would travel on the seas."

"Many people have gone to sea."

"She told me other things."

"Did you believe her?"

"I did not seek that knowledge senor, no man should, such things are not natural."

Tom noticed that Rafael had resumed the grip of his hand against his other wrist by which he clasped his legs, and had lowered his gaze. In an effort to lighten the conversation Tom said: "Perhaps she was an American spy." Rafael raised his gaze again, and observed the young man with eyes which knew another truth.

"No Senor Tomas, she was no spy. She told me that which we believe is real is but a dream; we do not realise this until we die, and then we awaken."

Tom looked about him. The house shimmered and wavered in the heat;

the implacable stone walls rippled and the scorching air filled his lungs. If this searing realm were a bubble of thoughts and memories, then what lay beyond was beyond human comprehension. Tom said: "I cannot believe in what I cannot see. I know that generations have been prepared to believe, to have faith, but I cannot."

"You cannot see the wind senor, yet you believe it exists," and Rafael laughed, "if you did not have faith in that, you would never climb into your aeroplane."

He relaxed again, easing his head back against the tree, stretched out his legs and unclasped his arms; he continued.

"When I grew up I went away to sea as a cabin boy in a freighter on the routes down the coast of South America, and then through the Panama Canal across the Pacific to the Philippines. You may know that America paid Spain twenty million dollars for the Philippines; but you may not know that the people of the Philippines did not receive a *centimo* of that money. In Manila I met more Chinese, mainly coolies who worked to load and unload the ships. They had their own beliefs, which they guarded from the Spanish and the native Philippinos. One of these men told to me a story about a king in ancient times who brought some blind men about an elephant. The king wanted them to tell him what an elephant was like. The first touched a tusk and said that an elephant was like a carrot; another touched an ear and said it was like a fan; a third grasped its tail and said it was like a rope. Not one could describe all the elephant to the king. Now each man had spoken truly, as he had sensed the animal, but they could not describe all that the beast was. If you had been one of those blind men I would not expect you to describe the animal to me."

"Am I blind?"

"No senor, not blind, and not about to die."

Tom next questioned Rafael about his life at sea.

"Oh! I went to the end of the world. Hard work, poor pay, danger. To the end of the world. Do you know that once Spain was the end of the known world? In Arabic, Spain is known as *El Maghreb El Aksa*, it means the Furthest West. We know now that is not true."

Tom had noticed that Rafael did not part company from his knife and asked him about how he had acquired it. The weapon never left Rafael's belt, unless he either had a use for it, or he went to sleep. It had a blade of worn steel, and a handle of yellowed ivory, a lanyard was fixed through a steel ring in the hilt. It had been purchased in Manila, as both tool and weapon against those uninterested in describing elephants to kings. Rafael crossed and re-crossed the Pacific with it, and worked the routes the conquistadors had followed throughout central and southern America. He however came in the wake of the Empire, and witnessed in the faded and collapsing colonial buildings of the ports of the former Spanish colonies the carrion picked carcass of imperial might and majesty. The lock knife was a poor substitute for a squadron of cavalry, but in dangerous back streets, it had provided a minimum guarantee of safety. Spain withdrew into herself following the humiliation of 1898; and eventually Rafael, keen to see what life was like in European Spanish society, followed the prevailing wind in search of the departed Spaniards. However, he would not be drawn as to the circumstances under which he had first met Arturo Bonar.

"What was he like?"

"Oh! He was a good man. He was a good lawyer. When he went off to the war I asked to go with him, but he forbade it. He insisted that I stay to protect Dona Consuelo and the house, and I swore that I would."

"Do you think that he will return Rafael?"

"All streams flow back to the sea."

"I have seen your mistress reading his letters at night; she cries while she reads. It must hurt her to be separated from him."

"Senor Tomas, the tragedy of their separation would only have been heightened had they never met."

They talked on, as Rafael wanted to know more of this young man who valued knowledge so highly yet came from an obscure part of society. Eventually, at Rafael's insistence, Tom transferred to the hammock, and stretched his frame over the pleated fibres. Rafael dozed by the palm tree, and Tom drifted into sleep, but thinking now of a tall rabbit leading an elephant by the tusk, stopping occasionally to pull an enormous watch from his waistcoat pocket, and pat the elephant's ear. Under his eyelids the hue changed from maroon to a light red, and he breathed without effort, looking up through his closed eyes, and allowing his body to soak into the fabric under his back. He fell asleep as this pendulum of light swung before him.

Without warning, Rafael let out a scream and jumped to his feet. Tom, momentarily disoriented, rolled out of the hammock and onto the ground, tense and expectant for the whine of aero engines and the crack of exploding bombs. Instead, Rafael plunged and jumped in front of him, tearing at the buttons on his shirt and cursing. The knife had fallen to the ground; grabbing it, Tom vainly struggled, holding the handle in his right hand and plucking at the blade with his left to open the knife up. But his fingers were clumsy, and the blade eluded him.

"I feel it, I feel it! It's a snake, dear God, there's a snake in my shirt!"

With the sound of rending cloth Rafael tore the shirt over his head and trampled it into the ground with angry short jerks of his feet. Then suddenly he stopped, a sweating dusky statue, eyes imploring help. Tom got to his feet, the still closed knife in his hands.

"Rafael where is it, what's wrong?!" he shouted in English, and then as Rafael's chest twitched added: "Oh God, has it bitten you?"

Rafael moved his hands slowly round to his back, then brought them together on his chest, as if in prayer. He said nothing, sweat dripping down his brow; then he held out his hands to Tom. Within the prison he had formed from his fingers protruded the head of a small lizard. Tom was appalled, but Rafael could not contain the joke any longer; his imploring look twisted into a wide grin, and then laughter rolled down his body in waves to his navel.

"You see Tomas, it is a baby lizard! Oh! Such a small fellow!"

The lizard twisted within Rafael's hands, anxious to be free.

"You bloody fool Rafael! I thought you had been bitten by a snake!" Tom shouted at him in English.

"¿Que?"

"Rafael, I thought it was a snake!"

"No, it was this little fellow, he was trying to find some shade, and slipped into my shirt while I was sleeping!"

Tom threw the knife down, and wiped his face with his arm, streams of sweat running under his shirt.

Rafael held the lizard, which fitted snugly within the living prison, its head caught between his middle and forefingers. Then he let it climb over his fingers; he transferred it nimbly from one hand to another as if his hands were ladders which the olive green infant reptile climbed without ever reaching a destination. He held the lizard out to Tom. "Take him!" he said. Tom held out his own hands over Rafael's, and the lizard continued to climb, transferring now from man to man. It was a strange sensation. As the animal alighted on Tom's right hand he could not quite sense it; as he guided it onto his left hand, the feeling returned, its minute feet pricking his skin as if needles were running across his fingers.

The lizard soon tired of the novelty however, and made a rush along Tom's arm; it was brought back under restraint by Rafael, who then released it onto the garden wall. Without a look backward, the green writhing arrowhead scampered away, until lost from view.

The Captive Summer

The Greater War

Spain maintained a relationship with Germany characterised by an inclination to enter the war on the Axis side, but under conditions so taxing of German generosity in equipping the Spanish Army, that the probability reduced to vanishing point. In the diplomatic dance of appearances both countries, at different times, gave the impression that they wished to consummate the relationship; yet at the last minute they yielded only to the most chaste and fleeting of embraces. Spain committed one division of volunteers, the Blue Division, to the Axis cause. They were despatched to the Eastern Front, where they fought and died ineffectually for two years. Franco asserted that there were two separate wars, and that Spain was solely involved in the conflict waged against Stalin. His erratic war diplomacy succeeded in confusing and exasperating the diplomatic corps of every major power. But his political genius allowed Spain to remain as a bystander to a vicious street brawl; although a bystander who shrieked in a piping voice his support for the thug wielding a cosh in an effort to overwhelm his opponent.

Few families in the town had sons away in Russia, but many had sons in Spanish prisons. The Russian campaign however was closely studied by Oleanza and his friends, who believed that they were witnessing the final crushing of Bolshevism; and took much reflected pride in their own contribution to that cause in the proceeding years. Denied the opportunity from taking their place in the trenches, they drank toasts and banged their fists on tables, as Radio Seville announced the unstoppable eastward sweep of the German armies.

Cafe Alejandro was their gathering place. It was named in honour not of a Spaniard, but a Greek, Alexander the Great, on the grounds that, irrespective of nationality, he was a warrior and empire builder; and Franco, like Alexander, was a builder of empires. Tables with stained damask cloths erupted from its mouth like bad teeth, and spilled onto the pavement. Old men who claimed to have fought in Cuba in 1898 drank black coffee at the tables by day; young men who dreamed of the *cruzada* drank whatever they could afford and listened to the radio by night. Enrique Morales was the owner; he prided himself on his clientele, which included many of the Civil Guard, Falangist party members, and Oleanza.

It was Oleanza's habit, once he had grown tired of sleeping in his chair in the afternoon heat, to stop at the cafe to drink and talk amongst his cronies, before venturing home. He sometimes took Ferdinand Aguado with him on these occasions, so as to have someone with whom he could not only have a conversation, but who would have to defer to him if their opinions differed. He knew most of the men he met at the tables, and they were eager to know him; but he did not let their flattery impair his judgement, which he considered as sound as that of King Solomon.

"Aguado," he called out from his office, "let's get a drink at the pig's sty."

Aguado, sitting at his desk, winced, and stroked his moustache. Since the notification of the outbreak of cholera he had hoped that he could avoid visiting the *Alejandro*. He got up and answered the summons.

"I have some papers to prepare for the Comisaria," he said, vainly hoping that he would impress his boss.

"So what? I've had enough of this place. Let's get a drink."

There was no option but to comply; he swiftly closed the office, and the two men made their way out of the building.

Morales possessed a broad nose and thick upper lip, which suggested to Oleanza something Neanderthal in his origins, but he nevertheless tolerated him, as he did anyone who might be of use, whatever their social or physical limitations. When Morales saw Oleanza emerge from the Town Hall and make his slow way across the square, he disengaged himself from the customer with whom he was talking, and made great show of the warm welcome he extended to the civic dignitary.

"Your Honour," he whined, "a pleasure to have your company again. Please," graciously indicating a table adorned with a permanently fixed sign bearing the legend *reserva* on it, "I have the best table for you."

Oleanza, without hint of acknowledgement, squeezed into a seat, and Aguado made the best that he could of the limited space remaining across the table from him.

"Is life to your satisfaction Enrique?"

Morales beamed, his lip almost rolling upward like that of a horse, to denote his own gratitude at the familiar tones Oleanza used to address him.

"The Mayor," being a form of speech idiosyncratically used by Morales to denote that the figure of the Mayor and the body of Jose Oleanza, were distinct, "knows that life provides challenges to the true Spaniard, which we rise up each day to conquer." He flattered himself on the use of idioms favoured by Franco; but where that failed to impress his guests he set his face in honour of his other hero, Mussolini. He continued, "In point of fact, life is currently very much to my satisfaction, on account of the reduced level of competition."

As he said this he nodded in the direction of *La Alverjilla*, which following the death of Gabriel and Elena Soto, had been closed intermittently.

"For once that damn fool Hernandez has done some good," said Oleanza, twisting in his seat.

"The order to close that Republican den to properly disinfect it has undoubtedly benefited trade," Morales beamed.

"So you're happy?"

"Yes senor, very happy. And now may I enquire what you gentlemen would like to drink?"

"A beer and a glass of water for me," and Oleanza pointed a stubby finger in the direction of Aguado.

"I'll just have a bottle of beer, no glass."

Morales scuttled away to find one of his waiters. Aguado had decided that it was prudent not to drink the water, as the source of the cholera outbreak was still unknown. He sympathised with Dr Hernandez, as he had children of his own, but dared not say this. He considered the Mayor's action in drinking water only a few doors away from a building with a recent case of cholera foolish, but a desire to remain in employment stifled his tongue. Oleanza looked at his watch: it was almost time for the evening news bulletin on Radio Seville.

"Turn the radio up!" he shouted into the cafe. An invisible hand turned the volume control, flooding the tables on the pavement with the dying refrain of a light music programme. The disembodied harmonisations of a small band of musicians in an airless studio in Seville, dehydrating rapidly as they crouched around microphones to imitate sanitised American band music, filled the evening air. Then the announcer introduced the news broadcast; conversations died away, and bodies turned in their seats the better to catch the latest herald of triumph over the Bolshevik enemy.

"The German High Command in Berlin," began the announcer, "has released the following communique for today August 5th. The German Sixth Army under the command of General Friedrich Paulus continues to make good progress toward the River Don," and a shout went up and warm applause, which had to be silenced by urgent gestures from those impatient to hear the rest of the bulletin, "Panzer units, supported by squadrons of Stuka divebombers, have relentlessly pounded the Bolshevik forces of the Red Army. Sources close to the German High Command believe that the Red Army is close to total collapse. The Caudillo has congratulated the commanders of the German Army for their successes, which he said guarantees the security of all Europe. He expressed his gratitude on behalf of the Spanish people, and gave assurances of the bonds of friendship between Spain and Germany."

The cheering echoed into the square, as those unlucky enough not to be shoulder to shoulder with their German allies, made the most of the achievements on the other side of Europe.

"I still believe that the Germans will enter Moscow," announced Oleanza, speaking to nobody in particular.

"The campaign is proceeding smoothly," was Aguado's dry comment, mindful that in the autumn of 1941, when the Red Army had counterattacked, Oleanza was uncertain what to do with the little pins he used to mark the positions of the German divisions on the map in his office. He had said then, "Surely they can't be forced back all the way to Berlin!" and paced relentlessly in front of the map, as if he himself were in a field tent commanding an army corps. Spain hoped for an Axis victory, Aguado was grateful that he was of an age when he could not be conscripted to help procure it. Morales returned, slapping the shoulder of a passing Civil Guard, with whom he had just conducted some blackmarket business.

"Your Honour, the news from Berlin is good. Soon they will push the Bolshevik scum right across Siberia and into the Pacific Ocean," and the corners of his mouth turned down in tribute to his Italian hero, unaware that Italian troops had played little part in the fighting.

"They seem animated tonight," and Oleanza jabbed with his finger in the direction of a group of men who had been particularly pleased with the news from Russia.

"Yes Your Honour. The man with his back to you, his son is in the Blue Division. They have been notified that he has received a decoration for valour. I tell you, these Reds are beaten."

In a gesture of civic pomp, Oleanza ordered brandy and water for all the men at the table, and then rose to accept a toast from the father of the war hero.

Their attention was distracted by the arrival of a car in the square. Motor transport of any description was still a rarity, due to the lack of petrol; so the passage of trucks or cars along the streets could arouse interest in a population with little else to occupy their time. Also, large saloons were unmistakeable statements of economic and political power. Therefore the arrival of a gleaming green Citroen caused heads not otherwise engaged to turn in its direction. The vehicle progressed round two sides of the square before stopping outside the Town Hall; the Civil Guard driver then climbed out and opened the rear door to admit two men onto the steps of the building.

"What business has Mendoza with me at this hour?" said Oleanza, who shrugged resignedly and prepared to meet his fate.

After a short interval the men re-emerged from the Town Hall and walked across to the *Alejandro*. Mendoza was accompanied by de Rozario; he appeared the more relaxed of the two, and could have been ambling socially in the warm night; de Rozario however was as perfect and measured in his step as a cadet on a parade ground. As they reached the cafe some of the off duty policemen at the tables rose to salute Mendoza, who impatiently waved them away.

"Ah! So this is where the Mayor conducts council meetings!" he said tucking the thumb of one hand into his leather pistol belt.

"You have me at a disadvantage capitan. It is rare for me to have the opportunity for a little relaxation."

Aguado said nothing and drank down a mouthful of the beer.

"I am conscious of the burdens of political office, particularly at times of moment Your Honour." He also jerked his head in the direction of *La Alverjilla*, where a few customers had now taken seats outside and were served by Andres.

"Please join us," Oleanza said with feigned civility, then directing himself to Morales added, "bring some glasses, a bottle of brandy and more beer." Mendoza and de Rozario removed their hats and seated themselves at the table. There was an exodus of a group of the police seated elsewhere, making excuses about the time and the need to see their families.

"What brings the chief of police to seek the Mayor at this hour?"

Mendoza leaned forward and spoke in a lowered voice.

"It's Dr Hernandez."

At the sound of his name Oleanza's face contorted a little, as if in expectation of bad news, and then he relaxed his facial muscles. He looked out into the square where two ragged men had taken positions by the fountain and now watched the people who drank and ate at the tables. The presence of the policemen prevented them coming closer to beg for food or money.

"What has he done now?" he asked, still watching the wraiths by the fountain.

"Nothing, as far as we know. But," and his eyes scanned the neighbouring tables to see if anyone was paying too much attention, "he is threatening to write to the Civil Governor about the cholera." He leaned back in his chair, letting Oleanza absorb the full implication of the intelligence he had just imparted. Oleanza's face hardened once more, and he turned to face the men seated around him.

"Cojones! That man is a threat! He has no respect for authority, and he doesn't care how many careers he will wreck in his determination to save the lives of some diseased Red peasants!"

"What should we do about him?"

Oleanza thought for a moment, caressing the glass of brandy he held, and casting his eyes over Mendoza, de Rozario, and Aguado. He summarised them in his own mind as the fat man, the hatchling viper, and the mute idiot.

"Nothing."

"But Your Honour, if word should...," but a raised hand silenced him.

"We have only two doctors in the town, let them do what they must. You," and he jabbed his finger again, at de Rozario, "look to me like an officer who would relish the opportunity to ensure that our wayward physician is kept in check."

"It would be an honour senor."

"Capitan, keep Dr Hernandez under observation. The time to take action is when the cholera has passed."

Satisfied with his authoritative control of the problem, he allowed himself a brief smile, and drank in the background chatter of the other customers. He decided that it was time for a toast of his own, but decided not to rise to his feet.

"Gentlemen, let us salute the German Sixth Army, which will not stop until it reaches the doors of the Kremlin! The Sixth Army!"

They drank, and brought their glasses down on the table in unison, confident of Axis invincibility. As they drank and talked, night drew across the town.

And across the Russian steppes their German allies pushed steadily eastward, eventually halting, not in Moscow, but Stalingrad.

The Captive Summer

The Silver Screen

"What about Chaplin?" The question, posed by Mendoza, was as innocent as a dusty grenade in the hands of a baby. Had the question been formulated as 'Is Charlie Chaplin an exponent of the corrupting Masonic-Zionist-Bolshevic hegemony in contemporary American society?' it would have proven more acceptable to its audience, although been somewhat less clear as to its meaning. Mendoza swung his head in one direction, then the other, but was regarded by the others seated around the table with nervous indifference.

"What about Chaplin? As an intellectual I must reply! Am I supposed to compare his comic technique to that of the Marx brothers? Should we regard the silent cinema as a metaphor for the emasculation of the male sex in industrial American society?"

The exasperated and sneering retort came from Oleanza; Mendoza sat erect on his chair, and fell into a resentful silence. Oleanza was not quite finished, and like a volcano harbouring one last pool of iridescent magma, erupted again.

"Do I look like that little shit Samuel Goldwyn? What about Chaplin? Fuck Chaplin!"

For over a sweltering hour, as perspiration was wrung from them, they had argued when each one would rather have sat under the shade of an almond tree, as madmen and sick dogs loped in the full heat of the day through otherwise deserted streets. The meeting was testament to the paranoia and sense of foreboding that was enveloping Oleanza like a fever, as the fourth anniversary of liberation approached.

Oleanza's fever was all the more virulent because not only was the planned triumphal procession of military force to take place under the baleful gaze of the Civil Governor, a man more disposed to bursts of acerbic whimsy than even the Mayor, but the Governor had suggested that there should be a cinema presentation in the town on the eve of the parade. Deciding what to include in the programme was not a task for one man alone; and today was the last available to submit proposals to Granada for the Governor's endorsement. Oleanza surveyed the members of the town's *ad hoc* committee of cultural affairs, daring them to oppose him, yet desperate for an idea from one of them which he could adopt.

His eyes fell on the only female present, Dona Victoria Zardoya, head of the women's branch of the Falange, the Seccion Feminina. In a dress of rustling chiffon and a hat decorated with cherries fashioned from paste, she called to his mind the image of an ornamental layered dessert which was slowly subsiding in the heat; but this confection was sour to the taste. Moulded in the acceptable image of Spanish womanhood, as a builder of home and family, she yet possessed a cold withering mind; and although she welcomed the limited social role for women prescribed by the government, this she interpreted as applying to *other* women, not herself. She regarded Oleanza with a look of deep affront. She had always been contemptuous of him, considering him to be an ill mannered and ignorant man, but now she would add a new item to his list of failings: deafness. He had sworn in her presence, but was either deaf to his own mouth or ignorant of social etiquette.

As her look of distaste increased, her face narrowed and elongated, her mouth forming a purple eruption between her nose and chin. They exchanged looks of mutual distaste, then Oleanza's eyes passed on, taking in Bucaro, Father Abarca, Mendoza, and Aguado: each looked blankly back at him. All that was required of them was that they made suggestions which were acceptable to Oleanza, and hopefully, the Civil Governor; hope, like the light over the mountains on a winter's afternoon, was dissolving.

A not inconsiderable problem was that San Cristobal no longer possessed a cinema. Few buildings in the town had been razed during the fighting that resulted in its 'liberation'; unfortunately the cinema was one of them, as it had been the last outpost of the Republican forces. The shattered and blackened shell was now boarded up, and for the last four years had been a secret memorial to a way of life, to a means of communicating ideas, as well as the men and women who died in the projection room and the aisles. With no other public building of sufficient size, the performance would have to be held in the open. There were only two open spaces in the centre of the town of adequate size: the *Plaza de Toros*, and the waterfront area around the harbour. Issues of public order, not comfort, were uppermost in their minds in making the decision. Mendoza rejected the use of the habourside, as there were too many narrow streets into which potential Republican troublemakers could escape. The cinema would therefore be built in the square; a huge canvas was to be suspended at one end against the walls of the buildings, and the projection equipment mounted on a platform next to the fountain. But what to show?

Bucaro, as a journalist and member of the Falange, which was a condition of employment, was expected to be sufficiently familiar with art, guidelines on censorship, and what films were being shown in neighbouring towns along the southern coast. The Mayor also expected him to prepare notes for the meeting. He sat next to Oleanza, a grubby exercise book in front of him, in which were set down numerous headings, each one neatly underlined.

"I suggest," said Oleanza, not expecting any contrary view to be expressed, "that the programme must commence with a newsreel. Russia is on the verge of collapse. We need to promote Axis invincibility, and the contribution of the Blue Division to the defeat of Bolshevism."

Aguado reflected on the events of the previous winter once more, and again declined to comment.

"We cannot exclude Franco!" affirmed Dona Victoria, still smarting that she had not received an apology.

"But he is not in Russia!" replied Oleanza.

"If we could include film of him inspecting the latest group of volunteers for the Russian front, perhaps with the Archbishop of Madrid in attendance," offered Father Abarca, eager to press the case for clerical endorsement of the campaign.

"Make a note of that Bucaro," Oleanza imperiously instructed.

"But what about Chaplin?" Mendoza again weakly suggested.

"In a newsreel?" enquired the Mayor contemptuously.

"No, no, no! One of his earlier films, something to get people laughing."

"Before or after the newsreel of the Russian front?"

Eyes full of uncomprehending hatred turned on Aguado, the perpetrator of this verbal outrage. At that moment he considered that he would have been far safer on the Russian front, where he could have drafted reports and memoranda from the comfort of a deep and reeking shell crater.

"Charlie Chaplin," and Oleanza rolled his eyes and puffed out his chest as he spat out the words in a minor melodrama, "is an agent of Bolshevism, and a co-conspirator with decadent Hollywood moguls to promote American values!"

Bucaro cast a glance at his notes; the next two categories of film to be discussed were American westerns, and gangster movies. In the column marked 'Actors', the names John Wayne, James Cagney, Tom Mix, Humphrey Bogart, Paul Muni and Joel McCrea were prominent. He swallowed, and moved an arm across the book to hide the offending entries from view. He had heard rumours that a copy of Chaplin's *The Great Dictator* had been smuggled into Denmark, and that secret audiences had laughed until they wept at the antics of the inept European dictators. He thought it desirable to turn the discussion away from its current course.

"The Vice Secretariat for Popular Education has approved *Ninotchka* for distribution."

"A Bolshevik poem!" and Oleanza pointed a finger to the ceiling, whether to give warning of divine retribution or the presence of police in the room above his head was not clear. "We cannot allow the screening of a Bolshevik poem!"

"But Your Honour, the film is a satire on Bolshevism, and Garbo is a great star. They say she even laughs!"

And to emphasise the phenomenon Bucaro laughed, but alone in the confined chamber, the sounds dying in his throat.

"What does that leave us with?" asked Oleanza, resigned to failure.

Bucaro made a feint of referring to his notes.

"If I may make a suggestion?" and Dona Victoria saw the hesitation of the newspaper editor as her opportunity to assert moral values in the discussion. Oleanza waved in her direction, in a gesture which could as easily be interpreted as an attempt to strike Bucaro about the head, as to denote that he had granted her request.

"I find it extraordinary that we have not yet selected a film which espouses the Spanish character. My niece wrote to me recently from Valencia, where she is organising moral education for the poorest women. There is a desperate need. Father Abarca, would you not agree?"

The priest, who was experiencing difficulty staying awake in the afternoon heat, raised a hand in acknowledgement.

"I agree, the sin of ignorance is widespread. We must cast the light of truth where there is darkness. We must save the souls of the poor."

"Thank you Father." Emboldened by clerical endorsement, she continued. "My niece informed me that she recently saw a patriotic drama resonant with the majesty of Spain. It not only combines Christian values, but alludes to the Caudillo's heroic career in the desert, and above all, to unflinching loyalty unto death."

The possibility of providing moral education, entertainment, and telling the story of a young Franco, appealed to Oleanza. The muscles in his lower jaw eased; and he sat back in his seat, thrusting his stomach outward, a sign that the proposal met with some degree of approval.

"May I say a little more?" she asked, and Oleanza briefly nodded. "The film is called *La Patrulla*, and is set at the time of the uprising in the Rif. A young officer, possessing all the values of youthful manhood, and eager for glory, arrives at a Legionnaire fort. He serves with distinction, gaining the respect of his superiors and the loyalty of his men. One of his brother officers," by which she meant another poorly trained adolescent with a death wish, "is ordered on patrol the day before he is to marry his sweetheart. His friend intervenes, requesting the honour of leading the patrol in his place, so that the wedding may proceed."

She paused, to ensure that she still had their attention.

"The patrol ventures far into the desert, where it is attacked by overwhelming numbers of tribesmen, and the soldiers die to the last man. But the Spanish flag proudly flies over their bodies; and as he breathes his last, the young hero clutches his crucifix to his lips and blesses the young couple for whom he has sacrificed himself."

This vision of violent and repeated death had evidently aroused her to some kind of sexual rapture, and a flush came into her face. Oleanza looked at Mendoza, Mendoza looked to Bucaro, Bucaro to Abarca, and Abarca to Dona Victoria. For a moment no one spoke, the only sound being the faint scratching of Bucaro's pen in the exercise book, as he took notes of the plot of the film. Oleanza grunted.

"We can agree on this. A newsreel, and *La Patrulla*. What else?"

His baleful gaze, and expectations, again fell on Bucaro.

"The Caudillo," began the hapless journalist, hoping that by invoking the name of warrior-king he could draw about himself a magical power to ward off evil, "enjoys watching American motion pictures. To select a film from Hollywood, would signal that the political leadership of San Cristobal shares Franco's good taste."

In making this suggestion he had been put in mind of the slogan, popular in Russia, that "You can't say it better than Stalin!", which no one at that time attempted. He contemplated shutting his eyes tight, in the hope that by so doing the magical power would increase. He could not bring himself to look directly at Oleanza, but with an effort forced himself to keep his eyes open. To his surprise, it was Father Abarca who spoke next.

"We must be careful Bucaro, America is morally degenerate, and a democracy, which is even more dangerous. However, if we select with care, and the appropriate moral safeguards are in place," which meant that the film was censored and dubbed into Spanish, "then I would endorse such a decision."

"If Father Abarca finds the proposal acceptable, we should agree on a suitable title," interposed Oleanza.

Oleanza relaxed further, satisfied that he had witnesses who could be called upon to blame the priest if the selection was not to the Civil Governor's satisfaction.

"I have prepared a list of three approved films," and Bucaro cleared his dry throat, as if about to read a causality list, "these are *The Roaring Twenties*, which is a story of Chicago gangsters, *Stagecoach*, set in the American west, and *Mutiny on the Bounty*." His eyes searched their faces in vain for signs of approval.

Each one in the room now looked to someone else, so seemingly burdened by the responsibility they had to discharge that they dare not risk eye contact. Again Abarca spoke.

"We should not seek to glorify criminal behaviour in any form, or bloodlust," he said, placing his palms on the table and half closing his eyes, as if preparing for a seance. Dona Victoria, taking her cue from the priest's hint that they should favour neither the gangster nor western movie *genres*, then intervened.

"I have always appreciated the similarity between Franco and Clark Gable," she offered, oblivious to the reaction to her statement, "but of course the Caudillo is much the more virile."

"And if I recall," Oleanza commented, as unaware of irony as Dona Victoria had been of the evident disparity in physical characteristics of the two men, "the story is that of an uprising against a tyrannical officer."

But just as the road lay open before them, Father Abarca roused himself from his transcendental state to hurl another moral barrier in their path.

"I would of course be concerned about any suggested lewdness. The native women depicted wear little clothing, and they are evidently not Catholics. The Church's teaching is quite clear, the depiction of immoral lives is a sin. It is forbidden."

Oleanza noted the time, he could not credit that he was still imprisoned in this room, as if with a jury afraid that it was about to convict itself. As for women wearing little clothing, he had seen enough of those, certainly many more than the priest. He resorted to a political allusion to break the stalemate.

"But let us not forget that the rebellion is against an English tyrant, this Capitan Bligh. And today Spain is herself threatened by an English tyrant, the degenerate Churchill."

Gable for Franco, Laughton for Churchill: in the afternoon heat it made perfect sense. And whether it made sense or not, as long as the flickering images they had selected distracted the minds of spectral rows of pallid men and women from the futility and pain of their lives, it would serve its purpose.

The Captive Summer

The Needs Of A Man

While Josef Stalin projected a favoured image as the Father of the Soviet People, in San Cristobal, Oleanza liked to be known simply as Uncle Jose. Gestures were cheap; as he went about his work he knew that a handshake, or a glancing slap on the shoulder, went far to further his image amongst those who were of no political use to him, but at little cost. For those who were of use to him he had to resort to more tangible rewards. He had to publicly support the high morality initiatives of Father Abarca and Dona Victoria, such as designating those beaches that were reserved for women and those reserved for men; and then to provide a hut for the beach patrol which Dona Victoria had organised amongst the sexless zealots of the Seccion Feminina. In private however, he was an unreconstructed Spaniard.

He favoured the brothel at which Andrea worked, which was situated in *Calle del Rosa*. The house had no distinguishing features, nothing which would suggest to an unknowing eye that the property was used for anything than a family home. However this family was not only extended, but exhibited marked fluidity in its membership, as the women who had to work there changed with the seasons, and the tides of economic necessity. Since the end of the civil war necessity had become more urgent and the *madame* who owned and ran the house had a waiting list of young women and girls who were eager to work there.

The house had a large bare cool entrance hall; its curling stairway clung to the flaking stone walls as if afraid to venture out into the space between them, and creaked in protest at the overuse from tens of thousands of heavily shod male feet. The main rooms, possessing high ceilings adorned with cracked and chipped plaster decoration, were respectable imitations of marital bedchambers; the beds were comfortable and clean, but flowers, not religious icons, adorned the tables. On the ground floor a corridor led from the hall to an annex, along which were the cheaper, and therefore smaller and more squalid rooms: Andrea worked in one of these. The madame's own apartment led directly from the hall on the ground floor, and her drawing room looked through an iron barred window onto the street.

Although prostitution was a crime, and periodic campaigns were launched by the police, and organisations such as Action Catolica, it was tolerated. This toleration did not, of course, allow Uncle Jose to confide to anybody what he got up to. If the house were raided the madame would simply claim that the young women which filled the place like kittens in a litter, were her nieces visiting from the country; all of them, at the same time. Oleanza took precautions to ensure that his visits would not be interrupted by police raids, and for this he resorted to Alexander Graham Bell's gift to humanity: the telephone. Whether it was his agitation at the amount of time it had taken to agree the films that were to be included in the programme for the celebrations, or the proximity of Dona Victoria's solid but forbidding form in the heat of the office, he decided that it was time for Uncle Jose to visit his favourite niece. He picked up the telephone and dialled.

"Good day," he said in a voice suddenly bereft of its usual acerbity, "can you tell me if you are expecting a delivery today?"

A mature woman's voice, weary, bored, but still full of seduction, replied.

"A delivery senor? But of course, we are expecting a delivery."

"At what time will this delivery be made?"

"At the usual hour senor."

"Thank you."

He replaced the receiver, and let out a deep moist breath: agitation had turned to contentment. The exchange had been coded, the delivery being the reference to his own visit. If the madame had suspected that the police or Dona Victoria's spies were watching the house, she would have told him that no delivery was anticipated. He looked at his watch; it was a little after five o'clock, he had nearly three hours to wait.

Most of the police in the town made their way, at one time or another, to the house; their bedroom confidences regarding the surveillance activities of their brother officers the principal means by which the madame could anticipate trouble. Most, but not all; the leading example of virtue and abstinence being Carlos de Rozario. His Catholicism, sense of duty, and gnawing inexperience with women held him in check like three overlaid strait-jackets. On the evening that Uncle Jose had decided to visit his extended family, de Rozario was patrolling the town with a reluctant Sargento Pelean and two Guards. Few people made themselves visible, and Pelean, reliable but laconic, could not see who they were expected to arrest. At a street corner de Rozario halted, motioning to Pelean to come up to him.

"Take one of the men," he began, "cross over here. At the next junction, turn left, then left again at the end of that street. That will bring you back into.."

"Calle del Rosa teniente, I know this."

De Rozario was irritated that Pelean had interrupted him, and waved him away. The empty scene presented no threat; in the warm crimson listlessness of approaching night, the shuttered and blind buildings dozed unconcerned. De Rozario craned his thin neck, but the only other living thing in view was an old and emaciated dog sitting in a doorway, dutifully licking inflamed skin on a hind leg. He resented being ignored by the world; he walked on, leaving his holster unbuttoned, in the vain hope that an armed uprising was in progress in the serpents' nest of streets ahead.

At same time, which was a little before eight o'clock, Oleanza was across the other side of the *Plaza de Toros*, and about to commence his own patrol, that took him on a circuitous route along minor streets until he gained an alleyway which ran along the back of *Calle del Rosa*. He was as concerned not to be observed, as de Rozario was to let the citizenry know that the Civil Guard was taking the security of the State seriously. After ten minutes' walking, he reached the door that gave access to the narrow yard at the back of the house, carefully picking his way over intervening heaps of refuse. It occurred to him that this open filth was what angered Dr Hernandez, and he held his handkerchief to his mouth as he navigated his way through pools of deep shadow and effluent.

"Senor! Oh what a fine man!"

This was the madame's customary greeting, no names being exchanged, as she opened the yard door to him and led him into the house and up to a bedroom at the back. There he found his favourite niece, a girl with fake blond hair which fell to her shoulders, and a pliable body; he undressed before her, placing his trousers across a chair, and talking to her in a soft but excited voice, as sexual expectation rose within him. The madame left them, counting a roll of banknotes as she descended the stairs to return to the drawing room.

The two police patrols rejoined and halted. De Rozario knew that there was a brothel further down the street, but had no orders to inspect it. He stood, quietly forlorn, as if in a pit, and stared up at the rooftops; a few people stole past the cluster of men in green uniforms, on their way home or to the square. A thick set man approached them out of the side street that Pelean had emerged from a few minutes before. His stride was more purposeful, as if he had to get somewhere in a hurry. He wore a beret, which he had pulled down to obscure his eyes. His hands were thrust in his trouser pockets, and he carried a beard of several days' growth. For an instant he broke his stride, as he realised that there were four Civil Guards before him, blocking his way. Then he stepped nimbly to one side, and carried on, walking past them with his face averted. Pelean tapped de Rozario on the shoulder and nodded in the direction of the disappearing figure. De Rozario had already noted him; after a few seconds of mental effort, he matched the hidden face to one of the photographs at the barracks, and he called out.

"You! Stop!"

The man continued to walk away, but faster now, head bent.

"You there! In the name of the Civil Guard, stop!"

De Rozario and the other Guards now moved forward as a group; he ordered them to prepare to fire and called out one more time. As he did so the figure broke into a run, his arms furiously pumping the air; de Rozario drew his pistol.

"Follow me!" he called out, his heart pounding now.

Ecstatic at his success in forcing a fugitive into the open, his earlier disappointment evaporating, de Rozario ran on, the other police following close behind. Their quarry sprinted away, reached a house toward the bottom of the street, and banged at its door; before de Rozario could raise his pistol the man disappeared, and the door closed after him. Cursing, he reached the door, bringing the butt of his pistol down against the weathered timbers.

"Open up! This is the Civil Guard!"

From the other side came, first panic stricken female voices, then the deeper resonance of several male voices.

"Where's the door?! How do I get out?!" shouted one.

"You said they had no reason to come here tonight!" exclaimed another.

"Get out of my way you old bitch, don't you know who I am?!" bellowed a third.

"This is a mistake!"

De Rozario spun round; Pelean was standing close behind him, out of breath, gripping his rifle in both hands, biting his lip. He continued.

"Teniente, not *this* house!"

Unable to comprehend what Pelean meant de Rozario turned back, and banged again. The sounds of panic and people running in many directions to no purpose increased.

"Open the door or we'll shoot the locks out!" he shouted.

He ordered Pelean and the two Guards to raise their rifles, as if they were an execution party and the door itself was to be despatched. As he was about to give the order to fire, he heard the sound of the bolts being pulled back. He raised his own pistol, and aimed for a knot in the wood at about chest height.

The madame stood before them, dressed in a robe of patterned Chinese silk, drawn over a dress of faded blue velvet. She screamed as de Rozario launched himself at the small gap and pushed her aside, sending her spinning onto the hall floor.

"Where is he?! Where did he go?!" he almost screamed.

"Who?" she pleaded, feigned girlish innocence in a cracked face covered in powder like a relief map of a mountain range.

He bent low, and put the pistol barrel to her mouth.

"Don't argue with me old woman! The man we saw run into this house! Where is he?"

"There's no one here but my aunt and my sisters."

The voice came from within the hall and somewhere above him. He stood up; on the stairs were three young women, all loosely dressed as if they had just risen from their bed. Then he understood. He turned around; Pelean and the other Guards were standing shamefaced in the doorway: they were all clients of the old woman.

"Teniente, please, he cannot be *here*, not *this* house," and Pelean's eyes pleaded with him to end his questions. But de Rozario ignored his agitated subordinate.

"Search this stinking den!"

Oleanza, his legs shaking with fear, and his hands trembling with rage, worked at the buttons of his trousers. He was back in the alleyway, panting, his thick fingers ineffectually pushing the buttons through the neatly stitched flap of material. He stood upright at the sound of another set of footsteps in the yard through which he had moments before run. He stepped back and pressed against the wall. A short sallow faced man, his shirt and jacket thrown skewed over one shoulder, but wearing his hat, emerged and ran past him. He recognised the Mayor immediately, and raised his hat in tribute as he skipped down the alley. Oleanza looked into the yard to see if anyone else was likely to interrupt his efforts to regain civic dignity, but only obtained a brief glimpse of one of the women, her heavy breasts flapping under a shawl, as she moved to the yard door and slammed it shut in his face. I don't recall having her, he thought, and continued working at his attire. Content finally with his appearance, he withdrew his handkerchief and mopped his face and neck, now puce with effort and running with sweat. He waited briefly in case of further interruption, then set off along the alleyway, cursing Mendoza, and reliving his fear at the sound of the Civil Guard storming the house.

"That bastard Mendoza will pay! We have an understanding, that bastard will pay!"

When he rejoined the street he looked about him, but the only people in sight were walking in the opposite direction. He returned to the square; on the far side he could see that the cafes were doing a little business, and recognised the sallow faced man, who was now seated at a table at *La Alverjilla*, intently reading the menu. He had no reason to return to the Town Hall, and in his agitated state did not trust himself to sit at a table and sip wine. He decided that he had been spared by God from being discovered in the brothel; he turned smartly back into *Calle del Rosa* and walked to the front of the house. A Civil Guard stood outside as sentry, and a small crowd had gathered to watch as several of the prostitutes emerged protesting their innocence. They were escorted by Sargento Pelean. Still seething, but outwardly composed, Oleanza went up to him.

"So your fishing expedition was a success," he said in mock comic tones, "and who should take the credit for this?"

The prostitute standing next to Pelean also recognised Oleanza, but when she cried out, Pelean slapped her, and cursed her for impugning his name. Then he spoke.

"The teniente saw a fugitive and gave chase Your Honour. The man came into the house but escaped through the yard, the women aided his escape." Then he added by way of apology: "The teniente was not familiar with the neighbourhood."

Satisfied that he could blame de Rozario for his humiliation, Oleanza resolved to see Mendoza the next day. More Civil Guards arrived to escort the women, who spat and cursed in equal measure, even in the face of raised rifle butts.

"What a disgrace," Oleanza proclaimed to the crowd, and faces turned toward him, "this will not be tolerated, I promise you, this immorality will not be tolerated!"

The Captive Summer

A Public Disgrace

As a sanction against the moral degeneracy of the women, three of the prostitutes were to suffer the cropping of their hair in public. Oleanza selected Andrea and two of the others, because he had no carnal knowledge of them, and could therefore claim untainted moral outrage at their occupation. Like the Moors who remained in Granada after 1492, the women were regarded as of no consequence in society, to be tolerated or abused as the victors decided.

As the three women had not been held in custody, Pelean rearrested them on the morning they were to be humiliated; they were marched together through the streets to the square. Andrea did not fully comprehend why she and the other two were taken, and as she walked along waved with childlike innocence to those she passed. The crowd was not as extensive as had been hoped, due in part to the absence on urgent business of several patrons, but in the pages of *Ascenso* the gaps would be filled and the murmurs amplified to full throated roars. Oleanza addressed the crowd from the platform built to dishonour them; Bucaro, prominent at the front, a copy of the Mayor's impromptu speech in his hands, read as Oleanza warned of the danger to the essence of Spanish life from the Republican creeds of free love, divorce, women's emancipation and education. Then he took a pair of scissors out of his waistcoat pocket and held them aloft.

"With these vigilant blades," he began, "I cut away at the mantle of shame on the heads of these base women. Thus we cleanse the motherland, thus we take away shame, and renew the earth which bore and nurtured us."

Having singularly succeeded in confusing his audience about the impending spectacle, he turned and approached the first of the three. They had been made to kneel on the platform; with bowed heads they awaited their fate. With a hand clammy with sweat he grasped at a lock of lank hair and hacked away. He moved onto the other two, Andrea being last, drops of his sweat anointing their heads as he toiled away above them. The ritual completed, he turned back to the crowd, now holding the locks of black and blond hair in one hand and the scissors in the other. In times past his ancestor would have held aloft the severed head of a Moor. Under encouragement from the Falangist activists in their ranks, the crowd responded with warm applause. Then to complete the *coup de theatre* he graciously stood aside so that Dona Victoria could take a central place on the platform and deliver her personal diatribe while the serious shearing began. He stepped down and made his way through the ranks of the self righteous, Bucaro in his wake eager to interview the man he had already written up in his editorial as 'The Moral Guardian of San Cristobal'.

Finally understanding, ashamed and with a bloodied scalp, Andrea made her way back to her lodgings. Some people spat on her, some looked away; she washed her face as she walked with the tears which had flowed freely on the platform when she had at last realised that the people had gathered for entertainment, a torture of mediaeval sensibility. The cropping was uneven and imperfect, and looked as if a wild animal had bitten her head in several places, tearing out the hair in clumps.

She sat on the front step weeping, her head pressed down between her knees. In her despair she thought only of her children, and took comfort that they were not here now to see their mother's agony. She had nowhere to run to, no possible friend. She remained in this state for some time, a low moaning eventually replacing the sobs. Then, as she had done once before, she thought of Consuelo; she resolved to make another journey along the coast road, not quite sure what the woman could do for her, but eager to leave her torment behind. She rose from the step, and walked away.

Maria opened the door and found Andrea slumped against the wall, her face bizarrely streaked with what Maria assumed was dark red pigment so difficult was it to distinguish from the dust. Andrea screamed when Maria tried to lift her up, and crouched down as if the brittle earth were her only friend, and she would not be taken from it. Maria's anxious calls brought Consuelo, Rafael and Tom to the doorway.

"Maria, Maria what is wrong?" but Consuelo could see very easily what was wrong as soon as she saw one bare leg of the crouching figure who would have burrowed into the searing earth to escape. Seeing that Tom was also present she stopped.

"Tomas, please go back inside, go to your room, it is too dangerous for you to be here."

"Can I do nothing?"

She would have replied but Andrea screamed again as Rafael crouched down beside her, turning her face away from him and clawing at the stones. Consuelo stepped out into the heat, the colour of her clothes immediately washed out in the intense light; Tom reluctantly turned back.

Consuelo took Rafael's place while he surveyed the land in front of the house, in case they had been observed. Their immediate concern was that Andrea had been attacked, but Rafael could find no sign of any one within the screen of trees that ran down to the sea, and he returned to the house.

"Andrea, Andrea, please look at me," Consuelo whispered, not daring to touch the girl, even though the wounds to her head were still weeping. Andrea kept her head turned away, whimpering like a child that has tasted a leather strap across its face.

"Madam, should we call for Dr Hernandez?" asked Maria, knitting her hands in her apron as the outward sign of her distress at the sight of the distraught young woman.

"No Maria, get some hot water, and the bottle of iodine and clean towels." Then Consuelo returned to Andrea, whispering to her, consoling, imploring her to let them help her. Eventually Andrea relented, but insisted that Rafael leave them, which he did without affront. Bent double, with Consuelo's arms about her, she stepped haltingly into the entrance hall, and from there into the same bedroom which had been Tom's first sanctuary.

Tom had no recollection of Andrea's earlier visit, as he was lost in his dreamworld inhabited by pursuing demons. Consuelo had told him afterward, of how Andrea had stood over him while he slept, as if cradling a baby. From the gallery he could not see where they had gone; curious, he decided to go down. He did so in time to see Maria's form disappear along the corridor, and he followed her. Andrea was sitting on the edge of the bed with her back to him, crying still, attempting to explain in a rapid babble what had happened to her. Consuelo sat beside her, washing the wounds with a gentle circular motion of her hand, and she also cried as she did this. Maria's eyes opened wide as she saw Tom enter the room, and Consuelo swung round to face him.

"Tomas," she said in a hoarse and urgent whisper, "please go back."
But it was too late, Andrea's head swivelled round to see to whom Consuelo was talking.

"It is the Englishman!" she exclaimed, her voice moving from tearful terror to childlike innocence in one breath.

The three women looked at him, Maria and Consuelo in apprehension, Andrea with something like the loving look a parent has for a child. Tom walked over to them, and knelt down.

"You must be Andrea," he said, "I've heard a lot about you. My name is Tomas."

He took one of her hands in his own while Consuelo continued to clean and wash Andrea's head.

"But you speak Spanish! This cannot be so!"

"It is so," and he laughed, "I am now as Spanish as you are!"

She was fascinated by him, and released her hand from his to feel his scalp where the wound had previously shown through as a vivid scar. Then she ran a finger down his face to his lip, which had now healed, leaving only a faint scar. To see that he was recovered calmed her; and she sat quietly while Consuelo attended to her. Maria departed with a bowl

164

containing water stained a muddy red, returning later with a night dress and bath towel. As they pieced together her story, Consuelo cut her hair, in an effort at least to leave it an even length. Where Tom could not understand what Andrea had said, Consuelo translated for him, the young woman's eyes darting rapidly between the two. Finally satisfied, Consuelo announced that Andrea would now have a bath, and be put to bed. The girl protested.

"It cannot be! Tomas, you must stop them! I'll drown!"

"Andrea, you will not drown! It is only a bath; do you think Consuelo will tie a rock to your big toe and let Rafael throw you from the cliffs into the sea?" he replied.

Tom left the women; as he retraced his steps he could hear clearly Andrea's protestations and squeals along the corridor as he emerged once more into the courtyard.

The next morning, as Tom read for the second time a copy of one of the few books in English in the house, *Gulliver's Travels*, and occasionally raised his eyes to the mountains, he again reflected on the nature of the society which lay beyond the walls of the garden. The shame which had started to prick his consciousness did so again, and he decided that he would take up with both Consuelo and Dr Hernandez what possibilities he had to escape. He had been warned that it could not be contemplated until the celebration was over, as many troops were expected to attend. It was now the middle of August, he had arrived in early June. Consuelo brought Andrea out to the terrace to say goodbye to him, as they were now all so deeply in common peril that it could not make any difference. Andrea's head was covered by a scarf, which made her look younger. Consuelo departed with her arm in arm; she was still not certain that Andrea might not inadvertently betray them.

"Andrea, do you remember what we said before about Tomas?"

"Yes Consuelo, that I would only tell God about him."

"And you will?"

"Yes. It will be known only to God."

"Only to God."

They kissed and parted, Andrea's slim form merging within the trees as the sun blurred all the shapes on the sharply sloping ground.

She walked in the dry air, the waves hurling themselves at the foot of the rocks far below, and sang to herself. She feared the town, and the people there, but started to swing her arms, and walked at the very edge of the metalled road surface, just at the point where the dry earth clung to it. She walked thus for some distance, absorbed into her own world, and wondering what games her children were playing, far away in a happier place. She looked up briefly as a vehicle passed her, but did not see who was in it. She did not hear it halt along the road.

"You! Prostitute! Stop!"

She froze, and started to cry, not daring to turn around. Two men approached her, their heavy boots making repeated dull thudding sounds on the roadway. Pelean and de Rozario walked round to face her.

"Where have you come from?" asked Pelean.

She did not speak, but crumpled before them, sobbing audibly, afraid that they would cut her hair again.

"Answer him! Are you stupid you little slut?!"

She only shook her head, and held one hand to her head in a faint attempt to protect it. Then Pelean took a step forward, but sideways also, which effectively shielded her body from de Rozario. He spoke again, but not as harshly as before.

"We only want to know where you came from. If you cannot speak, then point to the place."

Still averting her head from the men, she raised a hand and pointed in the direction of the rapidly rising ground beside the road. Although El Faro was by now completed obscured by trees, Pelean guessed what she referred to.

"There is a house about a kilometre along teniente. That's where she has been."

When Rafael opened the door in response to the impatient ringing, he retained as much composure as he could given the circumstances. Senses alert to the sound of a car engine prompted him to look to see who was approaching the house. The ensuing panic mirrored that in the house in *Calle del Rosa*, with the important exception that there was no alley to escape along. Even so, as he opened the door to the figure of de Rozario, his mouth slipped to his stomach.

"I am Teniente Carlos de Rozario of the Civil Guard, I wish to see the head of the house."

"Of course senor, please...please follow me."

The young man strode across the threshold with the air of a young torero; martial elegance, good looks, vanity, pride and a desire for glory combined within one body, yet maintained by the rhythm of one beating mortal heart. Pelean had answered his questions as to who owned the house, so he knew that he faced an audience with a woman. Then Rafael, dressed in worn trousers and a tattered linen shirt, led the way to the terrace, as he had done once before when Jesus had asked for their help. De Rozario saluted smartly, and removed his hat, which was so polished that the sun sparkled on its surface. Consuelo was seated at the table, one hand at her chin, the other resting on a book, her eyes looking far away.

"Good morning senora. I am Teniente Carlos de Rozario, I apologise for arriving unannounced."

She turned to face him; the banality of his introduction, and its civility, a surprise to her. She rose, and stepped forward to shake his hand, as she did so running one hand over her abdomen in short downward strokes to straighten her dress.

"Good morning teniente. I am Dona Consuelo Arranquez. How can I help you?"

For a moment he did nothing. It was as if all motive power and all feeling had been taken from him, all that remained was the sensation of being in that space with her. The universe fell away to leave only the sound of her voice and his heartbeat, nothing more. Then he composed himself, and accepted her outstretched hand.

"Thank you for seeing me. I wanted to ask you a few questions about a young woman who I believe you know, Senorita Andrea Perez."

If either were subsequently asked what questions were posed, and what replies given that day, neither could remember. Consuelo because she was convinced that Andrea had betrayed them all, and that the policeman was merely biding his time before reinforcements arrived to shoot them, de Rozario because he had never met a woman before who stirred passion in him in the way that she did.

As he resumed his journey with Pelean to the outpost in the mountains, his mind returned again and again to the short sweep of her hand across her stomach as she walked toward him, and how the folds of the dress fell away under her touch. He gripped the hanging strap in the car because his hand was trembling, and seemed to Pelean to be unusually distracted.

When he had left the house, he took his leave of Consuelo with genuine courteousness. She waved Rafael away to escort the young officer to the door, ran to the balustrade as soon as they were out of sight and vomited over it, gripping the stonework to stop herself from toppling forward. She remained there for some minutes, retching and crying all at once, and shaking like a child.

The Captive Summer

Decisions, Decisions

The Civil Governor agreed to the schedule of films submitted for his approval; in his letter, he even went so far as to commend Oleanza for his artistic sensibility. Oleanza, keenly aware of the significance for his own advancement of such praise, read the letter over and again while he rehearsed his speech of welcome. He paced his office, stopping in front of an ornate mirror which hung on the far wall, delivered his lines, paying close attention to his posture and facial expression, then brought out the sheet of paper from behind his back, and read again the words that promised so much.

"And I note with satisfaction," he read aloud, "the appealing synthesis of themes and subjects in the selection submitted for my consideration. I commend your judgement, and trust that the people of the town will gain suitable instruction as to the values and achievements of the new Spain, led once more to greatness by the Caudillo."

He looked up at the mirror, vainly pompous, and beheld the future civic leader of a great city like Barcelona or Madrid. Interrupted by the shrill ringing of the telephone, he walked across to his desk, threw down the letter and picked up the receiver. His countenance changed once more: the caller was Don Rondolfo Juan Cabarro de Navarre, the largest landowner, and therefore wealthiest man, within fifty kilometres.

"Good morning Don Rondolfo. It is a pleasure to hear from you. How may I help you?" he said.

Don Rondolfo had decided that it would be desirable to mark the eve of the fourth anniversary of liberation by hosting a dinner for its leading citizens. His farms grew more grain, olives and citrus fruit than all the others in the area combined and he hunted game on his own land. He boasted that his only concern was in having tables strong enough to withstand the feast, the devouring appetites of his guests his only salvation. The highest Spanish tables never had to resort to a diet of boiled grass seasoned with salt; indeed the many banquets held in Franco's honour became such an official embarrassment that mention of them was banned from the newspapers. But for poor Spaniards, hunger, like the secret police, lingered on every street corner, and rose before the sun.

The key people from the civilian arm of government, that is Oleanza, Castellon and Lupion, were invited, as was Bucaro (to ensure that the event was accurately reported in the pages of *Ascenso*), Capitan Mendoza, and other close and personal friends. The close and harmonious relations of Church and State would be signified by the invitation of Father Abarca.

Dr Hernandez and Dr Marin would probably not attend even if invited, so no invitation had been extended to either of them. There were a few foreigners living in the town, two retired Italian brothers and a White Russian emigre, who could be counted on to provide international sanction. He considered that by inviting the Russian, Vladimir Dolovsky, he would provide an exquisite riposte to the bloody but ultimately futile intervention of the Bolsheviks in the civil war.

His principal home was a large villa on *Avenida Isabella*, set well back from the street with a garden studded with date palms. In the summer, when the heat and stench from the drains became too oppressive, he escaped to a hunting lodge. For the August celebrations he had deigned to descend from his mountainous retreat and live among mortal men and women, a gracious gesture of personal sacrifice that was from time to time expected of people of high birth. He was a distinguished tall man of sixty years, as he had never been subject to hard physical labour, with leathery skin, wide flowing moustaches and a mantle of lustrous grey hair. He was a feudal lord in spirit, but as Franco's Spain was still a republic he had to content himself with his money, the influence that bought, and his family name. He was of course a Monarchist, and although he admired Franco's ability as a war leader, he grieved over the death of Alfonso XIII, only desiring to live long enough to travel to Madrid to pledge his allegiance to his successor in the audience room of the palace. A descendant of the Dukes of Navarre, he was reassured by Franco's defence of the Church but alienated by his ambivalent statements on the restoration of the monarchy: in his eyes the only legitimate authority in Spain under divine will.

"Good morning Oleanza," in private he only referred to Oleanza by his family name, as the man was clearly not his social equal, "I need your advice with the table plan."

The dinner was to be as carefully prepared as the parade itself; and the perfect arrangement of guests around the table required Don Rondolfo's skills at both politics and chess. Oleanza, already exultant about the Governor's letter, was further flattered that he had not only received a prestigious invitation, but was now being courted as to his views on the seating arrangements. That he was also due to attend the film presentation that night was a minor detail which could easily be resolved: by not attending.

"But of course Don Rondolfo, I would be honoured to offer whatever assistance I can."

"As you know Oleanza there will be fourteen of us seated at dinner. I have decided to sit in the centre rather than at the top of the table, as my position is then symbolically alongside those who wield civil power. My question is this, how to arrange the other thirteen?"

Before Oleanza could offer any suggestions to the crackling disembodied voice, Don Rondolfo proceeded to answer the question himself.

"One possible arrangement would have been for all fourteen to sit along one side of the table, as at the Last Supper, but I have decided that this might have unfortunate connotations."

The line fell silent, and Oleanza wondered whether he was now expected to contribute; but as he formed the first vowel sound in his throat, Don Rondolfo resumed.

"The supreme power in the country is civil, so Oleanza, you should sit to either to my immediate left or right side. The Church sanctifies the government of course, and, as a blessing will be called before we eat, I think that Father Abarca should sit on the other side. How does that sound to you?"

Oleanza formed in his mind's eye a picture of a long table draped with damask and overflowing with silverware, at which empty chairs had to be filled with the bodies of fourteen men, such that no one felt slighted, or was obliged to sit next to anyone they disliked.

"I think that your proposal is commendable," he said, at a disadvantage as he did not know who else was on the guest list.

"This however threatens my good relations with Eduardo Castellon," and hearing this Oleanza winced, "so I will compromise by putting him directly across the table from you."

Their distrust and dislike of each other was rooted in the past; so long as they were kept far enough apart not to be able to stab each other with fruit knives, he would tolerate this imposition.

"I need you to speak candidly Oleanza."

"But of course Don Rondolfo," he replied, with no intention of doing anything of the kind.

"What do you think of Lupion? I have to cultivate him, so to speak, but I cannot stand him. He reminds me of Goebbels with a bad skin condition. In the days before National Syndicalism people like him could have been disposed of late at night, now they are deferred to. He acts like a crack toothed, unwashed, repellent lizard who had gained access to a nest of rare eggs," and Don Rondolfo spat out the words as if they were poisoned grape pips.

Everybody hated Lupion: Oleanza was on safe ground.

"I do agree, Don Rondolfo."

"But where shall I put him?" he asked, exasperated at the potential checkmate he faced across the table. Oleanza guessed that Mendoza would also be present, as he knew Don Rondolfo was fond of the police chief.

"May I suggest next to Capitan Mendoza?"

"Mendoza? I like that idea! He can keep an eye on the little reptile, stop him stealing the silver!"

Oleanza smiled to himself: his suggestion had gained approval in the rich man's eyes.

"May I ask who else will be in attendance?" he enquired, hoping that the proximity of Castellon was to be the only indignity he suffered.

"Oh! Quality people, people who appreciate what we have done for Spain."

And with that enigmatic reply, and having no further use for Oleanza, Don Rondolfo put the telephone down.

On the morning of the film show, a truck arrived in the *Plaza de Toros* laden with the projection and sound equipment. It was followed soon afterward by three Guards under the command of Sargento Pelean. They erected barriers to vehicles across the narrower streets, then maintained a careful watch on the technicians, who busied themselves by rolling out reels of electric cable, positioning the loudspeakers, and finally, draping the canvas screen from the second floor balconies of the farthest houses. Quite what crime the police suspected the technicians were about to commit they were themselves uncertain; but cinema was a powerful agent, and these men had to be kept under protective surveillance.

From his office, Oleanza also watched the cinema technicians, but motivated by habitual boredom, not considerations of national security. On his desk lay a report from Bucaro and Father Abarca that detailed the final edits they had agreed to the main feature, *Mutiny On The Bounty*, to ensure that it neither offended public decency nor excited susceptible minds with its story of rebellion against tyranny. Oleanza remembered Dona Victoria's comment about the similarity between Franco and Clark Gable; but try as he might, and he attempted various ploys, he could not quite see the connection. As on so many days before, he decided that he had exerted himself sufficiently in the interests of the town by reading the document, and took an early lunch.

As evening came, a stream of expectant people made their way to the square, drawn by a desire to secure places on the rough benches that had now been placed in neat rows, with a central aisle, facing the screen. The screen flapped lazily, drawing the eyes of all who entered the square, even though at that time it was only a stained and dirtied piece of canvas, and held no fables. A few hawkers had been granted permission to set up their stalls, from which they sold oranges, nuts, and even stale bread, but it was not practical to open the cafes, so both remained closed. The children were allowed to stay to watch the newsreel and the screening of *La Patrulla*; but as Father Abarca was concerned that grainy images of South Pacific natives in little clothing might be corrupting on young minds, with which Dona Victoria readily assented, they were to be sent home during the intermission before *Mutiny On The Bounty* began.

Oleanza had resolved his social dilemma arising from the conjunction of the open air cinema and the dinner by deciding that he would only stay to watch the newsreel, then discreetly leave, return home to change, then summon his driver to take him to Don Rondolfo's house. Looking down from his office for one last time before departing, he noted with satisfaction that the square was now almost full; the benches, save those reserved for special guests, were all taken, and late comers were standing on the pavements. He emerged from the Town Hall escorted by two Guards, who forced a way for him through the crowd. As soon as he was recognised applause broke out, the Falangists clapping with greatest enthusiasm; he graciously acknowledged his role as the provider of the entertainment, sweeping the air with short strokes of his hands. Since the bloody demise of the town's cinema no film had been shown in San Cristobal, and many of the children present had never seen a movie.

Two young men in open necked shirts, with sleeves rolled to their elbows, stood on the projection platform, reels of film at their feet. As the ambient light faded, and the sky filled with crimson, they surveyed the murmuring crowd around them, winking suggestively to the young women, making faces at the children, and relishing the attention they received. The crowd was hushed, but excited; many looked about them, awed by the novelty, and unsure what would happen next. Oleanza looked to his watch, it was now a little before eight o'clock; he raised one arm, the agreed signal for the technicians, and the projector whirred into life.

The Captive Summer

Patriots' Banquet

As he drove through the darkened streets Oleanza had only one regret: there were few people in the vicinity of Don Rondolfo's house to witness his arrival. He had assured himself, and his wife, that this evening marked only the beginning of his rise to prominence. He saw himself as a man trusted by the Caudillo, a civic leader whose opinions and patronage were courted. In his mind he placed himself at a State banquet, rehearsed a conversation with the American ambassador and a smutty joke with the French military attache. So enraptured was he by this dream that he did not notice that they had arrived at the house until the driver, holding open the car door, coughed.

"My dear Mayor, I am so pleased to see you. I trust that the heavy burden you carry may be lifted from your shoulders, if only for a few hours," said Don Rondolfo, his telephone abruptness forgotten in the presence of guests, in his own home, as he greeted Oleanza.

"Don Rondolfo, I am delighted to be here. I thank you for your sentiments, and embrace you as a patriot," replied Oleanza, determined to prove that he was as capable of courteous speech as any gentleman.

Most of the guests were already present and engaged in conversation; Oleanza noticed that across the reception room Father Abarca was furtively passing intelligence to Mendoza, who regarded the cleric with a look of mild irritation.

"A young man, who gave his life for the Patria in Russia, is to be commemorated in a service on Monday. There are rumours that Republican agitators will make some gesture of defiance and violate the ceremony," confided Abarca in a low monotone as he sipped from a glass of pale sherry. Mendoza drank off the rest of the contents of his own glass before answering; experience had taught him that Abarca sometimes attached too much significance to tales of human fallibility, and on occasion, outright deranged ranting. Occasionally the information was useful.

"I had not heard these rumours Father, but then the police do not always lurk in the darkest corners," he said.

The priest offered a faint smile in reply, the thought occurring to him that Mendoza could not even be trusted to stand in a shaft of bright daylight if he were told that Archangel Gabriel insisted on it. Abarca continued making his report, which Mendoza largely ignored, apart from a confession of egg stealing, and the attempted robbery of a bicycle pump.

Don Rondolfo introduced Oleanza to those guests, such as the Italian brothers, and Dolovsky, with whom he had only passing acquaintance. The brothers, two elderly bachelors, were full of praise for Mussolini, although they were not challenged as to why they preferred to live in Spain rather than the land of their birth, under Mussolini's protection. Dolovsky, who had gravitated to Don Rondolfo as a fellow man of noble birth, and who found the world he now inhabited not entirely to his liking, was a blustering red faced pot for depositing alcohol. He spent his time playing cards or backgammon and assisted Don Rondolfo in drinking his way through his wine cellar.

As Oleanza discussed his hopes for the town, his eyes strayed to the other compact clusters of men huddled in spasms of conversation. Mendoza was now talking to Castellon, Father Abarca to Bucaro, and Don Rondolfo to Lupion. The young man was engaged in animated conversation; for his part Don Rondolfo betrayed no sign of his true feelings, but rather by his alternately sage or engrossed countenance gave the impression that he revelled in the opportunity to discuss the State price for lemons.

A servant appeared at Don Rondolfo's elbow, and advised that the staff were ready. He broke away from his conversation with Lupion and graciously turned to his other guests, ushering them toward the dining room like a shepherd rounding up a noisy flock, assuring them of the culinary delights that awaited them through the heavy oak doors. For Don Rondolfo, the essence of a good dinner was abundant food, alcohol, and prolonged conversation. There was a certain protocol, a certain ritual, and two unwritten, but unbreakable rules. The first was that he expected the decanters that made the circuit of the table to be regularly emptied, and the second was that he did not expect anyone to rise from the table before he did. This clearly gave rise to a trial of strength, a test of skill and courage as searching as a bullfight, but fortunately for the participants, not as deadly. The objective was subtle: it was not to demonstrate how much each man could drink, but how well he drank it. As the decanters passed they were expected to stop talking only for so long as to draw off another glass, then continue either in their conversation with their neighbour or with the group in general. Those adept at the art of conversation, and who could limit the quantity of alcohol that slipped down their throats, would win. Losing meant an undignified exit in search of relief for the bladder, and triumph in the eyes of those left behind. The torture would only end when Don Rondolfo took up his napkin, and then let it drop, declaring: "Gentlemen, let us take coffee outside." At this signal, those in danger of flooding could make a hasty but honourable exit, a dripping trouser leg the only outward sign of their brush with humiliation.

But first they had to eat. They were presented with seven courses:

heaving platter upon heaving platter of food. There was enough to feed an entire street, but to be shared only amongst a cluster of men already tending to corpulence. Wine and spirits slipped down their throats along with tender strips of beef, pork, squid, fresh salads, and venison basted in brandy. They argued good naturedly, spat food as they spoke, drank, grunted, called for more wine, and did justice to the stomach of Franco. After three hours the feasting concluded; they looked out on a battlefield of meat bones, toppled glasses of blood red wine, crumpled napkins like abandoned bandages, and heaps of punctured grapes. Cigar smoke now filled the air, obscuring faces and filling their lungs with mind altering toxins.

Don Rondolfo scraped back his chair and rose to address his friends and allies. Minds now fogged and slowed struggled to control colliding images of their benefactor, the sad but inevitable legacy of immersion of the visual cortex in alcohol.

"Gentlemen, it has been my privilege to be your host," at which Oleanza and Castellon in quick succession clapped and banged the table, "at this hour in the history of our beloved Patria. Tomorrow we shall celebrate the fourth anniversary of the liberation of the town by Nationalist forces. I give you now a toast to the men who gave their lives. They are glorious in the eyes of God. Gentlemen, to the fallen!"

At this point they all rose, whatever their drunken condition, and raised their glasses. Whether the suggested glory of the righteous dead in the eyes of the Divine, arose from the efficiency with which the liberators had despatched the wounded in the Republican field hospital as the town fell, none of the gathered celebrants would have cared to comment on. They resumed their seats; Don Rondolfo, now eager to impress upon them his erudition, continued.

"In Spain since that day, truth has triumphed over falsehood, light over darkness, health over sickness."

Lupion coughed; suddenly and acutely aware that he had become the focus of attention, he made desperate attempts at suppression. "Health over sickness, indeed," he said, coughed again, reached for the glass before him on the table and drank off the last of the wine it contained. Castellon scowled at him for the interruption. Don Rondolfo went on, praising Franco, denouncing the Reds (more table banging) and finally, making passionate reference to his desire for the return of the monarchy. He sat down, exhausted by his exertions; his guests rose once more, clapping or saluting him with their glasses and baying for Red blood.

As the night had worn on, Lupion had became more uncomfortably aware of his filling bladder; but either through lack of skill or ignorance of the rules, continued to drink. To distract his mind, he paid close attention to other conversations, in particular the counter-battery exchanges between Oleanza and Castellon. Castellon and Oleanza eyed each other with suspicion and malice through the cigar fog as the evening progressed, but maintained an appearance of decorum whenever Don Rondolfo looked in their direction.

"When will that orphanage of yours be completed Oleanza?" Castellon asked.

"That orphanage of mine, is the orphanage for the town, I hold no personal interest."

"Whether you hold an interest or not, it must be dusty work," and Castellon arched his eyebrows.

Before Oleanza could return the hostile fire, being the insinuation that Castellon knew that some of the cement purchased with public money went to private building schemes, Lupion interjected.

"After whom will the building be named?" he asked, as he thrust his knees together to divert his mind from the growing pain in his groin.

"I have written to General Ochoa, he led the Nationalist troops that liberated San Cristobal, and have his consent to being so honoured," explained Oleanza, not taking his eyes from Castellon's face for a moment.

Lupion was not alone in his discomfort; although the pain that both Oleanza and Castellon experienced was increasing steadily, neither would give way and lose face. Oleanza filled his glass with sherry; noting that Don Rondolfo was in conversation with Father Abarca, he slid the decanter across the table cloth, as if it were a chess pawn looking to take a rook. Castellon rose to the challenge, filled his glass, then passed the decanter to the unfortunate Lupion, who squeezed his thighs ever tighter, in the vain hope that he could stop the rising waters from breaking over the lip of the dam.

Then, still deep in conversation, Don Rondolfo's hand edged forward and grasped his napkin; eyes and heads turned toward him as he replied to a point made by Father Abarca. He rose, and uttering the words that had attained the significance of a secular blessing, called the ordeal to an end. Dolovsky stood, bowed low to demonstrate impeccable Russian manners and breeding to his host, then led an urgent procession of three to the toilet. Don Rondolfo nodded to Oleanza, rose, and withdrew from the torture chamber; the aroma of fresh coffee now drawing him and a small party like an Iberian Jason in pursuit of the golden fleece. Soon only Oleanza, Castellon and Lupion remained; Oleanza and Castellon resisting the desire to rise only from their mutual determination not to lose face, while Lupion was so drunk he was not sure that he could stand upright. But Lupion needed to piss, and he needed to piss very quickly, or he felt that he would rupture where he sat. Castellon and Oleanza were in the same condition, but they still persisted in facing each other down.

Suddenly, Castellon threw back his chair and made a dash for the french doors at the far end of the room, which opened to the front lawns. Oleanza and Lupion were soon after him, and all three men, rivalry forgotten now in their common jeopardy, struggled to open them. They were frustrated.

"It won't open, the lock's jammed!" hissed Castellon through grinding teeth.

"And is that my fault? Am I to be held responsible for the locks in this house? Please wait until I make a note of that, so that I remember to discuss the state of the locks in every house when I next see the Civil Governor!" replied Oleanza sarcastically, but with as much dignity and coherence as a drunk middle aged man on the verge of wetting himself could muster.

"This is not the time for humour Oleanza, we need to break a pane of glass, then open the door from the outside!"

"Why don't you just send one of the servants to do it?! Then we could ask for towels to wipe our hands on once we have pissed all over his lawn!" They were saved by Lupion; looking around him through blurred kaleidoscopic eyes for a weapon, he saw a cheese knife on the dining table that had been missed when the table was cleared; he lunged for it, turned round and thrust the blade between the two arguing men in one movement, aiming for the gap between the wooden frames. The lock yielded, and all three almost tumbled out onto the lawn.

Although they had a common purpose and need, the pride of each ensured that they sought out a separate patch of grass on which to relieve themselves. They stood with their backs to each other, humming to hide the sound of the trickling water, but not so loud as to attract the attention of anyone within the house. Lupion swayed between the other two, his mind moving between lucidity and opacity as the moon moves through cloud; he was strangely satisfied that he had rendered this service to two of the most powerful men in the town and had perhaps demonstrated how he might help them in the future. When the torrent had subsided, no Ark or other vessel being in sight, the three drunks turned their backs on the well irrigated pasture and teetered forward once more to rejoin high society.

The Captive Summer

The Big Parade

In the early hours of the morning, while the townsfolk were either lost to deep dreams of the South Pacific or nightmares from the Rif mountains, the now bleary cinematic technicians returned to the square and set to work to dismantle the projection equipment, loudspeakers and screen. They coiled the long ropes of electric cable; wrestled with the heavy loudspeaker boxes, heaving them up onto an open sided truck; and attacked the wide canvas screen as if it were the mainsail of a schooner, and they, sailors anxious to furl it before their ship was struck by an impending storm.

As soon as they had departed, and the square had sunk back into silence, a team of municipal workers arrived armed with brooms and a water cart. They swept the ground and washed down the roadway and pavements; as the sun rose above the rooftops it became reflected in thin slivers of water, as if a mirror had broken on the ground into a hundred pieces. The last task given to the men was to transform the platform which had served as both site of mock execution and projection booth into a temple to the national flag: with slow reverence they draped four bright rectangles in Spanish colours that flapped and cracked as they unravelled in the dawn air. The dreary and dirty streets had been banished; posters of Franco now occupied every spare piece of wall, offensive graffiti had been obliterated, and bunting strewn from balconies and rooftops.

Nothing was to be allowed to sour the atmosphere of martial celebration as the town prepared to acknowledge its deliverance from the forces of darkness, or deliverance into hell, depending on individual perspectives. Oleanza had fretted and tyrannised about every detail of the arrangements for the parade, with the exception of the time the sun should rise and set, which he conceded was God's province and not his own. The sun rose higher in the sky, its rays eviscerating the water in the gutters; the first dignitaries and local worthies arrived at the Town Hall and were shown to a reception room well stocked with alcohol. Ferdinand Aguado spent his time reassuring Oleanza, checking with the police and the stewards as the square began to fill, and parrying the petty complaints of Dona Victoria. The Falangist illusion for the day demanded that the townsfolk were as extras in the epic story of their own lives; and Dona Victoria had assumed responsibility for the costume department. The agents of Seccion Feminina handed out sets of clean clothes in exchange for the shabby and worn garments in which most presented themselves; but as soon as the Governor departed, the costumes were to be returned, held in readiness for the next visitation.

The Captive Summer

Oleanza had never served in the military, although on one occasion he practised loading a rifle, yet he was in awe of all military symbols and emblems. When he received the letter of confirmation from the Military Governor's office of the detachments that would take part in the parade, he memorised and reverently recited the names and unit numbers as if they had been taken from scripture.

"The second squadron of the fourth armoured car regiment of Navarre. The third regiment of Moorish lancers. The Black Arrowhead company of the seventeenth infantry regiment. The one hundred and sixth independent mountain company," he then paused, momentarily uncertain, "or was that the six hundred and first independent mountain company?"

But his ignorance of logistics, and his bombastic responses to Aguado, and even Mendoza, concerning the preferred parade route had condemned the troops to follow the narrow streets from the northern outskirts. They were to proceed to the *Plaza de Toros*, take the salute from the Civil Governor, and exit on the road that led to the open country to the east of the town. He could not understand the negativity of his subordinates, and would not listen to their requests for the route to be varied, thereby sealing both his and their fate.

Petrol and diesel fuel was in as short supply, and as strictly rationed, as food. The fuel tanks of the trucks and the armoured cars were almost dry when they reached the town's outskirts in the early morning, and arrangements had been made in advance for refuelling from an Army fuel truck laden with petrol held in large galvanized cans. Petrol for civilian use was even scarcer, and more closely rationed; Dr Hernandez had petrol coupons, but would resort to buying petrol on the black market through Enrique Morales if he had to. As he knew that the Army was bringing petrol, he decided to exchange his coupons for some of their fuel. After an early breakfast, he walked out of town to where the vehicles were drawn up.

Along the line of trucks and armoured cars the drivers and crews were passing glinting cans from hand to hand, patiently pouring their contents into the cavernous fuel tanks of the vehicles or filling large slate grey fuel cans placed at the side of the road, their caps opened like the gaping mouths of fledgling birds. One soldier spilled a little of the precious fluid onto the ground as he poured, the tinted liquid soaking into the earth and leaving a dark stain in the soil. A corporal came up to him and kicked him on the shin for his clumsiness. The admonished soldier stood erect, the can in one hand, and in a mechanical voice apologised for his crime. There seemed to be no one in charge of the fuel truck however, so Dr Hernandez bent down and picked up two of the silver cans that had been passed down and placed

The Captive Summer

beside it. He then walked toward the truck's cab, in the hope of finding one of the soldiers supervising the allocation of the fuel, so that he could exchange his petrol coupons. A voice called to him from behind.

"Dr Hernandez, please doctor, do not take those cans."

He turned round, and faced a young man who could have been his own son. The soldier's uniform was ill fitting, but he wore the insignia of the transport corps.

"But I have coupons," said the doctor with irascibility, "I have almost run out of petrol, and I need more. Do you know how difficult it is to get petrol in this part of the country?"

"What I meant doctor, is that those cans are for the Army, the cans for civilian use are still in the truck."

Suspicious that this was yet another scam, whereby he had to hand over coupons and an extra sum of money to be given 'civilian' petrol, Dr Hernandez tightened his grip on the carrying handles.

"What difference could there be between the two?" he asked in a voice betraying resignation at the petty corruption.

"It will only take a moment doctor."

The soldier called up to the truck and a head appeared above the silver rampart. Two cans of 'civilian' petrol were carefully handed down. Dr Hernandez and the young soldier faced each other; the doctor scrutinized the cans the young man now held.

"I see no difference between the petrol you have and the petrol I have," he said, "therefore I will give you the coupons and go, because I have infinitely more valuable ways to be spending my time."

The soldier took a step toward him, and spoke in a soft voice.

"But you see doctor, there is a difference. The petrol you have is sweet, while the petrol I hold is unsweetened."

There was something in the tone, and the soldier's familiarity with him, which caught the doctor unprepared. The soldier put down the cans he held, and prised those which Dr Hernandez held from his grasp. They were then exchanged. As Dr Hernandez looked down he noted that between the carrying handle and the cap of each new can there was marked in red chalk a small irregular cross. He looked hard into the face of the soldier, and began to wonder why the uniform and the face did not go together.

"How did you know my name?" he asked.

The soldier only saluted, his fingertips brushing a dark lock of hair that had slipped from under his forage cap.

"It must be a miracle. Good day Dr Hernandez."

Dr Hernandez walked along the line of vehicles, carrying his precious cargo, and curious about the incident he had just experienced. At the head of the line was an open staff car; two officers were lounging against its side, lightheartedly smoking and talking, while their driver filled the fuel tank just a metre from them. It was only then that the doctor realized that he had not been asked for the coupons: but when he turned around he could see no sign of either of the men from the transport corps.

Eventually the vehicles' thirst was slated; their drivers climbed up into the cabs or into the bodies of the vehicles, and started the engines. Military policemen showed their impatience at the length of time it had taken to refuel by loudly cursing the drivers. The staff car pulled slowly away, and was followed by a military band, the bandsmen marching with mute instruments; then came the armoured cars, spitting dirty blue-grey fumes, and the mechanised infantry, by which is meant that the soldiers rode in the open trucks. The company of mountain infantry were ordered forward by the police from a side street, incongruous with skis and sticks thrown across their shoulders in the heat of summer. The Moorish lancers rode forward, headed by a Spanish officer on a white mare that kicked and plunged until he showed the animal his whip. In flowing scarlet robes and saffron turbans, the tips of their lances adorned with streaming pennants, the Moors could have been a contingent of the Arab armies that had conquered Spain so many centuries before. Finally the town's band, led by an Army veteran, and additionally containing several former Legionnaires, struck up a march and walked forward, haphazardly co-ordinating music and motion.

In the Town Hall, the Civil Governor, held in deep conversation by Oleanza over a second glass of excellent Jerez sherry, was roused when his personal assistant, a lieutenant in jodhpurs and creaking leather riding boots, politely interrupted to remind them that the parade would soon move off, and that it was time to go out to the balcony to address the gathered crowd. The balcony was not a large structure, which oversight Oleanza blamed on the Town Hall architect being a Socialist, but it was ornate, the iron filigree work especially repainted in honour of the day. There was enough room for only a few, and consequently the privilege of standing next to the Governor for a quarter of an hour was highly regarded. Beside Oleanza, it fell to only Castellon, Father Abarca, and Don Rondolfo.

By eleven o'clock the crowd numbered many hundreds; they were held in check by barriers and a line of Civil Guards in front of the Town Hall. As the Civil Governor stepped through the open doorway to the balcony a shout went up from the people, aided by well placed Falangists who had been whipping them up for half an hour with patriotic slogans and songs. He held out his arms to them, gave the Falangist salute, then applauded them. The noise of the cheering rolled from one end of the square to the other, and the police struggled to keep the traffic lane clear where the troops were soon to pass. He approached the microphone.

"People of San Cristobal," he began, "it is my privilege to be here today to share with you the celebrations for the fourth anniversary of the liberation of the town. Today we have an opportunity to publicly thank those brave crusaders who saved, and purified, the motherland with their blood!"

Encouraged by the Falangist stewards, he was rewarded by further applause; he continued his speech.

"I would like to thank the Mayor, Senor Oleanza, for the warmth with which I have been received," at which there was a further spasm of clapping, "and I give you my assurance of the regard with which I hold San Cristobal and its people."

The cheering and clapping was taken up again, but this time, on cue, the town's dignitaries stepped forward to absorb the palpable energy released by the ascending waves of public approval; but a casual observer might only have noted how much strength yet remained in arms and lungs weakened by two years of malnutrition. The Civil Governor concluded his address: "God bless Spain! Long live Franco! Our motherland: One great, free, nation!" Hunger, repression, and bereavement all forgotten, weak hands clapped and thin faces smiled upward at the men on the balcony.

Then the sound of the military band came to the ears of the crowd, and they turned expectantly for the arrival of the troops; children and adults alike waved small national flags, with the children held aloft on the shoulders of the men. The staff car entered the square, the groomed and sleek officers sitting proud and erect. Then the military band appeared, freed from the confines of the narrow streets; the strident but sorrowful sounds emanating from the bugles and drums erupted into the square, rolled outward and struck the walls of the imprisoning buildings. Ecstatic, the crowd cheered and clapped; but behind the shutters and locked door of *La Alverjilla*, Andres and a few regular customers played cards and drank wine, determined to ignore the hysteria in the streets outside. Andres paused before taking up a card, then spoke softly but with deliberation.

"Plato said that the dead know the end of war, but I say the living shall know the end of hope."

The Captive Summer

Full Stop

The music swelled; the crowd pressed forward, eager for a glimpse of the soldiers. The glinting bugles swung in unison, each rising wave of sound splashing across the jostling faces and luminous eyes of the crowd; the tight drumheads reverberated, their silver fittings flashing in the sunlight. On the balcony the Civil Governor alternately beat out the tune on the iron filigree at his fingertips, and raised his hands to applaud. Oleanza stood at his shoulder.

The first sign of trouble came when the leading armoured car entered the square. It moved slowly, seemingly stuck in a low gear, but spitting steam and jolting violently as if it were convulsed by a mechanical fit, finally coasting to a halt directly below the Town Hall balcony. The vehicle's sweating commander emerged through the turret and smartly saluted the bemused dignitaries; they returned his salute, arms outstretched. The young man stood in the turret for a moment, in urgent conversation with the still hidden driver; he saluted the dignitaries again, and they returned the second salute, their arms swinging in unison. But when he saluted for a third time, both the dignitaries and those at the front of the crowd began to wonder why a gap had now opened between the car and the rapidly disappearing column of bandsmen.

"What's happening?!" Mendoza hissed into de Rozario's ear from their vantage point on the Town Hall steps. De Rozario stepped quickly into the roadway and knocked on the armoured car's side hatch. It opened, and the perspiring driver, goggles perched on his forehead, thrust his head out.

"Why haven't you driven on?" de Rozario questioned him.

"The engine is dead teniente, it seized as we came into the square. We're fucked!" he replied with no regard for the sensibilities of rank.

De Rozario looked up into the expectant and questioning faces of the Governor and the Mayor. He walked more quickly back to Mendoza and reported. It was fortunate for them both that the hapless Aguado had provided a team of workmen for such a contingency: on Mendoza's orders de Rozario went to find them.

When those at the front of the crowd saw the workmen arrive to push and heave against the crippled vehicle, their cheers turned to laughter and their applause to a slow handclap. Those behind could not see what was going on, and so continued cheering, the Falangist stewards amongst them clapping furiously to maintain the tempo of their adulation. Heads turned as the second armoured car arrived, was forced to slow down, and then stop, as the workmen put their backs to the obstruction, in an attempt to push it out of the way. Steam now began to spit from the engine compartment of the second car and rivulets of scalding water trickled onto the road and blindly sought sanctuary in the gutters.

"I am sure that it is only a minor mechanical problem Your Excellency," was Oleanza's attempt at a message of reassurance in the Governor's ear as they watched the unfolding calamity.

The third armoured car arrived; exhibiting no signs of mechanical fault it drew up on the far side of the square, with the fourth close behind it. The Falangist stewards threw garlands of flowers as if worshipping Biblical idols of rubber and welded steel; the crews emerged from the turrets and hatches to catch the flowers, and used them to adorn their uniforms or hang them from the barrels of the machine guns.

But as the iron hearts of the iron bulls siezed, so the mood of the crowd changed, in spite of the efforts of the stewards to maintain patriotic fervour. Derisive calls and whistles met the efforts of the panicky drivers to restart engines that were now pumping plumes of superheated steam; the crowd pressed forward, chanting now, taunting the crews and spitting at them. The situation was getting out of hand; on the balcony, the Governor shifted uneasily on his feet; although no mechanic, he sensed that random engine failure could not account for the unravelling farce. He signalled to his aide to come out to him, ignoring Oleanza's offer of assistance, and despatched the creaking officer to obtain an explanation.

There was no sign of the mechanised infantry. The leading truck had broken down some distance from the square, at a point where the mirrors fixed to the cab doors almost brushed the ancient stone of the buildings to either side. Trapped behind it the remaining vehicles in the convoy groaned and spat steam as their pistons seized one by one, the sound and jolt of metal tearing against metal clearly registering in the cabs. The soldiers were ordered down from the benches by their officers; they squeezed past the oily spitting hulks in the narrow gap left between them and the houses, and reformed on the far side in two columns. The mountain infantry followed, complaining loudly and dragging their sticks against the sides of the trucks as they edged past. The officers commanding the two detachments of infantry consulted about what to do: they were now far behind the bandsmen and the armour, had no radios, no maps, were without detailed knowledge of the labyrinth of streets, and anxiously looked around them as they spoke, expecting the morning air, suffused with steam and the stench of hot oil, to crackle with bullets.

"But what about the Moors?" asked the commander of the mountain troops, pointing to the column of cavalry.

The other officer looked first to the trucks, then to the towering cavalrymen behind them. Men could edge past the hissing trucks, the horses could not.

"Let me talk to their commanding officer," he said, and strode to the horseman on the white mare.

"Why have you stopped?" asked the cavalry officer.

"Our trucks have failed, the engines are hot," replied the infantryman, as he craned his neck and looked up into the other's face. Beside him the mare's eyes swivelled, and the animal pulled at its bridle and pawed the stones; man and beast alike united in apprehension.

"That's no use to me teniente! Who is to blame for this?"

"We don't know capitan, perhaps they have been sabotaged."

"Then we must get away from here before those Red bastards start shooting at us!"

They agreed that the cavalrymen should dismount and lead their horses by the bridle to find another route to the square, while the town's band squeezed past the trucks and followed the infantry. The order was given; the Moors dismounted, their scarlet cloaks fluttering like giant poppies, while the horses threw their heads to the sky and kicked the ground to demonstrate against their confinement in the unfamiliar narrow space.

While the officers discussed the manoeuvre through the streets, the leader of the town's band, already affronted at the view of the rolling hind quarters and lifting tails of the cavalry horses, decided to take the initiative back from the Army. He turned his back on the military planners and faced his musicians.

"In the current situation, we cannot go forward, but we will not go backward! So we must play where we are! For the glory of Spain!"

And the cluster of men in dark blue uniforms cleared their throats, drew breath into their lungs and commenced the opening bars of the national anthem.

At once, the officers in deep conversation, the Moorish cavalrymen whispering to their mounts, the vexed infantry soldiers standing impatiently beyond the steaming trucks, all jumped rigidly to attention as if an electric charge now flowed through the air. The officers exchanged glances, but dared not challenge the band leader and stop the music, while he, oblivious to everything but the music and his efforts to force the musicians to keep time, continued. A few people peered down from the upper windows of the houses as the music rose upward, by turns curious and disbelieving. They too stood mockingly to attention, but made no attempt to conceal their delight at the discomfiture of the angry soldiers below them.

The final notes of the anthem died away, and were greeted by a desultory fusillade of claps and whistles from the unseen audience. The infantry commander walked briskly up to the band leader, pointed a pistol at his head and ordered him to stop or face arrest for undermining military morale.

A relief column, in the person of a solitary Guard sent by de Rozario, arrived by a side street and reported to the Army officers; he briefed them about what was happening in the square, and volunteered to guide the cavalrymen through the streets by another route. Orders rolled along the column of troops; the Moors led their horses into the side street in single file, and with instruments held above their heads, the town's bandsmen navigated a narrow channel past the trucks. The Guard was only too conscious of the responsibility he had assumed, and wanted to be free of it as soon as practical. He brought the cavalrymen to a tributary street lying to the south of the square, where the Moors remounted, while he went in search of de Rozario, but only found Sargento Pelean.

Pelean had no idea where the infantry were, but quickly assessing the urgency of the situation, and the consequences of losing his pension if the situation got any worse, decided that the cavalry must pass: between them the two policemen pushed back the crowd standing across the mouth of the street and waved the cavalrymen forward.

The cavalry entered the square at the same time as the infantry, but not from the same direction. The two columns of soldiers converged toward the Town Hall, on a collision course regulated by the tempo and rhythm of the town's band, which had resumed its efforts. The Governor and the Mayor, alerted when fresh cheering rose up from the crowd in two places at once, were initially at a loss what to do. The Governor turned to his left, and saluted the infantry. He then turned to his right, and saluted the cavalry. He could see that they would arrive in front of him at the same time, but desperate reasoning convinced him that this must be a military drill. He frantically continued to salute, first one group, then the other, the other dignitaries following his example. The only people not assured that this was the intention were the officers in the two columns, each expecting the other to bear away. Neither did; the columns converged.

At the last possible moment the two files of cavalry parted, and the infantry and bandsmen passed between them, and out of the square. The cavalry made one more circuit before they too exited, dipping their lances in tribute to the Governor as they departed, to cheers and applause from the crowd. A word in the Civil Governor's ear from his aide brought the news that the parade had been sabotaged; and that in addition to the armoured cars, every truck and even the staff car were crippled. As soon as the last of the cavalrymen were out of sight, the Governor hastily withdrew, followed by Oleanza, who, as usual, was desperate to salvage something, or blame someone.

"How? How is this possible?!" shouted the Governor, confronting Oleanza, and shaking with rage at the audacity and scale of the atrocity.

Oleanza, rapidly absorbing the latest intelligence from Mendoza, in which only sporadic words were clear to him, hastily composed a response.

"The petrol, yes the petrol, delivered today....was contaminated with sugar....the engines seized. But we have closed the street where the trucks have broken down....and are pulling them out with horse teams!"

As he spoke, Oleanza looked like a man trying to talk his way out from a firing squad; his narrow eyes darted, and he licked his lips repeatedly, not able to look the Governor fully in the face. He had built his dreams of advancement on this day, only to see them turn to ashes in a few minutes. From beyond the windows the sound reached them of jeering and old Republican battle slogans, as the Civil Guard set about the task of dispersing the crowd which only half an hour before had warmly applauded the representatives of the new order. Oleanza had to blame someone, to save his career.

"Who supplied the petrol?" snapped the Governor.

"The Army Your Excellence!" Oleanza replied emphatically, bringing a fist down into the palm of his other hand. "The fault entirely lies with the Army! They allowed saboteurs into the town!"

Unimpressed, the Governor turned about and strode off, closely followed by his aide. Still uncertain whether the firing squad was being readied, Oleanza looked blankly about him, seeing but not registering the faces of Castellon, Mendoza and Father Abarca. He broke out in a great sweat, and his heart thumped irregularly, as if it too had been sabotaged and was about to seize.

He hurried after the Governor, trotting at his side, offering reassurance that the police would ruthlessly hunt down the perpetrators, while again blaming the Army. But even his powers of locution failed him, when the Governor turned to him with clouded eyes, as if he had been addressed by a prison inmate and said: "But I hold you responsible."

The Moorish cavalry searched for the fuel truck, which they found abandoned on the road to Granada; the discarded uniforms of the soldiers from the transport corps lay where they had fallen by the road. The dignitaries made their way to the orphanage in whatever reliable transport could be requisitioned, the contaminated fuel spreading faster than the cholera through the town's water supply. As Oleanza slumped down in the back of a crowded limousine which he shared with Aguado, Bucaro and Don Rondolfo, he said despondently over and again to himself: "What have I done to deserve this? Merciful God, what have I done to deserve this?"

The Captive Summer

A Glorious And Excellent Nation

Dr Hernandez had worked at the clinic that morning, and so escaped a visit from the police demanding that he make his Mercedes available in the emergency. He spoke to no one about the incident at the fuel truck; when he returned home he went into the garage, carefully rubbed out the red crosses on the cans with a rag, and hid them under a tarpaulin.

Oleanza, angry and embittered, returned to his office in the evening. He opened his desk drawer, and after a spasm of cursing, produced a bottle of brandy and a dirty glass from its depths. He was already drunk, and past caring. He held the glass up to the light, then spat into it to clear out a layer of dust which coated the bottom. He filled the glass to the brim and drank it off in one go, swallowing hard as if he were committing a piece of tough beef to his stomach. He had worked so hard to gain the favour of the Governor, only to suffer the humiliation of seeing his prize slip away like grains of sand. He began writing, setting down the names of men whom he suspected of having Republican sympathies, men who should be taken for questioning. He stopped as suddenly as he had started, picked up his telephone and called Mendoza. Who could he blame? Someone had failed in their duty. The Army? The Civil Guard? Had he not delegated responsibility to the Civil Guard? Mendoza! Had not Mendoza's carelessness also resulted in de Rozario entering the brothel? But the accused had to be challenged in the presence of witnesses, justice demanded no less.

"And what have you found?" Oleanza asked, rolling his eyes toward Castellon, but with his question addressed elsewhere. Mendoza and de Rozario faced him across his desk, perched on creaking chairs of fragile antiquity. To emphasise his authority Oleanza was sitting in a heavy leather bound high seat which was a relic from the era of Republican mayors; it had been dragged into the room from the old council chamber to replace the customary furniture. The incident on the lawn outside Don Rondolfo's home had induced a temporary truce between the Mayor and the Party boss, but below the bluff and supine physiognomy of each, the enmity of years prevailed.

"We do not believe that this was the work of Reds from the town."

"Oh! Not from the town! And from where do you think they came?" intoned Oleanza in a voice of well practised theatrical sarcasm.

At the back of the Mayor's office, a secretary sat taking down in shorthand everything that was said. Aguado sat next to Mendoza, grateful that the comments, for once, were not directed to him. Mendoza ground his teeth, and faced his tormentor.

"We believe that guerillas are active in the mountains; some farmers have reported the theft of goats and sheep."

"No doubt for political education!" sneered Oleanza, propelling himself from his chair and walking to the window. He stood watching the square, his nose pressed to the glass.

"What prevents you apprehending these men?" asked Castellon, in an apparent attempt at impartial questioning.

"We have sent out mounted patrols from the high station, and the mountain infantry are searching along the valleys and the peaks. We will catch this scum! We will drive them down and catch them between our patrols and the Army."

"That may not happen soon enough," Castellon replied drowsily. Oleanza turned.

"Why not soon enough?" he asked, alert to any statement for which there was no immediate clear rationale. Castellon shrugged.

"Well," he offered, "do you think that the Civil Governor will wait before reporting on the incident to Madrid? It is you he blames Jose, don't forget that."

"I was not to blame for Army incompetence!" shouted Oleanza, so loudly that the secretary, a young woman, started at the sound.

"But you were ultimately responsible for security within the town," hissed Castellon, anger colouring his voice. "The papers of the men on the fuel truck were not checked! And that's why the Civil Governor will recommend your replacement!"

"The Governor has regard for my ability!"

"The Governor thinks you're a toothless whore!"

"Cojones!"

"Damn you Jose! He told me himself yesterday!"

Oleanza seemed to waver in the air, like an obelisk about to topple, stung by the severity of the insult against his masculinity. He turned to Mendoza and de Rozario, stabbing an accusatory finger at them.

"I want a curfew! I want searches of every vehicle, every suspect house! I want arrests; I don't care if you have to dig up the fucking cemetery to get suspects!"

As Mendoza walked down the steps of the Town Hall he halted, unbuttoned a breast pocket on his tunic and drew out his cigarette case. He offered a cigarette to de Rozario, took one for himself, tapping it against the case, and then taking a cigarette lighter from a pocket, lit for both of them. De Rozario noted that he seemed much older just in the course of the last day, and his hand gripped the lighter fiercely.

"And the worst of it Carlos," he said, "is that the Reds have done all this without firing a single shot at us."

De Rozario worked through the night to draw up a list of men and women who were known or suspected Republicans, starting with those who had returned from the war. He then added names from the intelligence bulletins, and lists of released prisoners. He handed five neatly typed sheets of paper to Mendoza next morning, bearing the names of more than one hundred men and twenty seven women. As he drank coffee Mendoza read, occasionally looking up at his subordinate.

"You have Enrique Morales here, why?"

"He's a blackmarketeer, his file says that he sold cigarettes to Republican troops."

Mendoza pursed his lips.

"No, take him off the list. Felipe Escolar, the undertaker, why is he here?"

"His brother fought for the Republicans."

"Who is Pablo Villasellos?"

"He is a school teacher, he arrived here earlier in the year. He has been linked to a fugitive arrested in Madrid."

Mendoza nodded his assent to the inclusion of their names. He did not sign any forms or documents to be put before a judge, simply nodded to each name to be included, or shook his head if the name was to be struck off.

"Do you know who Manuel Ibanez is?" Mendoza asked.

"He is a petty thief, steals eggs from the farmers, but doesn't possess the wit to take anything of greater value."

"He is also an informer. Take his name off the list, but speak to him, find out if he saw anything while he was busy raiding hen-coops. But," and he pointed now at a point at the bottom of one of the pages, "leave the names of Antonio and Jesus Gomez. Those bastards haven't caught a fish these last four years!"

He gave the pages back to de Rozario, the names of the condemned alongside the names of the fortunate.

"Thank you senor. Is there anything else?"

Mendoza reflected, the coffee cup held close to his lips, his eyes poised between the surface of the aromatic brew and a point in space beside his subordinate.

"Interrogate anyone breaking the curfew."

The imposition of the curfew was the immediate and universal sign of the determination of the authorities to suspend what passed for normal life until they had captured those responsible. Notification of the ban was pinned up and plastered across the town, obliterating the notices of the parade and even Franco's image. The raiders had become folk heroes, and were referred to now as *Los Bandidos del Azucar*: the Sugar Bandits. That night the first curfew patrol set out from the barracks. It was comprised of ten men: de Rozario, Pelean, and eight Guards. People needed no encouragement to obey the curfew, as they did not wish to be interrogated by a rifle butt.

Before departing, de Rozario had decided that he should inspect the patrol, ostensibly to ensure that their weapons were in proper working order. He had another motive however: such was the immediate paranoia he could not trust that the Reds would not play their trick again. Pelean drew the men to attention in the yard; eight rifles and eight sets of pouches and belts gleaming in the crimson light. Satisfied, he turned and approached the nervous young man who keenly felt the slur on the reputation of the police of Oleanza's comments.

"Is the patrol ready sargento? Let's be quick about this!"

The inspection was perfunctory; and comprised repeated swift machine like movements, as de Rozario considered each man from head to toe, paying close attention only to the face of each. His Napoleonic address was similarly brief.

"Remember, it is now the time of the curfew, therefore no one should be on the streets. Arrest for questioning anyone you find, without exception. Now follow me."

They filed out of the yard and onto the deserted street. They were opposed only by two wild dogs, which sniffed the ground as they trotted along, oblivious to the posters proclaiming the curfew, and hungry for any scraps of food in the gutters.

Don Octavio sat down at his table, across which he had thrown a plain cloth of garish orange. His tableware was rudimentary, comprising a glass, a spoon and a knife. He had prepared a soup of watery potato for his supper, augmented by an onion, and a piece of bread. The spoon was of poor quality alloy; if he touched the tip of one of his teeth with its edge he detected a slight sensation, as electrons flowed. Today he had drunk very little, on account of the curfew, forcing him to abandon *La Alverjilla* and return to his apartment. He had prepared the soup on the hob in the little alcove where he cooked, and set down the steaming bowl on the table. He looked around him once he had taken his seat; satisfied that he was not sharing his meal with any uninvited guests, he closed his eyes and said grace. He opened one eye, and next the other, picked up his spoon and ladled some of the hot water with scraps of onion and potato onto it. He raised the spoon to his mouth, raising his eyes as he did so.

The child who now sat opposite him, had her chin cupped in her hands, and eyes that filled with wonder at the food he was about to eat. What soup Don Octavio did not choke on, he spat out in a fine spray. Throwing the spoon into the air and letting out a cry like that of a baby stung by a bee, he fell backwards and onto the floor. He pulled the chair in front of him as a shield, and cowered, looking between its legs to see where the child had got to. He remained like this for several minutes, visibly shaking, and gripping the legs of the chair with both hands. He looked to his apartment door, its surface a lurid mix of flaking paint obscured by a jacket and his hat, which both hung from a hook. Satisfied that he was now alone again, he got up and launched himself, as a drowning man will toward a piece of wreckage in the sea, at the door. Without looking back into the room, he pulled on one sleeve of the jacket, and then his hat, sideways.

In order to open the door he had to step to the side so turning around to face the room. Although his nerves were now shot to pieces, he knew that he had to do this, and summoned up the courage from dwindling reserves. The girl, who could have been no older than seven or eight years, was now standing by the table, and observed him intently. Tears filled the old man's eyes.

"I'm sorry, I can't help you," he cried. "Please, please, leave me alone!"

Then he ran out, the sounds of his feet echoing on the stairs. The curfew had then been in force for over two hours.

He did not travel far before one of the curfew patrol, lounging in the shadow of a building, spotted him, trotting along in the street, and shouted a challenge. The old man, the epitome of a non-Olympian, trotted a little faster, the empty jacket sleeve flapping around him, puffing heavily. He turned into a side street, and the Civil Guard now gave chase, heavy boots pounding on the stones. As the policeman reached the place where Don Octavio had disappeared from sight, Sargento Pelean came up behind him.

"This way! This way! We can get behind him!"

The two policemen ran in another direction, their rifles cocked and ready to fire.

"I saw them! I fucking told you I saw them! Do you not believe me? Am I a mad man?! They're here! They're in the town! They'll kill us all in our beds! But they won't kill me! I'll slice all those Moorish bastards!"

De Rozario and a Guard faced Alfredo Luzano. He was drunk and they had heard him swearing a street away. In one hand he held a bottle, in the other, an open razor. He swung at them with the razor, throwing his arm in wide lethal arcs which caught the light from the street lamps. When he desisted, he either spat at them or cursed, and then threatened to blind them with the bottle: he was troubled by visions of Moorish cavalrymen.

"Lozano, listen to me! They were soldiers, not tribesmen!" shouted de Rozario from behind the safety of the barrel of his pistol.

"No! No! I saw them! In the town with their horses! *Vive La Muerte*! Let them come! I'll kill them all!"

De Rozario could have shot him dead, but he knew that Lozano was a Falangist; they could have rushed him, but Lozano could have cut either of them with the razor, so they waited. They stood outside the shuttered cafe beside the harbour; Lozano made an ineffectual attempt to put the bottle down on one of the desolate tables, but it only toppled over. He turned to pick it up and fell headlong. The Guard leapt forward to prise the razor from his grasp, but Lozano was too quick for him, and still lying on the ground, brought the blade across the Guard's shin, cleaving it to the bone. The man fell screaming, clutching at his leg as blood spurted from the wound. And with the agility of a cat Lozano regained his feet and faced de Rozario before he could intervene.

"I have never forgotten what we were taught! Spain is a glorious and excellent nation! Vive La Muerte! Death to the Moors!"

Then he too fell, toppling forward, to lie unconscious on the ground at de Rozario's feet. Pelean stood in his place, his rifle butt raised at chest height. He moved the butt in a small circular motion, and winked at the young officer.

"And it's as effective at dealing with difficult women teniente," he said, with a wide grin.

Close Call

Don Octavio trotted through the echoing streets, his thin legs supporting his bulging stomach. He heard a voice, but assuming that the visions had now gained the power of speech, he would not look back, and he would not stop. The shuttered streets echoed to only his feet, but once or twice he was aware of blinds hastily pulled back as he went by, the inhabitants of the houses curious to know who should be so reckless as to challenge the police. Eventually he stopped outside the house of Dr Hernandez, still with one arm of his jacket in its sleeve, his hat askew; and knocked.

When Dr Hernandez opened the door to him, and seeing the flapping empty sleeve at the side of his body, he admitted him immediately, assuming that he had suffered a serious injury. He called for Senora Lopez, while he brought his friend into the parlour.

"Octavio, what happened to your arm?" he anxiously asked as he unbuttoned the garment, only to reveal the missing arm lying across Don Octavio's chest.

"Saw another...could not stay...ran...still strong as a young bull," and he slapped his stomach with both hands, "this did not stop me, did not get in the way, yes...ran, through the streets."

Don Octavio would not, or could not, answer any of the doctor's further questions, but it was clear that he had suffered another hallucination. When Senora Lopez entered the room, Dr Hernandez met her alarmed look, with one of sad resignation.

"Doctor, he has no right to bother you. He is a drunk, everyone says he stinks of drink, and staggers through the streets."

"Yes Senora Lopez, you are right," he said, "but it was not always so. Let's get him to bed. In the morning," and he paused, "he will need a bath, and a change of clothes before he goes home."

"Doctor, you are not obligated to him for all time," she replied, a little colour rising in her face.

"Oh, but I am Senora Lopez. He is my friend, and I am his. He was here that morning; he comforted her, and he tried to save her. I think that Constanza's death hurt him more than I. Yes, I think that. If I had been here, she might have lived. As it was, I was helping others."

They only mentioned the death of Dr Hernandez's wife infrequently. On the morning that she had suffered the heart attack, Don Octavio called by, on chance, to borrow a book. Dr Hernandez was away attending to a farmer's wife who was in labour with a breach birth. Senora Lopez found Constanza's body when she went to the door to admit Don Octavio. He stayed with the dying woman, while Senora Lopez made frantic efforts to find Dr Hernandez or Dr Marin. By the time that help came, she was dead. Since that time, no matter how harshly others judged him, Dr Hernandez would not speak against his friend. That he suffered the hallucinations more frequently as his drinking increased saddened him, but for the sake of his wife's memory he would not turn him away. Don Octavio was put to bed, safe from either pursuing visions or policemen.

When Sargento Pelean offered his advice to de Rozario, he was hinting at a change in the officer's behaviour which originated the day they had stopped Andrea at the roadside. As Pelean was the only witness, only he could guess why the young man who had walked up to the door of El Faro, was not the same man who walked back to the car and resumed the journey. There was a dossier on Arturo Bonar; de Rozario's questioning of the sergeant as to the family history progressed to a referral to the files during the night that de Rozario spent preparing the list of those to be taken for questioning. The yellowing papers that contained the dry facts of Arturo's past and culpability, the reports on his incarceration in France, the list of crimes with which he would be charged if he ever returned to Spain, had only passing reference to his wife, and gave no indication as to her character. The documents, already exuding the dry mustiness of a neglected archive, presumed guilt in both spouses, but could only lay one charge at Consuelo: that she had worked as a nursing auxiliary with the Republican army field hospital. As he sat reading the official version of Arturo and Consuelo's life, her image came to him: the curve of her body, her smell, of which he had previously no recollection, and the sound of her voice.

He questioned Pelean, he thought with subtlety, over the next days. But the sergeant guessed the true cause; he was not duped by his superior's apparent interest in those who grew food on the neighbouring terraces.

"But they could be aiding the guerillas, taking them food!" de Rozario said with grave conviction. This explanation did not strike Pelean as likely, the people were forced to work the narrow ridge bordering the ilex and cypress trees because they were hungry and needed food for their own families. As a pretext for visiting the area, regularly, he had to admit however that it was excellent.

He counted off the days until de Rozario made his next move. Pelean dared not give any indication that he suspected that de Rozario had become infatuated by a married woman, especially one married to an exiled Republican; as he was due a short period of leave, he declined the request to accompany him on his next reconnaissance.

The day de Rozario had selected to renew his acquaintance with

Consuelo began inauspiciously: she was not at home. She had not gone into town, but conscious since Andrea's second visit that they might now be under suspicion, had gone with Rafael to visit a neighbouring farmer and his family in a display of normality. The route took them beyond the ridge and into the deep mass of trees, then onto a track that climbed in the clear air over the next saddle of land and out of sight. The semblance of the old domestic routine was further reinforced by permitting Maria to bring her eldest child, Manolito, to the house that day, as his grandmother was taking his two sisters on the bus to Granada to visit other relatives. Mindful of Dr Hernandez's warning about the children betraying them, Manolito was given strict instructions as to which parts of the house he was allowed in, on the grounds that his mother did not want to search for him in the unoccupied rooms. The little boy loved Consuelo, whom he called his aunt; reunited with her after a long absence, and showering her with many kisses, he then ran down the steps into the garden to play. Consuelo watched the child before she departed.

"Madam, nothing will happen. Tomas is in the safe room. No one will visit, and if they do, they can wait here until you return."

"Of course," but Consuelo had been upset by the policeman's visit, "I am just a little anxious Maria."

Maria was attending to the laundry when the police car drew up outside the house; she did not hear the dull cracking as the doors opened, or the sound of boots as de Rozario and his driver walked over the crushed stones to the entrance of the house. Wiping wet and soapy hands on her apron she made her way from the laundry room at the sound of the bell, curious that Consuelo should return so soon, and not re-enter the house by the gate in the lower garden wall.

"Good morning," said de Rozario, alerted immediately that his appearance should produce stark alarm in the woman's face, "I wish to see Dona Consuelo. Is she at home?"

"No...no senor, she is visiting a neighbour."

"Then I'll wait for her," and he stepped past her, then stopped, "please show me the way senora."

Regaining her composure while drying her hands hurriedly on the apron, she led de Rozario onto the terrace, explained Consuelo's absence, invited him to sit and asked if he would like something to drink.

"Coffee, if you have it."

She nodded; as she walked away Manolito ran up from the garden, full of laughter until he saw the Civil Guard officer sitting under the awning, then he fell silent.

"My son senor, he comes here to play sometimes."

"Yes mamma, but not for a long time," said the boy.

Intrigued by the intelligence de Rozario sat upright.

"Not for a long time? Why is that?"

"I...I meant not since last time, senor," and the boy stood close to his mother, attempting to burrow into her body to regain the safety of her womb.

"And a fine garden to play in!" said de Rozario casting a hand over the lemon trees and the avenue of cypresses.

"Yes senor, it is a fine garden. Please excuse me."

Maria led the boy away, and de Rozario sat back to enjoy the view for the first time, as Tom had once done.

He attempted to make himself comfortable but was irked that his holster and pistol had ridden up and pressed into his side. He stood and unbuckled the belt, drawing the loops by which the holster hung through the polished leather until it was free. He placed the holster on the table next to his hat and rebuckled the belt. As he looked up, the thought occurred to him that it would be an excellent life to possess both the house and the woman who lived there; and he decided that he should survey this new domain.

In the kitchen, Maria scolded Manolito, making him promise to remember to remain silent in the presence of any policeman. Then she hugged the boy to her, ruffling his hair over and again. He sat quietly while she prepared the coffee; it was only his look of wide eyed alarm when she opened the bag of coffee beans, that saved her from facing further questioning as to how they could obtain real coffee in a time of such shortage.

"Here is your coffee senor. Of course it is only ground lentils, so I apologise now for the taste. Would you like something else?"

"No senora, no thank you. Tell me please," he paused, judging her reaction, "who maintains the garden?"

"That is Rafael, senor."

"Rafael...Rafael," he repeated slowly as if the name were familiar, but he could not set a face to it.

"Rafael Sabio senor, he is the other servant here. He is Cuban."

"Ah yes, the Cuban," and he drank some of the lentil coffee, trying hard to disguise his displeasure.

"Will there be anything else senor?" she asked with panic rising within her.

"No thank you senora, I will wait until Dona Consuelo returns."

When the police car had advanced through the trees, Tom, now hidden in a locked room, had done as he had been told, and stretched out on a mattress. He lay there for some time, occasionally looking at his wrist watch, and blowing hard to relieve the tension. The safe room was in the unoccupied part of the house, and possessed a second door to the steps of the tower. With the door to the gallery locked, he could retreat onto the steps and either climb the tower to the turret, or descend to the courtyard. If he was forced to do either he knew that detection and arrest would be imminent.

Just as he was lulled by the treacherous silence, he heard the first footsteps on the gallery. They were slow and deliberate, and made, he guessed, by someone who did not know the house. He started upright, as the handle of the door to the next room turned, his blood rushing and thumping now through his ears. The footsteps moved toward him, and stopped. He stared hard at the door; the old ornate handle first moved slowly down, and then rose upward. His head jolted slightly with the force of the pounding blood. The footsteps resumed, but fading now into the fabric of the stone. He lay down again, wondering why he had not been surprised to have lasted so long. Should he stay or move? Was the house being searched, or subject to casual inspection? He swung upward, stepped lightly to the tower door, and let himself out.

Maria was frantic; Manolito had vanished from the kitchen, and she wasted time looking for him, before deciding to return on some pretence to discreetly observe de Rozario. She went to the reception room, and proceeded to dust a clean bookcase. The policeman was walking in the garden, and she saw him amongst the fruit trees. She gasped each time he disappeared from view, and let out a sigh when he reappeared.

The lumber room confronted Tom as a collection of broken furniture covered in dust sheets. He had decided to climb, although that meant cutting off any possible escape, unless he jumped from the window. He forced his way past the groaning wardrobes and barricades of piled chairs, and sat in a prepared space at the back. Too late he had realised that he had no key, so could not secure the door, and cursed himself. For the second time he heard footsteps, but lighter than the first set. He tried very hard to stop breathing, so as to become both silent and invisible, but the light tap, tap, tap on the steps continued. The handle turned, but this time the door yielded. If it is a policeman, Tom thought, it is better that I take him, before he has a chance to draw his gun on me. He tensed his body, ready to jump forward, and strike his adversary. A small head appeared around the door, it was Manolito.

Angry and alarmed, Tom beckoned to the boy to come forward. The child scampered beside him, clearly delighted to have a new playfriend. They exchanged hurried whispers.

"Who are you?"

"I'm Tomas, who are you?"

"I'm Manolito."

"What are you doing here?"

"I'm hiding from the policeman, my mother said I should not speak to him."

"Where is he?"

"I saw him walking on the gallery."

Then more footsteps, heavier, rising toward them. Tom leaned back, but with too much force, and upset the tall wardrobe at his back, setting it rocking slowly. Still crouching, he raised his arms to steady it, straining against the deadweight. He could hear something stir; with a sickening feeling he realised that its contents had dislodged. The movement of the wardrobe had thrown dust into the atmosphere, which he now inhaled. He struggled against the toppling wardrobe and the pungent dust laden air in his head. He screwed his face in an attempt to close his nostrils but could not withhold the breaking air dam; as his head, fully cocked, threatened to come down in a sharp action like that of a hammer on the striking plate of a bullet, Manolito's hand shot upward, and the child's small but powerful fingers closed around his nose. Tom sneezed: the pistol did not fire. The boy laughed silently, but Tom shook his head urgently; the wardrobe regained equilibrium, and they sat together, watching the door with eyes that bulged outward like marbles.

On the steps de Rozario halted; he thought that he had heard a noise from above, but had also regard to noises from the courtyard below. He had strayed over the building when Maria had departed after serving the coffee; what he saw impressed him, but he judged that Maria might return at any moment. To avoid an embarrasing encounter he turned back, descending the steps to the garden as Maria entered the reception room. Tom and Manolito waited until they were quite certain that the listener had withdrawn.

"What a game senor!" said the boy.

"Tell no one Manolito," and Tom's eyes pleaded with him.

They shook hands, and the boy scampered away and into the stairwell. This is no game, thought Tom, as he dusted himself down, this is no game.

The Captive Summer

Appearances

An hour passed; with reluctance de Rozario decided to leave, there being no sign of Consuelo, and his interest in the garden and building waning in the dry heat. He woke his driver, who was asleep against one of the ilex trees, with a kick, and climbed into the car. At the road junction he looked back once, but now the house was obscured by the trees and clouds of dust thrown up by the tyres, and he turned his gaze to the shining road.

Maria sank down in a chair in the reception room, and wiped tears from her face. She regained her nerves with a glass of sherry, and then inspected the house and gardens for signs of the policeman's presence. Manolito had returned to the kitchen, but made no attempt to save himself from a beating, by explaining that he had been hiding with the man in the turret room. She left the whimpering child on a chair, with orders now to neither speak nor move, and went in search of Tom. She ran to the door of the safe room, and unlocking it found him sitting cross legged on the mattress.

"Has he gone Maria?" he asked.

"Oh! Tomas! He walked all over the house, through the garden, outside this room!"

"I know Maria, he also followed me when I went up to the turret room," but seeing great alarm on her face added quickly, "don't be concerned he didn't find me."

"I prayed to the Virgin, I prayed over and again, that he should not find you."

"Then perhaps the Virgin sent your son to me."

"Manolito! What was he doing there?"

"He was hiding from the policeman, he sat with me in the turret room. He," and he ran a finger over his nose, not quite able to bring himself to fully explain the circumstances, "encouraged the policeman to go away."

"He didn't say where he was!"

"I told him to say nothing. I had to."

Maria now understood the child's silence. They walked down together, until Tom stopped and touching her arm, added.

"Are you sure that he has gone?"

"Yes. I heard the engine senor."

"But could others be watching the house from the trees?"

She hesitated in replying; Tom returned to the hiding place, and waited for the return of Consuelo and Rafael.

It was not until the early evening that they arrived, Consuelo's satisfaction with the day evaporating as soon as she stepped across the threshold. Maria tearfully retold the story, showing her where de Rozario had walked, and even holding up the cup from which he had drunk.

The news of the visit confirmed her worst fears. Her home had been violated; his eyes had spied on her life, his hands had touched her possessions, his thoughts had placed himself in her company, perhaps in her bedroom. Dejected and angry, she looked out from the terrace. Rafael went out again, by the gate in the lower garden wall, and made a circuit round to the front of the house. Satisfied that the police were not watching, he returned and released Tom.

"May the Virgin protect us! He must know, he must know!" Consuelo repeated, her brow furrowing into three distinct ridges.

"Perhaps not Consuelo," said Tom, "if he was looking for the saboteurs he would have properly searched the house, if he suspected that I was here, then he would have challenged you. He came to see you, and he came not on official business."

"What can we do?" she asked.

"In any event I have to get away now, I cannot threaten your safety. What about the fishermen?"

"Rafael, we must find Antonio and Jesus!"

Rafael nodded, then said, "I agree madam. I will go to the town. But this policeman may become suspicious because you so rarely leave the house. You must go to the town, and let people see you there. It may draw him away."

She stood with her hands cupped over the lower part of her face, then let them drop.

"I could ask to see Don Rondolfo," she said.

Maria had come into the room with a tray bearing a coffee pot and cups, and exchanged glances of surprise with Rafael.

"Who is he?" asked Tom.

"He was a friend of my father, and knows my uncle. I can write to ask whether I can meet him to," and momentarily she struggled to think of the necessary pretext, "discuss selling some land to him! He owns thousands of hectares, but never loses the opportunity to acquire more."

The civil war had created jagged fault lines in Spanish society; her uncle, the judge responsible for her meeting Arturo, had become a Falangist, and knew many of the wealthy landowners in Andalucia. This connection ensured that she would be granted a meeting.

"Will he agree to see you?" asked Tom.

"If he thinks that he can cheat me out of part of my husband's estate, he will see me!"

There was one thing more that had to be discussed.

"What about the boy?" Tom asked, watching Maria's reaction. Manolito had been confined to the kitchen, as if he had become the house's second captive, and had remained on the chair where his mother placed him.

"I am sorry madam, deeply sorry," she said.

"Maria, what is there to be sorry about?" said Consuelo. "He saved us today. Bring him here."

Maria departed, and returned a few minutes later, dragging Manolito by the hand. The boy reminded Tom of his own nephew; his large brown eyes bore the signs of crying, and it was clear from his demeanour that he expected the adults to be angry with him. Consuelo knelt down and opened her arms to him, and he ran to her, burying his face in her breasts. She cradled him, then taking him by the hand, pointed to Tom.

"Manolito, do you know who this man is?"

He shook his head vigorously.

"Yes you do Manolito. Don't be afraid, this man is my friend. Do you know his name?"

"Tomas," he replied, looking at Tom with suspicion.

"Tomas is your friend also. Will you be his friend?"

Manolito shook his head vigorously again.

"Oh! Manolito! Tomas has to stay at my house," and now she turned the boy around, and looked deep into his face, "but no one can know that my friend is here. No one. I am so proud of you Manolito, so proud that you did not betray him today. Would you ever betray him?"

The boy looked from Tom to Consuelo, and shook his head a third time. Consuelo kissed him, and Manolito skipped back to Maria; as he passed, Tom ran one hand through the boy's hair, and with the other he held his fingers to his nose, as the child had done. Manolito looked up, and for the first time he laughed, and returned the salute.

Consuelo wrote a letter, in which she alluded to her desire to meet Don Rondolfo, hinting that it was in relation to a legal issue, but one in which she was invested with full power of attorney on Arturo's behalf. She believed that he would immediately understand that she needed to dispose of part of her husband's property. Franco's rise to power had ushered in a return to conservative Catholic family values in Spain; Consuelo was not considered the equal of Don Rondolfo, but he would see her because she could act on behalf of her husband. His reply was gracious, and welcoming.

The meeting was to take place in the late morning, two days after the receipt of the reply. Consuelo and Rafael set out for San Cristobal before the heat became too strong. As the town came into view around the headland she surveyed the red roofed houses with disdain; to her mind they were undertaking a journey away from civilisation not toward it, and she prayed that the cool glittering sea beyond the rocks would rise up and wash the filth and contamination of the new Spain away, and return to them their former lives.

They had been on the road a short time when a Citroen passed them, but soon decelerated and stopped. Apprehensive, Consuelo continued to walk, Rafael following close behind her. A door opened, and a young man stepped onto the road and turned to face them: it was de Rozario. Consuelo stopped, and turned briefly to see that Rafael was still close with her. Her mouth drying rapidly, and the vein in her neck pulsing as if regulated by a frantic metronome, she watched the vision in green cloth approach her. His sudden appearance, at the very moment that she set off to meet Don Rondolfo could not be a co-incidence, she reasoned. She looked quickly to her left and right, but neither the jagged rocks nor the sea gave ready sanctuary. She had not expected to be arrested here, on a squalid stretch of road where the dry wind tugged at the grasses; a lonely place, where sump oil stained the ground. She waited for de Rozario to emerge through the heat haze; she lowered her head, which tipped her face under a sliver of shade from her hat, and awaited her fate.

But de Rozario simply walked up to her, paying scant regard to the presence of Rafael, saluted, and enquired with grave politeness whether he could be of assistance.

"May I ask where you are going Dona Consuelo?"

"I have business in town teniente."

"If I may say, it is too hot to walk all the way. I would deem it an honour if I could place the Civil Guard at your disposal."

In the heat haze, the Citroen wavered in her sight like a hearse; she was scared, but she would see this through, her ordeal was slight compared to that of others, and she yet had Rafael with her.

"Thank you teniente, but the exercise would be beneficial."

"Do you ride?" he asked.

"Yes, by which I mean I used to. We have no horses now."

"I ride," he said excitedly, "I ride in the mountains, I ride with a patrol, through streams and over the passes. That is exercise Dona Consuelo; walking in the heat of the day is an imposition, even an outrage."

Consuelo wavered; to refuse his offer of help might arouse further suspicion, and as he stood before her, a boy dreaming of manhood, with his lean shining face, she began to doubt that he knew anything.

"I would not want to distract you from your duties teniente," she said.

"But assisting you would be my duty," he replied.

She relented, and they walked slowly together to the car, as if beginning a courtship. She took her seat with him; Rafael sat beside the driver, a man with the face of a prizefighter, who had propped the muzzle of his rifle on the dashboard. As the car pulled away again the rifle slipped and fell toward Rafael, who caught it cleanly, and returned it to an upright position. He looked at the Guard and said: "It's as well it wasn't loaded," but received no reply. Rafael assumed that the man resented having to share the vehicle with him.

"As you know Dona Consuelo," de Rozario began, "I visited your home again recently. I wanted to ask you some questions concerning the activity of guerillas, and to warn you."

At the sound of these words, Consuelo both relaxed and tensed. She wondered whether the invitation had been a ploy after all, and hazarded a glance at the door lock. She would have made an elegant fugitive among the rocks which plunged toward the sea. Looking ahead, the road clung to the hillside where it had been blasted and hewn twenty years before. There was barely enough room for two vehicles to pass, and to her left the rust coloured rock rose in huge steps. The vehicle rocked and whined as it made its way; the thick set head of the driver inclining one way, then the other as the twisting road tested the little mechanical shell.

"Warn us teniente? Are we in danger?"

"You may be. We are hunting for a gang; ruthless, dangerous men."

"I heard that they are all starving and steal only food," she replied, trying to conceal her amusement at this attempt to impress her.

"Even for food they will kill. They attacked a farmhouse near Cartagena, killed the farmer, raped his wife; all for two hams and a sack of potatoes. A disgraceful crime."

He was unskilled, she thought, and his sexual reference, of a vile nature: the violation of a farmer's wife, an atrocity against which he would protect her, if only she would grant him access to her bed. His intention became clearer to her; he wanted to seduce her, to replace her husband. This boy, no, this awful youth, wanted to become her lover. For the first time she became aware of her sexual allure, and her sexual power, over him. She wondered whether he had been with any woman, whether or not payment was made. And she also from that moment, began to believe that de Rozario did, after all, suspect nothing of her secret guest.

"But you are taking action to find these men?" she asked, for the first time looking at him directly.

"Of course Dona Consuelo, we have patrols, and you may see my men from time to time," he replied.

"Surely teniente," she said coyly, "you have more important duties than protecting one isolated farmhouse?"

"There is no higher duty," he said, looking casually beyond her to the sea. The car had now reached the outskirts of the town, and she was conscious that some people might be alarmed to see her, arrest being a common hazard. At her request they stopped by the harbour, so that Rafael could ostensibly make his way to the hardware store, then to a seed merchant. De Rozario was insistent that they convey her to her final destination, and when she relented and advised that she had a meeting with Don Rondolfo, he was suitably impressed.

The car swept along the drive of the villa and halted. De Rozario himself exited and opened the door for her, saluting impeccably. As he took his leave, he assured her of the protection of the Civil Guard, at all times. She walked away, the tension of the encounter subsiding.

"Protection for me, my husband, and for my English airman," she said under her breath as she walked away from him, a faint and lingering smile on her lips.

The Captive Summer

In An Andalucian Garden

Consuelo was greeted by Don Rondolfo's steward, who was resplendent in a starched white jacket, and reeked of rose water. As she walked behind him to the reception room, she noticed that the jacket exhibited no fluidity in movement whatsoever, obliging him to hold his arms a little from his body. She normally did not smoke, but when he offered her the silver cigarette box, she accepted, an action that brought Arturo to her mind; and she smiled to herself as she took the cigarette. The room was decorated in a Spanish baronial style, with an immense fireplace over which hung a painting of a group of hunters on horseback; she did not doubt that the ferocious men depicted were some of Don Rondolfo's ancestors.

A young man with crooked teeth and spectacles came out of Don Rondolfo's study, nodded in her direction and was shown out of the house by the steward. It was Carlos Lupion, with whom Don Rondolfo was developing an understanding with regard to the minimum price for grain. In truth, whether the official price was two pesetas or two pesetas and twenty centimos per kilo, was of little significance, as most grain was sold on the black market at higher prices; and Lupion would be rewarded for not querying too assiduously discrepancies in the records of the size of the harvest. She finished the cigarette hurriedly, allowing herself the luxury of exhaling a plume of smoke, which settled her nerves.

Don Rondolfo exhibited a graciousness only granted to those who have not had to work for their wealth; when he bent to kiss her hand the scent of rose water filled the atmosphere around his mane of white hair, and she wondered whether he and his steward used the same brand. He directed her to the terrace, where a table had been prepared for lunch.

As they ate, he made a point of referring to Lupion and his work for the SNT, by way of introducing the subject of the value, and potential sale, of land. Now more relaxed about the nature of de Rozario's interest in her, Consuelo had spent some time thinking of an alternative need for her to seek the landowner's help.

"Don Rondolfo," she began, "what do you know about goats?"

He stroked one side of his moustache with slow care.

"Stinking creatures, but they give good milk, and the meat is palatable."

"How easy is it to demonstrate ownership of them?"

"Do you have goats Dona Consuelo?" he asked, aware that there was no stock left on Arturo's estate.

"We appear to have acquired some. That was the issue I wanted to speak to you about," his look of surprise amused her, and she detected a little disappointment, "they appeared one morning, a small herd, that must have wandered from the mountain pastures."

"Oh!" he replied, not certain what expertise he could direct to the problem.

In truth there had been only one goat, a kid, that had become detached from its mother. Rafael caught it, and carried it across his shoulders back to the neighbouring farm from where it had strayed.

"They seem happy on our land," she rapidly improvised, "and livestock is so scarce, I do not want to give them up. Should I see the notary?"

As de Rozario had insisted on driving her to the town, so Don Rondolfo insisted on making his limousine available to return her to El Faro. His steward also provided the services of chauffeur, and changed now into a jacket of sober grey, he drove Consuelo home; his head, as she noted, also swayed from side to side as the powerful saloon swept around the snaking road. She sat in one corner, an arm draped on the back of the seat, her hat beside her; she suppressed a bout of giggling, and found that she was amused with life for the first time in many months. Her daring lie, to enquire of Don Rondolfo how she might purloin property rightfully belonging to someone else, suggested to her that in spite of the aridity of life there were still moments of joy, and this buoyed her soul.

Rafael had returned separately. His search for Antonio and Jesus was fruitless; no one claimed to know where they were, and he did not pursue the issue with the fishermen. The first of the arrests had taken place, and each man he spoke to was sullen and silent by turns. It was dangerous to be seen speaking in the open. One fisherman, Ignacio Quiros, who sometimes worked with the Gomez brothers, spat a few words out of the side of his mouth as he sat gutting squid at the quayside, and refused even to look at Rafael.

That evening Dr Hernandez visited them. The worst of the cholera outbreak had passed, and with what he called a cynical irony, he noted that the recent efforts to clean and disinfect the streets had contributed to the containment of the disease. He sat with eyes closed in the garden bower, waiting for Consuelo. The sickly sweet perfume of the jasmine competed against the slow swishing of the boughs of the fruit trees for his attention; he imagined the delicate petals slipping through the breeze as if caressed by the fingertips of angels. Hearing footsteps he opened his eyes once more, in time to see Tom appear and take up a seat opposite him.

"Hola Tomas!"

"Hola Dr Hernandez!"

"The flowers are talking Tomas, they say that life is good!"

The doctor's face was dappled from the sunlight which fell in shafts through the boughs of the trees. In the shade beside him he nurtured a glass of lemonade, from which he took brief sips. Tom also had a glass, and placed it on the ground.

"The flowers are optimists doctor."

"That is their disposition. When the sun shines they turn and embrace it; when it is hidden they wait for it to emerge once more. Remember that."

"I will try to doctor," he replied, as he caressed the back of his right hand, "although other thoughts claim my attention."

"Then discipline your mind Tomas. Or talk to Rafael, his philosophy is quite unique."

"What sustains you Dr Hernandez?"

The doctor looked to the ground, and then up at Tom again.

"In truth?" he said. "Poetry and," and now with a rare smile, "a cigar and a glass of brandy after dinner."

"Do you believe that life endures?"

Aware of the real issue, the doctor became more serious.

"Are we talking about your life, or life in the general use of the word?"

"Let's talk about my life first."

"Quite understandable. I do not have a full diagnosis Tomas, you know that much. I am pleased that you have not suffered a spasm for, four weeks?"

"Five."

"Good. That's good, five weeks. Your symptoms are abating, the sensory and motor functions are returning. You may yet make a full recovery."

"But the RAF doctors may not let me fly again."

"I cannot say what the English doctors will advise. We Spanish have a saying - *Vive La Muerte*! Long live death! It is a statement of passionate conviction, but in all honesty its sentiment cannot have endeared Spain to the International Committee of the Red Cross." He laughed again. "It is a sentiment at odds with what we all believe, regardless of whether we believe or do not believe in the endurance of life in any sense beyond the physical. Life is profound, and unique, and sometimes brief. Celebrate it Tomas."

"Do you believe in another life?"

"Rafael does, and certainly my friend Don Octavio Montero, although he is regarded as a madman and shunned for his pains. For me? Have you read Tolstoy? Do you know *War and Peace*?

Both men laughed at the unintended joke.

"No doctor, I haven't read it. Too much time taken up studying Air Ministry pamphlets on pilot etiquette. And I prefer Shakespeare anyway."

"Well you should. In any event, somewhere within the labyrinth, Pierre Bezukhov undergoes a crisis of belief. He is on a journey, after taking part in a duel against a man called Dolohov. He is waiting for fresh horses before he can continue his journey. You understand the metaphor?" Tom nodded. "Good. How does that passage continue?" and he stopped, pressing his hands down onto the bench as if the knowledge were contained in the timbers and could be drawn up through his palms. "Yes, I remember most of it," and sitting back he recited from memory. "*What should one love and what hate? What is life for, and what am I? What is life? What is death? What is the power that controls it all? And there was no answer to any of these questions, except the one illogical reply that in no way answered them. This reply was: 'One dies and it's all over. One dies and either finds out about everything or ceases asking'.*"

The doctor's features had softened in reciting the words, as if they had provided him a release from the memory of the first time he had witnessed a woman die in childbirth, to the young men in bloodied lorries during the civil war.

"We will know, but not while we are yet living," said Tom.

"Yes. There will be a moment of truth for each of us Tomas. We will either find the answer, or stop asking the question. Can you wait until then?"

"I don't know if I can."

"We all have to."

"There's faith doctor."

"There is also torment. There is holding a dying child, and trying to understand why a loving God would take that child away from its mother. Who has the greater need Tomas? The mother who wants to love the fruit of her body, or God?"

"I can't answer that question."

"I don't expect that you should."

Consuelo joined them, bearing on a tray a glass pitcher of opaque juice with fat slices of lemon spinning around an invisible axis. She refilled their glasses, then filled her own.

"And what is the news tonight?" Dr Hernandez asked, aware that Consuelo would have listened to the news bulletin on Radio Seville.

"Oh! Let me think," she said, tapping a finger to her forehead. "Of course! Axis triumph in Russia!"

"Another one?" replied the doctor in tones of mock surprise.

"Another day, another victory for Fascism!" she replied.

"And how is General Franco?"

"Alive."

"The Hippocratic oath forbids me to pass comment."

"Were you aware," asked Tom, "that English people helped General Franco escape from the Canaries before the mutiny?"

"Yes, but don't blame yourself Tomas. Many Englishmen came to fight for us," said the doctor, drinking down the lemonade.

"I did not know this!" exclaimed Consuelo.

"It's true," said Tom. "Franco escaped the Canaries in a chartered DeHavilland Dragon Rapide with an English pilot. In order to get to the islands without being suspected, three English people made the journey in the aeroplane on the pretext of taking a holiday. I saw their photographs in a newspaper. They were saluted as heroes."

"Who were these heroes?" asked Consuelo.

Tom scratched his head as he brought up the grainy image of the triumphant trio carrying riding whips and wearing bowler hats.

"There was Major Pollard, and his daughter Diana. They travelled with one of the daughter's friends. I think her name was Watson."

"Why did they do it?"

"I don't know. If the Rapide had dropped into the sea with Franco in it, then perhaps all this misery could have been averted."

"Tomas! You sound like a Red!" exclaimed Dr Hernandez.

And Tom made a fist with his right hand and said: "*No pasaran!*"

Dr Hernandez and Consuelo applauded him, and then Consuelo refilled their glasses with lemonade, and proposed a toast to the Royal Air Force. They talked on in the languid early evening, drinking lemonade and sunlight; Dr Hernandez told Tom of his own past, of what had happened to the town in the war, of politics, of Franco's grand schemes, of Oleanza's suspected visits to the local brothel, of Spain before the war. They spoke without fear, lightheartedly, sharing and enjoying Consuelo's account of the journey with de Rozario, and her encounter with Don Rondolfo. Where Tom's Spanish failed him, they encouraged him, helping him with pronunciation, and if that failed, Consuelo translated.

Eventually Tom took his leave of them, as Dr Hernandez still prescribed rest as a general cure. Then they retired to the loggia, in order to watch over the garden as the sunlight caught it in dying horizontal beams. They said little to each other, as they waited for Rafael to serve lentil coffee, the supply of good coffee being then exhausted.

Dr Hernandez placed his hands on his thighs, leaned forward and levered himself up from his chair. He crossed to the far side and stood alternately gripping and caressing the worn stone of the balustrade beneath his fingers. He reflected on the processes by which the brain passed signals to the muscles in the hand to accomplish this task, and how this activity could be disrupted. He was so absorbed in his thoughts that he did not hear Rafael approach, and was only brought back into the present when Consuelo and Rafael spoke.

He took the offered cup of hot dark liquid, and then turned back to look out over the garden. The branches of the fig and almond trees waved desultorily; he sipped the coffee, making a channel out of his tongue so as to guide the infusion of ground lentils and hot water through his mouth with least offence; maintaining his lookout, he spoke over his shoulder.

"He is making good progress. But he worries about whether they will let him fly again."

"But he is recovering," said Consuelo, a little pensively.

"Yes. He is recovering," then the doctor turned around. "Rafael, can I ask you a question?"

There was a pause; Rafael looked down at Consuelo, who in a gesture of support waved her own cup toward him and motioned him to speak with an open but silent mouth. The furrows on his brow became a little deeper, he coughed and cleared his throat.

"If I may be of service to you doctor."

"Is it easier to know a man's heart or the working of his brain?"

"Only God may know a man's heart doctor, learned men may discover the paths of memory."

"And if that man is our young Englishman?"

"It would be easier if Senor Roberts were Spanish."

Dr Hernandez was silent for a moment.

"What did you say?"

"Senor, I only offered that if Senor Roberts were Spanish, the problem would not arise."

"If only he were Spanish," Dr Hernandez repeated, as Tom had echoed his own words earlier in the afternoon.

"Federico, do you believe that Tomas could go to a hospital?" Consuelo asked.

"No," he said, "but we may not need a hospital. If only he were Spanish!"

A simple and obvious deception had taken form in Dr Hernandez's mind, a conjuring trick with words and letters. If it was too dangerous to send Tom in person, then he would go in writing, as a Spaniard.

"Why didn't I think of this before?!" he said, putting down the cup.

Rafael and Consuelo were both at a loss as to how the matter of fact reply could have made a difference.

"Think of what Federico?"

"If Tomas were a Spaniard, then I could write to the professor of neurological science at the general hospital in Barcelona to seek his opinion. Tomas will therefore become an honorary Spaniard!"

He drafted the letter that evening seated in Arturo's study, and gave Consuelo a small supply of his stationery, taken from a box he kept in his car; Consuelo typed the letter that night rather than risk this task to a secretary. Dr Hernandez signed it, and put it in an envelope.

"I think it will work," he said, "there's no reason for the neurologist to suspect."

"But what if the letter is opened by the police?"

He turned to her, his eyes, for once, laughing.

"My dear Consuelo," he said, "what would a secret policeman know about the working of the human brain?"

The Captive Summer

To The Stars

The *Alice* like world that Tom thought he inhabited finally dissolved in one brief moment. As he sat under the awning's protective shadow two days later, the sound of an aero engine came to his ears. Aircraft had flown overhead before, but had maintained altitude and passed out of sight. But this time the aeroplane came in low from the sea, and turned to follow the coast westward; the droning of the engine changed pitch as it came near, like a man with a mouth full of stones attempting to sing through a musical key. Its shadow passed directly over the house, the slipstream washing the roof tiles; so low in fact that Tom briefly saw the pilot's leather bound and goggled head as he craned around to observe the ground. It was a Fiat CR42, an Italian built bi-plane in the colours of the Spanish Air Force, and Tom knew that it was searching for someone. The aircraft was already obsolescent, an open cockpit fighter with a fourteen cylinder radial engine, and a stubby lower plane. He was surprised at how easily the aircraft recognition briefing they had received at Gibraltar came back to him; he was confident that his more heavily armed and faster Hurricane would have claimed the Fiat, but then remembered that his own aircraft was now a home for silver backed fish and lobsters.

As the aircraft cleared the far garden wall, Tom rose and stepped out from under the awning, the better to see its shape compress into a scurrying dot against the sky. He imagined what the pilot must be sensing at that moment, his feet on the rudder bar, the resistance in the control stick as his gloved hands pulled back, the wind lash in his face spitting specks of oil and dirt from the engine like tiny bullets. With a pang Tom wished he could have exchanged places with the anonymous young Spaniard, his past life returning as easily as if he had forsaken Arturo's clothes and again slipped on his own tunic.

For no reason he could conjure, as the bi-plane disappeared from sight, he remembered how one cool and fog bound afternoon, frustrated on the ground and digesting the latest piece of news from the Far East as the Japanese Army swept through the Malayan peninsula, the pilots had entered into a discussion of war aims, a topic not without peril for enlisted men. He remembered very clearly that Hilliard had composed a poem in jest, and was reprimanded for it by Breeve. Tom had written the poem down afterward, for no reason that he could justify, and committed it to memory.

In unknown glory lie we
Who chafed at life and gazed skyward.
To seek the high domain we rose

In glinting chariots that grazed the heavens.
But earthward again we plunged
And in the cold earth of England
Made our final bed.

Breeve, determined to bring the war speculation to an end, turned on them all rebuking them with: "Let's leave cynicism to another generation gentlemen, it ill suits those of us who measure our lives by the hour."

His duty was to return, to seek out that high domain; but now as he stood before the garden, his mind brought forward reasons why, now detached from the greater world, he was released from all previous oaths, allegiances, obligations and duties to it - except that to live. He inhabited a world bound by high walls, in which the fragrance of Spanish jasmine and not glycol lingered on the afternoon air. He had stumbled upon a reality more vivid than any lingering dream, where past realities became distorted by time into fragments of a half remembered nightmare. His past life had departed, the fabric of Arturo's clothes next to his skin had eased away discipline and struggle like fine sandpaper, leaving an unblemished self. He realised that he was crying, and shamefully wiped the tears away.

He had found life. He wanted more, and he was afraid that it would be denied him in the world beyond the garden. And yet he was also aware that the life he led now in the garden was a bubble, that without the garden walls the Civil Guard patrolled while common Spaniards starved. Consuelo stepped out onto the terrace, alerted by the engine noise. Freed from some of the worry of police suspicion she had regained her former sensuousness of movement, and in confident strides came to stand beside him.

"What was it Tomas?"

"A fighter, it must be on patrol."

"Perhaps it is looking for bandits in the mountains."

He almost added that it might be looking for him, but they were as satisfied as they could be that neither Andrea nor Manolito had betrayed them.

"It is a large country, he'll be looking all day," said Tom.

"Could you fly that aeroplane?" Consuelo asked, as if a sudden plan had formed in her mind.

"Yes, I should be able to," and now relaxing he added, "but I would prefer it if they sent a Catalina for me."

"What is a Catalina?" she asked.

"A flying boat, they have them at Gibraltar. They hunt down German U-boats."

Consuelo went back into the house; Tom went down to the garden, and walked among the scented bower to expunge the shame of his temporary lapse of conviction. He considered that this penance was inadequate, so he then went in search of Rafael, to offer his assistance among the vegetables and fruit trees.

That night he dreamed of his old life. He dreamed that he was in a night club, a plush room, with a brightly illuminated stage, dance floor and band. He sat at a table, which was covered in a silk cloth, and adorned with a shaded electric light; he was curious because the light had no discernible flex to provide power. The table had a good view of the dance floor, and was on a raised terrace, so that he looked down onto the next row of tables. The other guests were all elegantly attired; the men were either in dress uniform of the various services, or in tuxedos with dazzling white dress shirts. Some of the women were in uniform, but very few; the remainder were all wearing the most exquisite gowns, and all wore jewels. People were talking around him, laughing at jokes that Tom could not hear, or simply looking out as he was; they all seemed very, very happy. He looked down, and noted that he was still wearing the blue and white striped pyjamas in which he had gone to bed, but he did not feel inappropriately dressed. The band struck up, and the drummer gave a furious roll on the drums. Everyone else looked to the stage; when Tom looked across he saw Ken Maguire and Bill Mitchell standing there, both still in their khaki drill uniforms. Mitchell held his flying goggles in one hand, and a microphone in the other, while Maguire, standing behind him, had a hand placed on his shoulder. Then they started to sing *Underneath The Arches*, as if they were Flanagan and Allen, but with soft Australian accents.

Tom looked down, and now on the table before him he saw his silver cigarette case, the one he had lost when he had to exit the Hurricane. Although he knew he was wearing pyjamas he started to pat his chest as if looking for a cigarette lighter. Then he heard a voice behind, and looked round.

"Would you like a light Tom?"

He looked up into the face of the most beautiful young woman he had ever seen. She had a soft round face crowned by honey blond hair, drawn up into a comb, and cherry red lips. Around her throat was a string of pearls, and she was wearing a dress of deepest blue silk. Without speaking he took a cigarette from the case and put it to his lips. She produced a lighter, and Tom inhaled, drawing the smoke into his mouth as the tobacco caught. On the stage, Maguire and Mitchell sang on, and Tom turned back to watch them. The song finished, they bowed and walked off, to strong applause.

"Are you enjoying it Tommy?"

Tom looked round again, and his eyes now fell upon Alan Stanley. Stanley was dressed in a double breasted dinner jacket, his hair brilliantined and smooth like polished leather. He looked younger than Tom remembered him.

"Alan, are you here too?"

"Of course Tom, I'm the manager so to speak. May I join you?"

Tom gestured to Stanley to take the other chair drawn up at the table. He was so pleased to see him, he had never had the time to get to know him before.

"Have you had anything to drink yet?" asked Stanley.

"No not yet, I haven't been here long."

"Don't worry we'll soon sort that out," and Stanley got the attention of a passing waiter and ordered two glasses of champagne.

"Alan, do you own this place?" asked Tom in a hushed voice.

"Me? No Tommy, as I said I manage it," and Stanley leaned backed in his chair.

"I didn't know that Ken Maguire and Bill Mitchell could sing," and Tom gestured to the stage.

"Neither did they Tom, it's surprising what you can achieve if you put your mind to it. And they're not the only ones here; look at the band Tommy, do you recognise the pianist?" and Stanley pointed across to where the band was set up to one side of the stage. Tom looked, the pianist, who had been partly obscured before by some drapery, now leaned forward at the piano: it was James Hilliard.

"I remember that all ranks party in our mess when the film crew finished up, he played then. Oh! He was good!"

"Yes Tom, and with practice he has got better. I must say, we do all like it here, best little club going. Would you like to visit us again?" and Tom, delighted to receive an invitation to such a place, readily assented.

"That's good, but," and Stanley stood up to leave, holding out his hand to shake Tom's, "not too soon Tommy, old boy, not too soon." As Tom held up his hand he hesitated, worried that any weakness in it would be an embarrassment; but he felt no weakness as Stanley's fingers closed around his. Now, as he sat looking around him, the room darkened, and then the figures at the tables next to him started to dissolve. He tried very hard to keep the room in view, but it just melted away, until not an atom was left. He awoke to find that he was shivering in bed, even though the season was only just tending away from the warmth of summer. Now he could not sleep, and getting out of bed and cursing the pilot of the CR42 he dragged a chair to the bedroom window, opened it, and sat listening to the world.

The hard and sparkling whiteness of the stars, that hung about the mountains like diamonds cast among velvet, triggered further images; the Angel of Sleep bowed low and exited the room, leaving Tom alone to his thoughts.

There had been one incident in his earlier life when his career hung in the balance, and it had not been due to a flying accident. He had purchased a bag of icing sugar from the officers' mess, which was to be a gift for his sister. A small thing in itself, it was intended for his nephew's birthday cake, as a means of augmenting meagre rations. Unfortunately for Tom the station commander did not appreciate the gesture; Tom and the NCO responsible for the mess, Sergeant Mulvaney, were brought before him. Mulvaney did not like Tom, believing that the RAF was becoming overrun with non commissioned pilots, and had done his best to paint the worst possible picture of the true nature of the transaction. The station commander coldly eyed both men drawn to attention in front of him.

"Sergeant Roberts, you do know that selling foodstuffs to civilians is clearly black marketeering, for which I can have you court martialled?"

"Yes sir."

"Do you have any explanation?"

"I wasn't going to sell the icing sugar sir, it was for my sister."

"So am I to assume that she, like yourself, has a particularly sweet tooth?"

"No sir, she needed it for my nephew, it's his birthday tomorrow, she wanted to bake a cake, but with rationing, she just couldn't get any."

The station commander looked down, and then out of the window to the hangars and aerodrome apron.

"I understand that you are something of an athlete Roberts, is that correct?"

Tom was taken aback, and not able to make the connection between football and icing sugar.

"Well Roberts?" and this time he looked back and directly into Tom's eyes.

"I play a bit of soccer sir."

"I am told by your squadron commanding officer that you do rather more than 'play a bit of soccer', I am told that you can run pretty fast as well."

"Yes sir, even in full flying kit, I can run pretty fast."

"How far is the officers' mess from here?"

"I would think eight hundred yards sir."

"Yes, I would think so too. How old is the boy?"

"He will be eight sir."

"Roberts," he said slowly, "it would be a pretty poor eighth birthday don't you think, to have no cake? Does your sister need any other," and he looked now at the ceiling, searching for the right word, "ingredients?"

"She did ask whether I could get some raisins or sultanas, sir," the surreal turn of the conversation rendering him totally confused.

Slowly, Tom was daring to believe that he might not be put on a charge, but he remained rigidly at attention, trying to control his breathing.

The station commander rose and stepped to the window. Mulvaney had become concerned, his plan to compromise the young airman was not proceeding according to his scheme. The station commander turned back, and this time addressed himself to Mulvaney.

"Sergeant, I assume that the officers' mess has sultanas?"

Mulvaney felt indignant at this line of questioning, but knew better than to show it.

"Yes sir."

"Good," then turning to Tom again, "Roberts, I will give you eight minutes to get to the officers' mess, purchase half a pound of sultanas, and return here. If you can, you, the icing sugar and sultanas will travel up to London tonight to deliver the ingredients for your nephew's birthday cake. If you cannot, the icing sugar and sultanas will return from whence they came, while you will be placed in the Guard Room."

Tom gulped, nodded, and replied that he understood the condition. He was dismissed and left the room. Outside the administration block he took off his cap, and ran as if Hermann Goering himself were pursuing him.

"Clearly Mulvaney, the mess orderly has no inkling that such a human whirlwind is about to descend," commented the commander drily, "therefore, you will ring him now so that he has the item ready for collection."

"I will sir?" asked an incredulous Mulvaney, his face darkening.

"Yes damn you, you will!"

Mulvaney had intended his comment to be interpreted as a statement, but in his surprise at the commander's leniency it had gained an unfortunate interrogatory intonation.

"And Mulvaney," he said stepping closer, "don't think that I am ignorant of the circumstances surrounding the disappearance of half a case of whiskey. If there should be any further problems, I assure you that you will lose your stripes."

Mulvaney blinked, his ruse of attributing the loss to an air raid had been found out, and perhaps his guilt had been known all along.

Seated at the bedroom window, Tom remembered that as he sat on the train for London, his precious cargo hidden in a knapsack, he had watched the stars through the grimed window of the railway carriage as it made its halting way to the capital. His life had changed, but the same stars filled the sky.

The Captive Summer

The Unwelcome Suitor

In *The Merchant of Venice*, Portia uses three caskets, made of gold, silver and lead, in order to frustrate the efforts of her suitors. Neither the Prince of Morocco, nor the Prince of Aragon correctly deduces which casket contains her likeness, and their suits fail. Consuelo had no recourse to such devices, and believed that she had no need of them; this opinion was not shared however by Carlos de Rozario, who each day became more deeply infatuated with her.

When he sat down to eat a meal, he imagined her seated beside him, sharing the same food; as he walked through the town he imagined her walking beside him, raising her face to his, her dark eyes emerging from beneath the brim of a hat as the sun emerges from clouds. At night in his quarters, he wrote letters to her of dark passion; letters that he read over to himself under the frail light of the electric lamp on his desk, carelessly caressing the oiled leather of his pistol holster as he did so. He hid the sheets of paper in a cigar box, which he bound with tape and kept close by. Some evenings were given over to reading each letter again, acting out a virtual love affair, laughing at the those passages which would make her laugh, trembling at those which were intended to alert her and arouse her to the passion that inflamed him. The agony of the prose once moved him to tears, which he wiped away contemptuously as they mocked and derided his own manhood. She had become his shadow. His only experience with a woman had been as a cadet, when he and his class mates had visited a brothel; this was not like the establishment in *Calle del Rosa*, but a place where they considered young gentlemen were entertained, even though the rooms stank and the women were listless. At the end of a session of fetid grunting he had risen from the bed to dress. As he buttoned his tunic the woman, who still lay behind him, vomited and broke wind at the same time, spitting into a bucket that she pulled out from under the iron bedstead. His glory offended, he hurriedly completed the task, threw a few bank notes onto the dressing table and marched from the room, humiliated and smarting.

His parents had planned for a marriage to the daughter of one of their friends, following a long and formal courtship. It is difficult from the perspective of an age without formality, to appreciate the intricate rituals then observed in Spain; in his turn de Rozario had walked out with a young girl who, to his eyes, was as imbued with life as a porcelain doll.

The disparity in his age to Consuelo, her marriage, the fact that Arturo was an exiled Red, who faced execution if he returned to Spain, and

Consuelo's own appearance in police files for her work in the Republican field hospital, were of no consequence. He was blinded by desire, and the object of his desire was blind to him. The imperative of apprehending the saboteurs precluded any serious efforts at wooing Consuelo, while she, more secure that Tom's secret had not been betrayed, showed little inclination to venture into San Cristobal. His frustration ate at him like a sexual disease.

He could at least escape to the high station, where he led the mounted patrols through mountain pastures and woods of olive and pine. The country was deserted, as the only people who now risked travelling over the paths and trackways beside the clear running irrigation channels were dispossessed strangers unfamiliar with the area. These patrols scouted the open land that rose steadily from the sea to the base of the mountains; as he encouraged his horse onward over boulder strewn rising ground, or sat high in the saddle while he swept an arc with his field glasses, his thoughts still returned to Consuelo, who had become for him elusive and imaginary, lost in the faint mists which ran to the sea.

On the second afternoon of his next patrol, the Guards halted to rest at a rock pool beside a high stream. De Rozario assigned the men to their tasks, then settled to write under the shade of a large rock that threw its shadow across the pool. Those not on watch took off their uniforms and hung them from the branches of a shrivelled solitary olive tree, and plunged into the water to escape the sun. The horses were tethered to clumps of lavender bushes, where they could reach down and drink from the stream, their reins straining and the bushes bending and twisting as their tongues struggled to lap the clear swift running water. Lost in his thoughts, his thighs sore from the saddle, the young officer cut an isolated and despondent figure, while the men under his command enjoyed the rare and simple coolness of the waters. He began, and scratched out, several attempts for his latest letter, commencing them with the words 'My darling', 'My darling Consuelo', 'My love'. The hard dry voices of the men irritated him as they joked and talked amongst themselves, their rattling throats amplified by the whinnying of the horses. That she was so aloof to him, had been so physically close to him once but so disdainful, he could barely contain. That she had a husband was of no consequence: the man dared not to return to Spain. Why then, could she not accept him as her lover? He closed his notebook with an audible slap of leather cover on leather cover, and jumped to his feet.

"You, and you," he shouted at two momentarily startled bathers, "get your uniforms, we have more riding ahead of us!"

He gave orders to the corporal who stood in place of Pelean, and waited impatiently while three horses were readied. Marked by short pillars of dust they rode out of the encampment, along the road to the sea, and the walls of El Faro.

It was Maria's turn to raise the alarm; as she replaced the linen in Consuelo's bedroom her head and her eyes rose just at the moment that three horsemen emerged over an undulation of land, to disappear again in the next fold. With a shriek she ran from the room to find Consuelo and Tom. Their much practiced routine was put into effect, and Tom secreted away. Manolito was again at the house, this time entrusted to Rafael's care, and worked with him in the garden. Consuelo opened the door herself, an unusual event, but she needed to experience the physical act to dissipate the tension which welled within her at another test of endurance and nerve. The surprise on de Rozario's face was palpable, but the surprise had the benefit of robbing his mind of his opening request; in the dark and awkward silence that followed, the balance between the two potential and unresolved adversaries was reset.

"I had not expected you to open the door yourself," he said.

"Teniente de Rozario, I cannot afford a house full of servants to do my bidding."

"I need to speak to you Dona Consuelo."

Consuelo hesitated, behind her she could just hear Maria's soft footfalls in the courtyard, but had no reason to believe that they would be discovered.

"Please come in teniente."

She led him not to the terrace, but the reception room, where she established herself in one of the chairs, while de Rozario sat across from her. She was almost within his reach, he could clearly make out the pulsing veins in her throat, and was aware that her breasts rose and fell within her blouse. She had a fresh soap and water smell, with the faintest hint of perfume, and the heat appeared not to have made an impression on her. He, sore and stained from the hard ride, was aware of the dust on his tunic, which also adhered to the hairs on the back of his hands. So Portia met the gaze of the latest suitor; his senior in years, she almost pitied his immaturity and earnestness: they said that Franco had been like this once. The room was her audience chamber, to which she had graciously allowed admittance to a courtier from a foreign kingdom.

"Intelligence has come into our possession that a group of guerillas are planning attacks on remote properties from San Cristobal to Almunecar."

Consuelo considered it axiomatic that the intelligence to which he referred came into the possession of the police by force.

"What would bandits steal from here, teniente?" she asked in a dusky voice.

De Rozario looked around the faded and worn furnishings, sensitive that she did not acknowledge the hinted threat to her safety.

"They do not only steal Dona Consuelo, they use violence, extreme violence."

"The walls are high, and the birds do not like to have their sleep disturbed," she said, suppressing her pleasure at his discomfort.

"What use are the damn birds!"

"All birds defend their young teniente."

"Dona Consuelo, it is your safety that is my concern!"

"I am flattered."

In an instant his attitude changed; he stood suddenly and strode to the window, his sense of insult at the hands of this disdainful older woman who would not yield her body to him, twisting within him like a knife with a serrated blade.

"What do you know!?" he shouted. "What do you know of that old Cuban, of the people who work the land outside the walls!?"

Too late she realised that she had provoked him: she attempted conciliation.

"I am grateful for your concern Teniente de Rozario, I did not intend to infer ingratitude and," she paused, "I am aware that as a solitary woman, there are dangers to which I am particularly vulnerable."

She dared not look up, and with time itself suspended she waited for his reply. He stood looking out across the terrace to the garden, silent but quaking.

"The boy is here again," was his sole answer, as he witnessed Manolito standing beside Rafael and working a small pick on the baked earth, mechanically dragging at a film of topsoil, then returning to drag more earth along a shallow cutting.

"He helps Rafael when he can."

"If anyone should harm the child," he said, "such an innocent little boy, it would be a sin. Do you not agree?"

"Yes, of course."

"I can protect him Dona Consuelo, I can ensure that no one will harm him. It is what I am sworn to do."

She gasped involuntarily, and clumsily tried to suppress the sound. It was no longer a game between them. She sat instantly dejected, one hand thrown protectively between her thighs: the Prince had discovered in which casket Portia's image lay. She had lost the sexual struggle, and they both knew it. He walked back to her, and calmly resumed his seat.

"And Maria is his mother?"

"Yes."

"A good woman?"

"Of course, she has worked for me for several years," she said, her head lowered a little.

"She has no husband?"

"He is in prison."

He leaned forward, his voice once again assuming the querulous tone of the lusting youth.

"My concern is only, and you must believe me, for your safety. Can you trust the people who work the land?"

"They work the land because they are hungry. I do not believe that they would kill me for a little food."

"Even so, the guerillas are active here. We will protect you, and I believe that you may be placed in danger."

"I am grateful for your concern."

He stood up, but now proud and glorious in his own eyes. He had raised within her mind the prospect of a horror without limit. But he could not be satisfied until he had convinced her that he was *her* protector. He could use the boy as a way of gaining access to her, but he would have only her body, not her love.

Without exchanging another word they parted, Consuelo remaining with her head averted from him, tears welling in her dark eyes. He strode from the house, and roused the two Guards who had ridden with him. He stroked the mouth of his horse, a piebald mare, feeling the soft quivering flesh beneath his fingers; yet restraining the animal from pulling its head away by holding firm on the bridle. Then he mounted and rode away.

The Captive Summer

An Innocent Man

That the name of Felipe Escolar appeared on the list of suspects which de Rozario had prepared was, in some regards, unusual. He had the essential qualities to guarantee his inclusion, in that he was not a Falangist, and his brother had fought for the Republic. However, there was nothing to directly associate him with the Republican cause; and his own trade, that of undertaker, was of direct use to the authorities. He had attended to the needs of the deceased under Primo de Rivera, Azana and now Franco. He had learned that whatever the colour of the flag of government, the sick and the unfortunate, the slow and the careless, all died. The only thing that varied was the rate at which they departed this world; when that rate speeded up, business increased. He was not a callous man, but he had learned to detach himself from the essence of the business, something that Dr Hernandez, who was a soldier in the struggle to save life, had never mastered. He expounded to anyone who would listen, his philosophy of death.

"God has ordained it, we don't quite know why, but as we trust in Him we accept His judgement. As for me, I provide a final dignity where often there was none in the life itself."

He had built up a good business, that supported himself, his wife, four children, two horses, and a mule. The horses and the mule were used to pull a hearse and a cart respectively, depending on how much money was to be spent. For the poorest funerals, there was no assistance from any of the quadrupeds, but only a communal coffin with a false bottom, that was borne to the grave by four or six bearers. At the grave the false bottom dropped away, and the shrouded body fell into the hole. Little time elapsed between death and the funeral; for the poor that meant that they were simply washed and put into clean clothes prior to despatch.

Escolar did not expect to be under suspicion, but fear was arbitrary. One night the police had called at his neighbour's house, searching for a man who had escaped from a Labour Battalion. The fugitive was not there, so the police took Escolar's neighbour in his place. In common terror Escolar and his wife followed the sound of the struggle along the wall, as the man was dragged, punched and kicked to the door of the house. As he was thrown into the road Escolar pulled back the blind, but let it fall quickly when a policeman looked up. His wife wept and prayed for their neighbour all through the night. In the morning he went to the house; climbing over the wreckage of the street door and furniture he found the man's wife, sunken eyed and with no tears left in her body, holding the youngest child to her breast and rocking back and forward in a chair with only two legs unbroken.

The night that the police came for Escolar he had completed work to prepare a well-to-do woman for burial. As he smoked in the yard, passing a cigarette to his assistant, a youth with no longer or more definitive appellation than Ramon, he was glad to exhale the smell of death and the embalming fluids from his lungs; exchanging them for tobacco smoke and the pungent dung of the horses and the mule. He walked over to the stable; throwing the weight of his upper body on the half door, he spoke to the horses, asking them how they liked their work, which he reminded them, represented regular employment. They were two jet black mares called Sol and Sombra, and he loved them as he loved his wife. Then he called to Ramon.

"Ramon, if God Himself descended from the sky and mucked out the stable, cleared all their shit, they would still stand there with that look on their faces."

"But they know what we do for them Senor Escolar."

"I'll try to remember that the next time one of them stands on my foot!" The horses' ears pricked up and rotated toward the house. A thudding sound, at first muffled then more insistent and distinct, came to them. Escolar realised now that it was his own front door which was under assault. He stubbed out the cigarette, and heedless of the danger, ran to the building. In the dimly lit corridor his wife was pleading with voices in the street, as rifle butts fell on the timbers like rain. Escolar pushed her back, calling for Ramon and his own mother, who lived with them. His children sat at the top of the stairs sobbing; everyone was shouting or crying or uttering oaths at once. He opened the door to Sargento Pelean and two Guards.

"Felipe Escolar?" asked Pelean, knowing full well who the man was who stood before him.

"Yes; why do you come here?"

"We want to talk to you."

With that he was taken, a Guard on each arm. As they marched him away he managed one look over his shoulder at the rapidly diminishing oval of light that his own doorway had become, and the sobbing images of his wife and mother, clutching at and supporting each other.

He found himself sitting on a bench in a room with six other men, all of whom had about them the air of the wrongfully accused: it was in their sweat. The door opened and a Guard stood in the doorway and motioned to one of the others. From somewhere behind him they distinctly heard the sounds of blows being struck in one of the anonymous rooms which lay in shadow. The man who had been selected stood up, but not to his full height, as if fear had robbed his legs of the strength needed to lock at the knee. He shuffled forward, his head bowed, in the vain hope that by this act of submission he would be spared a severe beating. The door closed behind him, and with it the sound of the fists, or clubs, or boots in the rooms on the other side of the corridor.

When it was Escolar's turn he started up when he was summoned, as he had waited into the early hours of the morning and had grown weary. The Guard took him by the elbow, as if doubting his capacity to walk, and pulled him along the corridor from shadow to shadow. In the last but one room a man was sobbing, his voice a deep baritone which reverberated into the airless space. The door of the last room was slightly ajar; a pillar of light like the blade of a knife escaped between the door and frame. The room had no window, and was furnished only with a table and two chairs, set in the centre. A shaded bulb hung over the table, its pool of light regulated by a thin chain in place of a switch. Escolar was forced down onto one of the chairs, and the Guard departed. His eyes were immediately drawn to the table top, which was heavily marked by cigarette burns and numerous messages scratched into the grain and fibres. There was one near his left thumb which he could make out as '¿Donde esta Dios?' while a second which ran perpendicular to it read 'Muchos besan la mano que desean cortar': 'Many kiss the hand they wish to cut off'. He could not decide whether this was rendered as a piece of advice or a warning.

The walls were bare, but speckled here and there with dark spots and blotches, which as he peered closer he realised was dried blood. He shrunk back, and for strength gripped the sides of the table as if it represented the known universe and human consciousness. He thought of his wife and children; he did not know if they could go on if he did not return. Ramon was only a youth, he could master the horses, but knew little else; he did not know how to prepare a body, how to remove and store organs, how to treat the skin: the boy had never seen a body cut open.

The door opened and an officer and two Guards entered the room. De Rozario was tired and agitated, the top of his tunic was unbuttoned, exposing his neck; he motioned to the two Guards to stand against the wall behind Escolar; as Escolar's head moved round to observe what was happening he shouted at him.

"I have not given you permission to look away from me!"

"I am sorry senor, I am sorry," and Escolar now sat as if neck and spine were fixed, allowing only his eyes to swivel.

"You are," and de Rozario referred to several sheets of paper which he carried in one hand, "Felipe Escolar. You are an undertaker in this town, and you have lived here for twelve years. Is that correct?"

"Yes senor."

"Your brother, Emilio, fought for the Republic, and is now in a detention camp for combatants of the illegal former government. Is this also correct?"

The Republican government of Manuel Azana was the legitimate government of Spain in 1936, but to acknowledge this under Franco was dangerous, so Escolar agreed with the statement without dissent.

"Yes senor, he was a combatant of the illegal former government."

"So what does that make you Escolar?"

"I am a loyal Spaniard senor."

De Rozario pulled back the second chair and sat down at the table, dropping the papers containing the names and records of the other men to be interrogated that night, onto the table at his side. Under the penumbra of electric light he looked even younger than he did under the rays of the sun; but in spite of his youth the fatigue of several days and nights of interrogating scores of men and some women still made itself known in his eyes. He had not eaten properly for two days and the only respite had been when he left the Guards to extract what information they could with their fists, while he returned to his quarters. In the solitude of his room Consuelo soon crowded upon his mind; to escape thoughts of her he returned to the windowless interrogation rooms, often in time to see another interrogatee beg for his life before slipping into unconsciousness on the floor. The interrogations had not produced one single piece of information about the attack on the parade. Several men had confessed to other crimes: three to robbery, one to rape and one to smuggling corned beef. He did not doubt that some were so desperate to avoid a beating that they would confess to anything, but the punishment to be meted out to the Sugar Bandits was to be exemplary.

"A loyal Spaniard? Is that what you are? And as a loyal Spaniard do you plot to assassinate the Civil Governor?"

"No, no senor! Ask anyone, I am not a political man, I love Spain, I love Franco."

"Are you a member of the Falange?"

"A member of the Falange? No, senor; but with these hands I wrote to the Mayor to voice my anger that such impudence could have arisen!"

"With those hands?"

"Yes senor, with these hands!" and he implored with outspread fingers, turned so that the electric light fell full on them.

"Put your hands on the table."

"Senor?"

"I said," and de Rozario narrowed his mouth and spoke slowly and with precision, "put your hands on the table."

De Rozario nodded to the Guards and they sprang forward, grabbed Escolar's forearms and pinned his palms on the table. Escolar looked from the Guards to de Rozario and back, a wild terror in his eyes, as the possibility arose in his mind of what was about to happen. De Rozario unclipped a rubber baton from his belt, and placed it in front of him.

"I don't know anything senor, I beg you, please, I don't know!"

The Guards restrained him, but Escolar closed his fingers instinctively, mouthing silently as he begged for mercy; tears filled his eyes.

"Open your fingers."

"Please, senor, I don't know!"

"Open your fingers or I will break your jaw." As he said this, de Rozario picked up the baton, laying the tip of it against Escolar's face. Escolar opened his clenched fists, hesitantly allowing his finger tips to slip across the worn and marked table surface; the Guards held him by the wrists and shoulders.

"What do you know about the attack on the parade?"

Before Escolar could give an answer, de Rozario removed the tip of the baton from his face, and brought it down between the thumb and forefinger of Escolar's left hand. Tap. Escolar winced, and dry mouthed, swallowed hard.

"Teniente, I don't know anything about the attack. You must believe me."

"Spread your fingers further apart," to which Escolar complied in a jerky action as if in a spasm, "I do not believe you," and again he brought the baton down, first between the thumb and forefinger, then the forefinger and middle finger, and so on: tap, tap, tap, tap.

"I am the undertaker senor, no one talks to me, they say it's bad luck."

De Rozario said nothing, but staring hard into Escolar's face continued to bring the baton down, but now with greater force and speed. Tap! Tap! Tap! Escolar was sweating now, not the sweat of being exposed to the sun, but the sweat of fear; beads moistened his eyes and formed on his upper lip like a translucent thin moustache.

"Why were you not at the parade?"

"I..I was working teniente, we were preparing the hearse for a funeral. Ask Senor Hidalgo, it was for his father!"

"But the funeral was not for another day, you could have prepared the hearse later. Why was it so important that you clean and polish it at the time of the parade?"

The simple reason for this was that Escolar had first to remove blackmarket cigarettes with which the hearse had been loaded; he realised that whether he told the truth or a lie he was caught.

"I am a busy man teniente, there are many funerals."

De Rozario now turned his attention from Escolar's left hand to his right; this took Escolar by surprise, and the baton struck his right thumb. He cried out, but the Guards fixed his wrists to the table as he tried to withdraw his throbbing hand.

"Don't waste my time Escolar, we watch you because we know that your brother is a traitor to Spain. If you ever want to see him again, you will tell me what I want to know. Now show me your fingers."

Tap, tap, tap.

"Please senor," he cried out as the pain pulsed through his hand and along his arm, "by the Virgin I don't know! I don't know! I am the undertaker, the undertaker!"

De Rozario had now lost all patience; as his fatigue had increased, the sight of the pathetic figure grovelling and begging for mercy sickened him. He raised the baton over his shoulder, and brought it down in a gracious arc as if it were a sabre. The bones of Escolar's left hand cracked under the impact, and he let out a scream, a long dark scream like the sound a soul will make as it is thrown down into a boiling pit in the depths of hell. He was losing consciousness as de Rozario brought the baton down for a second time, exacting the same punishment on his right hand.

He motioned to the Guards to release Escolar; like a serpent he slipped down from the chair, and lay crumpled on the floor, holding his battered hands before him and shaking violently before mercy came in oblivion.

"I don't think he can tell us anything," de Rozario said, then he replaced the baton on his belt, gathered up the papers, and left.

The Captive Summer

Three Unwise Men

When Escolar regained consciousness, he was dragged out of the interrogation room and deposited on a bench set along one wall in the main office. Next to him were seated the relatives of other men who had been taken for interrogation. The Guard slouching against the counter, like the concierge of a hotel dedicated to human misery, ignored him, even though a few drops of blood from his throbbing hands now marked the floor. Eventually another man stood and, after futile efforts to procure help, tore up a neckerchief he carried with him to bind Escolar's hands. As he dressed the wounds he spoke softly to him, drawing him a little way out of the pain trance into which he had withdrawn. With the assistance of a woman who had gone to the barracks to seek news of her son, he raised Escolar from the bench and moved him slowly toward the main door.

It was now morning; pale light filtered into the office, driving out gloom but not despair. As they neared the doorway they were obliged to stop to allow a Guard accompanying another suspect to enter. The new suspect was a young man with intense eyes and a broad forehead, dressed in a threadbare suit that did not look as if it had ever fitted any man correctly. For a moment he and Escolar stood looking hard at each other; the younger man with fear in his eyes prompted by Escolar's mask of bewildered agony. They passed; the young man was presented to the Guard slouching at the desk.

"This man is Pablo Villasellos," announced his escort. The sloucher, without even looking up, nodded, and made an entry in an open book before him.

The escort pulled Villasellos, the teacher with associations in Madrid, away from the desk; together they disappeared into the corridor from which Escolar had earlier emerged.

De Rozario drank a cup of coffee in the mess hall. As he reviewed the names set out before him , turning the pages back and forward, his irritation and fatigue agreed to an uneasy truce. He ran a finger down one page, stopping twice to read the scribbled notes he had made, 'petty criminal - no convictions for violence', and 'violent only if drunk'. He had expected that from a list of fifty he could have extracted three or four names, yet none possessed the vicious temperament he sought. He decided that it was a futile exercise; as his irritation returned he pushed the sheets of paper away. At another table two Guards were eating breakfast, earnestly discussing something; from the tone and gesticulations the dispute was clearly about money. He remembered that he had seen them drinking at the

Cafe Alejandro; he reasoned that if they drank there they did business with Morales. Corrupt police regulated the transport and sale of contraband for Morales; anyone other than one of his people found in possession of illegal goods faced arrest. The confiscated contraband was quickly transferred to one of the store rooms behind the bar; Morales passed something back to the Guards for their diligence, passed something more onto Mendoza, and retained a substantial profit for the application of his commercial skills. Everybody was happy with this arrangement, except the original owners of the goods, and Carlos de Rozario.

"Can you do this?" he asked that night, sitting in Morales' office, awkward in civilian clothes, unused to the rough brandy he drank, and despising himself for the action he had taken.

Morales had been surprised when de Rozario had asked to speak to him privately; but never lost an opportunity to do business. He had expected that de Rozario wanted to discuss terms for selling confiscated blackmarket goods; but names, like cigarettes or rolls of silk, were also commodities.

"May I ask what it is you require these three men for teniente?" Morales asked, a false smile revealing a gold tooth.

"That is my concern; I am paying for names, what happens thereafter is between myself and these men. I assure you senor, you do not want to know."

"I understand," Morales answered, an ingratiating grimace denoting that it was a thing understood between two men; and hid his disappointment.

"Can you do it?" de Rozario asked again.

"But of course teniente, but of course."

"And how much will it cost?"

"For three good men? Fifty pesetas each."

"Fifty pesetas? Do I look like a Habsburg?" he spat out, anger rising clear in his face.

"Carlos, Carlos," Morales whined, irritating the young man further, "I am your friend, and friends can negotiate."

Had de Rozario taken his pistol with him to the meeting, he would have drawn it then and shot Morales dead. But he had no gun, and needed this favour. They negotiated and agreed a price; de Rozario departed, avoiding the eyes of the people sitting at the tables outside as he walked away.

Morales was only to tell the men that they would receive twenty pesetas each in advance, and three hundred pesetas more if the job was successful: it was a fortune. They were not to know who was recruiting them, and were not to contact Morales again. The gang he selected were occasional farm labourers, hard men with faces and bodies on which were etched the recent history of Spain. They were instructed to meet at an abandoned and isolated farmhouse, a memorial to forgotten generations who had trusted in God, ploughed the bitter earth with mules, and died dreaming of the wealth they had not known.

De Rozario reached the farmhouse as dusk cast a veil over the scrub, and made preparations to receive his guests. What had once been the main room now provided a home for wild goats and turtle doves; in a wreck of broken furniture piled up at one end of the room, he recovered a chair and table which were still usable. From a knapsack he produced an oil lamp, a bottle of wine and his pistol, wrapped in cloth. Having satisfied himself that he was not observed, he sat down by the window which gave views to the south, and waited. From the breast pocket of his shirt he brought out the latest letter he had written to Consuelo, which like the others, she had not seen. In the failing light he could not read what he had written, and so ran his finger tips over the paper, reciting from memory. Love had driven some to kill themselves, and some to kill others: it simultaneously denied and embraced life. De Rozario had decided that his love would have to lead to the death of others to gain reciprocation.

He was quite alone; as night drew across the land, he sat with one elbow resting on the table, his eyes either fixed on the open doorway, or out across the land that rose and fell in dry waves of crumbling red earth. He wondered whether the men would come, whether the prospect of so large a sum would dispel mortal caution. He waited, looking alternately to the doorway or out at the land. He was at peace; he had decided on a course of action, his love for Consuelo demanded no less a deed. Black night fell; the men appeared as three silhouettes, moving across the land, with the sea at their back, walking in single file. De Rozario took the pistol from its cloth, loaded a round into the chamber, and slid the barrel between his belt and the waistband of his trousers. He breathed in shadow, his form removed from starlight, although one or two impudently shone down between ragged holes in the roof.

"Go no further!" he cautioned as the first of the silhouettes stood framed at the door.

The figure turned toward him.

"We were told to come here," the man replied.

"You were paid to come here!" de Rozario protested, closing his right hand over the grip of the pistol. "Tell the others to come in!"

They entered, and stood before him. They had no faces, and he believed that they could not see his. With his free hand he struck a match on the table, and lit the lamp. The three men were instantly revealed to him, their shadowy alter egos projected behind them into the shadows. The first had been the shortest of the three, the second the tallest, and the third was somewhere between the other two in height. They wore a patina of dust, which made the stubble on their faces look like beards of the finest gold. They were ragged, and the tallest harboured the pained expression of a man subjected to a mild electric shock. The last man said little and hung back, as if from shame.

"We were told that there was a job for us," offered the first, who had assumed the authority of leadership among them.

"What do you know of this job?" asked de Rozario, his fingers drawing comfort from the pistol grip.

"We were only told that there was a house, nothing more."

"Do you know the country to the west of the town?"

"Yes, I and my brother," answered the leader, indicating the tall man, "have worked in the olive groves on several of the cortijos."

"There is a house, about four kilometres along the coast road. In parts the building is no better than," and he kicked at the table, shaking the lamp and the wine bottle, "this shack. But there is wealth there, hidden in a room. I want what that room contains."

He explained what they had to do, but never stirred from his seat, and kept his hand on the pistol. They agreed, nodding but in an unsynchronised way, to affirm their decision. As they turned to leave, the tallest one halted and turned back, a look of pain still on his hollow cheeked face.

"Will they have guns senor?" he asked.

"No, they will not have guns," de Rozario answered, the smooth metal of the pistol beneath his fingers.

He extinguished the lamp, and waited in the dark. He rose to check that they had departed, then opened the wine bottle, and taking a small tin cup from his knapsack, filled it to the brim. The three wise men of the Bible story had brought gifts, and taken away the knowledge of the birth of Jesus. These three, he reasoned, the three unwise men, would bear no gifts and take no knowledge away with them. He drank to that, and made preparations to return to the town.

The next evening de Rozario told Mendoza that one of the men he had interrogated, although he professed no knowledge of the attack on the parade, had told him that a robbery was planned on the farmhouse known as El Faro. He asked permission to take a squad of men to lay a trap for the robbers, who were to attack the house that night. Mendoza agreed, and Sargento Pelean organised a squad of eight men and motorised transport. De Rozario was more than usually preoccupied; although he took care to examine the rifle of each man, and to question Pelean as to which of them were marksmen, he behaved as if he had recently received bad news from home. They drove out of the town and along the road as the orange red sun dipped below the horizon in its struggle against the inevitable triumph of darkness over light. At de Rozario's command the truck halted at the side of the road, and the Guards dropped down from the tailgate. Rifles in hand they moved up through rows of ilex, until they reached the ground close to the house, where de Rozario ordered Pelean to take four Guards further to the west, while he and the remaining men skirted around the house to the north. Breathlessly stepping through the scrub grass, they took up firing positions in a shallow gully, the rifle barrels protruding like broken black stalks of grass.

Within El Faro, Consuelo, Tom and Rafael ate a dinner of salted cod and rice in the kitchen. Dance music from Radio Seville lifted their spirits, in spite of the news bulletins, but each one of them sensed that the season was slowly shifting, and each one at some point during the meal wondered for how much longer they would enjoy the company of the others. Rafael had succeeded in getting a message to Antonio and Jesus, and they expected that the fishermen would visit them in the next few days. The two subjects of conversation from the town were the arrests, and a new case of cholera; the latter had forced the authorities to demolish and burn a row of shacks in the slum district, but Dr Hernandez was not convinced that it would prevent a recurrence.

"Maria says that her children do not understand why they cannot play in the street," said Consuelo, "they are beginning to hate their mother, they cannot see the cholera and don't believe it exists."

"They would be safer here than in the town," responded Rafael, curious that he found it necessary to qualify the protection which the house afforded. Consuelo, her hands folded one over the other before her face, looked quickly between both men to show her amusement at the notion of the house becoming a refugee camp.

"Let me talk to Maria, there are things which have to be discussed," she concluded.

Consuelo tapped out with her fingertips on the table top the tune of the music playing on the radio, and rocked her head gently from side to side in time with the music.

"It's not as good as the music from the gramophone," Tom said.

"It has no soul, it has been approved by a Francoist committee, as music suitable to listen to while giving the Falangist salute at the same time," she replied.

Tom turned to Rafael.

"Rafael, did you ever learn to play a musical instrument while you were at sea?"

"No, too little room senor, and not enough time. I preferred to listen to the stars."

The music programme from Radio Seville conveyed pure and chaste Iberian love, but the sound did not carry outside the walls of the house. In the surrounding fields men checked their weapons, and waited.

The Captive Summer

The Assault

They came down from the mountains, crouching and running at the same time across the open stretches of land, moving silently in measured tread. They had darkened their faces with burnt cork, and wore crude smocks made from sacking. Each man carried a club, and the leader of the band a canvas bag also, to deposit whatever else they could carry off. While still several hundred metres from the house they sprinted to an olive grove, from where they could watch in safety.

"There are still lights showing, they should be dark by now!" said the Tall Man.

"Perhaps the old man has indigestion, perhaps he cannot sleep," offered the leader of the group, adding, "but he'll sleep soon enough and long enough."

They had been told by de Rozario that the house was occupied by an elderly farmer and his wife, who would put up only limited resistance to an assault. The old woman kept a jewellery box in the bedroom; it was to gain this prize that they waited among the olive trees while the last nightjars swooped noiselessly across the open ground before them. They sat with their backs against the trees, occasionally spying around the trunks; but each time the lights of the house winked defiantly back at them. Not one of them possessed a watch, and so they could only calculate the passage of time by the brightness of the sky, and the track of the moon. Eventually the light in the bedroom on the north side of the house went out; the three men stirred, and shook out numbed limbs.

In front of them and to their left was the silent gully in which de Rozario and four of the Guards were waiting. As the night wore on, de Rozario again began to doubt that the gang would come, the thought occurring to him that it would be the supreme irony if another Civil Guard or Army patrol had discovered them. Lying on his stomach at the top of the gully, he had an uninterrupted view of the house, and the land that stretched beyond; Pelean and his men enjoyed the same advantage from their positions among the far cluster of ilex trees. Anyone attempting to cross the open land would be caught in a cross fire; they would never reach the walls of the house. To his right, a shape separated itself from the trunk of an olive tree, as if the tree's spirit had stepped out, quickly followed by a taller form; de Rozario tapped the shoulder of the Guard lying closest to him: the time to kill to prove his love had arrived.

They came on in glorious ignorance, not crouching now but striding across the open land at full height, and with a relaxed gait, as if they were coming home from the fields to their families and a meagre supper. They maintained the order in which de Rozario had seen them: the Leader, the Tall Man, and the Ashamed Man. In the gully the Guards edged forward on their stomachs, trained their rifles and took aim. The Tall Man was the easiest target, his head like a practice watermelon in their rifle sights; the Leader was more difficult to make out against the folds of land and the trees, while the Ashamed Man seemed to dissolve in the envelope of darkness like an apparition. The distance between the two groups closed, the hunted oblivious to the hunters, their heads full of schemes for surprising and overwhelming the illusory old man and his wife.

De Rozario crushed a handful of dirt between his fingers, the beads of earth crumbling like ancient skull bones; his heart beat so violently that his body appeared to twitch on the ground, and his mouth was so profoundly dry that his tongue stuck to the roof of his mouth. The gang came on, gaining in form and filling the sights of the rifles. De Rozario drew his arms to the sides of his body, the palms of his hands pressing and squeezing the earth. He tensed, then he rose swiftly, as if emerging from a trench at the moment of assault, held his pistol aloft and shouted a challenge to the men to stop.

Only his voice broke the stillness of the night. The gang members froze as they stepped; struck dumb they peered into the hole in the ground from where the voice emanated. Without waiting for a response from the gang, de Rozario ordered the Guards to fire. One shot spat in the night air, then in quick succession two more; the Tall Man toppled forward like a felled tree, and the other two scattered like frightened deer. Pelean's men now opened fire, their shots flaring among the far dark curtain of trees. Exhilaration coursing through his body, de Rozario shouted to the Guards to pursue the gang; both squads now rushed forward, firing as they went.

The broken firing ranged across the open ground as the police chased apparitions, whispering scraps of grass and the boughs of olive trees. Bullets spat and whined, the flaring barrels moving swiftly across the ground. The policemen plunged and spun in the darkness, stalking each other, losing sense of location or direction. More than once a rifle was raised against a fleeting silhouette, only for a desperate shout to identify the phantom as another policeman. The two groups of confused men slowly converged, squeezing down the available open space in which the gang members could hide.

By a clump of tufted grass they found the body of the Tall Man, with a wound in his neck. A shout from one of Pelean's men brought de Rozario breathless to the place where the Leader's body lay. But of the Ashamed

Man, there was no sign.

"Where is he? Where the fuck is he!?" de Rozario shouted in their faces, as the perspiring Guards clustered around. No one knew, and no one ventured an opinion.

A Guard tapped Pelean on the shoulder and pointed behind de Rozario. De Rozario turned abruptly; the lights of the house were again lit. It was only then that the awful possibility broke into his consciousness.

When they had retired for the night, Rafael had sat at the edge of his bed, considering why he had been unable to assure Consuelo and Tom of the safety the house could afford to Maria and her children. He rose and opened the bedroom window, and looked out into the whispering blackness beyond the walls. The window was barred, as were all windows on the north side of the building, and so gave the room the appearance of a prison cell; it was a cell however intended to protect its inhabitant. He stood and walked across to the washstand, removed his shirt and shoes, and washed his face and body, letting the water drip from his chin and fingertips back into the basin. He dried his hands and regarded his grizzled face in the mirror, lifting his top lip the better to see a tooth which gave him a little pain. He turned out the electric light beside the bed, and stretched out, not bothering to turn down the sheets. He retrieved his knife from a pocket and inserted it into his belt; casually caressing the blade, he lay in the darkness and contemplated what it was that troubled him. Neither Tom nor Consuelo shared his undefined misgivings; they, in their respective rooms, slept soundly.

When the first rifle shot spat out an orange flare beneath his window, Rafael leapt to his feet, but doubted his own hearing, as he had experienced dreams in which he had heard the main door of the house reverberate, as if someone had just departed.

The second and third shots convinced him that he had not dreamt, and he was at the door of his room in a stride. Moving stealthily but with speed he reached the edge of the courtyard and stopped in deep shadow. The night was still again; the starved light from the sky barely illuminated the floor, and none of the cloisters beyond. Rafael removed the knife and opened its blade with slow care. He stepped noiselessly in pools of blackness, breathing softly, carrying the blade behind his body in case even the weak light from the sky was reflected in its lethal steel tongue. He stopped again, and resumed his watch. He heard two more shots, at some distance from the house. Without warning, Consuelo's bedroom lamp flooded the courtyard with a waxy light; as its beams struck into the cloistered space close to the garden passageway, the light reflected in the eyes of a man standing with his back pressed against the wall. The lamp as suddenly extinguished, Rafael slipped silently toward his prey.

The Ashamed Man's reluctance had ensured that he escaped the fate of his comrades; when the firing started he ran toward the trees, and hid among them until Pelean's men joined the fight and moved across the open ground. Finding himself now behind the police, he followed the treeline; as shots and curses and challenges intensified he sprinted for the garden wall, climbing desperately he assailed it and dropped into the garden. He could not tell what had happened to the others, but knew that bullets could not penetrate stone; he ran through the garden, gained the steps and crossed the terrace.

The muscles in Rafael's chest twitched in the cooler September air; as he moved his attention did not wander from the place where his enemy's eyes had reflected the bedroom light. But a quick shadow with a long arm leapt out of the night at him; Rafael withered under a blow from a blunt object. He collapsed to his knees but still held fast to the blade in his hand. As he looked up he saw a demon with a blackened face raise his arm once more to strike him dead. He struggled to regain his feet and lift his knife to parry in his defence; the arm of the demon arched backward, but became fixed at the top of its arc. A voice called out, and another arm gripped the club and restrained it. Conscious that the demon was in check, Rafael swung his body and arm and knife with all the strength and energy left in him; the knife found a new home in soft tissue. The figure staggered back, the club dropped from him onto the ground, and with a gasp of escaping air, he fell.

Tom looked from Rafael to the body of the Ashamed Man, then back to Rafael, who had now fully regained his feet, but clung to one of the pillars for support.

"Rafael, are you hurt?" he asked in an urgent whisper.

Rafael could not answer immediately, but only put out his hand to the younger man; they shook hands and surveyed the battlefield.

"Go Tomas, hide, there may be others!"

"Then you'll need help to stop them. You're bleeding Rafael, you can't fight them all."

Tom hesitated, aware that Rafael struggled to hold onto consciousness. Consuelo ran into the courtyard, carrying a large meat cleaver taken from the kitchen. The three of them stood together for a moment, but before they could speak, several deep reverberating thuds warned them that someone was breaking down the main door. Terrified, but holding the cleaver in front of her, Consuelo ran to the door, vowing to kill the first of the unknown assailants to pass the splintered timbers. The beating stopped abruptly, and a familiar voice called out.

"Open! Open the door! This is the Civil Guard!"

"What do you want?! Why can't you leave me alone?!" she screamed back.

"Dona Consuelo, this is Carlos de Rozario! You must open the door! You are in danger!"

Consuelo pushed back the bolts with her free hand, and turned the two heavy keys. As she pulled the door inward, she was dazzled by the light from several torches.

"In the name of the Holy Virgin, what do you want here?!"

"Dona Consuelo, a man may be hiding in your house!"

She would subsequently reflect, that de Rozario had not then appreciated just how close to the truth he had come. He stood before her, fear in his own eyes, his face framed by the rifles of the men who stood around him, their faces thrown into darkness by the light from the torches which some of them held.

"Yes...yes, he is in the courtyard," she said in a matter of fact voice, emotion draining away. De Rozario led his men in an heroic charge; they surrounded the body of the Ashamed Man, perhaps in expectation that he would try to get up and run from them, their rifles ready to shoot or bludgeon as required.

"Are you satisfied teniente?! He is dead! Dead! Can you see? Is that what you wanted?! Are you happy now?!" she shouted to them through streaming tears.

De Rozario was at the same instant relieved and affronted; relieved that she had not come to harm by his scheme, yet affronted that she showed no gratitude for his arrival. Rafael had suffered a cut to his head; blood trickled down the side of his face and onto his chest. In a rare act of graciousness, de Rozario ordered two of the Guards to carry him back to his room. Determined to retrieve something from the near catastrophe he went to Consuelo.

"Dona Consuelo, I apologise for alarming you, but you see here," and he pointed to the body, "the danger I warned you of. Your servant is clearly a capable man with a knife. I hope that you will always have someone close to you who will act in your defence. I will leave one of my men here tonight for your protection."

"No! No! No!" she screamed with emphasis and venom, almost spitting her tears at him.

"But there may be other men watching the house!"

"Then go and look for them teniente! But be under no illusion that you and your men are welcome here! Get out! Leave my house! Go!"

Although he was offended, he knew better than to risk losing all, even if he could still threaten Manolito. He saluted, and ordered that the Ashamed Man's body was carried out. As he was about to withdraw over the threshold, he bowed and spoke finally. She faced him with the cleaver still in her hands.

"I am, and always will be, at your service."

With trembling hands Consuelo locked and bolted the door. Crying and distressed at her situation, and begging God to return Arturo to her, she went to find Rafael. He lay on his bed; to her surprise Tom was already attending to him, cleaning the head wound from a basin of water stained red. Uncertain what to say, Tom looked up at her for a moment.

"Isn't it strange," he said, "once I took the part of the wounded man, and now I am the nurse."

The Captive Summer

Questions Answered

Rafael wanted to resume his watch, but Consuelo fiercely resisted; she spoke angrily, even accusing him of stupidity, before relenting and apologising. She spoke to Tom only in low whispers, as she believed that de Rozario had placed police around the house. They hurriedly discussed whether the assailant could have been a spy; although Consuelo could not hide her anguish, which left tangible tracks at the sides of her mouth, they agreed that if the man was a police agent, de Rozario would have arrested Rafael for murder. Neither Tom nor Rafael would accept full credit for their actions, each seeking to point out in their turn the significance of what the other man had done. Promising Rafael that they would keep watch in his place, they withdrew, and walked back to the courtyard.

As before, all was silent. What little moon had been in the sky had disappeared, and the stars threw down only a faint light over the terracotta battlefield. They stood together, peering through darkness to the place where the body had fallen. She turned to him.

"Tomas, I can smell his blood," she whispered, as the proximity and dread of death came upon her.

"I'll wash it away in the morning Consuelo, I'll scrub the floor."

"No Tomas, if we leave the blood until the sun rises, then it will stay with us, there will be more deaths. We must clean the ground now, while it is dark, we cannot let the sun find the stains."

Tom brought two rusting buckets from the store room, which he filled at the courtyard pump; he poured their contents over the drying inky stains on the ground. With heavy brooms they set about scrubbing the bricks, washing away the blackness which had a short while before meant life in a man's veins. They set no lights, and judged their success in sluicing away the blood only by what they could see as the streams and rivulets washed back and forth over the floor. They stopped whenever they thought they heard a noise from beyond the wall, and waited, bucket or broom in hand, for doom to descend once more. Satisfied in the almost darkness that they had cleaned the blood away, they went into the house, leaving the tainted water to seek an escape by evaporating into the night or soaking into the already dusky pink of the bricks.

Consuelo handed Tom a glass of brandy, and poured a generous measure for herself, before sitting down in the high backed leather chair and drawing her legs beneath her. They drank in silence, stopping with glass to lips, at the suggestion of a sound from outside, before guiltily resuming. The reception room was in darkness save for a solitary candle, and this emphasised the room's appearance as a Hispanic hybrid of baronial hall and mausoleum. Consuelo's head drooped lower, and then jerked upward, as she fought the fatigue which drew her to a troubled and temporary oblivion.

"Consuelo, you should go to bed. I will keep watch for the rest of the night."

"I cannot sleep Tomas. It is as if we had returned to the war: this is the last strongpoint, the enemy is massing in the darkness around us, and we must prepare to die."

"No Consuelo! What if de Rozario spoke truthfully? What if that man was a bandit?"

She raised her face to his; the little light in the room exaggerated the signs of care and exhaustion in her face. For the first time Tom glimpsed what Consuelo might look like as an old woman.

"I do not know what would be worse Tomas, if de Rozario spoke truthfully or lied. If that man was a bandit, then others will follow him. If he was a police spy, then de Rozario will return. I am a woman imprisoned, as assuredly as my husband is in France."

"Could you leave Spain? What about trying to cross the border into Gibraltar?"

"Tomas, this is my home, my husband's home. I protect it, as Rafael protects me. I will stay," and she cupped one hand to her forehead, as if the full implication of the decision wanted to force its way out of her mind, "and perhaps I will die."

"Do you fear death?" Tom asked.

"Yes. I fear being consigned to a hole in the earth, and the soil falling on my face. Do you know why Catholics have to be buried Tomas?"

"No."

"The Church forbids cremation because on the day of judgement we shall rise bodily out of our graves to go before God. Cremation is a sin."
Given his own uncertainties on the subject, he was disinclined to pursue that line of discussion.

"I think the judgement we receive in this life is the more important. How we deal with others, and are dealt with by them."

"Often the judgement of others in this world is transformed into cruelty. Rafael understands this, he has suffered a crooked judgement, but he has the strength not to allow it to break him."

"What happened to him?"

"Rafael has worked for my husband and myself for eight years," she said shifting in the chair, a sign to Tom that she was feeling more comfortable in herself, and continued, "so most of his life was a memory when he came into our lives. My husband defended him in court, when no one else would. Arturo was himself judged for that action, but it was of no importance to him what others thought."

"What had Rafael been charged with?"

"Rape. He was living in a rooming house in Cadiz, in the barrio favoured by sailors, although he was no longer a seafarer then. The wife of the owner of the house accused him of raping her, when he would not sleep with her. A Cuban, a negro. To this day people assume that he is Moroccan, and Spain will not tolerate the Moors."

Tom now began to understand Rafael's loyalty, and his determination to put himself in the way of whatever harm might be directed at Consuelo.

"Was he acquitted?" he asked.

"Yes. Arturo saw to that. The woman was cheating on her husband, the men staying at the house provided too much temptation, and she was stealing from him. She planned to take Rafael as her lover, then force him to kill her husband. No one would help him, until Arturo saw the case papers. But the world judges the acts of decent men harshly."

"Then Rafael believed himself under obligation to you?"

"No. It was worse than that," and she laughed sarcastically in the darkness, "he had nowhere to go. The trial was held in Seville, where we had an apartment. That night, it rained, rained very hard, the bell rang. We expected no one, and Arturo went down to the hall. When he opened the door to the street, Rafael was standing in the rain, soaked to the skin. Even though he had been acquitted, no one would give a Cuban a room for the night. So we did."

"And he has been with you ever since?"

"Yes Tomas, ever since. He told me once that he believed that God had sent Arturo to save him from the liars. He promised God that he would defend Arturo and I, even if it cost him his own life. And," but she hesitated before proceeding, "he told me that he believed God wanted him to protect you."

Tom felt ashamed at the idea that another person would be prepared to sacrifice his life to save him, even though by taking up arms he had shown his preparedness to do just that himself. They sat in silence, maintaining a strained state of alertness, until by the luminous hands of his wrist watch, Tom made out that the time was then beyond two o'clock.

"Consuelo, Consuelo," he called to the figure whose regular breathing in the darkness was the sole warrant of life, until she stirred and pulled her head from the arm of the chair, "there is no use in both of us being here, go to bed. I will stay."

She would have protested her right to remain, but Tom, determined to assert his own claim as a sentry, was insistent.

By turns he either sat by the water pump or loitered in the centre of the courtyard gazing up at the sky. He remembered an earlier period of night time guard duty, while still at flying school in Scotland, when he and three other L/ACs were issued with rifles, but only one bullet each, and entrusted with the protection of the Tiger Moths. There was hangar space for only a few of the aircraft, so most were left in the open, drawn up at the edge of the runway in a long line of doped fabric. As the aircraft were light, they were secured to the ground by stanchions, with pegs driven into the frozen earth. A gale, like a late arrival at a noisy party, rolled in from the Irish Sea; soon the aeroplanes were bucking against the high ice bearing wind in their efforts to escape. The Liverpudlian comic among the guard detachment, Leslie Nash of chattering teeth fame, threw himself in an act of heroic madness upon the lower plane of one Tiger as a stanchion and peg parted company. Tom and the others dropped their rifles and clung desperately onto struts, stanchions and wheels: but the aircraft wanted to fly. Nash clambered into the rear cockpit, perhaps believing that his body weight would tip the balance in their favour. It was his bad luck that the fury of the wind increased at that point, and the stanchion on the starboard side of the lower plane also came away. Tom remembered the sensation as he was lifted upward, and looked to the sky for an explanation. He briefly saw scurrying clouds which caused the stars to flicker like signal lamps; but was then dropped unceremoniously on his back.

As he got to his feet, he was conscious that now there was a gap in the line of aircraft. They found the Tiger on its back beyond a hedge, Nash hanging from the straps, which he had had the good sense to fasten. As Tom looked to the skies again, the clouds that passed over the house produced the same effect; he wondered what Morse message the stars were sending out on this treacherous night.

The sky lightened. Tom walked around the courtyard inspecting it for signs of the struggle: there were none. From outside the walls he heard the first innocent song of the birds. He considered going to the kitchen to prepare breakfast, but this was not possible. He patrolled his square of light, only taking a detour to inspect the door from the terrace for signs of damage. The splintered timbers bore evidence of the determination of the dead man to gain access.

Rafael was the first to rise; he tapped Tom on the shoulder as he sat at the pump. He held a finger up to his lips as the young man swung round, and then made a gesture with his hand to indicate food. Even though no one outside could have heard lowered voices, they maintained this pantomime, and Rafael went to the kitchen. They ate together with Consuelo, under a restraint of fear and exhaustion.

"Rafael, are you sure that Quiros succeeded with his message to Antonio and Jesus?" asked Consuelo, sipping lentil coffee.

"Yes madam, but I will go into the town today to enquire again. The Guard has been looking for them; their names are also in the list of suspects."

"The danger to you all is now so great," offered Tom, "it would be better if I took my chances."

"And walk to Gibraltar in your uniform?" retorted Consuelo.

"I cannot put you at risk any longer."

"Then let us organise your escape," she said.

"There are so few of us here, another assailant could get in and find me, and then you would go to a firing squad," Tom replied.

"There should be more of us," and Consuelo looked to both men as she said this, "Maria is afraid that cholera will return to the town. If she and her children were to live with us, we would be a little safer. But I won't force this. You also must agree to it."

There was a silence; both men were aware that there was both safety and danger in numbers. Manolito had said nothing following his encounters with de Rozario and Tom. The two younger children, both girls, had little knowledge of evil, and would only think that they had the privilege of staying with their adopted aunt in her large house overlooking the sea.

"If Maria consents," Tom said, Rafael nodded.

That afternoon Rafael went into town; at the harbour he sought out Quiros. The news of the attack on the house had passed quickly into circulation; as he walked through the narrow streets he was aware that he was the subject of general attention. He was credited with killing not one, but two or all three of the gang; people looked upon him as if he were a man possessing superhuman powers. Some resented that a Cuban negro should have killed a Spaniard, and yet be allowed to walk the streets. However, his journey seemed in vain as no one knew where Quiros was; he turned back. As he approached a street corner coming away from the harbour, his path was blocked by two men. They, like the gang, were farm labourers, when there was any work to be had, and when not, they propped themselves against a wall and waited.

"Ah! It's the Cuban, the one who thinks he can kill good Spaniards!" said the first.

"Cuban! No, he looks more like a Moor to me! I thought that Spain had rid itself of these people? Which is it, Moor or Cuban?" questioned the other.

Rafael stood his ground, but was aware that the altercation was drawing the attention of others.

There was a sudden disturbance behind him, as if a group of people were moving forward through the crowd at great speed.

"Do you have a problem?" asked a voice.

"No Quiros, we were only..."

"I don't fucking care, get lost!"

Rafael turned, to face Quiros and a handful of the other fishermen.

"I heard that you were looking for me Rafael," he said, "so, you've found me."

Quiros was a hard man, who would resort to violence if provoked; but he also respected bravery, and he hated the Civil Guard. He and Rafael walked back to the breakwater together, and plotted an escape over the sea.

The Captive Summer

The Trial Of Galileo Galilei

Pablo Villasellos had expected arrest from the moment of his arrival in San Cristobal. He was a Republican. To be discovered to have broken the Law of Political Responsibilities would cost him his licence as a teacher, and prevent him from working. But this was not the end of it. It was true that he did not actively participate in the defence of Madrid in the war, as he had a temperament ill suited to fixing a bayonet, but he had been one of those engaged in another war. He had written a play, *The Trial Of Galileo Galilei*, a criticism of a Church so assured of the divinely imparted revelation which it guarded, that the Inquisition sentenced Galileo to house imprisonment for life for advocating the theory of Copernicus. The play had been denounced as a Bolshevik love poem, its performance or publication deemed an arrestable offence.

To Villasellos, Galileo was a hero of an earlier struggle; he had demonstrated that the mysteries of creation could be unravelled through experimentation and observation. In presenting Galileo's trial, he drew parallels to Spain in the twentieth century. He could not trust himself to fire a rifle, but he could set down on paper a struggle of ideas and beliefs which would rank alongside the deployment of a corps of trained men.

Who had betrayed him to the police? Perhaps he had betrayed himself, perhaps his own enthusiasm for enquiry, had encouraged a child to relay his views to an adult; and the adult had then simply relayed them to the Civil Guard. Perhaps word had come from the Ministry of the Interior in Madrid that he was suspected of Republican sympathies; perhaps an old friend, now in the Civil Guard headquarters, had offered up Pablo's name when he could no longer tolerate the blows and kicks. He did not know, and it did not matter whether he did or not, it was enough that he was suspected. When he had entered the Civil Guard barracks, Villasellos did not know the man with bleeding hands who passed by him in the main office, and that did not matter; Spain was a nation replete with anonymous men with bleeding hands and pleading eyes.

As he returned to his apartment he took care to observe whether he was followed; he halted to tie a shoe lace, asked a stranger for a match, lingered on a street corner as the air vibrated around him in the afternoon heat. As he resolved to complete the journey without further delay it occurred to him that no one need follow: they knew where he lived, and he could not live in another town without the permission of the authorities.

When he closed the door of his room behind him he surveyed the floorboards intently for any sign that one had been disturbed: he knew of unsuspecting men in the civil war who had walked across creaking floors, only to detonate a hidden grenade and die. Satisfied, he stepped lightly to the wardrobe, and pushing aside the clothes hanging there, felt for the edge of the back panel. It came away; he turned and put it down against the bedstead. The buff parcel was where he had left it, safe in the false compartment. Pausing to listen in case anyone was outside the room, he took and opened the parcel and sat on the bed. He was faced by the proof of his guilt, the only surviving typed copy of *The Trial Of Galileo Galilei*. As he turned the rough pages he absorbed the words which could send him before a firing squad. Rousing himself from his reverie, he looked to the cold fireplace. To start a fire in summer would be as subtle as walking into the street handing out pamphlets accusing Franco of being a Mason: but even now they might be coming to get him.

The fire came easily. He knelt down by the grate, and fed the sheets of paper into the devouring flames. Some pages however drew his attention; he paused to read for the last time, the words he had first scribbled under a guttering candle, as dust from the ceiling plaster, loosened under the impact of the shells which dropped vertically in the streets around him, powdered his hair and obscured what he wrote. Often he wiped away dust and inky scrawl from the sheets of paper to create a lane for his metal tipped plough to furrow through the stony field. As he wrote he cursed the Fascists, and he cursed the shells, and he cursed the broken pen. As Madrid was pounded he deliberated on the procedures of the Inquisition, and the arguments put forward by the Judges; he considered how Galileo would have defended himself. His greatest difficulty was in deciding on the form of words by which Galileo eventually acquiesced to the judgement of the Court.

Two scenes had resonance for him: he remembered that he had nearly died writing them, his sole warning being that his candle blew out just before the shockwave from the shell reached him. He threw himself down, the window frame and shattering glass splashing across the table above his head. When, stunned and deafened, he had regained his feet and extracted the pages, his own blood was soaking into the cellulose fibres along with ink blotches and dirt. He took this as a sign; clearing the table with a sweep of his arm, and pushing away splintered timbers, he sat down and resumed writing. He read on one sheet the following.

[A cell beneath the Court of the Inquisition. Galileo is visited by the Jailer.]

JAILER: It is dark senor, I will light a second torch.
GALILEO: I have need of no light, but I thank you for your concern. What

is your name?

JAILER: My name is Marco senor.

GALILEO: Have you been in the service of the Inquisition many years Marco?

JAILER: I have held the office of jailer for three years senor.

GALILEO: Does your work trouble you?

JAILER: I serve the Church, and therefore God, my work is a duty against heresy.

GALILEO: Marco, do you regard every man and woman who you have had cause to deposit in a fetid cell as a heretic?

JAILER: It is the determination of the Court.

GALILEO: I ask not what the Court determines, but what you believe.

JAILER: Senor, there is no determination but that of the Court.

GALILEO: You believe it so.

JAILER: Have you eaten senor?

GALILEO: The questioning of the Judges tends against a want of food. I have eaten all that I wish.

Then the beginning of the next scene, once the Jailer had left Galileo and reported what he had observed to the Judges.

[A private chamber of the Judges. The Jailer enters.]

FIRST JUDGE: And did you observe him as you were instructed?

JAILER: Yes senor, I did.

FIRST JUDGE: Well, what of it? Did Galileo converse with Satan, as we suspected he would?

JAILER: No senor, he did not.

SECOND JUDGE: Then how did he pass his time jailer?

JAILER: By juggling senor.

SECOND JUDGE: Juggling? Was this some trick?

JAILER: No senor, he sat quietly, in the half darkness, and tossed an orange between his hands.

FIRST JUDGE: An orange? He threw an orange between his hands?

JAILER: Yes senor, like so. [The Jailer takes a coin and tosses it from one hand to the other and back again.]

FIRST JUDGE: What explanation did he offer for this behaviour?

JAILER: He said that he was observing the trajectory of an object falling in space. He held his hands together so, only a little apart; then on each throw of the orange increased the distance between his hands. He caught the orange cleanly each time, and after a moment seemingly to weigh the fruit, passed it back to the other hand.

SECOND JUDGE: Did he not eat the fruit?

JAILER: No senor, he said that he was without bodily hunger, only desiring to understand the laws by which such things could be.

SECOND JUDGE: What laws?

JAILER: He said the laws governing the motion of objects in the heavens, laws which applied universally regardless of the size or position of the object.

FIRST JUDGE: Jailer, are you sure that he did not did not enter into a conversation with demons?

JAILER: Senor I swear that he did not. I sat beside him, there was none in the cell but he and I.

FIRST JUDGE: When did you leave him?

JAILER: Shortly after midnight. I counselled him to sleep, as he would be called for early in the morning for further questioning.

SECOND JUDGE: Was his mind troubled?

JAILER: No senor. He appeared to be at peace. And he thanked me for my company.

FIRST JUDGE: [Pauses.] You may go, here is the gold. Say nothing of this.

[Judge gives the Jailer a small purse containing some coins. Jailer exits.]

SECOND JUDGE: Is this man to be trusted?

FIRST JUDGE: In my experience yes; before he became a jailer he assisted with the extraction of confessions. His faith is strong.

SECOND JUDGE: Can we devise a prison sure enough to hold Galileo?

FIRST JUDGE: It matters not if a man stand at the heart of a desert or on a high plateau. If his mind is captive, then he is our prisoner.

SECOND JUDGE: And how are we to build a prison which will bind his mind without denying his mind access to his beating heart?

FIRST JUDGE: We will devise a method, have no doubt, his heresy will be ended.

He hesitated, but then relinquished each sheet from his hand and cast it into the flames; the pages curled in the heat, darkened and shrivelled before his eyes. He sweated readily, his shirt collar becoming a dark noose.

Villasellos expected to be re-arrested that night, and sat back on the bed once the manuscript was burned away. He imagined the hurried departure of the policeman keeping watch on the house; saw him running breathless to raise the alarm, and a returning procession of men bearing rifles with bullets washed in holy water. He watched the door, and listened intently for any noise in the street. Would he resist? Would he scream a final denunciation of Franco as they subdued him? He thought how strange it was to have survived the war, to have escaped searing fragments of shell which tore holes in those around him, only to be captured now.

There was no commotion outside, no suggestion that his true crime had been discovered. He rose and went to the window; the street was deserted, but at that time of the early evening, when children had been called in from play, and labourers were returning from the fields, that was not unusual. Perhaps the police did not know, but they must suspect. He went out, ate at the cafe at the harbour, watched everyone who passed. When he had spent his last few pesetas he returned to the house before the curfew fell, climbed the stair, threw himself down on the bed and waited. Eventually he succumbed to sleep, secure at least that the manuscript existed now only in his head. He awoke at dawn, and looked about him: there was no policeman at the foot of his bed, by the wash stand or the wardrobe. He arose, washed, and changed his shirt.

He decided to arrive at the school punctually; he walked through the streets, as cautious as before, but not to the extent, he thought, of giving himself away. At the school he passed the Principal, Senor Garcia, in the corridor as the children filed in. They exchanged greetings, but Garcia was as agitated as a lamb before the slaughterhouse. Villasellos began the first class, which was Spanish history. Although his mouth was dry, and there was a physical pain in his stomach, he became calmer as he faced the children: their open faces, as yet untainted by the full horror of life, gave him hope; he addressed them.

"Children! The history of Spain," and he hesitated, surveying the rows of docile faces set before him, faces too young to know what he knew, faces shaped by play, faces which so far had only learned that this was a hungry country, "the history of Spain is a story of courage and forbearance, written in the blood of the martyrs. Spain is a nation set apart by God to receive His divine blessing, united under the banner raised by the Caudillo. Today we will learn how Spain came to greatness under God's will and grace." What he wanted to say was that Spain was a nation descending into barbarism, where the light which God caused to fill the sky had been obliterated by the smoke from the fires of Guernica and Barcelona, from the burning flesh of children like themselves. There was a knock at the door. He stopped and looked across, Senor Garcia was standing at the open doorway, and beckoned to him. He went over.

"Senor Villasellos, the Civil Guard is here, they want to see you." Through the barely opened doorway he could taste Senor Garcia's breath, and over his shoulder stood the form of de Rozario with another Guard behind him.

"Let me tell the children that I have to leave the lesson Senor Garcia. Please, grant me one moment." To his surprise, Garcia agreed; before de Rozario could dispute the decision the door was closed, and Villasellos turned back. He walked to his desk as if in a dream, his heart pounding in his ears, unconscious of his steps across the wooden floor. Were the children to form his firing squad, was this room to be the place of his execution? When he turned once more to face them should he ask for a blindfold and wait for the crack of the last sound which would ever pass his ears?

"Children!" The rows of faces grew attentive once more, "I must leave you now, as I have to answer some questions. I had not expected to leave you so soon, when there is so much that I had wanted to tell you. It is difficult to compress all that I had wanted to say to you into a few words. But I have no choice," vaguely indicating the closed door with an outstretched hand, "and must therefore be brief." He paused, struggling to control his feelings, but then found strength in their faces. "If you remember me when you are older, when you have attained adulthood, and taken your place in our society, remember me as one who counselled you that gentleness in a human being is a sign of a surplus of strength, not a want of it."

With that he bowed before them and turned away. As he left, young uncomprehending eyes followed his form to the door. Then he was gone. He faced de Rozario in the corridor without fear.

"I am ready teniente. But before you take me, know this. If there is a God, and if Franco rules Spain under divine will, then it is God who should be judged, not the Spanish people."

This was more than de Rozario could tolerate, and Villasellos was felled with a blow to his jaw delivered by the Guard's rifle. As he stood up, he wiped the blood from his mouth with his sleeve, and laughed at his tormentor. He did not doubt that his life would soon be over, and that de Rozario might live much longer than he; but every day the policeman would have to remember what he had said to him, and consider its truth.

The Captive Summer

The Fate Of Arturo

Conscious that Oleanza had in anger advised that he would accept corpses dug up from the cemetery, Mendoza contemplated the simple device of claiming that the El Faro gang members were the Sugar Bandits. Their death removed the tedious necessity of an interrogation, and prevented the unfortunate calamity of an escape. There was one obstacle however: the three dead men were already suspected of a robbery that had occurred on the day of the parade near Almunecar; the Civil Guard commander there was adamant that the corpses were, in a manner of speaking, already his. The search continued.

Like the action of a set of beaters on a pheasant shoot, the nocturnal raids of the police on houses throughout the town flushed out both those they expected to arrest, and sometimes those that they did not. Like the fugitive who had escaped through the house in *Calle del Rosa*, men with no identity papers, and no desire to apply for any, regularly passed through the town, taking refuge with former comrades or family members; at night they defied the curfew and slipped like spectres through the streets and into the fields once more. Some men had been on the run since the end of the civil war, others had escaped from prison or a Labour Battalion. But each man hid his face, and slept lightly, if at all.

In a house like a fractured tooth in the slum district, two such men, who had beaten a soldier over the head with a length of chain and fled from a work party repairing a railway bridge, enjoyed sanctuary provided by the father of a man whose name did appear on the list of suspects. The suspect was Julio Saez, who had fought for the Republic and then disappeared; his location was as much a mystery to his father, Luis, as it was to the police. The house was set in a steep lane passable only on foot or by mules, where neighbours across the way could almost reach out to shake hands. Although a hovel, with no running water or sanitation, it enjoyed the defences of a castle, and an escape route unknown to the police. The land fell sharply away in an escarpment at the back of the lane, and sanitation pits dug into the sloping ground ensured that the night soil dropped clear of the hovels. Some closets were little more than stinking shacks made up of a mosaic of unmatched pieces of timber collected from ruined buildings or the beach; others were more luxurious, with a measure of dignity for the occupant and obscurity for the waste as it fell to the pit below. The house of Luis Saez had such an enclosure, with a ladder giving access to the pit, and a hatch beside the base of the ladder.

Sargento Pelean was ordered to arrest Julio Saez, on impeccable intelligence that he had returned to visit his father. He was astute enough to send one of his men to the back of the lane; the Guard took up a position upwind of the shacks but at a point where he could observe anyone leaving the houses through the yards and making for open country. Satisfied that he had set a trap, Pelean and another officer trotted through the darkened lane, brought the butt of their rifles down on the door of the house, flakes of ancient paint falling like petrified flower petals from its warped timbers, and demanded entry. The occupiers of the neighbouring hovels looked anxiously to their own portals; a sucking child broke off from feeding to cry at its mother's breast, and gaunt young men nursing aching stomachs spat onto the floor; none looked out. But the intelligence was wrong: there were two fugitives not one, but neither of them was the son of Luis Saez.

As the storm broke upon them, the fugitives, with noiseless precision, took up small bundles of food and made for the rear door. Their host, with a nimbleness which belied his age, dropped a piece of timber into brackets across the front door, and squealed in a high pitched voice at the Civil Guards in the street, demanding to know what was going on, and feigning infirmity when it came to taking the cross timber up again. The two men let themselves out, but instead of crossing the tiny yard and out through the gate, entered the closet, pulled up the seat, climbed down the ladder to the pit.

"Ughh! This stench! I'm going to vomit!" said the first.

"Shut up! Some of it is yours!" hissed his companion close behind him.

When the seat had dropped back into place above them, they were left completely in darkness. They held their breath against the fumes of the decomposing excrement, and listened. The Guard who was watching the gate ran forward when he heard the rifles pounding from the lane; the fugitives then removed the wooden pins securing the hatch in the base of the closet, and let themselves out into the sweet, clean night air. Both wanted to vomit, but this would have in an instant betrayed them; hand to mouth they crawled away, folding their bodies into the curves of the dry earth like snakes. They skirted the perimeter of the town, running blindly through olive groves, orchards, and scrub; they climbed over walls and crawled like lizards; they swam through dirt and refuse, alert for any sign that the police were pursuing them. Eventually, exhausted, bruised and bleeding, with wounds washed only by their own sweat, they halted. They had reached the north western outskirts, and found themselves in a walled garden, with a large brick and concrete building in its centre: unknowingly, they had reached the new orphanage. The building was unlit, as it had yet to receive the first children. The fugitives lay panting in the screen of bushes which lay against the garden wall, uncertain where they should go. In the Labour Battalion they had no identities or history; they had once been known as Gutierrez and Bautista. In their work party it was Gutierrez who struck at the guard, and the nearest man to him, Bautista, ran with him as they came under fire. Gutierrez nursed his left leg as they lay in the cover provided by the foliage: he had struck his knee climbing a wall, and the joint was now swelling and painful.

"Let's rest here, I may have broken my knee cap," he said, gripping his knee with both hands, in an effort to stop the pain rolling up to his groin.

"Can you walk?" asked Bautista.

"No, not on this leg, I'm done."

"May the Virgin save us."

"May the Virgin save Spain!"

For perhaps a quarter of an hour they thought that they had evaded the Civil Guard; and the earth on which they lay became softer as sleep overtook them. They were jolted awake by the sound of a heavy truck approaching along the road on the far side of the building. The vehicle stopped, shouting and the sound of heavy boots striking the roadway replacing the sound of the night.

"They found us! Get out Gutierriez, get out!" shouted Bautista, as he scrambled through the branches, only to emerge into the beam of a powerful torch. A second beam cut the darkness, and he was illuminated in the light of both. Gutierrez pulled himself to his feet and staggered out to meet his own fate.

"If you have the chance," he said, "go back into the bushes and climb the wall. I'm done."

They heard a voice, which came from a point of impenetrable blackness between the beams of light, it was de Rozario.

"Stay where we can see you, or I will give the order to fire!"

They walked forward, arms raised, Gutierrez limping from the pain in his knee. He was a veteran of the war, had faced exile in France, and recklessly returned to Spain to find his family. That was when he had been taken, crossing the Pyrennes, and imprisoned for his crimes. He did not believe in God or the Apostolic Church, and did not accept that after this life of pain he would awake in a better place. He understood the Spanish fascination with death; he had run and crawled and cowered long enough: if death was coming he would meet it here, in the garden of the darkened house. He spat on the ground as he hobbled forward; lowering his hands, he tore open his shirt, revealing his chest. As he did this he took a step in front of Bautista, thereby obscuring him from view by the approaching Guards.

"Come on you bastards! Shoot me! Can you see my nipples?! They're as good as those on your whores, and they're easy targets!" he screamed at them. "Are you waiting for a sign from your God?!"

"What are you doing, you crazy bastard?!" hissed Bautista into his ear, not wanting to be caught in a storm of bullets.

"Go! Run! Get away now!" Gutierrez hissed back at him over his shoulder.

The Guards were closing, and emerged now around both sides of the orphanage; they came on, silhouettes holding out long sticks, three or four with torch beams processing before them. The building stood mute in the middle of the sloping ground, its dormitories and classrooms virgin spaces, without memories or the imprint of children. The structure stood on its foundation of weakened concrete, set on the sloping earth which pressed down upon it from the silent mountains to the north. The workmen had completed their tasks as required, but to a man they were glad to leave the place and move onto other sites. The fine cracks that had appeared at ground level before even that was completed were hidden; but as more weight was added, the cracks deepened and lengthened, floor by floor, day by day. Had the building been occupied, its imminent collapse would have been a tragedy; as it was, it provided the last opportunity for the men to escape.

There was a loud crack; bricks and timber began to tear from the building in a plume of dust. A pillar of bricks shuddered, slipped in the earth, and with a roar like the wounded Goliath, collapsed, shaking the earth and throwing down several of the darkened figures in the garden. But Gutierrez and Bautista stood transfixed, unable to comprehend what had happened, but aware that the torches which had shone full in their face were now extinguished. Gutierrez turned, and with both hands pushed Bautista, again exhorting him to run.

De Rozario stood with his mouth agape, aware that something terrible had happened; and through his stupefaction assuming that a grenade had been thrown into the garden. As silence returned, he remembered that they were pursuing fugitives; he took his torch and played its dusty beam first upward over the broken orphanage, and then across the ground. He stopped when he found Gutierrez standing alone, his shirt open to the waist, and laughing hysterically.

Mendoza, found it hard to believe his dust stained subordinate when he returned to the barracks with Gutierrez.

"Did he plant a bomb?" he asked, curious as to how Gutierrez could have arranged for the building to fall.

"There was no bomb capitan, the orphanage collapsed without warning as we searched the grounds."

"Does the Mayor know?'

"I have not yet informed him."

"Good. I want to speak to this prisoner first. Bring him to an interrogation room," and Mendoza left de Rozario to wipe himself down.

Gutierriez was held at each elbow; Mendoza went up to him, intently looking over his face, amazed that an emaciated, exhausted and wounded convict could have caused such mayhem. He stepped back.

"Take the table out, tie his hands at the back."

The room was quickly cleared.

"Now," he said turning to de Rozario, "I'll show you how to conduct an interrogation Carlos that does not require the walls to be repainted. Put him on his back."

Gutierrez was forced down, and lay on the floor looking up at the two officers, who appeared to him as giants. Mendoza bent over.

"Gutierrez, this is how the world will appear to you when they lay you in your grave. Does life seem a long way from you?" he asked, thumbs tucked into his belt.

"Yes, very far away."

"Good. Let's see how much farther away we can take it," and he placed one foot across Gutierrez's windpipe, and slowly applied pressure. A look of terror spread across the crushed man's face, as the supply of air was cut off. His body bucked under the trauma, but Mendoza's foot remained in place. De Rozario was in awe of his superior, and looked from Gutierrez to Mendoza and back, deeply impressed at the calm and effective torture. Mendoza relinquished; Gutierrez recovered like a man who had suffered a fit.

"All I did was to escape. I wanted to see my family again," and he gasped and gulped air into his lungs, knocking his head on the floor as he did so.

"Why did the building collapse?"

"I don't know," and Mendoza raised his foot as if to bring it down on his throat, "I don't know! I don't know! We were hiding in the grounds, and it fell!"

Mendoza lowered his foot, he was aware that there had been stories, from reliable sources like Morales, that cement intended for the foundation had found its way into other buildings. Perhaps the man was telling the truth.

"I will not let you up from the floor until you tell me something of use to me. What do you know?"

Gutierrez looked from Mendoza to de Rozario; in his terror his mind was blank. He had nothing of value for them, and although he wanted to face the final agony, yet he wanted to say something to placate them. Impatient, Mendoza applied his foot once more; Gutierrez kicked at the floor, Mendoza relented. Then from his memories of imprisonment in France, a word came back into his mind, the only hope of his salvation.

"Bonar," he croaked.

"What did you say?" asked Mendoza.

"Arturo Bonar."

The name meant little to Mendoza, but de Rozario seized on it immediately.

"What about him?"

Gutierrez gulped, this was the only piece of information which might stop the torture.

"He is dead."

"That isn't possible, he writes to his wife from the internment camp at Bram."

Gutierrez shook his head vigorously from side to side.

"I knew the men, one of them was a forger. Bonar was killed at the Ebro. These men were with him, they took his papers, letters, money. They knew he was wealthy, knew where he lived. They forged letters, sent them from France, as if he was still alive. His wife sends money and food parcels. To a dead man."

Mendoza looked to de Rozario, who appeared stunned by the information.

"Is this of any value?" he asked.

"Yes capitan. I know the woman, it was her house that was attacked by the gang."

Mendoza signalled to the waiting Guards; Gutierrez was pulled from the floor, and his hands untied.

"Take him away," then turning to de Rozario he said, "perhaps you should let her know that she is a widow."

De Rozario nodded, numb and wondrous. The final obstacle had been removed from his path; Arturo would not return home, and Consuelo would soon discover that she needed his protection more than ever.

The Captive Summer

Discovery

Those who had known San Cristobal when Lindbergh's exploits filled the newspapers on both sides of the Atlantic, or Art Deco swept the salons of Paris, recalled a corner of Spain ignored by the outside world. Some foreigners made the journey, but mostly the open barren spaces and ilex plantations were known only to the people of Andalucia. No one of note ventured as far as San Cristobal itself. Its capture in the civil war merited a brief note in the London newspapers, then it returned to glorious obscurity. But the sabotage of the parade and the collapse of the orphanage changed that, to the despair of Oleanza and the delight of those who believed that men and God were engaged in a common guerilla struggle against Franco.

The circumstances surrounding the destruction of the orphanage attained Biblical significance; Gutierrez acquired the status of a new Samson, as rumours spread that the fugitive had simply pushed the building over with his hands, and that it had taken twenty Guards to restrain him. In the morning a crowd gathered to look in at the ruins from the lower garden wall, until the Civil Guard forced them to disperse. One of the onlookers was Maria, who was full of Catholic rapture at the possibility of a miracle, and gossip, in equal measure. She talked amongst the large number of women gathered at the wall, each one of whom possessed a new piece of information as to how the building fell, or were eager to re-circulate an old piece of news with a twist to it. The Guards were watchful and sullen, holding their rifles across their chests, but conscious also that the wrecked building behind them might collapse without warning. They nervously looked around from time to time, and stayed close to the safety of the road.

A car came up from the town and drew to a halt; from it emerged Oleanza, Father Abarca and Bucaro. They walked into the garden, escorted by de Rozario. The Mayor stood and surveyed the damage; from his vantage point he looked directly into one of the classrooms, which now adopted the aspect of a room in a large doll's house. He clamped one large fleshy hand across his mouth and jaw, and walked back and forth, stepping over bricks, roof tiles and broken lengths of timber. Finally despairing at the injustice in the world, he cursed his mother, his conception, his life long bad fortune, and the Madrid prostitute who had passed to him a sexual disease. Strutting in a violent rage he then threw his hands into the air, walked back to the car, wrenched open the door, climbed in, and sat sulking on the rear seat.

Maria and her children had been in residence for a week or so. Manolito and Isabella, the eldest girl, were old enough for school, and so walked into town with their mother each morning. To Maria the distance of four kilometres provided safety from the cholera, which she believed still persisted. The re-arrest of the teacher Villasellos, the fate of the orphanage, and the Mayor's evident anger and dismay were the principal topics of conversation when she sat with Consuelo later that morning to relay the intelligence.

"Madam, it just collapsed!" and Maria made a downward gesture with both hands to emphasise the force of the demise of the building.

"All of it?" asked Consuelo, still not believing the scale of the disaster.

"Well, one entire side! They say it will have to be demolished, it is unsafe. Thank God and the Blessed Virgin that no children were inside," and she hugged her other daughter, Emilia, to her. The child, oblivious to the danger she had not faced, continued to suck her thumb.

"I do not think that God had any part in its demise Maria. Why destroy the orphanage and leave the Town Hall and the Civil Guard barracks standing?"

"Madam, it was a warning to the Falangists from God. I know it."

"And Rafael knows of men who loaded a truck in the depth of night with many bags of cement from Oleanza's warehouse, and drove away."

"Madam, God does not love Franco."

"If only Franco understood that," replied Consuelo, "our suffering would be muted."

Their conversation was conducted in the reception room, from where they could observe Tom and Rafael working together in the vegetable garden. Quiros had succeeded in relaying a message to Rafael from Antonio and Jesus, and the two fishermen had visited the house late on the previous evening to discuss how Tom was to be extracted from Spanish soil. They discussed the plan in the kitchen, all interested parties huddled around the table, sharing a bottle of coarse wine, which rasped on their throats, and some cheese. The two brothers were not only amazed that the near dead young man had been restored to life, but had developed the ability to converse in their own language; for his part, Tom had the opportunity to thank the men who had saved him from the beach and the fierce naked sun.

"When can you take me?" he asked, aware both of the need to go, yet also sadness at the prospect of departure.

"Five days senor. Your countrymen in Gibraltar send a motor boat along this coast on its way to France. It carries various types of cargo," which Tom understood to mean intelligence agents, "we know when it is next returning, and we will take you and row out to meet it. Until that time we will have to remain in hiding ourselves, as we have an appointment with

Capitan Mendoza which we prefer to avoid."

"I understand, thank you. But I don't have anything to pay you with."

Antonio put his hand up to stop him speaking further.

"Senor Roberts, we need no payment, you will be returned to your comrades. Our fight against the Fascists is over, your struggle continues." Tom was still unclear whether he would be allowed to fly again, but he resisted saying this. Their business concluded, they all shook hands gravely, as if they had been delegates at a peace conference, and the fishermen departed.

Tom had promised Rafael that he would help him cut down and remove a group of old plum trees which were failing to bear fruit in useful quantities. As his remaining time at El Faro was now limited, they set about the task. Tom had suffered no further attacks, and the feeling in his right hand returned a little more each day, but he would occasionally stop, and scratch and rub his hand when the tingling sensation irritated him. As Consuelo and Maria watched, the men wrestled with the trunk of a plum tree that clung to the earth with a tenacity which derived from a long period of occupancy. They rocked back and forth, hoping to tear the tree complete with the larger part of its root system from the ground; their goal eluded them.

"It loves the ground Senor Tomas, it does not want to part from it," Rafael said.

Tom reflected that he understood how the tree felt (if trees had feelings) and to a degree, shared them.

"Rafael, we need more leverage. I'll climb the trunk, and you hack at the roots with the pick."

Tom scaled the tree, holding on to the slimmer branches as he rose. The tree groaned and creaked its protest at the deadly assault, and slowly bent toward the earth. Rafael set about the roots, bringing the sharpened pick down in a series of swift strokes. Just as Tom turned around the better to see what success Rafael was having, one large root snapped like a taut hawser, and the plum tree dropped. Tom disappeared under the foliage, to emerge moments later with twigs and plum leaves in his hair. They stood by the fallen tree for a moment, as if it were a dead comrade, sad that its life was over. Then they set about cutting and clearing it away.

The final days passed quickly, as Tom helped Rafael and tried to attune himself at the same time to the world to which he was about to return. He had only limited time to get to know the children, which was as well; they were less likely to question his presence, accepting what their mother told them, that Senor Roberts was a friend of their aunt, and would be leaving shortly. To Manolito of course, Tom was more than a shadowy figure, a stranger in one of the bedrooms: he was a pilot, he had flown a real aeroplane. To the child, it was as if one of the Gods had descended from heaven, and become his very best friend.

The day before Tom was due to leave, being a Saturday, Maria went with Manolito into town to visit the market. Outside the house several families were working their own strips of land on the terraces; some had brought their children with them, including a number of Manolito's school friends. On their return, Manolito wanted to stay outside and play; he badgered his mother.

"Mamma, can I play?"

"Where Manolito?"

"With the other boys on the open ground."

"Yes, but do not go into the trees, stay where the adults can see you," she said, gripping the boy by the shoulders and fixing him with a look of adult displeasure, to ensure that he understood the conditions of his parole. He nodded, she released him, and Manolito ran away to his friends, while Maria entered the house.

Manolito's group of friends were all of an age, where outside of open war, the tribulations of the adult world made little impact. Some of the boys had lost an older brother or father to the civil war and its aftermath. At that point in their lives while there were still opportunities to play in the sun, they took them as their right. As they grew older they would question the absence of the other men. Games of war, conflict and aggression were as much part of their lives as boys anywhere. It was natural therefore that when it fell to Manolito in his turn to nominate a game for them to play, the choice of 'Bombers and Fighters' should have been greeted with wild applause. The boys separated into two groups: Manolito was to lead the 'Fighters', while his friend Pedro, became the commander of the 'Bombers'. They selected their teams, assured that their respective pilots would acquit themselves with distinction. The objective of the boys who were nominated as Bombers was to run across the open land from one side to another, carrying in closed fists and outstretched arms stones which represented their bomb loads. The objective of the Fighters, who could deploy themselves wherever they wished on the land, was to chase after them, also with their arms outstretched. If a Fighter intercepted one of the Bomber force, the boy was to reach out and touch the other on the shoulder: this was a 'kill'. If a Bomber succeeded in reaching a designated area, he could open his hands and release the stones. The total number of stones was counted when the 'raid' was over, and became the score for that team. They then switched roles: the team with the highest number of bombs on target won the war.

As Tom was Manolito's hero, he naturally wanted to command the Fighters, although he was a little confused that the Hurricane MkIIb that Tom had flown was both a fighter and a bomber. However as Tom flew alone, he must be a fighter pilot. His young mind never attempted to analyse the reversal of the roles between the two groups of boys; Fighters were still Fighters, even in the role of Bomber: the intrinsic logic of slaughter.

Their war game started, each side carrying out its allocated role, with high pitched sound effects to match, as their parents worked the land under the September sun, occasionally rising stiff backed to pause and watch them. The boys wheeled back and forth, their engine mouths droning, as they banked and ran up and down, the gentle slipstream cooling their faces as they puffed their cheeks and pumped the ground with their legs. One bomber tried to reach the target by running close to the edge of the trees and avoid the screen of fighters: but Manolito set off in pursuit, making a machine gun noise as he grew near, banking and wheeling as the other boy tried to shake him off. Their aerial combat did not go unnoticed however; as they turned away from the trees, a man emerged and stopped to watch them. Manolito gained on the other boy, and with a final effort, got to within reach of him, put out his hand and touched him. The boy ran on, oblivious to the kill; furious, Manolito ran after him.

"You're dead! You're dead!" he shouted. "I'm the RAF, and your dead!"

"No I'm not!" came the reply. "You'll have to shoot me again!"

Manolito ran as hard as he could, but the other boy increased his lead, and escaped, reached the target and dropped his stones. Anger welling up in his small frame, Manolito ran up, and confronted him.

"I shot you! I shot you!"

"No you didn't! I felt nothing!"

"I did! I am a Hurricane pilot, I fly with the Royal Air Force. I shot you!"

"I fly with the Blue Division. I am a pilot of the Spanish Air Force!"

Their arguing ended only because the raid was now over; Manolito took his pilots away to discuss tactics and commence their bomb run. The man at the edge of the trees, who held a cloth bag in his arms with great care, now took a few steps forward. He called to the returning boy pilots.

"Good work boys! *Viva Espana!*"

Manolito looked across to him, still annoyed that his success in shooting down the enemy aircraft had not been recognised. He made a boyish grimace, and walked on at the head of his squadron.

"*Coronel!*" the man called across to Manolito. "Why don't you fly for Spain?"

"Because my friend at my aunt's home is a pilot with the Royal Air Force!" came the innocent reply.

It was done. The work of three months to hide and protect Tom, was given away in a moment, from the mouth of an angry child. The man nodded, as if accepting the casual treachery, and turned away. Manuel Ibanez descended the slope, clutching the bag of stolen eggs to his chest, and carefully made his way back to the coast road.

The Captive Summer

By An Unlit Road

Ibanez entered the front office of the Civil Guard barracks without fear. He had left his house that morning with nothing more on his mind than a successful day of egg snatching; the chickens invariably offered little resistance to him, a farmer's dog, or a farmer's rifle, being the more potent threats. He was an emaciated and coarse man, but could yet sprint, weave and dart with the agility of a deer. He was tolerated by the Civil Guard because he lived in the slum district and was prepared to yield up, for a price, whatever secrets the place had. It was he who accidentally led the police to Gutierrez and Bautista, his suspicion aroused because Luis Saez had started buying more bread and vegetables than the stomach of one old man required.

The desk was once again defended by the sloucher, who looked up as Ibanez approached; dismissing him as posing no threat, and being of no social standing, he thereupon ignored him.

"Good evening senor," Ibanez said, the eggs rolling against each other under the cloth.

The Guard continued to have regard to a ledger which was opened before him, scratching at the margin of a page with a pencil.

"What do you want?" he asked without looking up.

"I would like to see either Capitan Mendoza or Teniente de Rozario," he answered with a calm voice, but one which yet hinted at excitement.

"Have you come here to surrender?" asked the Guard.

"No! I have business with them, important business."

"They're not here."

"But I must see them."

The Guard looked up; his dark eyes fixed on the bag.

"What do you have there?"

"This is my property. I was just going home, and I thought that I should see them on a matter of urgency."

"What is in the bag?"

Ibanez's confidence started to wane. He realised too late that to walk into the barracks with a bag of stolen eggs and ask to see one of the senior officers was not a good idea. The sloucher was becoming suspicious, and in any event his wife was always complaining that she did not have enough food to satisfy the hunger of their children. Rather than answer, Ibanez made the mistake of looking quickly around him for an escape route. The sloucher signalled with a finger; as Ibanez looked behind him he saw that he had beckoned to another policeman who had just come in from the street.

"These are eggs," he said.

"Your eggs?"

"Yes, my eggs."

"You don't look like a farmer. I think that we will take care of these."

Realising that he was caught, Ibanez relented; the Guard who now stood behind him reached round and plucked the bag from his arms.

As he stood on the pavement outside the barracks, Ibanez cursed and spat. At the desk the sloucher looked into the bag of eggs and agreed with his colleague how their haul should be divided. Ibanez fumed that this was the reward for being a good citizen: the police stole your property, even if it was not your property.

Tom would never know it, but this chance encounter of the egg stealer and the policeman, was one reason he escaped that night. Angry that the police had robbed him, Ibanez vowed not to help them; he skulked to the cafe beside the harbour to drink his anger into a drunken rage. He had a few pesetas with him, and drank weak beer. He shared a table with some of the fishermen. He was foul tongued and angry company, but apart from acknowledging that he had grievance against the Civil Guard, a common topic of conversation, would not be drawn further. As he turned the diminishing pile of coins over in his palm, and contemplated the lost eggs, and the lost reward for leading the police to an enemy of Spain, his anger deepened. He drank more, and became more garrulous; eventually succumbing to a glass of brandy offered by one of the fishermen, his tongue loosened.

"I'm a good Spaniard," he said, engaging the man sitting opposite him, "I love my country, and I keep my eyes and ears open."

"You mean you steal eggs, and salute Franco!" retorted the fisherman.

"No, no, no! I see and hear things. Today I heard something, something the Civil Guard would want to know, if they were not so busy making life hard for patriotic men!"

"What?"

"At that house," and he pointed vaguely in the direction of the coast road, "I heard that they are harbouring an Englishman, a pilot. And what thanks do I get?"

"Did you tell the Civil Guard this?" asked another man, who was seated with his back to Ibanez.

"No! I won't help those bastards now!"

The man turned round in his seat: it was Quiros.

"Good. Make certain that you don't."

Quiros fixed him with a look of imminent and lethal threat; recoiling,

Ibanez got up, pushing back his chair.

"I am a patriot!" he said, and unsteadily walked away.

As soon as Ibanez was out of sight, Quiros signalled to two of his men. He ordered one of them to find Antonio and Jesus, and tell them that they would have to travel that night; the second he sent after Ibanez, to observe where he went and to whom he spoke. Quiros then drank off his glass of brandy, and went in search of Dr Hernandez.

The absence of both Mendoza and de Rozario was explained by Oleanza's insistence on a meeting to discuss the hunt for the saboteurs. His hopes had risen when de Rozario provided three fresh corpses, only to plunge when they had to give them up. He was not happy.

"How many have you arrested for questioning now?" he asked.

"One hundred and fifty three men, nineteen women," answered Mendoza.

"And no one knows anything?!" he rasped, his anger and blood pressure competing in their struggle for ascendency.

"No Your Honour. These men must have come from another town, nobody here knew them."

"And do you find this an acceptable situation?" he asked with the heavy familiar intonation of sarcasm.

Mendoza sighed, he had now been subjected to this tirade for weeks: the wheedling sarcasm of a man who never expended boot leather, for the slow pace of the man who carried a heavy pack on his back. He contemplated going to his colonel in Granada and asking for a transfer, even back to the north, life could not get worse. De Rozario intervened, he appreciated their common jeopardy, and his estimation of Mendoza had risen following the interrogation of Gutierrez.

"Your Honour the situation is not acceptable, but the Civil Guard will find these men."

Oleanza had a little time for the young officer, he seemed to embody the best traditions of the police, and he at least had tried to bring back likely suspects; it was just a pity that they were the wrong ones, and not breathing.

"But how long will it take?" Oleanza asked, exasperated.

"We cannot know senor. At the academy I was taught that the Guard never stops searching." He saw that the Mayor was again unimpressed with this affirmation of the Civil Guard code; he decided to relate a story from his family history, in the hope that this would illustrate his determination, if not his ability to deliver swift justice. He began.

"When my mother was a young woman, as yet unmarried and living with her family in Barcelona she was attacked."

As he spoke these words, Mendoza's countenance underwent a change. His mouth became suddenly clammy, and he was aware that the blood was slipping from his head. He turned to face de Rozario, his own youth rising up in judgement against him.

"It was during the events of the Semana Tragica. One night two armed men stormed the car carrying my mother and my grandfather..."

At this point Mendoza began to feel deeply nauseous. Even Oleanza noted his sudden sickly pallor; Mendoza rose from his seat.

"What is wrong?" asked the Mayor.

"Nothing, I just feel a little giddy. Carlos, go on, go on. I need a little air Your Honour," he said in a voice stripped of its strength.

He walked toward the window, from which there was a view of the sea over the roofs of the houses. He opened it slightly and stood with his face turned to the breeze. His mind raced. Was this a joke played on him by the Devil? Was it possible that de Rozario had been sent because the higher authorities suspected that he was the man who had escaped? Could Carlos in truth be the son of the woman he had so nearly killed all those years before?

"You were saying teniente," and the Mayor encouraged him to continue, bored with the youthful prattling yet mystified as to why Mendoza should react so strongly to the story.

"One of the men was caught, and garrotted. The other was not found, even though the police searched all Barcelona for him. The story was retold in my family many times. I promised my mother that one day I, the youngest son, would find the man. And kill him."

Mendoza bit his hand, if only to prove to himself that he had both feeling and some blood left in his fingertips. Then he dropped to the floor.

He awoke looking up into the concerned faces of de Rozario, and Oleanza's servant. He protested that there was nothing wrong, he had simply not eaten that day and had become a little light headed. If nothing else, the incident stopped Oleanza's interrogation; the Mayor insisted that Mendoza go home, and a call was made to Sargento Pelean to drive over from the barracks. Mendoza waited with de Rozario in the Mayor's drawing room, his wretchedness of mind at the revelation of his subordinate's origins now compounded by that young man's evident concern for his health.

The car carrying Mendoza and Pelean disappeared along the street, emerging then falling back into pools of light thrown down by the weak electric lamps; de Rozario watched its progress, then began his solitary walk back to the barracks. He was crossing the *Plaza de Toros* when a vehicle entered the square. He looked up for a moment, as the two saloons were of a similar model, and expected to see Sargento Pelean at the steering wheel; however, he was surprised to see Father Abarca, and seated beside him the informer, Ibanez. It was clear that Father Abarca was looking for someone; when his eyes fell upon de Rozario, he pressed urgently on the horn and brought the vehicle to an abrupt halt.

De Rozario went over to the car as the priest and Ibanez got out; he saluted the priest, but largely ignored Ibanez.

"Teniente de Rozario, we have been looking across town for you!" said Abarca, the vexation and urgency clearly registering in his voice.

"I am sorry Father. We have been in a meeting with the Mayor. Is something wrong?"

"Is something wrong? If you do not act, it soon will be! Do you know this man?" he asked, pointing at Ibanez as if he were a rare species of insect.

De Rozario did know him, and wished that he did not have to do business with him, for information of little use.

"Yes," and he turned to face Ibanez directly, his hand instinctively dropping to his holster, "Manuel Ibanez. Has he stolen from the church?"

"In the name of God, no! But he does have information upon which you must act if you are a patriot."

This seemed unlikely to de Rozario and he could think of no reason why Ibanez should have been in the company of the priest.

The fact that their paths had crossed was an unfortunate circumstance arising out of Ibanez seeing Abarca in the street, just as the anger and resentment within him at the loss of the stolen eggs reached its height. The police would not listen to him, but they would listen to the priest; so he went up to him and, with varying degrees of coherence and truthfulness, explained what he had heard, and what happened afterwards. Setting aside the issue of the reward which he might claim for the arrest of a foreign serviceman on Spanish soil, Ibanez was more angry at the loss of the eggs, but succeeded in convincing Abarca that he acted out of a sense of patriotism. Abarca knew both Consuelo and Arturo Bonar, and disliked them for their Republican and anti-clerical views: now revenge had presented itself in the form of Ibanez.

"I promise you senor," said Ibanez to de Rozario, "I heard this from the boy's mouth. There is a British serviceman hiding there."

"What will you do teniente? This woman is a criminal, an enemy of Spain," Abarca said.

And yet, thought de Rozario, this is the woman I love. He stood alone on the pavement; the sounds of the evening barely registering in his consciousness, as people entered the shabby square from all sides to begin the ritual social promenade reserved for this night. Providence had removed the last obstacle in his path, only to throw down a new rockfall that entirely blocked the way.

"This cannot be," he said the words dying in his mouth, "it is not possible that she would do such a thing."

"She has! And it is your duty as a Civil Guard officer to arrest her and the man she is harbouring!" Abarca retorted with burgeoning judicial enthusiasm.

De Rozario looked into the faces of the two men, but could not hear them. His love was poisoned, and now duty must prevail. Almost as if he were detached from his own body, he heard a voice say that he had to go to El Faro, and prevent the escape of the airman. Abarca offered the use of his car. The three men drove to the barracks, where de Rozario made enquiries after Pelean, forgetting that he had given him instructions to stay with Mendoza in case he needed a doctor. Without explaining why he needed them, de Rozario ordered three Guards to follow him in the only other available vehicle. He drove away without waiting, Father Abarca seated beside him, and Ibanez perched regally on the back seat, quietly satisfied at the change in his circumstances. At the edge of the town they halted to wait for the other vehicle to join them; through the windshield de Rozario stared at the sheer rockface beside the road, now flattened and distorted by the light from the headlamps.The pitiless beams of light washed all warmth and allure from the stone, rendering it as an inanimate and petrified sequence of blocks.

The Captive Summer

To The Sea

But the police were not the first to travel along the coast road that evening. Quiros had found Dr Hernandez before Ibanez found Father Abarca. Dr Hernandez made a hurried call to Consuelo; suppressing his panic he told her that he had to see her, giving the agreed codeword. He put down the telephone receiver and surveyed the study; he looked out to the garden, to the place of his morning encounter with a specimen of the species hyla meridionalis, and wondered what had happened to the amphibian in the succeeding weeks. He stood quite still for a moment; then, taking up his medical bag, he left the house.

Rafael waited in the tower for the headlights of the doctor's Mercedes to cast their penumbra over the rocks and trees by the road. Only a thin sliver of crimson and gold now illuminated the western sky and the moon had yet to break above the horizon. The speed with which the car approached the house, and the squealing sound like a tortured pig as it braked, was the herald of the collective betrayal of all those within El Faro's walls. The heavy iron studded door was opened before Dr Hernandez had taken two paces, he entered, and it closed behind him.

"They know!" he said, speaking to everyone at once. "Manuel Ibanez has found out, and perhaps the Civil Guard also!"

"How? That isn't possible!" remonstrated Consuelo, her thin features flushed with anger and fear.

"Could Ibanez have seen me?" asked Tom.

"No, no, no. He said that he had heard that you were here Tomas, but he did not give a name or a description. But he knows that you are a pilot," replied the doctor.

"Who told you this?" asked Consuelo, as yet not able to comprehend what was happening, but fearing that the attack on the house was linked to it, as she led the little party across the courtyard.

"Quiros came to see me. By chance! By chance he learned of it! He was sitting next to Ibanez at a cafe, boasting of what he knew!"

"Then I'm done," said Tom, "they will arrest me," he paused, "they will arrest all of us."

"No, no! There is still a chance Tomas! Quiros has sent word to Antonio and Jesus; you must leave tonight, now!"

"But the boat from Gibraltar doesn't arrive until tomorrow!"

"Antonio knows where to hide you, you can be kept safe there for one day."

Then realising for the first time since his arrival that Tom was still wearing civilian clothes, the doctor added: "Oh God! Where is your uniform? They will shoot you as a spy if you have no uniform!"

Tom ran to his room to change; Consuelo sank into a chair, she tried to speak and held out one hand as if giving emphasis to an argument, but no words came. Rafael returned to the tower, to look for other vehicles on the coast road; Maria poured brandy and left the glass on a small table close to Consuelo, then went to see her own children, who had been disturbed by the commotion, and wanted to know why their beloved aunt was now crying.

"Consuelo, Consuelo, don't despair," said Dr Hernandez softly, "we will get Tomas away tonight, and there will be nothing for the Civil Guard to do but bluster and strut around the house. They can prove nothing."

"They...know, Federico," she replied, her mouth still making attempts to form sounds that her throat was unable to project. Under encouragement from the doctor she drank a little of the brandy, spluttering as she did so. Dr Hernandez had his back to the door, and so could not immediately see what it was that brought about a sudden change in Consuelo's expression.

He turned; Tom was framed in the doorway, dressed once more in military uniform. The RAF khaki drill suited him now that his skin had developed a deep tan and his fair hair was washed with gold. The doctor had forgotten that the young man was a sergeant; in his talks with him he had assumed that he was conversing with someone of higher rank, not that rank was a criterion he cared to use for assessing any man.

"Tomas, are you going to fly? Let me fly with you!"

It was Manolito who spoke; Tom turned to face the boy.

"No Manolito. I have no aeroplane with me, I cannot fly at the moment," he said kneeling down beside the boy.

"Can I fly with you one day?" Manolito asked in a husky voice.

"Perhaps Manolito, we will have to see."

"This afternoon I was proud to be an RAF pilot Tomas, I shot down many bombers!"

The air froze; and the attention of the adults became fixed on the sleepy child.

Tom looked to Dr Hernandez and Consuelo through the open doorway, his face combining despair with forgiveness: he knew that it was the boy who had unknowingly given him away. He rose slowly; taking the child by a hand, he entered the room.

The three adults looked from one to the other; the child stood between them, holding onto Tom's hand and staring up at the face of his hero.

"I cannot be angry with him," Tom said, "I owe him my freedom."

Manolito detected that something was wrong, and that perhaps it related to him. Seeking reassurance, he tugged at Tom's hand, imploring him to look down. Tom smiled at the boy, ruffling his hair with his free hand: he still reminded him of his nephew.

"Whatever happens," he said, "I don't want..." but his Spanish failed him, so he continued in English, "I don't want him to think that I blame him. Please let him know that."

Consuelo nodded. Maria came back, and gathered up the boy to take him to bed.

"What do we do now?" Tom asked.

"We must wait in the garden, by the gate, Antonio will come there to take you to the boat."

"Who is guarding the boat?"

"Jesus."

"This isn't how I thought we would say goodbye," Tom said, "I must go and see Rafael."

Dr Hernandez waited for Tom at the foot of the garden steps, Consuelo stood by the awning. In three months, she and Tom had shared no intimacy, even when they became dancing partners on the terrace. But that night they kissed, and Consuelo squeezed his hand as he drew away from her: it was only at the moment of parting that she realised how much it hurt her to see him leave. Still faithful to Arturo, she realised then that Tom had satisfied an emotional need she would not give voice to. The last that Tom saw of her was as he descended the steps from the terrace. She was standing by the balustrade, framed by the light from the house, and looking down on him with the intent gaze which she employed to remember something or someone with every atom of her being or pulse of her consciousness.

The two men waited in the darkness; a fusillade of pebbles from beyond the garden wall aroused them: the pre-arranged signal that Antonio was outside. As Tom was about to go through the portal, Dr Hernandez stopped him.

"This," he said, "I almost forgot this."

He thrust a letter into Tom's hand, with an urgency which surprised him. As Tom looked into his face, he had a sudden intuition of a desperate sadness.

"What is this doctor?"

"The letter from the specialist in Barcelona. He has suggested that your symptoms are consistent with an injury to the spine, high up in your neck, not your brain. Give the letter to the RAF doctors when you reach Gibraltar."

"Dr Hernandez, what are you going to do?" Tom asked.

"I am going to either find the answer, or stop asking the question Tomas. Now go."

He pushed Tom through the gateway into the darkness beyond, and shut the door. Tom wanted to argue with him, but found himself confronting the wooden panels barring the way to the garden. He shook hands with Antonio; the two men walked down through the trees, to the silent cove and the fishing boat.

"Consuelo," Dr Hernandez said, "I have an idea. If anyone comes from the town, they have to use the coast road. If I should drive down the road, by a kilometre or two, and park as if I have broken down, blocking the road, I could slow them. They would not be able to get here until well after Tom had escaped in the boat."

He hoped that as he related his plan to her that it carried conviction, and plausibility. Consuelo had already assisted Maria with collecting the clothes which Tom had worn; these were to be hidden, and later burned. But she did not appear to hear him as she scanned the reception room for any other sign they might have left of Tom's presence. She prayed that the police would not interrogate the children. Dr Hernandez repeated his plan, and she now considered for a moment whether it would work.

"They may arrest you Federico," she said pensively.

"For breaking down? I might annoy them, but it is not a serious offence," he offered.

She was still distracted, but agreed that it would be better if he was not at the house when the Civil Guard arrived.

As she went with him to the front door, Rafael descended from the tower and came up to them.

"Are they coming Rafael?" Consuelo asked.

"No madam, I thought that the doctor was leaving and that I should come down, as I might be needed."

"Needed? Yes...Of course. Rafael can show me how to disable the car," the doctor interjected.

He and Rafael stepped out into the darkness beyond the lights from the house, and walked over to the Mercedes; Rafael opened the hinged cover of the engine compartment; the smell of warm oil and rubber escaping from its recesses filled the night air. They confided in low voices.

"Why did you come down Rafael?"

"You are troubled Dr Hernandez, you have made a decision."

"What decision would that be?"

"To sacrifice the life that God gave you."

Dr Hernandez sighed, and held out his hands.

"Do you see these Rafael? I have to keep my hands in my pockets to stop them shaking," he said, then paused. "There is a bend in the road, two kilometres from here, where the road narrows. If a car, travelling sufficiently fast, in the centre of the road, struck a vehicle travelling in the opposite direction, a direct impact, then it would have a good chance of knocking it out of the way, and down to the sea. Do you understand me?"

"Yes doctor."

"Do you understand why I must do this?"

"Yes doctor."

"I know that I will not survive. But I am afraid to die Rafael! I thought that I would have had enough of this world, but I am still afraid of death! If I could believe in God it would be easier for me. But I do not, cannot, believe in God," and he paused again. "Perhaps by my death some good will come."

"Dr Hernandez, by your life much good has come."

"Then if He exists, may God grant me a good death."

"Many men fear death doctor. I can only tell you that I believe we do not die, and that good men and women are not forgotten, here or in another place."

"Do you truly believe that Rafael?" he asked, agitation now palpable in his face.

"Yes doctor, I do."

Dr Hernandez was silent, his head bowed over the engine. Then he looked up.

"I have never shaken your hand Rafael, in all the years I have known you. But I would accept it as an honour to do so now."

They shook hands like old friends; then Rafael lowered the bonnet and closed the engine compartment.

Dr Hernandez could not trust himself to say farewell to Consuelo, so he waved to her as he got into the car. He sat for a moment, then reached out for the ignition key, and turned it.

At the bottom of the drive he halted the car and extinguished the headlights. He shuddered and looked out across the sea, to the faint lights from the town that escaped around the headland. The rising moon was almost full that night, but obscured by clouds that moved rapidly inland. He called to God to stand by him, but had no conviction that anyone or anything could hear him. Then, as he sat with his head again bowed, he became aware that the cloud was breaking up from the west, progressively illuminating the stretch of road on which he had to drive, but keeping the road closer to the town, in darkness. He looked around him, in the moonlight he could clearly make out the road surface and its plunging edge that led to the rocks. He engaged gear, and pulled away.

Out in the bay, Tom sat in the stern of the fishing boat, one hand firmly on the tiller, while Antonio and Jesus rowed in unison. Without warning, there was a bright flash of light from the roadway; two balls of metallic fire tumbled slowly through the scrub and onto the rocks to extinguish hissing into the sea. Antonio and Jesus stopped rowing and watched dumbfounded; Tom sat with his back to the fires, the muscles of his stomach tightening.

"Shall we go on Senor Roberts?" Jesus asked.

"*Si! Vamos!*" Tom replied.

And the fishing boat, rowers, oars, helmsman, all, was consumed once more in the oily blackness of the waters of the bay.

The Captive Summer

Daybreak

The desultory promenade in the main square precluded many citizens from venturing out to investigate the cause of the flash of light. Fishermen further out in the bay saw a flare, like a giant match struck against the rocks. One boat came closer in, but apart from some burning scrub beneath the road, the men could see nothing more and turned back to resume their journey to the fishing grounds: there were hazards and troubles enough without seeking additional problems. Only the stray cats sniffing for fish heads, the representatives of the forces of law and order, and a handful of determined drinkers in the cafe at the harbour saw anything.

A Guard patrolling near the breakwater noticed the lighting of the sky, a distant clump of trees being thrown briefly into relief. Curious, he walked along the breakwater and stared out across the darkness that distorted space and form. It took a little time for his eyes to adjust to the dark from the pervasive yet gloomy lighting in the streets. As he peered out, the stealthy waves slapped at his feet against the marine stone, their sound distracting him. When he cast a glance back into the sheltered pool of water, the boats that lingered there bobbed up and down in unison, mocking him, as if affirming that they knew the secret of the light, but would not divulge it. Satisfied that he ought to report the incident, as the distant flare was too close to land to be from a boat, he returned to the barracks.

The sloucher was still on duty at the desk, but would take no action in the absence of Pelean, Mendoza or de Rozario. He made a note of the incident, and advised his colleague that he would tell one of the officers upon their return. In the absence of higher authority, there was no one to whom he could delegate the decision as to whether to discover the cause of the incident now, or wait until daylight. He had been told repeatedly that there was an undiminished need for vigilance against acts of sabotage by the Reds, and that the Caudillo himself had called for heroic and decisive action; but he preferred to wait, and return to a warm bed and his wife.

Pelean returned to the barracks near midnight, on foot, as he had decided to leave the police car with Mendoza, in case he should require it. "Where is Teniente de Rozario?" he asked, but no one had seen the officer since early evening. Before going to his quarters he checked what acts of minor lawlessness had occurred in his absence. The report of the flaring light close to the rocks caught his attention; he questioned what had been done about it. He did not want to concern Mendoza about so trivial a matter, but decided to send two Guards to investigate. The first problem was that there was no usable motor transport: de Rozario had ordered one car to follow him, Mendoza had the second, and the motor pool truck had no diesel fuel. There were however three bicycles, although they were not intended for the high speed pursuit of bandits, unless they were hobbled and on foot. The bicycles had no lights, and only worn brakes, but by the standard of a nation that had endured a vicious annihilating war, they represented sleek racing machines. With rifles slung across their shoulders the two men set off, bouncing across the cobbled streets and cursing under their breath as they struggled to avoid hitting the walls of houses on their unfamiliar mounts in the darkness; a kilometre or so from the town they gained their stride and settled down to an even tempo.

When they came panting to the scene of the car wreck and dismounted, there was little immediate evidence of what had happened. A small fire still burned in the scrub by the road, and there were two sets of tyre marks leading off the road and down the steep slope as it plunged clean to the sea. They swung their torches around in broad arcs; by their beams they saw a large wrecked car, in the narrow ditch which hugged the rock along the opposite side of the road. One torch caught a broken headlamp, the light refracting crazily in the shards of glass. They came nearer and dropped into the ditch, one of them with his rifle ready, while the second kept a torch beam on the vehicle, and looked through the shattered windscreen. There was one man, well dressed in a dark blue suit, lying crumpled and twisted. His head was flung back, which disguised the wound he had sustained; his right arm lay across his face, with the hand turned upward, as if at the moment of death he was making a gesture to the heavens.

It was not apparent to the Guards that the two cars that had plunged over the edge of the road, to tumble down to the rocks and the sea, contained de Rozario or Father Abarca. De Rozario's failure to return that night did not provoke concern because no other policeman saw him with the priest, and no one saw the direction he took leaving the barracks. The burning undergrowth by the road did not throw sufficient light onto the steep slope to illuminate what lay below; and the Guards had neither the means nor the inclination to climb down to see what had become of the other vehicles. Unable to see or do anything further, they made their way back to the town. It was only as the sun rose, that the final scene was presented. The second vehicle had burst into a fireball when it ran into the back of the car carrying de Rozario and Abarca: it left only a burning trail of petrol, before extinguishing itself in the sea. By some means de Rozario was thrown clear, as his vehicle, shunted off the road by the force of the collision with the Mercedes, tore down through undergrowth like a four wheeled dive bomber: but his neck was already broken.

As the morning sun pulled itself from the sea, Pelean sent another patrol to resume the search. Within an hour of being despatched, a dusty, breathless and perspiring Guard half ran and half fell from one of the bicycles outside the barracks, and presented himself to Pelean with the desperate information that de Rozario had been killed in the accident on the road; his body lay on rocks close to the sea. A state of panic and high activity followed; Mendoza was alerted, diesel fuel was requisitioned for the truck and fishing boats just back from the night's catch were sent out to the foot of the rocks to look for survivors. Mendoza swept imperiously into the barracks in an agitated state with his pistol drawn, evidently expecting an uprising or looking for the first reprisal victim to shoot. He was a man in a blind funk: when he had gone to bed he believed himself to be effectively under sentence of death, now he had been spared by the untimely but fantastical death of his subordinate. He shouted contradictory orders, then immediately reversed them; demanded to know where the Mayor was, then gave instruction that the Mayor was not to be told what had happened. He strode to his office, and setting his pistol down before him, acted out an imaginary conversation about the incident with his superiors.

"You must understand coronel," he said, "I had no idea, no idea whatsoever, that he was missing."

He stopped and looked up, distracted; Pelean stood in the open doorway observing him with curiosity.

"Sargento Pelean. What do you want?"

"We are ready to go out capitan."

"Yes. Good. Go out, of course go out, and recover the bodies."

Pelean saluted and turned away; Mendoza called him back.

"You are sure that he is dead?" he asked.

"Yes capitan, we are quite sure."

He was dismissed and went out to the yard; as he walked away he took with him the indelible impression that Mendoza was relieved to hear that de Rozario was gone.

The rumours started to spread through the town as soon as rough wooden coffins were loaded onto the back of the truck in the yard of the barracks. The Guards, presented only with the bare fact of a car wreck, were denied the emotional release of immediate sanction against the civilian populace in retaliation. In any event, people knew that when Civil Guards were killed, no matter what the circumstances, to stay indoors and keep out of the way. But word came that there was one other fatality; and the name of Dr Hernandez was whispered from mouth to ear through the sun splashed lanes. There was a palpable alteration in the consciousness of the town now; many would later claim that as they received news of the calamity, the heat of the sun dimmed for a moment. The communication had an energy bound with it, not as a breaking wave has energy which dissipates as the wave breaks upon a shore, but an energy which grew as the news moved along the streets and through the open doorways and windows: the self reinforcing energy of grief.

There was no one to claim Dr Hernandez's body but Senora Lopez. Mendoza refused that any help should be provided by the Civil Guard to transfer the coffin from the yard to the doctor's house: he held the doctor responsible for the yet fortuitous death of de Rozario, lack of any evidence being no barrier to guilt. But Quiros and several of the other fishermen, tired though they were from the night's activity along the dark coast, bore up the coffin and carried it with quiet reverence, Senora Lopez following them. A crowd had formed in the street; as the coffin came up people fell back to let it pass, some averted their eyes, others wept silently. They could not know that his death was a final sacrifice, and assumed that it was a tragedy without purpose in a land that could make a market in grief.

The fishermen were directed to take the coffin through to the back parlour of the house, which was hurriedly cleared of furniture. Two of the women from the crowd came to Senora Lopez to offer her help in preparing the body. Quiros and one other man stayed behind: Dr Hernandez's body had first to be carried upstairs to his bedroom to be prepared for burial.

When they laid him on the bed not a word was spoken by any of them; they stood numb to the moment, then the men departed. The women's tears flowed unobserved into the morning air, and they began their work. The two fishermen sat in the parlour, trying to avert their eyes from the coffin and concentrate on the framed pictures, statuettes and potted plants which adorned the shaded chamber; but time and again their eyes were drawn to the wood splinters, knots and badly hammered nails of what was little more than a crate, into which the doctor's body had been rudely pressed. At length Quiros felt compelled to speak.

"For such a man, they find a box in which I wouldn't bury a dog!"

His companion nodded in agreement, and both men sat on, grimly silent, hands gripping their knees, occasionally looking to the ceiling. A few minutes later there was a knock, and Quiros rose and went out. It was Felipe Escolar, who removed his hat with bandaged fingers as Quiros opened the door to him, and was shown upstairs.

"I am so sorry, so sorry," he whispered as he stood next to Senora Lopez, looking from his still bruised and painful fingers to the body of the man who had tended to him after his release from the barracks. She turned her head slightly toward him, red rimmed eyes betraying her feelings.

"I have seen many leave this world," she said, through lips which barely acknowledged the effort applied to them, "yet I never entertained the idea that a man whose life was life would be among that number."

It was Felipe who suggested that the town would want to honour the doctor and, when Senora Lopez seemed overwhelmed by the prospect, readily took responsibility for the arrangements. When Escolar referred to the town, he of course meant the people of the town, to distinguish it from the dignitaries and party officials. This latter group, given voice by the Mayor, was not in the least sure that there should be any sanctioned display of regret at, or acknowledgement of, the death of a man about whom there were lingering suspicions; and if news reached Madrid that San Cristobal had honoured a man who had been involved in the death of a distinguished and much regarded Civil Guard officer, this might prompt the further unwelcome attentions of the Ministry of the Interior. The new crisis called for decisive leadership: Oleanza convened a meeting with Mendoza, Castellon and Bucaro, to discuss the implications for them all of the latest disaster.

The Captive Summer

Final Honours

The four men took their seats; for once their habitual demeanour of casual self satisfaction replaced by mutual incomprehension. Prompted by a gesture from Oleanza, eyes turned toward Mendoza, the local font of temporal knowledge in a police state. From a sheet of damp paper he read out the names of the victims, pausing when he reached that of Father Abarca. The confirmation of the loss of the town's senior cleric produced a profound silence, broken only when Oleanza announced that he would personally notify the Bishop of Granada, to which there was nodded agreement. As to what had happened on the road, Mendoza was obliged to pad out the bare facts with animated gestures, bringing his fists together emphatically to suggest the dynamic of the vehicles as they raced together in the night. He regretted it as soon as his knuckles came into contact.

"Why was Dr Hernandez on the road at that hour?" asked Oleanza.

"We do not know," replied Mendoza.

"And do you know why de Rozario and Father Abarca were there?" asked Oleanza, shifting his weight onto one side, one hand with splayed fingers compressing the top of his desk.

"No Your Honour, that is also a mystery," he said, conscious of the inadequacy of the reply.

He was questioned as to whether there could have been any criminal involvement; although he would have liked to blame the Sugar Bandits, he was obliged to report that there was no evidence to support that view. It had been, they concluded, a most tragic accident. They had no way of knowing what de Rozario was doing or his intended destination; they were aware that the coast road passed El Faro, but for the sake of those at the house made no connection. Mendoza had contacted the provincial headquarters of the Civil Guard to report the death of his men. Oleanza proposed that de Rozario's funeral should take place in the town; without a trace of irony noting that there was an area set aside at the cemetery for fallen heroes. However, Mendoza pointed out that de Rozario came from Seville and that his family would want his body returned there; but perhaps a delegation from the town could travel to Seville to pay their respects, and at this prospect the atmosphere lifted.

"He was a fine officer, a fine man, a fine Spaniard," was Oleanza's final guttural comment.

"His death is certainly a great loss," interjected Castellon, "particularly as he was beginning to demonstrate his abilities in suppressing the enemies of Spain," he added with a curt sniff directed to Mendoza.

The Captive Summer

The only other issue was whether to allow any civil ceremony for Dr Hernandez. In spite of the fact that the doctor had, over a period of many years, without favour but with care and compassion, tended to the sick, comforted the dying and brought new life into the world, the four representatives of the new Spain were unanimous in declaring the folly of such an act. Bucaro readily agreed that there would be no report of the incident in the pages of his fearless publication, nor would any obituary for the doctor appear. He promised them that it would be as if the doctor had never existed. Satisfied with their deliberations, the meeting concluded and the quartet broke up to burden themselves once more with the responsibilities of public office.

While they went about their business, at El Faro life also appeared to follow its routine pattern. Following the doctor's departure that night, Consuelo and Rafael withdrew into the house. Maria had hidden the bundle of clothing in the cellar; they three gathered in the reception room, sitting stiffly, waiting for the sound of an approaching vehicle, trying to remain calm, but certainly for Consuelo and Maria, close to hysteria. Rafael sat between the two women, a little ashamed at the new deception to which he was a party. There was no noise save the creaking of the furniture on which they sat. Eventually Consuelo rose and went into the courtyard, spending some time pacing up and down, as Tom had once done, in an attempt to ease the nervous strain of the silent time. It was not until the early hours of the morning that they decided that the immediate danger had passed; only Rafael among them being able to guess at what price that may have been achieved. He alone now remained as a sentinel, while Maria went to bed with the children, and Consuelo retired for a few hours of tormented sleep.

In the morning they rose and, incredulous but still despairing, greeted the world. Even in a land of drought and sun the season was turning, and cooler autumn winds would soon arrive from the mountains. There was a strange silence among them as they shared a late breakfast, neither woman able to understand how they had passed the night. As it was a Sunday, Maria considered walking to church for Mass, but Consuelo resisted, out of fear for Maria's safety. Rafael offered to go into town, on the grounds that no one knew for sure what had happened on the road in the night. The truth was soon revealed to him.

In spite of the indifference shown by the authorities, the arrangements to remember Dr Hernandez nevertheless proceeded. All those who had reason to remember him: the defeated; the poor; the sick; all those who knew and understood what he had represented and what he had done, were determined to pay their respects. A priest from Almunecar agreed to officiate; all other arrangements being made in just two days. The night before, mourners were allowed to attend the house and observe the body, which had been placed in an open coffin in the parlour. All through the evening people arrived at the house, many carrying small tributes of flowers and grasses picked from the countryside. Some lit candles, and those who could not afford candles borrowed or shared them with friends or neighbours. The pavement around the front steps became crowded with little points of light; as darkness fell, those coming on along the street were guided by the lights of those who had gone before. The children were not allowed, but at the street corner groups of them gathered, fascinated by the procession of their parents and elders, until driven away from the scene.

Late in the evening Consuelo, Maria and Rafael arrived from El Faro. The absolute, implacable, unwearying foe had stolen their friend away, as it had taken so many others. Consuelo gripped Maria's hand as they entered the room, having first kissed Senora Lopez, who like a dowager was established in the kitchen. Dr Hernandez was dressed in a light grey suit, his greying hair was brushed and combed; and he smelled not of death but expensive hair oil. He was elegant, and looked as if he were about to step out for an afternoon excursion across the watered and beautifully kept lawns of a country club or hotel. When they left the house, Consuelo, blinded by her tears, had to be guided through the darkened streets.

Escolar worked through the night to prepare the hearse, which would be pulled by Sol and Sombra. He relied more on Ramon now, and as they went about cleaning and polishing, reflected that it was a strange land which could only offer ready opportunities for young men to train as undertakers or policemen. In the morning they brought out the horses from the stable and harnessed them. They breakfasted on coffee and bread, prepared by Felipe's wife; as he drank the coffee he talked to the two powerful jet black living engines, occasionally drawing a battered hand along their sides. Then they dressed in their formal clothes and, at the appointed hour, moved off through the streets.

The hearse drew up outside the house; Felipe climbed down, and leaving Ramon with the reins, went to the horses. They were proving fretful, kicking and tossing their manes, bothered by the number of people they had encountered on the way, and perhaps the prevailing atmosphere. He stood close between them, as if he were to impart a great secret or make a request which could not be overheard by anyone else but them. Patting them in turn he spoke, pleading gently.

"Sol and Sombra. You who have guided so many through these streets to their last rest, I make this request of you. Today we carry Dr Hernandez, a compassionate man," and then holding up his hands, "the man who bandaged these broken fingers, fingers that cannot hold the reins and instruct you as they have before. I ask of you to be patient with Ramon, for the sake of he who we carry."

Sol, which was harnessed furthest from the house, tossed her head and looked back across her flank into space. Her ears pricked up, and the mare intently regarded something close by; the animal saw and heard something, but to Escolar there was only a pillar of air. He patted the horses once more; now calmer, they threw their heads as if agreeing with his request.

It was the usual custom for those wishing to attend a funeral in the town, to assemble at the house of the deceased in the morning, make formal expression of sympathy with the near relatives, and wait quietly in the street for the time to move off to the cemetery in procession. Senora Lopez on this instance took the place of family; dressed in her finest brocaded black, she humbly accepted the words of comfort offered, and squeezed the hands proffered with a strength which spoke of her urge to cling to life.

However, what distinguished this funeral, was the number of those intent on making public recognition of the respect which they accorded the doctor. The death of a child or a young man or woman cut down by the scythe with indecent haste would, even in a land where the bloodstains of the civil war were still literally evident in the stones, provoke a deep emotional response. The response of the town to the death of Dr Hernandez went far beyond this. Clearly there was a political dimension, a rare opportunity to make a demonstration of resistance to the Francoist State, a chance to silently utter the words: "We honour the man whom you would disparage because he was not like you." But they also loved him.

As the morning came, people across the town made preparation and came out onto the narrow streets. If they had a presentable set of funeral clothes they wore them; if not they wore whatever constituted their best, even if these were threadbare and faded. In the isolated cortijos, they rose early and walked into town, joining the townsfolk when they reached the outlying houses. It was soon clear that there could not possibly be enough room in the little street for all the people and the hearse, so they walked on in the direction of the cemetery, taking up station along the way. As the *Plaza de Toros* lay between the house and the main road out of the town, that also began to fill with people, prompting panic in the two Civil Guards on duty there, one of whom ran to the barracks to report the unlawful assembly.

Don Octavio also wished to say goodbye to his friend; dressed in a dark suit he took up his hat and went out. He had not been troubled by visions for some time, and so did not resort to a careful scrutiny of the doorways close to his own. The street leading to the main square was choked with people, unusually sombre, moving slowly forward. Some whimpers were discernible above the sound of shoes on the stones, and a melancholy spread over them like a mist. Once in the square the crowd formed on the sides where the cortege would pass. In order to join the main road, the hearse would have to pass along two sides of the square before turning and leaving the faded elegance of the Town Hall, the statue of Philip V and the fountain behind. Don Octavio made his way to the corner where the hearse would turn onto the second side; flanked by a growing crowd he took station at the front of the narrow pavement.

Felipe went into the house with the fishermen who were to act as pall bearers; the coffin was taken up on their sinewy shoulders and brought out into the morning's light, presented to the hearse and silently guided into the glass chamber. He climbed back up beside Ramon and, looking around to see that all was ready, gave the order to move off once more. Senora Lopez, Consuelo, Maria, and Andrea, made up the principal mourners, each woman dressed in black; Rafael found himself shoulder to shoulder with Andres; those who had been able to enter the street formed up behind them. The streets were hushed, and apart from the distant crying of a baby, no human sound was heard. Heads dipped as the hearse passed, and the onlookers offered up silent prayers for the doctor's soul. Those who wished to follow the hearse to the cemetery now joined the procession, the tail of mourners growing steadily longer.

When the hearse entered the main square, the horses, being presented with so many faces, started: but soothing words from Escolar, who also extended a comforting hand on the arm of Ramon, calmed them; throwing their heads as if in remembrance of their agreement with their master, the animals walked on. The cortege drew level to the place where Don Octavio was standing, who could now barely see for the tears that rolled down his face.

Then something unforeseen happened. Don Octavio wiped his face with his hand, and as he opened his eyes again it was as if he had cleaned away a besmirched pane of glass: Dr Hernandez appeared before him, walking beside the hearse.

Don Octavio, his grip on his nerves tenuous at the best of times, felt his legs weaken and wondered if he would pass out. He stood, pale and twitching, and held his hat to his chest by the brim with both hands. Dr Hernandez stopped now; turning toward his friend, he bowed low from the waist. As he drew himself up, the doctor smiled. His form remained as he had been in life, but the weariness had gone from his eyes, and he had become again the distinguished gentleman unburdened by sorrow; he looked as Consuelo had thought, as if about to commence a leisurely afternoon excursion. Don Octavio blinked in an effort to make the apparition go away, but it, he, persisted. He looked cautiously from side to side to discern if anyone else could see the figure: after all Dr Hernandez was supposed to be in the coffin not walking beside it. Satisfied that none else could see, but conscious of his own reputation amongst the townsfolk, he smiled hesitantly back.

Dr Hernandez waved in farewell; he turned away and walked on, looking about him as he went at the people crowding in on all sides. Then he resumed his role as the otherwise unseen escort to the funeral party, as it made its way out of the square, and along the road that led to the little cemetery set on a rock outcrop overlooking the glittering sea.

All through that day, and into the hurrying night, a motor fishing boat punched a highway through restless water; on its deck, Tom, now huddled in an Army greatcoat, watched as darkness fell across the eastern horizon. The boat accepted no entreaty from Neptune, and only a light spray fell intermittently across Tom's face. He felt the sea wind, and the roll of the vessel beneath his feet; in the wheelhouse a solitary crewman maintained the watch, and below deck the diesel engines pushed the little craft ever closer to Gibraltar. His thoughts turned to those who had cared for him, those who he had left behind in the burnished land; and he awaited the rising of the sun once more.